A Novel by Pucasso

This is a work of fiction. Names, characters, places, and incidents either are the product of the author's imagination or are used fictitiously. Any resemblance to actual persons, living or dead, events, or locales is entirely coincidental.

ISBN-978-1-7339654-1-5

DUFFEL BAG BOYS

&

MOST VICIOUS PEOPLE:

BOOK #1

"THE LIME-LITE"

DEDICATION

I dedicate this book to my dearly departed cousin, Dominique "Nique" Bullitt. Your presence has touched the hearts of many people. Although you're gone, your name alone deems worthy of remembrance for an eternity. Tupac said it best, "The good die young." Furthermore, being acquired by the skies above makes you (Nique) even more a "Ghetto Star." Rest in Heaven, cuz. -PUCASSO

A Novel by Pucasso

DUFFEL BAG BOYS

&

MOST VICIOUS PEOPLE:

BOOK #1

"THE LIME-LITE"

TERMINOLOGY FROM THE AUTHOR

DUF· FEL· BAG·BOY /duf' el bag boi/ n. 1 Anyone who succeeds in the. event of "running up a check"; a breadwinner. 2. An outstanding hustler who demonstrates dedication, determination, and discipline when it comes to stacking gwop(cash). 3. A paperchaser known for being the big homey who've graduated from stacking dirty money in Nike shoe boxes and bed mattresses to putting it in a duffelbag and taking it the laundromat to get cleaned.

MVP abbr. (Mobs) most vicious people n. 1. Mt. Vernon Park. 2. A glorious clique of "go-getters" originated from the Washington Heights community. 3. Anyone who "get it out the mud, taking penitentiary and life or death chances in the event of securing a duffelbag.

THE LIME-LITE n. 1. A money-making scheme that involves doing some "street homework." 2. A sweet lick that's worth at least 10-bands or better; a money booster. 3. A fortunate glow that highlights the glamorous lifestyle; A stage or showcase where "Most Vicious People" gather up around and discreetly plot their next move.

A Novel by Pucasso

DUFFEL BAG BOYS

INTRO:

Class in Session

Spring '88

Swarms of kids played in various groups outside of Mount Vernon Elementary School, waiting for class to begin. The bell rang signaling everyone to come inside and report to their assigned classrooms.

Aaron "**Shawty Bankroll**" Mann was in the same third grade class as Keyon "**Kee-Kee**" Smith and Valentine "**Tino**" Kingpin. All three of them were from the Washington Heights Community of south Chicago, a predominantly black neighborhood known for gang violence, drug distribution, and robbery. Growing up in this type of environment you had to be built a certain way, mentally and physically, in order to survive.

From day one, Shawty Bankroll had just what it took to be a *HOOD HERO*. He came from a family full of con artists and crooks. Ever since he was running around in pampers, he'd been jacking swag and making it his own. It didn't take long for him to gain supreme popularity among all his contemporaries.

Shawty Bankroll and Kee-Kee lived on the same block (west of 104th Place and Aberdeen), which later became known as the "Fo'." (Four) Tino stayed right up the street on Racine; but due to all the action that was happening on the Fo', he ended up making it his primary turf. No doubt about it, the Fo' was the place to be. You seen everything there…gang banging, shootouts, crack heads, stick ups, prostitution, high speed police chases, etc.

Shawty Bankroll ended up making it to class late-once again. The new Jordan's had just came out, and he had to shoot up to Foot Locker to cop a pair before they sold out. On his way to school, he messed around and got caught up serving a crackhead who went by the name of **The Eight Dollar Man**. He got the name from always being two dollars short whenever copping a dime bag of crack. Each time, eight dollars was all he had…nothing more or less.

Shawty Bankroll learned how to bust drug juggs(deals) from his older cousin Lorenzo, "Zo" Mann. He was currently doing time in a federal prison for a number of class X offenses. His criminal background consisted of crimes that would make even the toughest convict bow down. Really, he is to blame for the direction Shawty Bankroll was headed in. As soon as he came up out of the stroller, Zo poisoned his head and exposed him to the wickedness of the streets. Ever since then, Shawty Bankroll fell in love with the hustle and never looked back.

He learned fast using jugg and finesse as a primary source of getting whatever he desired. The boy was a natural born hustler. Whenever there was a potential serve on deck, he outran everyone. He did not have the luxury of pussyfooting around; he had to provide a decent living for himself since his dope fiend mother could not. His granny, "Momma Mann," was the only person he could count on when times got rough. She was his rock, and he had every intention to look out for her once he got on.

On this particular day, Shawty Bankroll slid through the front entrance of the school building moving like a cat burglar. He crept pass the principal's office trying hard not to get busted for being tardy again. Mr. Jordan, the principal of Mount Vernon, had forewarned him that if he was to get caught being late to school one more time, without a valid reason, he would have no choice but to expel him for the remainder of the school year.

However, Shawty Bankroll didn't really care about excelling any further than he already did, school wise. The shit was cutting into his hustling time, which was a big *No-No!* He already accepted the fact that kindergarten would be the last graduation he would ever be awarded.

Shawty made it pass the front office without anybody of importance noticing. He shot up the stairs, skipping a few at a time, and then broke straight towards his classroom. He was rocking a Nike Air Flight jumpsuit with the new Jordan's on his feet... the ones with the elephant print on them. He was more flyer than the Jump man that was on the back of his jacket, with about six or seven hundred dollars in his pockets. Hell, the average teacher in the school building did not even have that kind of money in their savings account, let alone in their pockets.

Once he made it to the classroom, he took a peep through the door to see if the coast was clear. Immediately, Ms. Dawson, "Ms. Dee," caught eye contact with him and came to unlock the door. She stepped outside of the classroom easing him back, making it private what she had to say to him.

"Mr. Mann, your attendance is terribly unacceptable with me! And as far as your grades go, it is gonna take a miracle for you to pass onto the fourth grade with everyone else. What is going on son...are you having problems at home?" she asked, in concern of his well-being "What do your parents have to say about all of your tardiness and bad grades, or do they even know what's going on?"

Shawty Bankroll's face was buried deep into the floor and he had his hands wrapped around each other behind his back. He remained silent, answering no questions-none whatsoever. He just let her get her rocks off.

"Don't you care about your future?" she asked, giving him the third degree. Ms. Dee really cared though, she was a very inspiring lady. She loved all of her students and strived wholeheartedly to teach them all she possibly could, academically and socially. Shawty Bankroll wasn't really trying to hear shit she was saying though. All he had on his mind was sliding through the classroom's door and showing off his brand new Nike attire.

"Look, I'm not gonna keep allowing you to interrupt my classroom with your late attendance. There are some people in there who actually want to learn and move on to the next grade," Ms. Dee advised him. At this point, Shawty Bankroll had his head lifted looking her in the eyes. "You're a very special person, and I want to see you succeed in life, but you got to want it for yourself just as much."

Ms. Dee looked at her watch seeing that the lecture was cutting into her scheduled program. "Next time you come to my class, make sure you show up on time and well prepared to learn or don't even bother to come at all! I'm not giving you anymore breaks, do I make myself clear?"

Shawty Bankroll looked at her and nodded his head saying, "Yes, Ms. Dee." He gave her a slight smile, happy to be allowed to go into the classroom. All he could think about was how muthafuckas was gonna be on his dick; the new Jordan's ain't been out a good hour, and he already had them on his feet.

"I hope you do, because I mean it. Now, go get ready to participate in the class discussion we're having," Ms. Dee said.

Shawty Bankroll walked into the classroom with a big smirk on his face. He had one hand in his pocket, gripping onto his bankroll and the other hanging down by his side, swinging back and forth. He was bopping to his own rhythm.

Everybody in the class stared down at his feet as if they were on fire. "Look at them new Mikes, right there!" one kid said while pointing at Shawty Bankroll's shoes.

"Dang, them bitches sharp as hell! I thought they didn't come out until next week," another kid replied.

"Nah, they just came out this morning," Shawty Bankroll said, butting in on the conversation the two kids were having. They continued to ride his dick, throwing him all sorts of compliments.

Shawty Bankroll was walking on cloud nine. He loved getting attention, it was a feeling he would come to treasure the most-right next to revenge and getting pussy. Most of the girls in the class had a crush on him, and he knew it.

Finally, Shawty Bankroll made it to his desk, which was right in between Kee-Kee and Tino's. These were his day one niggas, whom he'd been shooting the shits with since preschool. They stayed fly also, but he was on another level with the shits. Unlike Kee-Kee and Tino, Shawty Bankroll was buying all his shoes and clothes himself. He took care of himself and was doing a damn good job at it. He was the lil big homie of the hood; taking care of the folks he loved became an everyday habit he enjoyed.

"Shawty Bankroll...what up, my boy?" Tino said while reaching his hand out to show a young player some love.

"What up, dawg, what it do?" he replied while shaking his hand.

"What up, Kee-Kee?" Shawty Bankroll greeted. "You over there all quiet and shit, looking deep into that book as if you're really reading."

Shawty Bankroll and Tino both busted out laughing. "Man, fuck y'all! I'm trying to stay on the honor roll, so I can be like you one day and rock new Mikes every time they come out." Kee-Kee said, giggling to himself.

Instantly, Tino looked down at Shawty Bankroll's feet seeing that he had on the new J's. "My mom's gonna snatch up a pair for me, as soon as she gets off work today. Them bitches go hard as fuck." he said while examining the shoe from front to back.

Kee-Kee wasn't quite sure if his mother was gonna cop him a pair. She found no sense in repeatedly buying the same shoe just because it came out in a different color. She would rather buy him something a lot more different, such as the Bo Jackson's, Huaraches, Air Maxes, Charles Barkley's, etc. These sneakers costed just as much as the Jordan's. However, the compliments you got from rocking the Mikes were incomparable. There was a popularity aspect that came behind having the Jordan's on the first day they came out…you were considered superior to anyone that didn't. It was a hood thang, and if you didn't have them on, you definitely wouldn't understand.

"You better hope them bitches don't sell out because they were going like hotcakes when I was up there, and that was only like twenty minutes ago," Shawty Bankroll explained as he pulled out his *gwop* (money) and thumbed through it. The girls that were around, watched in amazement as he flicked through a bunch of $20 bills like the shit was nothing. "Damn, I just spent over three-hundred dollars! I got to make that back, today."

Kee-Kee continued reading his English book, completing the assignment at the end of the chapter. He was a very intelligent individual, and English had become one of his favorite courses in school. He was the type of student that hurried up and finished his studies then distracted the rest of the class by cracking jokes. Yeah, he definitely was a class clown, but everyone knew not to try to play him like a chump. Along with being intelligent, he could turn vicious in a heartbeat.

Ms. Dee lifted her head up, taking a slight break from reading her teacher's handbook guide. Tino and Kee-Kee had their faces buried dead into their books. Shawty Bankroll didn't have a book to begin with.

"Mr. Mann, since you like to talk and disturb my class from their work, why don't you be nice enough to read the first paragraph of the chapter out loud to the class," Ms. Dee suggested, with a serious look on her face.

"Ooh!" the whole class sighed.

"Quiet now, class!" Ms. Dee shouted. "Go ahead, Mr. Mann,"

"I don't even have a book!" Shawty shot back, defensively.

"Don't worry, I'm pretty sure Mr. Smith or Kingpin won't mind lending you theirs. I know they completed the assignment by now, haven't y'all?" she said.

Tino lifted his head up from his book, catching Ms. Dee eyeballing him to death. "No, ma'am, I haven't finished yet." he said, feeling embarrassed from being put on the spot.

"Is that so," she replied, giving him a smirk. "How about you, Kee-Kee?"

Ms. Dee often called Keyon by his nickname. He was her favorite student, and everybody knew it. On many occasions she would remind him of how special he was, telling him that he would grow up to be something great in life. She always bragged about him to the upper grade level teachers, telling them how talented he was. She even recommended for him to advance a grade. Kee-Kee's mother, Gee, preferred for him to stay with his regular class though, she was afraid that he would grow up too fast and miss out on his childhood.

Although Kee-Kee was a bookworm, at times his conduct didn't match his academics. At any given moment, he could turn up and get real disorderly. However, that was nothing a good ol' disciplinary notice couldn't fix. Gee did not play that shit, she was real strict on him about school. Ms. Dee would often threaten him by saying she was gonna give Gee a call if he did not straighten his act up. Most of the time it worked, but every now and then, Ms. Dee had to get him together.

"Are you finished?" she asked, knowing already that he was.

"Yes, ma'am," he replied.

"Well, good then, let your homie from off the block borrow your book, so he can read out loud to the class."

Kee-Kee passed his book to Shawty Bankroll and showed him where to start reading at. At first, he did not want to take the book but got tired of Ms. Dee giving him the evil look.

"Okay, damn!" he said while snatching the book out of Kee-Kee's hand. He put his thumb under the first word of the paragraph and took a shot at it. "Pre-prep-prep,"

"That's prepositional, dumbo!" a teacher's pet piped in. The whole class began laughing, except for Ms. Dee, Tino, and Kee-Kee.

"Shut the fuck up, you baldhead ass bitch!" he shot back at her. He was embarrassed from being laughed at…that shit hardly ever happened to him.

"Who you calling a baldheaded bitch? Your mamma! At least I can read!"

"So, at least I know how to count!" Shawty Bankroll upped his *knot* (money) showing the entire class. Everybody was back on his dick again.

"Damn, that's a big ol' bankroll!" one kid chattered.

"Hell yeah, I've been telling you that homeboy had the mumps." his friend replied. The teacher's pet was lost for words.

"That's why your hype ass daddy owe me money, and if he don't run my scratch, I'm gonna blow y'all house up!" Shawty Bankroll said, frightening the lil' girl but only exaggerating the matter. However, she took the threat serious and began crying. The class got disorderly...everybody was laughing and making noises.

"Alright now, everybody be quiet, or I'm gonna have to pull out my ruler," Ms. Dee warned the class. However, the noises continued to grow.

Ms. Dee slid her drawer open, pulling out a thick measuring stick and then banged it against her desk. "*Whack!*" Immediately, the whole class got silent.

Shawty Bankroll shoved the book off his desk to the floor.

"Mr. Mann, pick that up right now!" she demanded.

"Man, fuck school! I'm missing out on a whole bunch of money wasting time up in this dumb ass place. I'm outta here!" he said, as he got up and made his way towards the door. Tino and Kee-Kee felt sad for their homie.

"Mr. Mann wait a minute," Ms. Dee said. Shawty Bankroll kept it moving though, pimping with one hand in his pocket holding onto his bankroll. This was his trophy... the bigger it got, the prouder he felt about himself. "I said wait a minute!"

He stopped in his tracks and turned around slightly to hear what she had to say. "Baby, them streets are only gonna get the best of you. I done seen it happen too many times before, it's my job to guide you on the right path in life" Shawty Bankroll just stood there taking all what she was saying into account.

"I see you all dressed up sharp, you making a lil' money and that's good, but where's that gonna get you without any education to go behind it? You're winning right now, but what about tomorrow?"

Shawty Bankroll paused for a moment thinking to himself, *If tomorrow comes.*

"Look, I'm not thinking about tomorrow right now, it's hard enough just trying to get through the day." he said.

Although what he said may have sounded very ignorant or awful to most adults, it touched Ms. Dee's heart deeply. This was a nine-year-old boy she was holding a conversation with. All Ms. Dee could do was shake her head. *It's crazy how the streets brainwashed this kid.* She thought to herself. She walked up to him and gently grabbed ahold of his shoulder.

"Baby, do you have any goals in life? The world is beautiful, you can be anything you want if you just put your mind to it. I know you got dreams…what is it that you would like to be when you grow up?" she asked. The whole class weighed in on the question, waiting to hear a response from him.

He looked at Ms. Dee and then at his classmates, answering emphatically, "When I grow up, I want to be a **Duffle Bag Boy!**" He turned on his heels and walked right out of the class. Ms. Dee didn't even bother trying to stop him. Shawty Bankroll had his mind made up, and it was nothing that could stop him from becoming what he set out to be.

A Novel by Pucasso

CHAPTER #1

ᒪIfe ᖴᒪTeᖇING

PRESENT DAY

A-1 pulled up at the MB Financial Bank in an SRT-8 Dodge Challenger. He backed into an empty parking spot, directly in front of the bank's main entrance, and shut off the engine. His crony, **Kick-Dough**, was in the passenger seat finishing the last of a Newport. He put it out, mashing it into the ashtray, and then got into position.

"You ready, my nigga?" A-1 asked, giving Kick-Dough a savage stare.

"Mandatory," he replied, rubbing both of his palms together. "Mandatory."

Good, because it's five minutes till 11 o'clock…he should be pulling up any moment now." A-1 said, looking at his phone.

Kick-Dough reached back and grabbed the license plate out of window and placed it on the floor. A few minutes later, a foreign hatchback pulled into the bank's parking lot and parked right beside them on the left-hand side. The driver hesitated to cut his car off, taking his time before getting out. Kick-Dough waited patiently for the perfect moment to strike.

"Okay, I just seen it, he put it on the right side under his jacket." A-1 said, with enthusiasm.

The driver of the vehicle was an elderly Caucasian male, military veteran, who co-owned a couple of liquor stores. A-1 and Kick-dough had been doing homework on him for several weeks now and were determined to take him down today. Money was running low, and it was only a matter of time before they would be broke again...the extravagant lifestyle they were living had taken its toll. They were supposed to hit this lick earlier in the week, but they were too busy wrapped up in new pussy.

"He's getting out," A-1 said, with a smirk on his face. This was the very moment they had been waiting for, and they were ready to set it off.

"Lights, cameras, and action!" Kick-Dough said as he reached for the door handle.

The **Lime-Lite** got out of the car, closing and locking the door behind him. Then he started walking towards the bank, oblivious of the crooked plot at hand. The element of surprise is a muthafucka!

Without hesitation, Kick-Dough sprang into action, running up on the man and snatching the bank envelope. *WHOOP!* This shit was an art. The victim was surely taken off guard, but he wasn't going down without a scuffle. He snatched right back at the bank envelope with all the strength he could possibly muster. "Somebody help me, I'm being robbed!" He screamed.

A-1 fired the car up and put it in drive. He watched diligently in all directions making sure there weren't any cops in sight. "Help me, somebody. Please!"

The victim clung onto the bank envelope for dear life. Kick-Dough struck him in the face and then the ribs with clenched fists. Instantly, the cracker let go of the bank envelope. Kick-Dough grabbed it and took off running towards the car.

A-1 pulled up beside him in the Dodge, and he jumped into the passenger. They calmly pulled out of the bank's parking lot drawing less attention as possible. A-1 looked through the rearview mirror and saw the victim slumped on the ground with a lady kneeling down beside him. She hopped on the phone and began pointing at the getaway car. He really didn't give a fuck though, he'd been doing this shit for some time now. If

the police got on his tail, he would just **Paul Walker** their asses—
VROOM!

"That peckerwood acted like he was willing to lose a whole arm the way he held onto that money," A-1 said, turning the car radio up a few notches. "I kind of thought he was about to do that to you boy."

"Nah, it was a lil' misunderstanding, he ended up seeing shit my way though." Kick-Dough replied, pulling a wad of cash out of the envelope. He sang along to **Chief Keef** while swiftly thumbing through the gwop counting it, *"All I care about is money."*

"Be on point, my nigga, it looked like a lady may have called the shit in." A-1 said. Kick-Dough paid no attention though, he just continued to thumb through the cash.

"That's it...$7,800! That old white muthafucka was willing to lose an arm and possibly a leg or two over this petty-ass cash." Kick-Dough complained, looking ahead.

"$7,800, that ain't shit but fuck off cash at **RED DIAMOND!**" A-1 said, busting a quick left before the light turned red.

"I should have you drive me back, so I can finish kicking his dumb ass...stupid muthafucka!" Kick-Dough said, looking disgusted.

Reality began settling into A-1's brain. "He must've moved the big money Monday. I knew it, we should've been on point then, my nigga," A-1 complained. "See what a funky-ass piece of pussy just cost us...50 muthafucking bands! We are lacking hard, Dough."

A-1 looked over at Kick-Dough with agitation written all over his face. "All this fucking eating we're doing...and the hunger's beginning to fade away!" he said, pounding his fists on the steering wheel.

The SRT-8 pulled up to a red light blocks away from where the robbery took place. Kick-Dough put the cash back into the leather pouch and grabbed the license plate from the floor, along with a screwdriver.

This was standard routine; after every lick they busted, they pulled up somewhere to put the plate back on the car.

The Dodge Challenger was a rental car that Kick-Dough had borrowed from one of his loyal **P's** (a personal customer). Worst case scenario, all the **P** would have to do is report the car stolen. A-1 and Kick-Dough had been busting licks for some time now and were schooled on all the ins and outs of the game.

Them boys done played with a whole bunch of money in their time. They threw the shit around as if it was just candy wrappers. They kept a *duffle bag* full of money with them when parlaying around in luxurious hotel rooms. $7,800 was nothing more than a night out at a hole-in-the-wall club. They partied like rock stars; at any given moment, they were willing to blow every single dollar they owned. To them, having fun was priceless. They had the master key to the city, so getting money was a cake walk to them.

A few months back, A-1 and Kick-Dough went on a frenzy snatching money bags. They managed pulling off several of them in just a week. The money calculated up to damn near a quarter-mil. The way they passed out cash through the hood, you would have swore they were printing the shit themselves. **Duffle Bag Boys** was the title they went by.

The light turned green, and A-1 pulled off again. He continued searching for a decent spot to pull over so Kick-Dough could put the license plate back on the car. A-1 was a few years older than Kick-Dough and had a lot more experience when it came to this street shit. Not taking anything away from K-D; when he was just a youngster, he had popped a notorious gang member in the back and left him paralyzed all over a piece of Harold's Chicken, crazy ain't it? Ever since then, he have been turning up his savage by any means necessary.

A-1 and Kick-Dough were two of a kind; if you saw one, you can bet the other one wasn't too far behind. Indeed, they were true fucking brothers. No fuck shit was involved between them, their main motto was **loyalty over everything**.

"Call Old Man, tell him that we had just come across a slight dimmer and need to be put in the Lime-Lite—asap!" A-1 said.

Old Man, *a.k.a.* **"Pops,"** was their golden-goose egg. To them, he was more valuable than a genie in a bottle. Pops didn't lift his feet unless the occasion had something to do with money. He stayed coming up with licks of all sorts like robbing the ATM cash refillers, gas station owners going to deposit their earnings in banks, smash and grabs, etc.

Pops loved A-1 and Kick-Dough genuinely as if they were his own sons. The game he gave them was priceless, no money was worthy of it. He sharpened them boys like cutting knives and used them accordingly. They were forever in debt with Pops and vowed to show gratitude by curving him off each money move they made.

Kick-Dough looked around in search of his phone and could not find it. "Call my phone, bro…I think I just tweaked," he said, looking in the back on the floor.

"Never," A-1 said as he quickly dialed him up. The sound of a phone vibrated underneath Kick-Dough's seat.

Instantly, Kick-Dough felt relieved. "All I care about is my phone," he rapped, mocking Chief Keef song that was still playing.

"I thought that white fucker was about to be Face-Timing some of your hoes tonight, trying to come up on some black pussy." A-1 snarked while looking deep into the rearview mirror. Flashing lights were accelerating right in their direction.

An off-duty detective in an unmarked car had heard the call come across his radio. *"Attention! A robbery has occurred at an MB Financial*

Bank parking lot in Country Club Hills on 173rd and Cicero. The robbery involved at least two suspects, one identified as being a young black male wearing a black hoodie and fleeing in a red and black Dodge Challenger. The victim is one Caucasian male, a military veteran, who claims to have been beaten badly and robbed for $30,000 dollars. I repeat, the suspects are in a red and black Dodge Challenger traveling northbound towards Markham."

It was pure coincidence that no more than a second after the call came, the detective so happened to run into them.

"Looks like we got company," A-1 said. He was a dog at getting ghost on twelve, that black muthafucka could drive his ass off. It got so embarrassing for the cops that pursued him in the hood that the Chief had speed bumps strategically placed throughout the area. That shit still didn't slow A-1 down though, he was a modern-day **Dukes of Hazard**…the boy had wheel.

Kick-Dough wasn't bothered by a high-speed cop chase either. He just kept reaching along the sides of his seat, trying to grab his phone. He'd been in so many high-speed chases with the law that the shit became a part of his nature. *Checking a bag and getting rid of twelve,* those were golden rules for two breadwinners.

"You already know what time it is, my nigga," Kick-Dough said. Before he could brace himself good, A-1 punched the gas pedal going from 20 mph to a 100, within a blink of an eye. He finally got stabilized and continued trying to recover his phone from under the seat.

"VROOM!" was the distinct sound heard as they flew pass cars, zig-zagging through traffic at top speed. "Ooh-wee," Kick-Dough said, expelling a monstrous laugh afterwards.

A-1 whipped in between two cars so close that it could have even made Vin Diesel shrink in his seat. The off-duty detective wasn't giving up easy though, he kept an eye on the SRT-8 good enough to pinpoint each direction it went. "Who is this muthafucka...the black cop from **Gone in 60 seconds**?" Kick-Dough said, looking back trying to get a good view inside the detective's car.

"I don't know, but I'm about to **Nicolas Cage** his thirsty ass, right now!" A-1 whipped around a Dodge Durango and came up to a red light.

Traffic was at a constant flow, crossing the intersection they were headed into. With no time to think, he leaned on the gas pedal and shot through the busy intersection, nearly being t-boned by a Mack truck. *VROOM!* The eager detective was left behind stuck in a mad traffic jam as the intersection clogged in chaos with cars and trucks skidding and swerving.

"On Scoobie's grave, you just did that!" Kick-Dough said, merching the shit on one of their favorable dead homies. Finally, he retrieved his phone from beside the seat and seen that he had three missed calls. One was from A-1, and the other two were from his baby mamas, Trina and Stacey.

Still moving at the speed of lightning, A-1 took his eyes of the road for a split second, giving Kick-Dough the savage stare, and that's when things took a turn for the worst.

Destiny looked at her face in the mirror, seeing the long scar that stretched from the top of her head to underneath her chin. She rubbed her hand across it gently, mentally feeling the very pain of back when the horror first occurred. It's been about 7 years since she had surgery on her face. A buck-fifty...that's how many stitches it took to sew up the left side of her face. She was left with a permanent mark that would have even made a *rag doll* feel alive.

She cried to herself silently, ashamed of the way her face had turned out. She once was a beautiful, nicely-shaped girl who attracted top-flight type of niggas, but now things were a lot different. During her years of being incarcerated, depression had taken over her soul. She had gained weight like a pregnant woman, her hair began falling out, and on top of all that, half of her face looked like the top of a football.

Destiny was doing time in Logan Women's Correctional Facility for first degree murder. She took a plea bargain for 20 years at 100%, that meant she had to run through twenty straight calendars before becoming eligible for parole. She had no family to lean on while being locked up. Her mother died of A.I.D.S., and her father went M.I.A. before she was even born. The only thing she had to look forward to going home to was her daughter, **Olivia.**

When Destiny had first gotten locked up, her baby's father, **Oly**, ended up getting full custody of Olivia, *a.k.a.* "Livy." However though, within a couple of years, he was gunned down in a random drive-by shooting. Taken to a nearby hospital, a doctor sadly pronounced him dead...what a fucking tragedy!

Fortunately, before Livy was handed over to foster care, a close friend of her daddy's grandmother agreed to adopt her. She moved to the northside of Chicago and was brought up decently, despite the horrible adversities she'd been through. Livy remembered her mother very well, just as much as she did her dad. However, she was very confused about what happened to them both and why. She often blamed God for her misfortune.

Her adoptive parents, Mr. and Mrs. Harris, were very loving people who did their best at giving her as much love and affection as they possibly could. Pops, a long-time friend of the Harris', vowed to be the girl's godfather, seeing how adorable she was. He loved and spoiled her as if she was his real daughter. Actually, he didn't have any biological children; A-1, Kick-Dough, and Livy were very precious to him.

The Harris' didn't block Livy's real mother out of her life, they did everything in their power to keep them in touch with each other. For years now, Destiny preferred for the Harris' to not bring Livy to visit her, she did not want her daughter seeing her locked up liked she was some type of animal in a cage. However, Livy was getting older now and curious about seeing her biological mother. This was a delicate matter, Destiny had to come up with something and fast.

Clifford Wright was taken to South Suburban Hospital in Markham, Illinois, shortly after the robbery attack at the MB Financial Bank. He really did not want to go, but it was standard procedure. A cop also rode along in the ambulance asking him questions about the robbery.

"Did the suspect have any tattoos or distinctive marks on him?" The cop whipped out a little pocket notebook.

"None that I can recall at the moment...it all happened so fast." Clifford responded while being attended to by a beautiful nurse.

"You said that the color of the car the suspect jumped into was red and black, right?"

"That's correct, it was a real nice one too."

"Did you get a good look at the driver?"

"No! What's up with my money while you asking me all these damn questions? That son of a bitch took $10,000 from me!" he exclaimed.

The cop flipped back a page in his notepad and said, "I thought you said that it was $30,000 in the bank envelope?"

"Yes, it was $30,000. What, now-I'm being interrogated about my own damn money?" the veteran groused while trying to get up from the stretcher. "I don't have to take this verbal assault from some weak-ass rookie cop. I served my country very well and deserve to be treated accordingly!"

The nurse and the cop calmed him down as they arrived at the hospital for a standard check-up. A couple of hours later, he was released, and the cop took him back to the bank where his car was parked.

"Livy's been asking the Harris' about coming to visit me," Destiny said to a group of females she was sitting with in the *chow hall.*

"Then let the girl come see you; I don't see it hurting the relationship between y'all one bit." one girl repelled.

"Yeah, if anything, it'll bring you two closer together." another girl stated.

"I know, but...it's just..." Destiny paused.

"It's just what, Destiny?" Both of the girls asked, simultaneously.

Destiny, *a.k.a.* "Dez," swallowed hard and continued what she was saying, "It's just...I'm scared."

"Scared of what, girl? You have a beautiful daughter who wants to see you." a friend of hers said.

"I'm not scared of seeing her, I'm worried about her seeing me. Look at my ugly face!" Dez said, tears falling from her eyes.

Her girlfriend Fate, *a.k.a.* "Fee-Fee," sitting right next to her, wiped her eyes off with a piece of napkin and then gave her a kiss on her scar and lips. "You're not ugly baby...you're a precious work of art." she said while looking deeply into Dez eyes. All the girls at the table smiled in admiration.

Fee-Fee was locked up for killing her abusive boyfriend. One day, she climbed through the window where he stayed and caught him in bed with another woman. A fight broke out which led to the kitchen where she grabbed a huge knife. He rushed after her and ended up getting *iced-up* (stabbed) multiple times. It was all out of fear, so she says.

She called the ambulance and they came, but he ended up bleeding to death. Her lawyer called it a crime of passion. She pled guilty to second-degree murder and was given 12 years at 50%. She only had three years and some change left on her sentence. Dez and Fee-Fee had a bond that's unbreakable, *most people would say,* but only time could tell how deep their love was.

"Thank you, honey. You always know how to make me smile when needed most." Dez said while wrapping her arms around Fee-Fee's neck and kissing her passionately. The girls at the table smiled warmly. "You know what...maybe it wouldn't be such a bad idea for my daughter to come see her momma."

CHAPTER #2

𝔸IN'T NO W𝔸Y 𝔸ROUN𝔻 IT

Muscles had 8 in on a 28-year sentence, and although he was going down the hill at the end part of his bit, he didn't feel short at all. The past calendar was the hardest one for him...his grandma, *a.k.a.* "Granny" died from heart failure...his mother, Gee, died from lung cancer...his cousin Scoobie died in a horrible car accident...and a few of his homies fell victim to Chiraq's gang violence. All this shit happened in the same fucking year.

His support system was steadily petering out on him, and prison was beginning to be the only thing he knew. If it wasn't for A-1, Tino, and his favorite cousin, Bible, shit would have been a whole lot worse along the way. A-1 and Tino were Muscles' day one niggas; they went way back to the days when Mount Vernon Park had sandboxes and seesaws.

Muscles, *a.k.a.* "Kee-Kee," was a stand-up, frontline type of nigga. Jumping off the porch at an early age, he learned how to be a problem just from hanging around Bible. Bible is a whole 'nother book. It didn't take long for Muscles to become one of Washington Heights' **"Most Vicious Peoples."** He was a prime shooter, and if you weren't a part of his circle, then you were fair game.

He was from the *Wild-Wild Hundreds*, where gun violence was a quick way to become famous. The **opz** (enemy) wanted him dead, so he never had the luxury of putting his tool down. Nah! Instead, he kept the shits on him like a diaper on a newborn baby.

He was involved in all sorts of crimes...drug trafficking, home invasion, and murder just to name a few. Twelve ended up snatching his ass off the streets, and the judge took care of the rest. He was given a 28-year sentence to serve out at Illinois Department of Corrections Max-prison.

Muscles was only eighteen when he was thrown in the slammer. The rumor was, the judge had thrown the book at him (due to his reputation mostly). He was one of the founders of a glorious group of individuals called **MVP** (Most Vicious People). Him, A-1, and Tino had started the group back in the 90s; ever since then, MVP had been the leading criminal element and the major focus of discussion and law enforcement attention throughout the hood.

The posse combed through Washington Heights like a plastic hair pick going through an afro. They pushed cola like a pop machine and busted more caps than cowboys. All the lil shorties looked up to them...they were titans. Their swag was duplicated so much that it's a pity they didn't patent the shit. MVP wasn't your average street gang...it was a fucking movement.

"Push-push, nigga, come on-keep pushing!" Double-O shouted to Muscles while spotting him. "Don't stop-you're almost there, keep pushing nigga!"

"Up-up," Double-O said while pointing his thumbs up in the air.

Muscles didn't hear a word he was saying though, and frankly didn't give a fuck. He was already zoned out with a pair of Sony earbuds in his ears listening to **Rick Ross**, *"Push it to the limit,"* off the 'Port of Miami' album. That song always got his blood going giving him the exact motivation needed when trying to reach new heights.

He often daydreamed of the very moment where the prison bars opened up, freeing him from captivity. Everybody in the hood looked forward to seeing him come home…lil' drillers (shooters), bitches, the opz, family and friends, etc. There are cops that haven't gotten a good night's rest knowing Muscles would be back on the streets again. He was mentioned in conversations so much that he became a modern-day urban legend. The impact he left on the hood was an ongoing event.

"Okay, lock it out-lock it out, nigga!" Double-O said, guiding Muscles. He attempted to grab the bar.

"Don't touch it," Muscles breathed. "I got this bitch…she's all mine."

This was Muscles' money, and nobody could take it away from him. He locked his back arms, pushing the 495-pound bar up and back into the rack; all eyes were on him. He hopped up from the bench flexing hard looking like **Tookie Williams**.

He began singing out loud, "Put it all on the line, at the drop of a dime. I be pushing them whips-yep, three at a time. I'm pushing it, I'm pushing it." He continued rapping, extending his arms out in a pushing motion like he was Rick Ross himself.

Other lifters on the weight-pile just stared at himself in complete amazement. "Damn, he pushed that shit straight up like he had a hydraulic jack under him." one lifter said to another, while doing curls.

"I feel sorry for the stupid muthafucka that pisses him off, for real." the other lifter replied.

"That ain't shit," Montana said. "If I was locked up for a decade straight, I'll be hitting more than that!"

Montana was a pack-worker, from out west, doing a wine head bit for a drug conspiracy charge. He was the ultimate hater. "Hell, the muthafucka weigh damn near what he just hit." he said, exaggerating the matter. You would think that a puny muthafucka, who only weighed a buck-sixty, knew how to watch his mouth when speaking about a full-blown killer like Muscles. But nah, Montana was a chaos agent, and it was only a matter of time before him and Muscles clashed.

"You banged that bitch, bro...it looked like you had another one in you." Double-O said while unloading the bar. Muscles was on the other side helping.

"That shit only looked like that I damn near shitted on myself pushing that muthafucka!" Muscles replied. "Okay, let's break it down to three plates and rep out till they call yard."

Looking up, Muscles sensed being mugged by Montana. Montana noticed that Muscles was looking back at him and turned his eyes elsewhere. Muscles kept his eyes focused trying to catch Montana eyeballing again, but he never did. *I'm tripping*, Muscles thought to himself. He turned his attention back to Double-O.

Double had been frustrated with the progression of his bench, so recently he joined Muscles' workout plan to improve his strength. It was a powerplay to say the least. Muscles rocked with Double-O the long way. They were both brought up in the Wild-Wild Hundreds and shared the same ethical background...kill or be killed...money over bitches...death before dishonor...trust no man only God. You know, that Mafioso shit.

Double-O had six in on a 17-year bit; but unlike Muscles, he felt short. He took a plea deal for an aggravated-kidnapping of a minor. Him and one of his cousins snatched up a big-time drug dealer's kid from school and held him captive for ransom money. A hundred-thou was the demand; but somehow twelve got involved, that's when the plot went sour.

"Lil' Bit supposed to be coming to check a pimp out next week," Muscles said while pushing the three-fifteen up and down easily, with his legs crossed in the air. "Ever since her husband got back from deployment, all of a sudden, she seems to have her hands tied."

"It's that nigga, he's home now. She got to go back to being a housewife." Double-O responded, standing behind Muscles watching him with the weight.

Muscles racked the bar, sat up on the bench, and said, "The nigga think he can turn a hoe into a housewife...my hoe at that." Double-O couldn't help but laugh as he switched places with Muscles on the bench. "For real, broski...that's my bitch She's just married to him under a financial agreement." He grabbed the bar off the rack and handed it to Double-O.

Lil' Bit was Muscles' high-school sweetheart. She was a five-foot, chocolate, sexy lady with a horse ass. Muscles loved him some Lil' Bit. When he first got booked, he winded up losing contact with her. He just got back in tune with her recently but wasn't too happy to hear about her current situation...unhappily married with children. Yeah, that **Carl Thomas** shit.

"Come on...push it up...up my nigga...give me one more." Muscles said while spotting Double-O. He pushed at another rep then racked the bar.

"Financial agreement...huh, that shit sound like some **Indecent Proposal** type of shit." Double-O said, as he sat up on the bench.

Muscles laughed and threw his workout gloves at him. "You got them bitches," Muscles said, referring bitches to jokes.

A guard yelled through the bullhorn, "Yard's over, come to the front gate." The two partners concluded their workout, sliding off the weight-pile chatting about jailhouse politics. They were super-jammed, and it goes without say that Muscles had every intention on looking out for Double-O once he hit the streets.

Double-O support system was at a minimum also, and times were beginning to get rough for him, financially. His dear mother was getting up there in age and already was taking care of his son. His baby-mama had got gunned down at a gas station, just shortly after him being found guilty. Although the homicide went unsolved, he suspected it had something to do with his case.

"What's on the menu tonight, Chef Boyer G?" Muscles asked as he rubbed his stomach. Double-O was a straight dog at whipping up anything and when the two boys feast, the shit looked just liked Thanksgiving Day.

"I got a taste for some gyros," he responded while moving his mouth as if he was chewing on something.

"Then gyros it is. Grab whatever you need from out of my box," Muscles said, handing over the key to his room. "I got to catch this horn right quick to make sure bro 'nem sent that bread off. Them niggas be high and shit, they liable to forgot."

"Go ahead, my nigga. I'm gonna hop in the shower first and then start throwing down." Double-O said.

"Alright, bet."

They entered their cellblock and Muscles skipped straight to the phone.

"Watch out for that car!" yelled Kick-Dough while bracing himself for a sudden impact.

"*Skrrr!*" screamed the Challenger as A-1 pumped hard on the brakes trying to maneuver his way around a Nissan Maxima that had suddenly took a pause right in front of them. He managed pulling it off, whipping the steering wheel like he was at the arcade room playing a race car game. *Easy!*

Kick-Dough could do nothing but watch as A-1 tried gaining back control of the car. A Chevy Malibu pulled out of a parking spot and into the lane the SRT-8 was fishtailing towards.

"*Smack!*" A-1 crashed into the Chevy, T-boning the rear driver side. The Challenger spun around in a half circle, leaving the rear end wrapped around a light pole. The Chevy was knocked back to the side walk. Airbags expelled inside of the rental, pounding A-1 in the face and Kick-Dough in the chest. All you could hear and see was the horn beeping and smoke coming from both vehicles.

"Fuck!" A-1 shouted as he grabbed ahold of his head and unbuckled his seatbelt.

"You alright, nigga?" Kick-Dough asked.

"My fucking head," he responded. "That damn airbag got one hell of a punch."

A-1 tried getting out of the car, but the door was jammed. Kick-Dough searched for his phone again; in the process, he found the bank envelope in between his seat and the door. When he reached down to grab it, he noticed blood all down the door. He was leaking from his right arm.

"Come on, we got to get outta here before twelve comes," A-1 said as he climbed out of the window with his phone in his hand. "You got the money, right?"

"Mandatory, but I don't see my phone."

"You and that damn phone," A-1 complained.

"I know, right. I'm leaking too, bro."

An older black man tried to get out of the totaled Malibu that was on the sidewalk, but the door was jammed shut. He yelled out his window towards the dynamic duo, "You young street punks must be on some kind of dope, driving like a bat out of hell! I hope y'all got some good ass insurance, because I sure in the hell ain't paying for this".

"Shut the fuck up...old man, 'fore I come over there and kick the teeth out your mouth!" Kick-Dough said fiercely, annoyed just off hearing the old man's voice. He had a bad temper and pissing him off was like running through hell with gasoline drawers on, somebody's ass was gonna get fried-deeply.

He got the name Kick-Dough from when he was younger. An older bully had put his hands on his lil' cousin. When he got word of it, he went looking for the fucker with a golf club. It didn't take long for him to catch up with the nigga. As soon as he saw Kick-dough, he took off running towards the front door of his house. He flew through the gate first and then up the front porch stairs.

Kick-Dough, being a superb sprinter himself, got right on him like a lion hunting a gazelle. The bully made it to the front door and opened it swiftly. He slammed it behind him and tried latching the chain on it, but before he could complete the task, Kick-Dough came stomping through the door like he was a college frat-brother.

Running in fear, the boy ended up tripping and fell to the floor in the front room where his grandpa was watching the classic television show **Good Times**. Kick-Dough walked up on him while taking a few short practice swings, as if he was up to bat or something. He looked down and seen the nigga had pissed on himself.

He pointed the golf club up to the boy's forehead and said, "Next time I won't be as nice." He turned about taking a half of a step like he was getting ready to leave, but out of nowhere, he swung back around and cracked the nigga in his skull—leaving a knot on it about as big as a golf ball.

The boy's grandfather didn't even bother to look up at his grandson getting punished; he just continued to watch J-J and the rest of the cast. Ever since that day, Anthony Moore went by the name Kick-Dough.

Traffic started to get congested from the accident. Out of nowhere, the unmarked detective car came speeding towards the wreck. A-1 and Kick-Dough took off running away from the crime scene, through a vacant parking lot and down an alley. Police squad cars began swarming in from every direction...up the block...down the alley...and through the side streets. A-1 and Kick-Dough hid out in a nearby garage, waiting for the chance to make their getaway.

"It's like they done assembled every pig in town. Look at 'em, they're everywhere." A-1 said as he peeped out the garage window.

"Damn...we gotta keep moving! Pretty soon they're gonna get the canines." Kick-Dough thought out loud. He took the money out of the envelope and held it in one hand while tucking away the leather pouch in a toolbox. Then he separated the cash in half and tried handing A-1 his proper chop.

"Here, bro," Kick-Dough said, stuffing his half into his Robin Jeans.

Waving him off, A-1 said, "Nah bro, you hold onto all of the gwop. In fact, here...take my phone too. I'm running out of breath, and it won't be long before my legs give out on me."

"Man, we done got outta worse jams then this. Ain't no need to give up now, nigga," Kick-Dough replied. "We just gotta keep it moving."

"Listen to me, my nigga, it's too many cops closing in on us, and they're not gonna stop either...not till they find somebody. I'll just be slowing you down." A-1 said, trying to make some sense of the shit. He was a realist; it would be hard enough for one of them to get away, let alone two.

"We gotta split up, right now."

"Fuck nah, nigga! You sound dumber than Ricky in **Boyz N The Hood**. We're in this shit together; if you go down, then I go with you and vise-versa." Kick-Dough said, with emphasis in his voice.

A-1 saw that Kick-Dough wasn't giving up, no matter what he said. The boy was about as stubborn as a mule, he was stuck on street law and wasn't thinking survival. A-1 taught him way better than that. It was just that Kick-Dough loved him just as much as he loved himself. He would die for him if it ever came down to it.

"Ain't no one man above the crew, you know that shit!" Kick-Dough quoted a line from Bishop off the movie **Juice**.

A-1 had to turn his finesse up and take a more deceptive approach. He just wasn't sold on all of the nonsense Kick-Dough was kicking, he knew better.

"Well, somebody gotta be making their way to come get us—immediately! You got any suggestions?" A-1 asked, knowing that he would bite down on the bait.

"Hell yeah, Stacey…she just called," Kick-Dough replied.

"Alright, get her on the phone now and let her know what the lick read." A-1 said while handing over his phone to him once again. "I'm about to take a quick peep out this garage to see what street we're close by, she'll need to know exactly where to come scoop us from."

A-1 went ahead and grabbed the cash that had been sitting in Kick-Dough's hand for the past few minutes. Kick-Dough began dialing his baby mama up. "Hello," Stacey answered.

"Bae, this me,"

"Anthony," she said, sounding really worried.

"Yeah, baby. Listen to me. Twelve on my ass, I need you to come scoop me, asap. I'm out here on foot." He turned around and looked for A-1, noticing that he hadn't returned. The sound of a souped-up engine came racing through the alley—*VROOM!*

Kick-Dough whispered outside of the phone, "A-1, A-1." He looked over at the door and saw a pile of money sitting on a wooden stand.

Instantly, his eyes went straight to the window, a cop car shot pass chasing A-1 down the alleyway.

"Fuck-fuck-fuck!" Kick-Dough spat as he put the phone back up to his ear. He made his way towards the door and grabbed the money from off the stand.

"Hello-hello," Stacey shouted through the phone. "Anthony, what's wrong? where are you?"

"Baby, you hear me? Kick-Dough asked as he peeped out the doorway making sure the coast was clear.

"Yeah, tell me where you are, and I'm on my way!"

Stacey was the baby mama whom he could trust and depend on-no matter what. It wouldn't matter if she so happened to be busy fucking President Obama, if Kick-Dough needed her she was on her way...in a timely fashion.

"I don't know exactly, just start coming towards South Holland and hurry up!" he said angrily. He was pissed off that A-1 had finessed him. *I got to get away,* he thought to himself as he exited the garage running in the opposite direction of A-1 and the cop car.

"Freeze," a cop yelled out while hopping out of the squad car, pointing his gun. A-1 didn't look back though, he just hopped over the fence and kept running.

"Suspect is on foot coming through the yard going towards Central Ave. He's a black male wearing all black. I repeat, I'm on foot in pursuit of the robbery suspect, gonnawards Central Ave." the cop said, calling it in on his radio.

A-1 rocketed out from the side of the house, looking like Usain Bolt in the 100 meters race. As he made it to the street, a cop tried to run him over, but he still managed to fly pass the front of the car without getting hit. Then he went hopping from yard to yard, diverting the cops as far away from Kick-Dough as possible. He gave them pigs a run for their money.

However, it wasn't too much longer before twelve painted A-1 into a corner. He was forced to try to hide under an abandoned car in the back of a house. The cops brought the canines through, and that was all she wrote for the infamous cop chase.

"Where are you, Anthony?" Stacey hollered into the phone.

Besides his parents and twelve, Stacey was the only other person that called kick-Dough by his government name. He didn't mind it though; she was green to the streets and highly educated. He had gained a decent lead on the cops' manhunt.

"I'm on Chicago Road hiding under a blue Infiniti. It's parked on the west side of the street," he said, breathing hard through the phone. "Where you at?"

"I'm right here, you don't see me? I'm driving my mother's car." she said as she looked at her mother dead in the eye. Her mother didn't like Kick-Dough but tolerated him only because of her precious grandbaby, Baby Aaron. She loved that lil' boy with everything in her, he was her rock. Seeing how Kick-Dough went hard for him, made her accept him somewhat.

Stacey's mother, *a.k.a.* **"Ms. Jackie,"** didn't appreciate the way Kick-Dough was treating her daughter. She stayed sneak dissing him every chance she got. "What the hell this boy done got himself into now? It's always something with him. Don't he know you're with your mother and son?" she complained.

"No momma, I didn't get a chance to let him know. He needs me though," Stacey said, feeling the negative vibe coming from her mother.

"Need you my ass! He only calls you when he's either in some shit or to check up on Baby Aaron," **Jeremiah** was playing on the radio, *"Tell me if you're bout that life right now, hope it ain't talk. I can take you to the mile-high club, what's up-let's take a trip."*

"And what in the world made him name my grandbaby after some low-life street punk? Goes to show you how much he's thinking about his son's future."

"Please, don't start that right now, momma." Stacey warned, trying to keep her cool.

"Why didn't he just call his other baby mama or one of them lil' stripper whores he throws all his money at?" Ms. Jackie said while looking in the back at Baby Aaron, putting his pacifier back in his mouth and gently pinching his cheek. "That's granny's baby there, yes shim is."

Stacey was frustrated, she didn't like the things her mother was saying about her man. However, in all actuality it was all the truth. She hated that Kick-Dough always put her in compromising situations. She was growing tired of being looked at like a fool, but what could she do...she was strung out in love with him.

From day one, Kick-Dough stole her heart putting an ugly spell on her. Regardless of how stupid he made her look with all his infidelities, she defended him wholeheartedly, even from her own mother.

"I don't wanna talk about this with you right now, momma! Sometimes you need to just mind your own damn business," Stacey shouted, with Kick-Dough still on the phone listening. "Maybe then you could find a man of your own, instead of sleeping around with Mrs. Johnson's husband!"

Stacey's words made her mother bristle up. She sat in the passenger seat looking at her daughter in total disbelief.

"I mean, I know he's a certified plumber and all, but how much pipe does the man have to lay before the kitchen sink gets repaired, momma?" Stacey said, exposing her mother's own flaws. "It seems to me, he's been laying pipe everywhere else except the kitchen."

Ms. Jackie was ready to blow...she had to catch herself from smacking the shit out of her daughter, kicking her out of the car, and riding off with Baby Aaron. Stacey never really disrespected her, she always held her tongue when it came to her mother and her affairs. However, today Stacey had reached her limit, she couldn't hold the shit back anymore. Ms. Jackie was hotter than a Saturday night special, and Stacey saw it all in her face.

"I'm sorry, momma, I shouldn't have said that," she pleaded. "Please, forgive me."

Her mother just turned away towards the door and acted as if she was deaf. She had reached an all-time high when it came to being enraged. Her thoughts began to drift off into the land of animosity, and Kick-Dough's face was there-front and center. *I'm gonna fix that muthafucka, if I don't get to do shit else in life. I'm gonna fix his ass real good!* she thought to herself while sitting in the car silently.

"You brought your mother with you, what the fuck?" Kick-Dough said, after hearing their conversation. He had stripped from out of the hoodie he had on, it was stained with blood. He was glad that Stacey had made it to him so quickly, he just didn't like her mother being in his business.

"I was already in traffic with her and the baby, I just wanted to get to you as fast as possible." she explained.

Ms. Jackie kept her head turned towards the window as she sang along to **Bill Withers** that was playing on the radio station, "I don't want to spread the news/—but if it feels this good getting used/—aw, then just keep on using me—until you use me up."

Stacey recognized the sarcasm behind the song her mother was singing along to. She just ignored it though; she was relieved that she was back talking.

"Don't trip, look in every direction and tell me if you see the cops." Kick-Dough said as he began easing from under the Infiniti.

Just as Stacey looked up in front of her, a couple of squad cars sped through the intersection. She re-focused and looked all around her in a complete 360-degree circle. Seeing that the coast was clear, she yelled through the phone eagerly, "Come on, now, you good. Hurry-hurry!"

Within a split second, the back door opened, and Kick-Dough came diving through it. "Pull off slowly, bae...real easy." Kick-Dough said while patting her on the shoulder as if she was just a good pal in the time of need.

"Until you use me up!" Ms. Jackie kept dabbling in sarcasm. Kick-Dough paid her no attention, not even the slightest bit. He knew that she was just a scorned old woman jealous of the fact that her daughter had something she didn't...a man of her own. Stacey never knew her father, and she had an older sister strung out on dope. Technically, Kick-Dough and Baby Aaron was all she had and ever wanted.

Kick-Dough looked at his son in the face seeing a spit image of himself. "What up, lil' nigga...what cha looking at?" he blabbered at his son while roughing him up.

"Da-da!" Baby Aaron cooed, clearly.

CHAPTER #3

FIRST 48

When the cops brought A-1 into the police station, you could clearly see where the canines had torn deep chunks of flesh out of his arm and leg. Detectives took his clothes and personal property into inventory for evidence. Although he wasn't picked out of any photo arrays by the peckerwood that was robbed, a security camera placed him at the scene of the car accident. The older man in the Chevy Malibu picked him out of a line-up along with another eye witness of the car crash.

Investigators retrieved Kick-Dough's phone from the totaled Challenger they had impounded. They also took DNA samples from the car door where Kick-Dough's blood was. They dusted the car thoroughly for fingerprints.

Carl Stucky, Kick-Dough's loyal P, name came back being the cardholder who rented the Dodge Challenger. Shit was beginning to look bad for A-1, detectives gather as much evidence as they could to solve the case.

A-1 sat in the cell with only his undergarments on. He was angry with himself for getting caught and worried about his partner, Kick-Dough. He paced back and forth in the empty cell, praying that he had gotten away with the lil' robbery money. It was real tough that A-1 had to take one for the team, but Kick-Dough was well worth the sacrifice.

A-1 understood the flip side of the coin. Jail was just a place where he got some rest and prepared for his next move. He was destined to be a **Duffle Bag Boy**; ever since he was in the third grade, he's been *jugging* and *finessing*. The O-G's in the hood gave him the name Shawty Bankroll cause he used to always whip out a wad of cash from one pocket, flash it, and then put it into the other. He kept all his dollars together arranged in their proper order. When it came to managing a bankroll, he had an adept quality about himself.

Not too many people could outshoot him on the dice either. He click-clacked with the terrific finesse, passing for hours at a time. He turned crap games into block parties; when he shot, everybody and their mommas gathered around to see him perform. Scuffing up a brand-new pair of Jordan's was quite necessary when it came to striking a pose.

One of his most memorable dice games was when he shot against this well-known baller named **Dolla Bill.** Dolla Bill done shot dice with **Puffy, Snoop, and J'Prince**, just to name a few. He had so much money on him that day while fading A-1 (*Shawty Bankroll*), he stacked all his cash up on the ground and took a squat on it. The money was said to have been tallied out to a hundred bands. "*Shoot your shot, lil nigga,*" was all he often would say, covering every bet available…no matter what it was.

He rarely even took a shot at the dice. No matter how many times A-1 passed on the dice, eventually the dice would always turn, leaving the big bank capturing all the smaller ones. And when it came to chips, Dolla Bill was a walking casino.

It's been times when Dolla Bill managed to let A-1 get away with some winnings, about 15 to 20 *bucks* (thousand dollars); but between passing it all out or losing it right back to Dolla bill, A-1 found himself back at square one…back hugging the block. It wasn't until Pops took him under his wings, giving him a beautiful game, that changed his life forever. Snatching bags…A-1 recalls back when Pops first put him in the Lime-Lite.

"A nigga would beat up or even kill his own kind over a measly hundred-dollar bill but would run up on a cracker who's holding 40 or 50 bucks and freeze up," Pops said, with a silky tone. "You see, it takes a special type of nigga to take away from the white man."

A-1 paid close attention, listening intently as Pops read the lick down to him. The teachings was very enlightening, he tried soaking up as much game as possible. He was at Pops pad, in the basement, where it resembled a mini-lounge. The **Four Tops** was bumping through a surround-sound stereo system, *"Still water runs deep…still water runs deep."*

"Shawty Bankroll, I know you're a go-getter, it shows from how you handle your business out here in these streets," Pops said. "But snatching a leather pouch filled with money from **Uncle Tom** just ain't yo' average day on the block. You have to be built for this type of shit, mentally and physically."

Pops pointed his finger at A-1 and continued speaking, "This type of game will last forever. As long as businesses are up and running, they gonna need somebody to deposit that cash into a bank account for them, and son, Mr. Brinks charges an arm and a leg."

Pops took a pull of his Cuban cigar and cracked open the bottle of Crown Royal that was sitting on the mini-bar. "I can take you to the water, son, but I can't force you to drink the shit. Nah…you already gotta have a thirst for this line of work." he said, pouring him and A-1 a shot. They tapped glasses against one another and then took the smooth drink down their throats at the same time.

"One day real soon, I'm gonna pull up on you and give you some real good news, or rather I should say…put you in the Lime-Lite." Pops said while shaking up with A-1 and giving him a fatherly hug. He loved him and really wanted the best for the youngster.

Hearing footsteps approaching outside the room, A-1 snapped out of the daydream and began to contemplate on his current situation.

Word got back to the streets that A-1 had gotten locked up for a robbery, and Kick-Dough was on the run. Nobody really knew the whole story behind the shit, all that was said was it was a robbery gone bad. A news reporter on WGN News said, *"One of the robbery suspects had gotten away with $30,000."*

"Them some lying muthafuckas." Kick-Dough remarked, cutting the television off. Ever since him and Stacey had dropped off Baby-Aaron with Ms. Jackie at her house, the day of the robbery, they been laying low in a hotel room outside of the city. Nobody knew where Stacey's mother lived except A-1. They kept Ms. Jackie's car and pulled Stacey's up in the garage.

Kick-Dough gave a band to Stacey to give to Ms. Jackie so she could keep all her suspicions to herself. She didn't know much, but possibly, what she did know could put him in a terrible position. Ms. Jackie was a money-hungry, conniving woman who always had her hand out for something. If she was to find out about Kick-Dough's involvement in the robbery...man down.

When Kick-Dough first hit the hotel room, he had perused through A-1's phone getting a few numbers out of it. Then he powered it off and smashed it up against the bathroom floor. He wasn't about to run the risk of letting the police track him down with Apple's latest device- **'find my iPhone.'**

"Damn...my nigga, A-1" he said, sadly as he dropped his face into his palms.

"Baby, don't move!" Stacey said while trying to clean his injured arm.

Since they been at the hotel, she's been taking good care of the wound making sure it didn't get infected. She put alcohol and then some peroxide on it, wrapping it up with a fresh bandage afterwards. She was an RN with hopes of becoming a doctor one day. Kick-Dough's other baby mama Trina was one already...a head doctor.

"I couldn't find my phone in the car, and I left my blood all over the car door. Them people gonna be coming back to look for me soon, baby." Kick-Dough complained, with his head still down in his palms.

"Don't think about it too much right now bae, just chill...we'll figure something out." Stacey said with confidence.

She eased up behind him while he sat on the edge of the bed and began massaging him on the shoulders, kissing him on the neck. Kick-Dough was always up for a good ol' back massage, not to mention the *sloppy top* (blow job) that usually followed.

Stacey was only wearing a Victoria's Secret matching bra and panties set, she was 5'8" weighing out to a hundred and twenty-five pounds. Most of her weight came from her breasts, thighs, and ass. She had no stomach at all, and her waistline was as thin as the line between love and hate. Yes sir, this girl was eye candy. Carmel colored skinned with hazel brown eyes and long natural eyelashes, Stacey's facial features were the epitome of beauty. It wasn't a secret that she had Indian in her family, evidenced by her black wavy hair stretching down her back.

Stacey was a bad bitch, no doubt about, but her glamorous attributes wasn't what had Kick-Dough's heart captured. The kid had a gang of vixens all across town; pulling a bad bitch wasn't a big deal to him. The short, light-skinned player had the swag of that trap music rapstar from

Bankhead, Atlanta—**T.I.** Kick-dough talked and walked that **BOSS-LIFE** shit. Being around A-1, he'd learned how to elevate his game to a whole 'nother level.

Kick-Dough loved Stacey not just because of her amazing looks; it had everything to do with how loyal she was to him. She never crossed him, the thought hadn't even crossed her mind once. The girl remained faithful to him, even after she found out that he cheated on her with one of her co-workers. The truth of the matter was, when it came to love, the only man she saw was Kick-Dough. Her love for him flowed fluidly like water coming out a faucet...but even a well runs dry, eventually.

"Lay down, baby. Let me take your clothes off so you can relax." Stacey said, pulling him up out of his POLO V-neck. Kick-Dough's physique was bricked up; he had a big chest, shoulders, and arms. His lower body matched the top, and his abs were solid.

Stacey got off the bed and knelt down in front of him. She unbuckled his Ferragamo belt sliding his Robin Jeans and Calvin Klein briefs down and off of him. She grabbed his dick and began massaging it gently, bringing it to a full being.

"Aww, baby," he moaned while putting his fingers through her hair, massaging her scalp.

"You like that, Anthony?" she asked, sounding like a porn start. She looked up at him in the face as he bit down on his bottom lip, tilting his head backwards like he was at the barbershop getting hair shaved off his neck.

"Hell yeah," he answered, eager to just snatch her ass up and fuck her on the mattress...the right way. He couldn't take being teased, and she knew it so before she let him take off, she made the first move.

She wet her lips with as much mouth juice as she could muster up and then put 'em on the tip of his dick. She began sucking up and down on it like it was a Bomb Popsicle. Deep throat had become her specialty. She took in his entire move without gagging, massaging the head of it with her tonsils...a little trick she learned over time.

"Aww, baby, I love you!" he moaned, in complete ecstasy.

Keeping her jaws as tight as possible, she sucked her way back up to the top of his dick, making a big smacking noise as she took her mouth off of it. You could see the saliva coming off her tongue connecting to the tip of his lil' mans.

"Oh...you're a lil' slut, huh? Alright then, show me what you're working with." he said as if he was talking to a stripper at Red Diamonds.

Stacey spat on his dick then grabbed it with both hands like it was a wet towel that needed to be wrung out or something. She began massaging it again, gently but efficiently. Then she took her tongue and lips, puckering up erotically, and sucked all around it in a spiral motion, going down farther and farther each time. Kick-Dough was overly pleased with this.

"Yes, baby, you're a big girl now," he said while maneuvering her long, wavy hair out the way. He wrapped it up in a big ball and held it tightly behind her head, showing off his name tatted on her neck. "No more daddy's little girl." he said, rapping one of **Nas'** songs.

She loved when he talked to her while she gave him sloppy-top. It was good confirmation that she was doing an excellent job. It also made her pussy extremely wet like Niagara Falls.

At the beginning of the relationship, the poor girl couldn't suck a dick to save her life. A-1 used to put her down about the shit, using it as an excuse to go and find other women who knew how to do the job right, perhaps Trina. It wasn't till she embraced the challenge, taking some *fellatio* classes, that she developed the ability to satisfy her man completely. She figured that if she didn't boss up and become a **Super Head**, eventually, she'd lose Kick-Dough to someone else that would.

"Oh yeah, right there, baby...that's my spot." he said, grabbing her head and pushing it down on his manhood. She knew that when he did that, he was getting ready to bust. She wasn't having that shit just yet though, she came off his dick making that loud smacking sound again.

"*Smuah*! Who's dick is this, tell me who it belongs to?" she asked, already knowing the answer. She licked her tongue down the big vein bulging out of his dick, all the way to his balls. Once she arrived in *Testicle City*, she put one of them in her mouth and began chewing on it gently. She did the same to the other as well. Before he knew it, she had both of them muthafuckas in her mouth humming. Kick-Dough was way past excited.

"Aww, aww," he kept moaning. "This is your dick, baby…all yours."

She licked her way back up to the top trying to catch his semen before it shot out everywhere. Out of nowhere, she took a deep dive at his piece again, this time she used no hands. She sucked up and down, repeatedly. Kick-Dough began shaking like he was having a seizure of some sort. Orgasms were kicking in back-to-back, one on top of the other. This was the best head he had ever had.

When the precum shot through Stacey's mouth, she moaned and mumbled, "You bout to cum, baby?"

"Yeah-yeah," Kick-Dough answered, sounding like he was about to cry. His eyeballs were rolling to the back of his head. This was definitely an *outer-body experience*.

"Me too, baby," she confessed, still taking his dick back and forth in her mouth, playing with her pussy at the same time.

"Here comes the boom!" he said, letting it shoot out all at once. She took it down her throat as if it was a cold glass of milk.

Stacey was hot and nasty, ready for Kick-Dough to be inside her pussy, asap. All of a sudden, her phone rang, but she ignored it as she came out of her bra and panties. She crawled up on him like a stray cat in the night. Around this time, he was just returning back from a sexual abduction. She kissed him on the chest all the way up to his lips. He grabbed her ass and smacked it. Right when she grabbed his dick and positioned it between her pretty-wings, her phone rang again.

"Answer that," Kick-Dough said pointedly, wanting to know who was calling her and why. Ever since the first time her phone rang, he had a funny feeling in his heart that something was wrong.

"But, baby," Stacey cried, looking like a sad puppy.

"Go ahead now, hurry up! That might be an important call." He lifted up and gave her a kiss. She got up and pouted her way to the dresser where her phone was.

"This better be the fucking President," she mumbled. Kick-Dough watched as her ass bounced up and down like two miniature basketballs from **Six Flags Great America**. He couldn't wait for her to get back, so he could dunk a couple baskets.

"Hello," she said, answering the phone angrily.

"Where's Kick-Dough?" Sheila, A-1's baby mama, asked. She was crying, making it hard for Stacey to make out anything she was saying. Kick-Dough watched nervously, from the bed.

"Right here, why, what's wrong?" Stacey asked while walking back towards Kick-Dough to give him the phone. Suddenly, she stopped dead in her tracks and said, "He died?"

A suited detective opened the door and walked inside the bright room where A-1 was currently being held. The detective had a manila folder under his arm. He closed the door behind him and then went to the table and sat the folder down. He grabbed his cuff key off his belt and uncuffed A-1 from the bench.

"I'm detective Hogan, and you're Aaron Mann, right?"

"Man, what's the fucking hold up with my phone call? Y'all got me sitting in this bright ass room, cuffed up to the wall like a I done killed a muthafucka or something!" A-1 complained while rubbing his wrists, feeling a slight relief from the cuffs being taken off.

"Could you please, take a seat?"

"Man, fuck that! I've been arrested for two days now and haven't even been charged with any crimes. And on top of that, y'all won't even give me a damn phone call. I know my fucking rights." A-1 argued.

"Just calm down, you'll be given a call shortly. I just need to ask you some questions first." Hogan said calmly while sitting down and opening up the manila folder.

A-1 zoomed in on the picture that was at the top of the papers realizing that his current situation was possibly worser than he'd imagined. He knew exactly what time it was.

"I ain't answering shit, call my lawyer!" he shouted, defiantly.

A-1 had planned for days like this, retaining the best defense team that money could buy...**Chuck Simmons and Associates**. A-1 had been using this powerhouse since his first robbery case. He was caught red-handed but ended up beating the charge on a technicality. The DA was enraged and had been at A-1's neck ever since. A-1 continued to pay Chuck and his team every so often for any future run-in's he might get into with the law.

A knock came from the other side of the glass window and Detective Hogan closed the folder getting up from the chair. "Thank you, Mr. Mann." he said, sarcastically.

"Alright, can I have my phone call now?" A-1 asked, standing by the table-half naked.

"Why sure you can. As soon as you get processed in, you'll be allowed to make one quick call," Hogan said, making his way towards the door.

"Processed in…what am I being charged with?"

The detective paused for a second and then turned around, answering A-1's question, "Felony Murder!"

CHAPTER #4
BREAKING NEWS

When Muscles made it to the phone, he took the receiver off the hook and began punching in a series of numbers, barely even looking at the dial pad. He put the receiver up to the side of his face and spoke, "Keyon Smith," then let it hang as he began stripping out of the soil stained t-shirt he had on. He grabbed receiver again and put it back up against his face.

"Thank you for using Securus, you may now start your conversation." the automated recording said.

"What up, T?" Muscles shouted, sounding pleased to hear from him. T, *a.k.a.* "Tino," was his day one nigga, whom him and A-1 had formed the glorious "MVP" clique with. He stayed in tune with Muscles throughout his bit, always keeping him updated with what was real in the field.

"Shit, just out here in traffic trying to make it happen. What's good with you, my nigga?" T replied, after blowing out kush-smoke choking off the shit.

"I see your ass is still at it, huh?" Muscles commented.

T couldn't help but laugh at his slick remark but only for a short moment. "Man, Joe, you heard what happened?" he asked.

"Nah, nigga...tell me!" "Man...A-1 got bumped for a robbery-murder. It's all over the news."

"Get the fuck out of here, hell nah, how?" Muscles responded, shocked by the latest news. This *snatching money bags* obsession was all new to Muscles; it came long after he was sentenced to prison. All he knew was that his team, MVP, was winning, and when he came home, he wouldn't have shit to worry about.

"They trying to say A-1 and another person had beat up a white veteran man and robbed him for 30 something thousand dollars." T said, before taking another pull off the dope.

"They just beat him up...well, how in the fuck did the muthafucka die?" Muscles replied, gripping on to the phone tightly as if he was about to crush it in his bare hand. The little bit he did know about the moves his team made had nothing to do with murdering someone...an old white man at that. Half of the times, they didn't even have to snatch anything from anyone. All they had to do was bust a car window and *BLAM!* There it was...a duffel bag full of money.

"Some ol' fluke shit, bro. All I know is they said the cracker checked in and out of the hospital the same day the shit supposed to have happen, and then died two days later."

"Damn, that's fucked up! I was just rapping with bro'nem last week; they were on their way to Vegas to see the Mayweather fight." Muscles said. He didn't mention Kick-Dough's name at all. He figured that the other person in the robbery must have been him, especially the way T talked around him. It was a given, Kick-Dough had gotten away.

"Bro got a bond yet?" Muscles asked, knowing that if he did, somebody was gonna be coming to get him—perhaps his cousin, Face.

"Hell nah, no bond, but you know Chuck is on top of the shit. Eventually, something will pan-out."

"You have one-minute left," the automated recording warned them.

"Man, T, put some bread on the phone. I got to finish hollering at you." Muscles said.

"Alright, I'm in the process of making that happen right now as we speak, my nigga." T replied, passing Gunna the blunt...he was riding shotgun.

"Tell that nigga I said what up," Gunna said.

"Oh yeah, Gunna said what up too."

"Yeah, he's in the car with you right now?"

"Yep."

"Tell him I said MVP. I been hearing about his wild ass out there in the shits." Muscles said in a rush, knowing that the phone was about to cut off any moment now. "Man, y'all put me something decent together too. I'm fucked up in this bitch, nigga. I'm gon' call back tomorrow."

"*Thank you for using Securus—goodbye.*"

T kept his distance and carefully followed the white F-150 pickup truck down Harlem Ave. Gunna was still riding shotgun and of course-blowing dope. Gunna, *a.k.a.* "Muff," was awarded the infamous name from how well he fired pistols.

A couple of miles away, Fat-Fat and Sco waited patiently in a First National Bank parking lot. Fat-Fat was in the driver's seat, and Sco road shotgun. They laid low, incognito to the random traffic going on around them. **Meek Mills** voice came out of the car speakers at a low volume, "*When it comes to stunting, I'm like money man Meech/get my clique together, and we're coming in a fleet.*"

Fat-Fat scrolled through his phone as Sco rubbed his hands together slowly, looking out the window for the Lime-Lite.

"Come on, muthafucka, bring your ass here." Sco said.

It was 10:30 a.m. when Fat-Fat's phone rang. Seeing Gunna's name on the screen, he quickly answered, "What the lick read?"

"The Lime-Lite is about a block and a half away. Y'all in position, right?"

"Hell yeah!" Fat-Fat answered, tapping Sco on the arm.

"Buddy's making his way towards us now," he warned Sco.

Gunna continued laying the lick down, "Stick to the script, we gonna be posted up across the street in that lil' strip mall parking lot. Don't tweak! Tell Sco to wait till the vic get out the truck and on his way towards the bank before taking flight. Get that fucking bag and then get the hell out of dodge, the shit's that simple." He moved his hands like a musical conductor, orchestrating a classical symphony.

T just watched, letting Gunna put things in its proper order. He'd been doing homework on this move for a month now, and he had all his t's crossed and i's dotted. He was very determined to get a bag today.

Now was the time to strike; a bunch of janky shit's been happening lately…niggas been freezing up on the targets…dropping money all in the streets…losing tails, etc. And what happened to A-1 and Kick-Dough just took the cake. Finances were in the red for T. He owed a bunch of money for drug consignments he hadn't paid back for a nice while now. Bible was one of those bill-collectors.

Everybody in the neighborhood knew that Bible didn't play about collecting debts, he was the epitome of a loan shark. It didn't matter if it was just $50 owed to him either; that very amount would get a niggas head bashed against the concrete.

T was down on his luck and had to make a move fast, he barely had kush money to blow. Unlike A-1 and Kick-Dough, Pops didn't take too well with him. Once Pops learned about his pettiness, he didn't even bother speaking to him, let alone putting him in the Lime-Lite. T didn't have any beef with Pops, he just felt that he didn't have to chop him in off his own personal moves…talking about, *"A muthafucka ain't never did shit for me."*

Whatever A-1 and Kick-Dough would do with their money was on them. T had different plans with how he handled his cut and passing it out wasn't in the equation. A-1 and Kick-Dough kept their oath unbroken and curved Pops off every move they were involved in, regardless of whether he knew about it or not. They were very loyal to him, and the return was definitely worth it.

T didn't give a fuck about an oath kept or broken…he never cared. He was out to get it on his own and within his own crew. A-1 was in jail now, and Kick-Dough was said to be in the same boat eventually once twelve catches up with his ass. The way T seen it, this was his opportunity to be the top **Duffle Bag Boy**. The moment had come for him to solidify that slot.

The white Ford F-150 pickup truck pulled into the First National Bank parking lot, just as planned, and parked right next to Fat-Fat and Sco. Sco was already on point with a can of mace in his hand. The driver of the pickup truck had a decent size on him, Sco didn't stand a chance trying to wrestle around with him. It would be much easier for him to just spray the vic in the face and then go to work, stripping him of the money bag.

"Make sure you spray him in the face good. Once you do that, everything else is a piece of cake." Fat-Fat screened Sco.

"I got this, scud. I'm official with this shit, just check me out," Sco bragged.

The heavy-set man hopped out of the truck, but instead of walking towards the bank, he went to the back of the truck. Paying no attention, Sco bailed out and made his way to the vic. He was just about to open the side compartment until something told him to look up. When he did, he'd seen a suspicious young black male in all black coming in his direction.

T and Gunna watched from across the street, helplessly. "I told them dumb ass niggas not to take off till the vic began making his way to the bank!" Gunna complained, looking disgusted. T just watched, thinking, *Some more fluke shit is about to happen, I can just feel it.*

The heavyset man took his keys back out of the side compartment and tried to put them back in his pocket. However, Sco was right up on him with the mace can out, spraying him excessively. Instantly, the man grabbed his face and screamed, "Help me somebody!"

The keys dropped on the ground, and Sco reached down scooping them up in one whop, *whoop!* It was multiple keys on the ring through. *Dammit! Which one is it?* he thought to himself. Fat-Fat watched nervously, not knowing what to do. He fired the engine up and waited while Sco thumbed through the set of keys trying to find a match to the compartment. Right when he found the key and opened it, the heavyset man grabbed ahold of him.

"Help me, somebody, please, I'm being robbed!" he yelled. The fumes from the mace were strong, both the vic and Sco were choking. People started taking notice of the robbery in progress.

"Fuck!" Fat-Fat said as he bailed out to help his partner. He came up from behind the man and threw him in the full nelson. "Get the money, hurry up!"

Sco reached in the compartment and grabbed the bank envelope. "I got it, let's get out of here!" he said, tucking it in his pants. The two thugs bailed back in the car and took off in a dash. A security guard came out and helped the injured man.

"Call them clown-ass niggas," T said while pulling out of the parking lot he was in. "Tell them to slow the fuck down they're fronting the move."

Gunna dialed up Fat-Fat, "What up bro?" he answered.

"Man, ease off the gas and drive like you got some sense. You got your **Ghost Speed-Racer** turned up on dangerous."

"Tell them to go towards the expressway and hop on, going the Indiana way." T commanded. Gunna relayed the message.

"Alright, bet." Fat-Fat replied. Sco unzipped the leather pouch and pulled out a bunch of grocery coupons.

"What the fuck...hell nah!" he shouted while digging deeper into the pouch pulling out another wad of coupons. "This ain't money...we got juked!"

Once Fat-Fat seen the coupons, he banged his fist on the steering wheel in rage. "Fuck, we just jagged the lick off!" He called Gunna back and relayed the bad news.

T seen it in his homie's eyes that some fuck shit had happened again. All he could do was shake his head in great disappointment. *I can't win for losing'* he thought to himself, wanting to cry.

"Are you alright?" the security guard asked while helping the vic up off the ground.

"My eyes are burning—I need some water in them" he complained, barely can see. He reached on the side of his waist and grabbed a healthy bank envelope, stuffed with money—$50,000 to be exact. He began laughing to himself, "Stupid muthafuckas!"

Muscles was torn by the devastating news about A-1 and Kick-Dough. Every time when the tables had seemed to be turning good for him, something bad always happened. Misfortune had become his best friend...the only friend he had for the moment.

The only thing worthy of keeping the beast in him contained was some good ol' rec, pushing some iron or pounding on muthafuckas heads...whichever one came first. He was so agitated a fly landing on him could cause him to go off on somebody. Now wasn't the time to get in his way.

"You got an extra pair of gloves that I can work out with?" Muscles asked Double-O while looking around on the floor for his. "I think a muthafucka picked mine up by accident or something."

Muscles zoomed in on a pair of gloves sitting on a table by Montana. *Them too ripped up to be mine* he thought to himself.

"I'm not sure, I have to go check in my room. How you lose yours? You just had 'em in your back pocket," Double O replied, helping look around for them.

Muscles patted his back pockets seeing they weren't there. He backtracked his steps all the way to his cell, making sure he didn't drop them by chance. He came back from the trek empty-handed. He questioned his cellie about the whereabouts of his gloves, but he didn't have the slightest clue.

Muscles' blood began to boil. It wasn't because of the expense of the gloves, which was petty-cash. It was the basic principle...a muthafucka shouldn't touch shit that doesn't belong to them.

I know a muthafucka didn't just jump my gate (steal) *for my damn gloves,* he thought to himself. Double-O started walking around asking people if they seen some gloves laying around anywhere. Yard was getting ready to be called in about ten or fifteen minutes.

The dayroom was packed with individuals standing around waiting to go outside. Double-O went back to his cell to check to see if he had an extra pair. Muscles marched to the T.V. area where it was a gang of people, including Montana, and shut it off.

"Ay, did anybody pick up a pair of brown insulated gloves that doesn't belong to them?" he asked, calmly. "Please, check and see. You may have picked them up by accident, thinking they were yours."

Muscles was a walking time-bomb, and the slightest thing could trigger him to go off. The whole dayroom was on notice, however, no one volunteered any information.

"Did anybody pick up a pair of gloves that don't belong to them? They're mine and I want 'em now! Stealing carries no probation." Muscles said, loudly.

"Man, don't nobody know where you misplaced your gloves! Cut the damn T.V. back on, would you...we're missing the news!" Montana said.

"Nigga, fuck you and that pussy ass news! If my gloves don't come up found within the next minute or so, I'm gonna turn this whole gallery upside down and shake it!" Double-O was still in his room looking for some gloves.

The entire deck got quieter than an abandoned church seeing the Muscle-man turning into another color. Montana stood up and pimped off talking under his breath, "Muthafuckas be letting them weights go to their heads...get a lil size on them and don't know how to act."

"What your bitch ass just say?" Muscles replied while making his way towards Montana in a hurry.

"You heard what the fuck—" Before Montana could turn around and finish what he was saying, Muscles had thrown a three-piece combo, connecting with his face. "*Peck-peck-peck!*" Muscles went from hand to hand, dropping blows on Montana. Just when it seemed like he was about to collapse, Muscles snatched him up right off of his feet. He lifted the bony nigga straight up in the air, horizontally, and then dropped him dead on his fucking neck...*twelve o'clocked* him.

When Montana's face smacked the concrete, the whole dayroom felt it. They shouted, "Damn!" all at the same time. Double-O heard the sudden commotion and hurried his way back to the day-room. There wasn't a guard present to save Montana's life. Muscles really didn't give a fuck if twelve was on location or not anyway, this was the very rec he'd been waiting for and wasn't about to let anyone stop him from enjoying every bit of it.

Before Montana's body got a good chance to absorb the pavement, Muscles sent multiple kicks, of all sorts, to the back of his skull and face. The boy was unresponsive, and the area began to get bloody; however, that still didn't stop Muscles from stomping a mudhole in his ass.

Double-O came up from behind Muscles and grabbed him by the shoulder, trying to calm him down. "That's enough, broski, you're gonna kill the poor boy!"

Muscles took a slight pause at working out his legs to see who it was disturbing him. Thank God it was his homie because if it would have been anyone else, he would of did 'em the same as Montana. He showed his teeth to Double-O, letting him know to back off, and then went right back to work—stomping Montana's ears together.

"Concussions, muthafucka! See, that's what I'm giving out, concussions!" Muscles yelled as he bounced Montana's head against the concrete like it was a basketball.

"That's enough, it's over-snap out of it, bro!" Double-O said, putting Muscles in a bear hug and pulling him away. Muscles slowly began turning from green, all the way back to his natural skin tone...charcoal.

CHAPTER #5

FꞦMILY TIES

Jesus Rodriguez, *a.k.a.* **"El Huncho,"** sat down at a cherry oak wood, laminated king-sized table looking just like the coldblooded **Mob Boss** he was. He was surrounded by a number of Surenos, all originating from one of the deadliest gangs in the U.S.—MS-13. It was a very urgent matter that needed to be discussed.

El-Honcho was a drug lord, a part of the notorious "Mexican Mafia," who controlled the cartel in the Midwest. The Feds had been running an investigation on El-Huncho and his infamous syndicate for some time now. They sought to link him to a catalog of crimes that could possibly have him thrown under a federal prison. He was heavily involved, making it big off of running a criminal enterprise, tax evasion, extortion, drug-conspiracies, contract murder, etc.

One of El Honcho's top soldiers had got jammed up on some federal charges. The Feds took him down with the help of a federal informant, Samuel Walters, *a.k.a.* "Sammie." He had been purchasing a considerable amount of raw cocaine from the cartel, linking it back to El Huncho.

A Sureno named Ruben Sanchez, *a.k.a.* "Rude Boy," was locked up in the feds waiting to stand trial for multiple drug offenses. Rude Boy had sent word back to El Huncho about the latest discovery he had retrieved. Sammie was named in his documents as a confidential source for the FBI. El Honcho may have met him once or twice, but never had an actual conversation with him directly.

It was a very touchy matter; but surely, El Huncho wouldn't risk Sammie trying to tie him to any crimes nor his loyal soldier, Rude Boy. He would rather find a way to get rid of the infiltrator before something like that happened.

"We have a little problem on our hands, gentlemen," El Honcho said. Even though there were a couple of women sitting at the table, they took no offense to being called gentlemen. "A federal informant who some of y'all may have done business with."

El Honcho took a pull off his Cuban-Cigar and looked at everyone at the table fiercely, before speaking again. "He goes by the name Samuel Walters, aka Sammie," He passed a picture of him around the table so everyone could see how he looked.

"Huh, Sammie the Bull...what a fucking coincidence!" Hector Gonzalez, *a.k.a.* **"Popeye,"** said. This was El Honcho's top soldier now that Rude Boy was locked up.

Popeye earned El Huncho a whole bunch of *dinero* and carried out all orders at his command. He definitely worked hard to become El Huncho's right-hand man. He had a solid foundation established in the Chicagoland; if there was anybody qualified at getting the job done, killing Sammie, it was Popeye.

When Popeye made the funny remark about Sammie, a couple of soldiers laughed out loud; however, El Huncho didn't find shit funny. He remained serious about the subject. "Look, we can't allow this cock-a-roach to come and lay an egg on our family, now can we?" he said, with emphasis. At this point, the group who were once laid back and *chillaxin* had become attentive to every word that came out of El Honcho's mouth.

"Hell nah!" the majority ruled. Everyone began conversing among each other about the latest news, wondering if they were being targeted by the Feds. The noise level turned up a few notches till El Huncho calmed the room down.

"*Shhh, quiet now!*" he said, waving both of his hands in a downward motion. "You all will be able to converse in just a bit, let me wrap this up first."

Two bad Spanish chicks, Mommi and Peebles, stood at his sides, one on the left and the other on his right. Both of 'em were holding M-16's with scopes and laser beams on 'em.

"I got a cool-mil all in American dollars for the person who makes Sammie the Bull disappear for good!" El Honcho looked over at Popeye while putting out his cigar in an ashtray, giving him a heartless look.

Federal Agent Henry L. Cunningham, *a.k.a.* "Bumper," was laying in the bed with his arms wrapped around his wife when he heard his phone rang. Trapped in the coziest comfort ever, he ignored the classical sound of his iPhone going off…he was in a coma surely worth staying in. As soon as the phone rang out and it seemed like whoever was calling had went away, the phone repeated the familiar tune. The shit was very annoying.

"Fuck…" he shouted, looking over at the clock seeing that it was 2 in the morning. *Who in the hell's calling me at this time of night, and for what?* he thought to himself.

Bumper turned aside, removing his arms from around his wife's body, and reached over to grab his phone. "Baby…" she complained, missing the comfort of his body pressed up against hers.

"Hello," he answered, sitting up in the bed and rubbing the side of his face. He didn't bother looking at the number first.

"Bumper, this is Carlos. I'm sorry for disturbing you this time of night, but I got some crucial information that you must know, immediately!"

Carlos Santana, *a.k.a.* "Loso," was an undercover federal agent who managed to infiltrate El Honcho's drug cartel, posing as a Sureno. Loso got a free opportunity to call and inform Bumper about the contract-murder just put on Sammie's head. From the time Loso said he had some crucial information, Bumper had gotten up and walked to the bathroom. He kept his wife out of his work affairs.

"I was at a Cartel meeting today, hosted by El Huncho, and the topic of the discussion was Sam."

Bumper's face dropped into a worried expression as he stopped dead in tracks by the bathroom door. "Sam...what was they saying?"

"El Honcho knows he's a federal informant... he called him a big problem that needs to go away—forever. He put a million-dollars on his head, and the way it looks, a Sureno named Popeye had already guaranteed to take care of the problem." Loso explained.

"How soon you expect this Popeye guy to move in on the hit?"

"Popeye is climbing the ladder, trying to become El Honcho's right-hand man. If you ask me, he's on his way to Sammie's crib as we speak. He got a deadly squad set up in Chicago already. You need to act asap, these MS-13 muthafuckas mean serious business. They won't waste the slightest second when executing a command."

"How close are you to taking this El Huncho fucker down?" Bumper asked, frustrated with the whole ordeal.

"Close, my brother, very close. Just hide Sammie out somewhere till all of this is over, but even then, I can't promise the safety of his life. These MS-13 fuckers are growing deadlier by the day." Loso said.

There wasn't any more for the two to discuss, so Bumper let Loso go, thanking him for the update. Once the call ended, Bumper hopped right back on the line dialing up Sammie. He tried twice, but each time he got sent straight to voicemail. He went ahead and left a brief message, "Sammie, this Bump. There's something very important I need to discuss with you. Call me back when you get this message."

Olivia sat nervously at a hexagon-shaped, metal table in Logan Correctional Center for women waiting to see her biological mother for the first time in over 7 years. She was eager and over-excited about the visit, hoping to recreate the mother and daughter relationship they once had. Livy was a lot older now and had so much to talk about, considering puberty and her start of high school.

The Harris' were very decent people and did a fantastic job caring for Livy. Among keeping a roof over her head...clothes on her back...and food in her mouth, they also gave her emotional support. She appreciated them a whole bunch, respecting and honoring any rules they laid down. They weren't too strict on her, they really didn't have to be...Livy was very responsible and stayed in her studies and away from the many peer pressures that troubled most teens.

Dez was blessed to have guardian angels watching over her precious daughter. There were a number of people in Livy's life making up for the absence of her real parents-the Harris; Pops; and A-1, all of which were awesome individuals. For the most part, Livy had a beautiful support system, and that alone lifted a lot of weight off of Dez's shoulders.

There was a bunch of food scattered out across the table where Livy was sitting that she had bought from the vending machine for her mother. Mrs. Harris brought her to see Dez right after she had agreed to the occasion. She gave them their space by waiting outside the visiting room.

A side door opened up letting a group of lady prisoners in, causing Livy to lift her head to see if she could pick her mother out of the crowd. Seeing a woman coming from the front desk towards her, Livy zoomed in and recognized the infamous scar that took up the whole left side of her mother's face. Without hesitation, she stood up—proudly.

"Momma!" she said, realizing in fact that it was her. A tear fell from her eye as she put both hands over her mouth, letting the sensational feeling absorb all the way in. This was the very moment she'd been waiting for, for so long.

"Livy, my beautiful baby…come and give momma a hug," Dez said while extending both of her arms out and shedding tears. The two girls hugged for a great while; neither one of them felt the need to let go of each other's body. If it was left up to them, they would have just stayed standing, hugging each other till the visit was over. That could have been for a couple of hours at least. However, there were standard visiting rules, and one of them was once a person hug and kiss their visitor, they must have a seat.

"Momma, you done picked up some pounds. You're bigger in person than you are in 'nem pictures you sent me." Livy claimed, still holding onto her mother. Dez laughed, still shedding tears of joy.

"Me and my…" Dez stopped herself before spilling the beans about her intimate relationship with another woman. She wasn't quite prepared to explain that to her daughter just yet. "…Cellie be making all types of dips, every night. Come on, let's sit down, baby…before these people try to terminate our visit and momma'd have to get wild up in here. You don't need to see me act an ass."

Both ladies took a squat. Livy couldn't keep her eyes off her mother. She stared in great admiration, happy to be in Dez's presence.

"What you are smiling at, baby?" Dez asked, catching her daughter all in her grill.

"You, Momma. I miss you so much, I tell all my friends about you and everything."

"And everything like what, girl?" she asked, hoping her daughter didn't spread the awful news about her mother being a killer. "You don't want people getting the wrong impression about you, misjudging you for the wrong I've done."

"Oh no...I don't even reveal my own personal business, let alone anybody else's. I'm 'bout that life, momma. Besides, it's none of their business." Dez smiled at her daughter, it felt good to see that she had a strong personality—resembling herself, every bit.

"'Bout that life...you teens are something else coming up with all these slick phrases. When I come home, I'm just gonna be *lost in the sauce.*"

"No you're not, momma, I got you."

"Girl, don't worry about me. Just make sure you got them books. What them grades looking like anyway?"

"They're on point, still on the honor roll like always. I just got a letter letting me know that I made the principal's list."

"My baby, that's great! I brag to all my girlfriends about you, showing off your report cards every chance I get. I'm so proud of you."

Dez began shedding tears. Although she was extremely happy to be in the company of her daughter, she couldn't help but feel hurt for missing out on the majority of her life. There was nothing she could do to get those lost years back.

"Don't cry, momma, you gonna make me cry too, and once I get to going it's gonna be hard for me to stop. I just got control of my tears a few minutes ago." Livy said, trying not to break out in tears. Although

Livy may have not shown it much, she was affected a great deal behind her mother being locked up in prison. It had become an emotional distress she'd grown to live with.

"Baby, I'm so sorry for not being there for you all these years. I'm doing everything in my power to get back out there to you at the earliest convenience possible." Dez said, reaching over and grabbing her daughter's hand. She began rubbing it gently as she spoke again. "I filed this thing called a "Clemency" about a year ago, and it's been on the governor's desk just waiting to be reviewed. If he rules in my favor, it's a possibility that I could be coming home real soon...possibly before you graduate."

Livy's eyes got bigger than a dead fish, and her smile stretched out wider than the **Kool-Aid** pitcher. "That'd be a dream come true. *Ooh*...I can't wait. I'm gonna whip your hair up real nice and take you to this nail shop called **Nail One**...get your hands and feet done. I got you G." she said, taking ahold of her mother's hand examining how long her fingernails were growing.

"What's up with all this 'G' talk...you ain't in a gang, are you?" Dez asked, giving Livy a straight look. She remembered the facial expression if she didn't remember shit else.

"Nah, momma-you're tweaking. I say 'G' meaning girl not gangster" she explained, while giggling'.

"You bet not be because if I find out you're in a gang, I'm gonna have *fo' nem* come and give your ass a *V*...and I put that on Oly's grave." Dez replied, talking that Chiraq lingo...*merchin'* it on Livy's beloved father. Livy busted out laughing, amused at the way her mother joked around. But then, suddenly, she got quiet. Dez sensed the sudden mood change, knowing exactly what it was about.

"Baby, I know you miss your daddy a whole bunch. Hell...I think about him daily. He's in heaven now, looking down upon you making sure nothing else bad ever happens to you again. Look at all the wonderful people you're surrounded by...God is good, ain't he?"

Livy wanted to tell her mother that she didn't believe in God, but instead chose to keep her religious beliefs to herself right now. She would find a better time, later in life maybe, to have this discussion. Dez looked at her daughter from across the table, seeing how much she had grown, mentally and physically. She was impressed with how good of a job the Harris' were doing, raising her daughter...their daughter. Livy didn't look anything like all she had been through.

"Momma, I want you to make me a promise that whenever you do come home, you won't leave me again. You got a pass this time; however, I wouldn't ever be able to forgive you if you abandon me again."

Livy had been holding that in for a long time; and now that she finally got it off her chest, she felt a lot better. Dez couldn't do shit but respect what her daughter had just said. It was some grown woman shit to say, and it showed a lot about her character. Let her tell it, once given the chance to be back in her daughter's life, she wouldn't ever risk losing her freedom again.

"I promise, baby...I won't ever leave you again, I put that on my momma." Dez replied, shedding a few more tears of joy.

Seeing how well-developed her daughter's figure had turned out, Dez couldn't help but ask the ultimate question, "Are you having sex yet?"

Livy busted out laughing. "Nah, momma...I don't even have a boyfriend," she claimed.

Dez gave her the *are you telling me the truth* look. "You're not lying to me, are you...because I really hate to be lied to."

"Nah, momma, why is that so hard for you to believe. I'm a virgin," Livy replied while picking through the food items on the table. She was beginning to feel uncomfortable with discussing the matter.

Dez sensed her daughter's discomfort and went ahead to close the matter on one final note. "I want you to look me in the eyes and promise to—"

"—Promise to stay a virgin till I die, momma!" Livy said, interrupting her mother from finishing what she was about to say. She began giggling to herself. However, her mother wasn't. "You gotta be kidding me, you can't be serious."

"Nah, not that long. What you take me for, a nun or something?" Dez replied, remaining in character, looking serious. "Just until you're 50."

"Momma!" Livy pouted, forcing Dez to break character. Finally, she began smiling again.

"Well, at least till you're up in age and happily married, okay?" she compromised.

"That's just about the same time I was thinking," Livy said, giving her mother a dap.

"They say *'great minds think alike'*," Dez responded, handing Livy a microwavable package of hot wings and a double-bacon cheeseburger to warm up so she could start maxing. These were her two favorite visiting room food items.

"I got these for me." Livy said as she reached and snatched the food items back from her mom, toying with her. "The pizza over there is for you, miss."

The girls went back and forth fake beefing about who was entitled to eat what, laughing among themselves. By far, this was the best day either one of 'em had in about 7 years.

Sammie met up with Bumper at an old abandoned warehouse building on the far southwest side of the city, right outside of Joliet, Illinois. The meeting was set to discuss the inside tip Bumper had gotten from Loso last night...about how bad El Huncho wanted Sammie dead, putting a cool million dollars on his head. Popeye's gang was already in effect, scouring the Chicago area, looking to smoke Sammie for the prize.

There wasn't too much the FBI or anybody for the matter could do to protect the lives of Sammie and his family, whom he loved deeply. The only reasonable option he had was to relocate for a while, at least till they brought the Cartel down, but who's to say how long that might take, or if it was even gonna happen. This was a complicated matter that had to be looked at and taken with extreme precautions.

"We have to get you up out of Chicago—immediately! The Surenos will be moving in to get rid of you any day now. They have extensive ties across the city. You're not safe here." Bumper said.

"How did they find out where I live? I mean, I never told anybody or done business here at all. I don't understand," Sammie replied while pacing the floor-back and forth. "The shit just didn't make any sense."

"None of that even matters right now...what's important is trying to find you a safe spot to chill till we pan this mess out. And we must move asap." Bumper said.

The truth of the matter was, the Feds never told Sammie that his name and location could possibly pop up in any investigation of the Surenos he helped take down. They didn't anticipate the case even going that far, they assumed Rude Boy would rat out his boss. They offered the boy damn near everything in the world to give up El Huncho, but he turned it all down. Talk about loyalty! Now that his discovery was beginning to unfold, people's lives were being put at stake just to secure a victory.

"I don't want to leave Chicago...it's all I know," Sammie complained.

"It's not safe here, and we just don't have enough manpower to watch over your every move. I'm sorry, Sam, but it's for your own good." Bumper said, sadly. He had grown a certain kind of liking for the ex-bank robber over the past years of dealing with him. For the most part, Sammie was an intelligent, savvy person who ended up going down a different path than Bumper.

"Just pick a city, anywhere, just as long as it's far away from here. It's a must that we get you the hell out of Dodge and in a hurry." Bumper said, walking over to Sammie and putting a hand on his shoulder. He was very sincere about the situation at hand. He knew the FBI had fucked up, and he was willing to do whatever he could to try to fix it.

Sammie thought about it for a moment, weighing out the pros and cons. At the end of the day, it was all about survival; and if he had to relocate to duck death, then so be it. Hopefully, he'd be able to reunite with his family again. As for right now, he had to do what was best for him.

"Atlanta, Georgia!" Sammie shouted, figuring he could do the '*A*' being that-it was somewhat similar to the Chi.

"Well, Atlanta it is. Pack your things...you're leaving first thing tomorrow".

"Tomorrow...I need at least a month to take care of my business before I leave," Sammie replied.

"A month...hell, how these Surenos move you're guaranteed to be dead in less than a week." Bumper warned, looking Sammie in the face. He felt a bit sorry for him. Instantly, he came up with a compromise, bending the rules a little for his informant. "I'll tell you what, you got less than a week to handle all of your affairs here, and then it's farewell to Chicago, okay?"

Sammie stood there thinking about the life he had become so accustomed to living. He thought about his family, how he would be abandoning them, but sticking around could very well put their lives in danger…if that wasn't the case already. He had to leave, there was no way around it.

"Okay," Sammie agreed, shaking Bumper's hand. Sammie liked him a bit as well. He never thought a cop could actually treat a criminal from the wicked streets of Chicago like a normal human-being. From the jump, Bumper made Sammie feel comfortable with communicating with him. "But as soon as y'all nail this El Huncho muthafucka, I'm coming home to be with my family…they need my presence."

The two fellas agreed on the matter, leaving the warehouse and going their separate ways.

CHAPTER #6

THE BIGGER PICTURE

Kick-Dough was broken by the news he found out about the dead peckerwood. A-1 was charged with Felony-Murder, and lab results had finally came back-linking him as an accomplice to the crime. He got up with Pops to discuss the situation at hand and future moves. They met up right outside of East Chicago. Kick-Dough bailed in the car with Pops, and he pulled off.

"What up, son?" Pops said, puffin on a big cigar. **Jerry Butler** was playing low in the background, *"Only the strong survives...you got to be a man, you got to take a stand."*

"Man, Pops...shits all fucked up for the kid right now. I don't know what to do," Kick-Dough said, bitterly.

"Well, first of all, don't go beating your head against a brick wall about it," Pops advised him. "What happen-happened, and it ain't shit a muthafucka could do to change it. That cracker is dead and gone...he ain't coming back, jack! What you need to be worrying about is your next move...how you gonna come from under this mess?"

Pops continued puffing on his cigar while pointing a finger at Kick-Dough. "And how do I suppose to go about doing that, Pops?" Kick-Dough asked.

"By snatching up as many money bags as you can, son. I mean, go trick or treating with the shit!" Pops hastened to reply. He took another pull off the cigar and got right in mode. "Shit looks bad right now, and it's gonna continue looking that way till you do something about it.

Money changes things…it could turn a horrible situation into a good one, just look at me."

Kick-Dough sat back and let Pops explain the matter further, "With the right type of people on yo' side, mouthpieces…doctors…and judges, you and A-1 could come from under this matter with a little to no time to do."

"You think so, Pops?" Kick-Dough asked, looking hopeful.

"Mandatory!" he responded, quoting one of Kick-Dough's favorite lines.

"The DA trying to say that the peckerwood died from the injuries he sustained, allegedly, during the robbery, right?"

"Right," Kick-Dough replied, eager to hear the punchline.

"I'm willing to bet all the tea in China that the muthafucka had died from a pre-existing condition, Cancer perhaps." Pops stated as he pulled over the midnight blue Lincoln-MKS they were in. "With the right amount of money and people backing you…coming from under this isn't far-fetched."

Kick-Dough continued listening, trying to make sense of what all Pops was saying. He knew that he had only struck the deceased man a few times; and even then, it wasn't with all his might. *Something else had to be wrong with that white muthafucka already,* Kick-Dough thought to himself. He remembered about the money he had for Pops and reached in his pocket to *curve* (hit his hand) him.

"Oh yeah, the shit almost slipped my mind. I got something for you, Pops" Kick-Dough tried handing $2,500 to him.

"Oh no, put that away," Pops said, turning down the kindly gesture. "I appreciate it, but I'm not the kind of father who would take from his son in a time of need. Nah, that's not me. I'm the type of father who gives meaning to his son's future, especially when it doesn't seem so bright!"

Kick-Dough just smiled in complete admiration. It was a true blessing to have someone in his corner who was as wise and kind-hearted as Pops. He always gave Kick-Dough and A-1 gifts, but none of them were worth more than the words he spoke. The shit was *verbal gold.*

Pops reached in the back of his car and grabbed a Gucci knapsack. He put it in his lap and thumbed through a bunch of papers inside it, pulling out a college-ruled notebook pad. This was a multi-million dollar blueprint, a hundred pages filled with names and addresses of all kinds of lucrative businesses, including the banks where the owners of these businesses deposit their finances; dates and times when the money gets deposited there; and how much at a time each business deposits.

The book covered areas all across the entire city of Chicago and included the surrounding suburbs as well. This was supreme homework mapped down to a science...the mother of all Lime-Lites. Pops was leaning toward retirement and felt the need to pass down the torch. Kick-Dough and A-1 were perfect candidates...the only candidates for the matter.

Pops trusted A-1 and Kick-Dough with his life, and he wanted them to come from under the black-cloud hovering over their world. He sought to help in any way he possibly could...this exceeded the measure.

"Wow...what the fuck!" Kick-Dough said, opening up the notebook and skimming through it. "It must be over a thousand Lime-Lites or better in this bitch."

"If not, then very close," Pops clarified. "Son, take that golden book and flourish. It's your time now, make the most of it. Being a king only lasts for so long. Keep that book someplace safe where only you know its whereabouts."

Stacey's mother's house, Kick-Dough thought to himself. "It'd be a great misfortune to lose it." Pops advised.

Kick-Dough was overwhelmed with joy; the streets would now be his, and it was nothing twelve or anybody else could do about it. It was time for him to step up and take on the role that Pops had played for years. Those were some very big shoes to fulfill, but he had great potentials.

"Man, this is a huge gift. I don't know what to say,"

"Son, when the money's talking, what else is there to say?"

Pops picked his cigar back up from out of the ashtray and flamed it up, taking a deep pull on it. He blew out smoke in circles and began speaking again, "I got a goddaughter named Olivia. I've been looking out for the lovely girl ever since an old friend of mine adopted her back when she was 9 years old. I don't think you ever seen her before, but A-1 has. She lives up north. I need you to make sure she doesn't ever want for shit after I'm gone."

"Gone where, Pops? Stop talking like that, you ain't going nowhere but straight to the bank." Kick-Dough said, quoting a line from Pops.

While giving a dull and dry laugh, Pops pulled back off maneuvering the *Stinking-Lincoln* into traffic and said, "Son, one day we all gonna have to go somewhere we might not wanna go, and all the people we love dearly or the money we done stacked up...none of that shit is gonna be able to go with us."

Not even a good week went by and already, Kick-Dough qualified as an official member of the **Hundred-Band Club**. Ever since Pops had given him the golden book, he went crazy. Immediately, he took off wasting no time at all, checking a bag. He took down Lime-Lite after Lime-Lite, utilizing every bit of power given to him by the golden book. It was precise and accurate every time...so reliable that he didn't even need anyone's help. Yep, the muthafucka made moves all by his lonesome.

He stacked racks on top of racks like Y-C 'nem. Hell, it wasn't till he reached a quarter-mil when he started playing the backfield letting other niggas get some money. He stayed hungry though, licking where ever he saw fit. Niggas just wasn't on point with the shit like how he was. If he tried putting someone in the Lime-Lite and they went pussyfooting around, he just went ahead and bust the move himself. Off each Lime-Lite he passed out, he demanded the same chop as Pops did—one third. That way, it was enough room for everybody to eat.

He squared A-1 off first, making sure lawyer fees were paid and potential bond money was put away safely. Commissary and everything else that falls in that category, was platinum…A-1 walked around Cook County Jail with a BLACK-CARD. After that, he kept his word with Pops and made sure Olivia was well taken care of. He adopted her as his sister as well. It wasn't too much of anything she wanted for.

Although Kick-Dough was a big player in the game, he did an excellent job staying low-key from the **Big Ol' Sharks** and twelve. That was, as of for the moment. Everybody in the Washington Heights Community loved him, just how they did the Lord. He became the Godfather of the neighborhood, giving out blessings every time he came around.

A-1 was in the middle of playing a good ol' game of chess when his name got called for a visit. He had been locked up in the county for several months now and was beginning to get used to it. Everybody knew him, from all the detainees and guards to the counselors and nurses. Good character and charisma pushed popularity upon the street legend quickly.

Not to mention, the black, cheesy-face trap star still had a big ol' *Duffel Bag*.

A-1's protégé Kick-Dough was out there in 'nem streets taking flight like an airplane. Snatching money bags had become easier than snatching bags of candy from kids on Halloween. He didn't have shit to worry about other than getting a bond.

A-1 was often saddened by the fact that he wasn't out there fucking it off with his boy, but he was nothing less than proud of how he'd risen up to the occasion. All the grooming he had put on the boy had come back with rewards. It's nothing like having a good friend in the time of need...I mean NOTHING!

A-1 showed up to his visit rocking a crispy, tailor made DOC jumpsuit with a pair of black Prada's on his feet and matching glasses to go with them. Visiting days were his most favorable times while being locked up, right next to commissary day. When he slid in the visiting room, all eyes were on him. He searched through the long, thick Plexiglas-window for a familiar face and seen Pops.

"Old Man," he shouted out, happy to see him. He walked up to the part of the glass window where Pops was.

"Shawty Bankroll," Pops replied, calling him by his childhood name.

A-1 took a squat down on the metal-stool and got right into his visit. "What up, Godfather, what do I owe this wonderful visit?" A-1 had a big Kool-Aid smile on his face.

"Nothing at all, the pleasure is all mine," Pops responded, staring at A-1's upper body, which was all bricked up. "What the fuck are they feeding you up in there, concrete sandwiches? You're real solid up top...looks like you could shit out a brick or two."

"That shit comes from going hard, no days off yet. I do a thousand push-ups and dips a day. Hell, it ain't nothing else to do up in this bitch...why not?" A-1 said, flexing his chest muscles back and forth at Pops.

"Look at there, you damn near look better than me in my hay days." Pops replied while giggling. A-1 just smiled.

"Your lil' protege is out here going crazy in these streets, jack!" Pops said, with emphasis. "It hasn't been a full week yet, and already he done mastered the Lime-Lite."

"Yeah, I hear...word travels fast. I'm very proud of the boy."

"Good boy, very dedicated and determined!" Pops hastened to reply.

"Wait a minute, you left out disciplined."

"Son, when you busy getting to the money...you don't have much time worrying about discipline." Pops replied while giving A-1 an old-school mug.

A-1 couldn't do shit but continue smiling. He always enjoyed Pops' company, and the feeling was mutual.

"It's something I gotta tell you, but I don't want you to get all bent out of shape about it, okay?" Pops said, with a serious look on his face. A-1 had been around Pops long enough to know that whenever the old man gave him the serious look, something was wrong. He didn't respond though, he just braced himself for whatever Pops had to reveal.

Pops was beginning to have a change of heart. He had initially come to visit A-1 to tell him about the cancer that's been eating him up on the inside for so long. He hadn't told anybody about his troubling situation. His intentions were to share the unfortunate news with A-1 first, but seeing how happy he was just melted his heart. Although Pops was dying to tell somebody about his conditions, he chose not to burden A-1 with the bad news. He figured that he had enough bullshit on his plate to deal with already...this would only make matters worse.

Pops took a quick detour in his chain of thoughts. "Son, I'm leaving the Mother of **Lime-Lites** to you and Kick-Dough and moving on."

"What do you mean when you say, 'moving on'?" A-1 asked, feeling a bit confused.

"Early retirement, it's time for me to travel the world," He answered sadly, trying hard not to burst out into tears. He had never cried in front of anyone since he was a kid and wasn't about to start now. "It's nothing else here for an old-timer like me."

"What you mean? You got family here—me, Kick-Dough, and Olivia. We need you here with us!" A-1 said, feeling some type of way.

"Son, try not to take this the wrong way, it's not personal. You, Kick-Dough, and Olivia aren't just here in Chicago with me, I got y'all embedded in my heart...always and forever. That's permanent, jack...nothing can change it." Pops said, putting his right fist up to the left side of his chest.

Pop's days on earth were numbered, he was given a short amount of time to live. "This won't change our relationship just as well as you being in there shouldn't change the relationship of you and the ones you hold dearly to your heart." he stated.

"You're right," A-1 responded, still feeling a bit disappointed. "When are you leaving?"

"I don't know right now, but I'm gonna come back up here to see you before I head out." Pops felt ashamed of himself for lying to his godson. The truth of the matter was, after this visit, it was a possibility that he wouldn't come back to see A-1 ever again. The cancer that's been eating him up on the inside had finally taken its toll.

"Well, I'm gonna hold you responsible for that day, Pops," A-1 said, giving him that serious look right back.

"Don't worry about me, son. Just focus on getting yo' ass up outta there and for good, you hear me?" A-1 nodded. "Kick-Dough is holding the fort down very well, so you don't have anything to worry about."

A guard walked into the visiting room saying, "Alright, that's it...visit's over!"

"I love you, Pops," A-1 said while putting his handcuffed fist up to the plexiglass-window.

"The feeling is mutual, son." Pops did the same with his fist.

Sammie was at O'Hare Airport with a one-way ticket waiting to catch a flight to Atlanta, Georgia. Leaving Chicago was a very tough decision to make but necessary in the safety of his life. El Huncho wanted him dead, putting a million-dollar bounty on his head. Popeye's gang had already moved in, looking to cash out on the deal.

Sammie didn't have any other choice but to abandon the very city he loved so much. He came from off the southside of Chicago, on the **Low-End**, where the environment was-poverty stricken. He grew up in the **Robert Taylor Homes Projects** and was introduced to the street life at a very young age. **Hoolio** was his childhood name, being that he was half Black and Hispanic. Sammie done brushed shoulders with some of the most notorious gang leaders, one of them being "**Larry Bernard Hoover.**"

Sammie earned recognition first from striking poses in crap games. He had mastered the art of using trick dice. He would often sit around the house all day long practicing different ways slipping trick dice into crap games without anyone noticing. It was quite easy when having a partner with him to help out. That way, Sammie would just give him the dice so that when he faded him, he could catch the real dice, cuffing them up and tucking them away, and throw the tricks back out into the game. This shit was definitely an art.

As soon as the tricks were in the game, Sammie would make outrageous bets across the entire board-no matter what the point was. It made no difference because with the tricks, you were a guaranteed winner. The times where he was alone, he just held the tricks in his hand, right behind his money. That way, as he shot the real dice, he could scoop them up and tuck them right behind his money after first, laying the tricks down. The constant snapping of his fingers made it hard for anyone to catch the switch of the dice when it occurred. Even the faders got lost in the sauce, and their eyes were planted directly on the process.

This shit wasn't simple at all, you had to have magnificent hand mechanics to go behind it or else...you could get yourself killed if ever caught. Although word on the streets was that Sammie had trick dice up his sleeves, never once did he get caught in the act of using them. The trick dice had him so rigged-up and extra confident that whenever he did shoot fair, he still struck an ultimate pose, breaking the entire dice game up.

Sammie was a bonafide crap-shooter with the great ability to perform magic, some would say. He had trick dice in all colors, so it wasn't no safeguards to his finesse. He learned this game in the projects back when he was just 8-years old and kept it with him ever since.

By the time Sammie was a teenager, he was thumbing through more wads of dollars than the average bank teller. He was named "*The Golden Child*" of the projects, but it wasn't till he started robbing banks that he became famous all throughout the streets of Chicago. Sammie and his malicious crew were lining banks up and knocking them down like dominos. It was a very profitable hustle that went well till some copy-catters fucked everything up. A couple of bank robbers who got caught in the act of trying to take down a federal bank ended up turning Sammie over to the Feds in exchange for a lesser sentence. Although Sammie was cut from a different cloth, he followed suit and cooperated with the Feds…gave them whatever they wanted in order to duck having to do any jail time.

The truth of the matter was, the FBI had handpicked Sammie to be a confidential informant. They watched his moves and was flattered by how he finessed to get what he wanted. Him having some Latino in his blood made it all official; the Feds needed a match like him to get up under El Huncho's regime in regards of destroying the Cartel.

They came to Sammie with a deal of a lifetime, not too many people would of refused it. The deal required his assistance, becoming a federal informant and helping bring down the Cartel. In return, they would allow him to be free of any incarcerations and gave him a certain amount of leeway to do whatever he needed to make a decent living…just as long as it wasn't violent. He was given large amounts of money and was authorized to use it to purchase *birds* (kilograms of cocaine) from top-flight Surenos, a part of the Midwest Drug Cartel. Sammie dealt outside of Chicago only, that way his cover could stay low-key in the land.

For years now, Sammie's been earning the trust of the Surenos working hard to get close to El Huncho. He had become a great asset to the Feds, and now they were getting set to wrap the investigation up all together. They had a decorated agent going undercover, posing as one of El Honcho's infamous syndicates.

Rude Boy was currently locked up in a federal jail, waiting to stand trial for a number of class x offenses. He had found out in his latest discovery that Samuel Walters, *a.k.a.* "Sammie," *a.k.a.* **"Pops,"** was a federal informant. Immediately, Rude Boy sent word back to his boss El Huncho, knowing very well he would quickly take care of the rat. The

Feds tried everything in their power to get Rude Boy to turn on his boss; but unlike some ducks that get cracked and quack, Rude Boy remained a loyal soldier to the game.

Pops was hurt with having to leave the people whom he had grown to love so much behind in Chicago. A-1, Kick-Dough, and Olivia really meant the world to him, he hoped for all of this to be over with soon, so he could get back to them. He couldn't fix his mouth to tell either of 'em about the cancer that's been eating him alive...that he was a federal informant. Pops sold his soul to the devil for freedom and money, and now came the time for him to lay down in the same bed he'd made.

All Pops could think about was how his godchildren would feel once they learned about him being a rat. He dreaded them looking at him pathetically, he would rather die first before being stripped away of the credibility he had with them.

To keep shit funky, it was the Feds that opened Pops eyes up and turned him onto the theory of snatching bank envelopes. Sitting at the airport waiting for his flight, he recalls back when Bumper first put the bug in his ear. "Robbing banks may seem lucrative at first, not evaluating all the risks you take and the extensive time you may have to do behind getting caught," Bumper said, giving Pops (*Sammie*) a lil game of his own.

Pops just looked at Bumper like he was crazy. "What do you know about robbing banks, Agent Cunningham?"

"Well—for one, I know that a person won't get away with doing it for long. The FBI have created a special intelligence used specifically for profiling robbery suspects and hunting them down." Bumper replied, talking like he was reading straight out a FBI criminal handbook.

"Profiling my ass, if it wasn't for that jive turkey ass nigga snitching on me, y'all would have never caught me!"

"Don't be so sure of yourself. We had you made out since your second bank robbery," Bumper said, with a deceptive smile planted on his face.

Pops wasn't buying the shit yet though. "Yeah right...if so then why didn't you hunt me down?" he asked, looking at Bumper dead in the face. "It wasn't like I disappeared off the face of the earth. Why allow me to continue robbing banks?"

"You see, it's certain protocols we have to go by. We're not like the police who takes shit for face value, we operate way further than that," Bumper said while checking the time on his watch. "While you were assuming to get away with the bank robberies scot-free, we were there on your ass each time profiling your moves. You're good but not that good...nobody is."

Pops just sat there with a blank expression on his face. Him and Bumper were at an old warehouse building. They often met up there for updates at least twice a month. Bumper enjoyed unfolding the plot out that had been going on right under Pops' nose. His next statement took the cake, confirming very well that he knew exactly what the fuck he was talking about.

"Remember that one robbery at First National Bank in Arlington Heights, Illinois, where a guy held the door open and waited until you came all the way from the grey Cadillac Seville that a Hispanic male was driving?" Bumper exposed his face so that Pops could clearly easily recall the time.

It didn't take but a quick second 'fore Pops to recollect. "That was you?" he asked.

"Maybe it was, or maybe I was the person in that green Jeep Cherokee parked right next to you...the guy whom you waved at when you first stepped foot out of the car," Bumper said, fucking around with Pops thought process. He was lost for words. "The FBI is everything they say we are. We hand-picked you for a specific task, your character and charisma were highly needed in getting close to El Huncho and his soldiers."

Pops couldn't do shit but smile, realizing now that them people been on his ass from the get-go. "If you ask me, I think you would have had a better chance with snatching bank envelopes from business owners who come to the bank at least two times a week, depositing money. It's easy and less risky. If you were to ever get caught, you'd only be looking at a 3 to 7 instead of a 6 to 30-year prison sentence." Bumper said, winking his eye at Pops.

Pops was in great amazement with the new-found discovery. Bumper had just given him a way to eat on a whole 'nother level. He would just have to come up with a team of go-getters to execute the underhanded scheme...his old ass damn sure couldn't fulfill the task all by himself, not this one. The Feds put him in the Lime-Lite. As soon as he seen that A-1 was ready to get glowed up, he went ahead and limed him up. Ever since then, the "Fo'" been eating like kings.

"Flight 103 to Atlanta, Georgia, gate is now open. Flight attendees may board the plane and be seated in assigned order. Thank you." a receptionist said, over the intercom.

Pops snapped back out of the days to his current situation, which was a harsh reality. He had a million-dollar tag put on his head by a notorious drug-kingpin, El Huncho. He was forced to go into hiding for sometime. He gathered all of his belongings and walked towards the plane's entrance. This was a new beginning for him, one that he prayed deeply to be over with soon.

A Novel by Pucasso

CHAPTER #7

GANG-GANG

Kick-Dough was gliding through in an all-black Porsche Panamera when he spotted Lil' Charles, *a.k.a.* "**Shoota,**" coming out of an alleyway. He blew the horn and Shoota came skipping towards the car, swinging his dreads along the way.

Shoota was the devil in teenage clothing—a young, wild muthafucka. He got a high off popping shit up. Although he was just a juvenile, he aimed and fired pistols like a sharp-shooter. His body-count was gradually growing by the days. No doubt, shorty had the murder-game on lock.

When Shoota was just 8-years old, his mother got blown down-right in front of him and his lil' sisters. A "PYT," pretty young thang, claimed Shoota's mother was sleeping around with her baby-daddy. The girl warned her of what she would do if she didn't stop the shit. Shoota's mother, Melissa Jones, *a.k.a.* "**Missy,**" didn't take the threat too well...she upped a box-cutter and got wild.

Later on down the line, the girl ended up catching Missy at a nearby park enjoying the beautiful weather with Shoota and his two sisters. She crept up on her and emptied a .38 revolver handgun right into her face, turning the gun on Shoota afterwards. Fortunately for him, the girl had ran out of bullets. Ever since then, Lil Charles became "Shoota."

"Oh, what up, Kick-Dough?" Shoota said, finally recognizing who it was piloting the spacious aircraft.

"Get in, lil' nigga—hurry up!" Kick-Dough looked in the rearview mirror, fully examining the car coming up behind him.

Shoota bailed in, pulling the *stick* (a handgun with an extended clip) off his hip and placing it on top of his lap. Instantly, Kick-Dough pulled off.

"This you, big bro?" Shoota asked, lusting over the car's interior.

"Hell yeah, something slight for the moment," he responded as he handed Shoota a wad of money. "Here."

"What's this for?"

"That's you. Go to the mall and have a lil fun," Kick-Dough said, while pushing a button, opening the glove compartment box. "Look in there and grab that Harold's Chicken bag."

Shoota grabbed the bag hoping it was a 6-piece chicken dinner...ketchup, hot sauce, salt, and pepper—hold the coleslaw. Instead, it was something much better...a *Halsted* (63 grams of raw cocaine). Although he wasn't much of a drug dealer, he had a team of hustlers who wouldn't have a problem with getting it off for him.

"Love, my nigga. That's right on time too, the block is dry." Shoota said as he dropped the shit right in his lap with the thirty, *Arm Violence.*

"Yep, yep—mandatory," Kick-Dough replied.

Chief Keef was playing low in the background, "*I got all my muthafuckin' jewelry on me.*"

Man, big bro, when you're gonna put me in the Lime-Lite. I appreciate all what you be doing for me, but I got a gang of wolves to feed. It's time for me to turn-up in these streets."

"Everybody got a part to play and in an orderly fashion, ain't no *jumping gates.* When your turn comes, believe me...you gon' get limed up," Kick-Dough responded while giving Shoota a savage stare. "Till then, go to school and fuck you some bad bitches. All of us can't do the same shit, especially not at the same time."

Shoota stared at Kick-Dough discreetly as he whipped the steering wheel with proficiency, showing off the expensive Yacht Master Rolex watch dangling on his wrist. He wasn't buying the shit Kick-Dough was kicking talking about…*"Everybody got a part to play and in an orderly fashion."* Shoota hated being denied and getting spoon-fed was beginning to get played out. He was eagered to get out there in the field and get his full jus-due.

Shoota was the leader of a gang called **"JRW,"** Juvies Running Wild. JRW were a bunch of dread-headed teenagers who burglarized their own community and brought down the property value every chance they got. They hit petty licks and glorified gang-banging as if the shit was the greatest thing in life. The crew of savages wore each other's clothes and posted up around abandoned buildings, vandalizing the premises.

Shoota had three lieutenants—Do-Dirty, Popcorn, and Shawty-Rough. The rest of the squad was nothing more than a bunch of send-offs willing to carry out any order given to 'em, just to be accepted. Unfortunately for Washington Heights, JRW was slowly destroying the legacy that the MVP regime had built.

Kick-Dough ended up dropping Shoota off at his cousin Dino's spot. "Be easy, lil nigga." he shouted out the window, hitting the horn and mechanically maneuvering the foreign back into traffic. It was a Kodak moment.

"Eazy died of AIDS, I ain't on none of that!" Shoota mumbled as he threw up four fingers to Kick-Dough-repping the block. He ran into the back part of the house and down the short stairway to the basement where Dino stayed.

Dino was a paranoid, clown ass nigga who always thought someone was out to get him, in one way or another. Being twice the age of Shoota, you would've thought he had more sense; but that just goes to show that age ain't shit but a number. Dino was dumber than a box of rocks. Everybody ran schemes on him; dick eaters finessed him out of his drug money, and the youngsters in the hood used his spot as a hangout.

Shoota came through the door, which was mistakenly left unlocked, and made his way towards the back room where Dino and Do-Dirty were blowing dope and playing "Call of Duty." When he got to the room, he upped his gun and crept in—silently. He pointed it at them, and imitating shots being fired, "*Boc-Boc!*"

"You niggas lacking hard, I could've just blew both of y'all shit back." Shoota advised them while shaking his head in disappointment.

Do-Dirty was stuck at a standstill, holding the Xbox controller in one hand and a lit blunt in the other. Dino was stuck too; however, he tried playing the shit off by continuing playing the video game as if nothing happened.

"Nigga, you couldn't have done shit. I'd been peeped your mop-headed ass running alongside the house," Dino argued, without even looking over at Shoota who was taking aim at his head again.

"Shut up, nigga. I should pop your ass for real just for lying, muthafucka! You knew your ass was smoked,"

"Cooked!" Do-Dirty hastened to say. He had no problems with keeping the shit real.

Shoota continued pointing his pistol at Dino's head, taking a precise aim. "Nigga, quit aiming that damn gun at me, because if it goes off—"

"—If it goes off, then that dirty white wall over there besides your fucking head, is gonna just get a crimson paint job." Shoota said, interrupting Dino's less threatening words. "Now, say you was dead!"

Shoota and Do-Dirty both busted out laughing. Dino had been exposed, to say the least. When him and Do-Dirty made it back in, coming from Harold's Chicken Shack earlier, it was him who had forgotten to lock the door behind him. He knew it too; however, he was the type of muthafucka who never liked owning up to his mistakes. He would rather fabricate some bullshit ass story and try to get around the shit.

Shoota, still laughing with his lieutenant, finally lowered his weapon from out of Dino's face and sat it down on the nightstand by the door. Then he reached over and tried giving Dino a handshake. "I'm just fucking with you, cuz." he confessed.

Dino ignored the gesture, he kept both of his hands wrapped around the game controller and continuing to play "Call of Duty."

"Damn, nigga…you all in your feelings now, I said I was just fucking with your soft ass!" Shoota shouted out while taking off his North Face fleece, flopping down on the couch. Do-Dirty wasn't laughing anymore.

"Nigga, we got guns down here!" Dino yelled as he slammed the controller to the floor. He snatched the Glock 40 out of Do-Dirty's lap and wave it around in the air. "If you would've came in here busting, I would've just grabbed the move from Do-Dirty, pushing my nigga out the way, and then clapped back and took cover behind the bed mattress after flipping it up in the air."

Dino demonstrated his exaggerated imagination live…in slow motion. The nigga was animated as fuck-straight out a comic book.

"Man, would you…" Shoota asked, rhetorically. "Knock it the fuck off!"

Shoota and Do-Dirty both went back to laughing again. They always seemed to get a real good laugh whenever being around Dino.

"Y'all some goofy ass niggas, always giggling...*Hee-Hee-Hee-Hee*," Dino replied, still being animated. "I see why the BROs don't want y'all around them."

"Get the fuck outta here, with your dick sucking ass," Shoota said, impatiently waiting to put some dope in his lungs. "Man, Do-Dirty, pass that shit with your leap frog looking ass."

"Don't pass that nigga shit, Dirty. He already talking about what he could have done to us...he might get high and just try to do it." Dino began laughing mischievously. The cartoon-character within him was fully in mode. "You been hanging around the BROs too much, that snake shit it starting to rub off on you. They're probably talking about murking me, and your stupid ass don't even know."

"Or maybe I do," Shoota responded. Instantly, Dino got quiet. "Man, don't nobody give a fuck about you one way or the other. Whether you live or die is solely on you...you ain't even got no opz, you just a fucking nerd."

"Where you just come from, bro?" Do-Dirty asked Shoota while handing over the blunt to him.

"Flipping a few blocks with Dough, he just copped that new Porsche Panamera. That bitch so *futuristic* inside out."

"Big bro don't be fucking around," Do-Dirty said.

"Not at all," Shoota hastened to reply.

Do-Dirty began rolling up another blunt of dope. **Rich Homie Quan** was playing in the background, "*A real nigga, he'll kill you and won't tell a soul. Pull up in a Phantom, thought you saw a ghost.*"

"Man, that ain't his shit...he be having hypes rent cars for him." Dino said, hating as usual.

"That's his whip, boy! Bro getting to it." Shoota replied.

"I know he broke you off with some gwop, nigga," Do-Dirty said. "Cut me in or cut it out."

"Man, you be acting all shy and shit. Tell him to hit you, he got plenty money," Shoota said as he reached down in his pocket and pulled out a bankroll. He swiftly thumbed through a number of bills and peeled off several hundreds. "Here, my nigga."

Shoota couldn't deny Do-Dirty for shit; they've been in the shits together forever. From sleeping in abandoned buildings to *jumping gates* (robbing niggas) just for the sport, they have been through it all together. Although Do-Dirty was the oldest, Shoota played the position of a big brother...he made big-boy gang moves.

"Oh yeah..." Shotta said, almost forgetting about the *Halsted* he had in his jacket. He took it out and said, "Voila!" like he just performed a magic trick of some kind.

He tossed it over to Dino. "Catch, nigga!" he said. Dino grabbed it out of midair, with one hand. This was right up Dino's alley. He wasn't a gangster nor a player—none of the sort. Nobody ever took him serious about shit other than getting rid of some drugs. The muthafucka made flips like an acrobat...all he did was sell coke each and every day. He sat down in that junky ass basement of his all day, playing the video game and blowing chronic smoke, catching all kinds of drug traffic.

"That's right on time, the block's dead on the work side." Do-Dirty said while flaming up some more dope.

"Man, he be hitting you with all this frivolous shit...what's up with one of them Lime-Lites he's been dishing out...is he gonna glow you up or what?" Dino asked, opening the bag of coke and looking at the fish scales.

"Yeah...is he?" Do-dirty asked, tagging in on Dino's question.

"He's talking some off the wall ass shit…saying, '*everybody got a part to play, ain't no jumping gates.*'"

"What!" Do-Dirty said, choking off the chronic.

"Man, y'all should rob that muthafucka! Who in the hell he thinks he is—Pops?" Dino implied. Do-Dirty handed him the blunt, still choking off the smoke.

"I was thinking the same thing, especially when he started talking that go to school shit—showing off his Rollie." Shoota agreed, scrolling through his Instagram-page. "That bitch ass nigga Rio really must think shit's sweet…all on the gram flexing…talking about we some broke ass shorties."

"*Ha-ha-ha,*" Dino giggled while getting up to look for an ashtray. "Y'all don't wanna see Rio and Taz…them niggas some real-live killers."

Dino continued taunting around with Shoota and Do-Dirty, saying a whole bunch of ignorant shit. Spreading negative syndromes and ignorant outbursts was something he had become so accustomed to doing ever since he learned how to talk.

"Man, if I catch any of them hoe ass niggas, I'm off at their heads!" Shoota replied, pointing the stick he had grabbed back off the nightstand at the screen of his phone.

"Bang-bang!" his lieutenant shouted.

Desire, *a.k.a.* **"Ray-Ray,"** had it real bad growing up as a child. On numerous occasions, she'd been sexually molested by her drunken stepdad, in addition to being enslaved to both physical and verbal abuse by her mother. Ira, her fraternal twin, was a *flaming fag*. Often, she had to fight against people who cracked cruel gay jokes on him. She wasn't for none of that shit.

A Novel by Pucasso

Ray-Ray's dramatic upbringing turned her into the type of girl that most teenage boys couldn't handle. She was *one of the guys*, and when she came around, muthafuckas treated her accordingly. It wasn't long before she got recruited as a JRW, becoming their first-lady. Shit...she turned out to be a lot harder than most of the niggas in the clique. She had hands like the late-great **Kimbo Slice**.

One day a big block fight jumped off and Ray-Ray ended up bumping with a whole family by her damn self. Long story short, she ended up beating up a pregnant mother and two of her kids, a teenage daughter and her older brother. Popcorn recorded the scuffle and posted it on Facebook. Instantly, the shit went viral and shot her street cred up there with the moon. It was a *WorldStar* moment.

A couple of niggas pushed up on Ray-Ray and tried to get her to become their girl; however, when it came to pairing up with someone intimately, she only had her eyes set on one person—Shoota. She loved him loved deeply, ever since kindergarten he's been the apple of her eyes. However, Shoota down played the way she felt about him and brushed her off each time she made a pass at him.

At first, Ray-Ray just wasn't Shoota's type, but now things done changed. The once, slim, tomboyish looking girl had grown into her clothes very well. Shoota couldn't help but take notice of the girl's *growth* and *development*. He went ahead and gave her what she'd been yearning for all along...dick and balls.

After Shoota cracked Ray-Ray, she became his ride or die bitch and was willing to do whatever he told her. He taught her how to shoot pistols accurately and laid the murder game down to her the same exact way it was laid down to him...nothing was left out. He made her vicious, and in return she gave him extraordinary loyalty.

One day a bunch of shots popped off through the front window of Shoota's granny's house. Ray-Ray dived and pushed Shoota out the way of gunfire. She ended up getting skinned in the head by a stray bullet. From that point on, she had earned a special spot in Shoota's heart, for an eternity. It was said that nothing could possibly break their bond.

Popcorn was unarmed and all by himself when he entered the Citgo Gas Station, located directly on the southeast corner of 103rd and Aberdeen. This was the outskirts of the Washington Heights Community, dividing the Tre from Fo' Block. Technically, it was said by street geographical measures that Citgo belonged to the Tre, and the Fo' ruled over the Shell Gas Station located on the northeast corner of 107th and Halsted. If either gang got caught setting foot on forbidden turf, it would be at the risk of getting beat down, shot, or maybe even killed.

Popcorn was bad at following rules though. He continued to come and go as he very well pleased. And that was *whenever*, *wherever*, and *however*! That same mentality was bred through the entire administration of "JRW," just a bunch of hardheaded muthafuckas.

Popcorn was very eager to get some dope in his system, and going to the Citgo Gas Station was the quickest way to fulfill that need. Not safe at all but very expeditious. He arrived to the gas station and slid in, looking around at the few individuals who were inside. He noticed that neither one of them were his *opz*.

Popcorn understood clearly the risk he was taking; however...he never cared. He didn't quite take them Tre boys serious, obviously. If so, he wouldn't of came this far—especially without a *blicker*. Let him tell it...he was the muthafucka niggas should be worried about. He went to the back cooler and grabbed a Mystic Strawberry-Lemonade, and that's when 103rd's very own stepped through the door—**Stunna**.

Stunna was a young card-swiper, licking for thousands of dollars at a time on all type of designer clothes. All he wore was expensive shit—Moncler, Giuseppes, Robin Jeans, etc. He got the swipe game from his big homie, Baby-Joe. Baby-Joe had been making a decent living off manufacturing and selling fraudulent credit cards since the 90's.

Stunna moved through the gas station rocking all Louie-V from head to toe, even his undergarments. The nerve of this nigga having on a $2,500 outfit and didn't even have a car or his own spot to hang his wardrobe at. These shorties in Chiraq definitely only lived for the moment.

When Popcorn heard the door open, he slightly turned around towards it to see who entered. At first, Stunna's face wasn't recognizable, being hidden behind a pair of Louis Vuitton stunter shades, but once the G-Herbo look-a-like handed a crispy bill over to the store cashier and said, "Give me 4-packs of white-grape Cigarillos," Shoota knew exactly who he was.

That's Stunna bitch ass, he thought to himself as he took a quick glance outside of the window to see if he had come alone.

Besides an older woman out there pumping her gas and two lil' boys dribbling a basketball, the scene seemed free of any eminent dangers. It was time to get it busting. Stunna couldn't have seen it coming.

"Ay, lil' bitch, what the fuck I tell yo' duck ass about lacking out here in these streets!" Popcorn said savagely, cracking Stunna upside the head with the Mystic bottle. *WHAM!* Instantly, the bottle busted open and fruit juices went flying everywhere, mostly all over Stunna's L-V attire. He fell out across the counter and tried holding on to it as if someone had mysteriously snatched the ground from underneath his feet.

The foreign cashier began yelling from behind the bulletproof window, "Take that nonsense up out of my store, or I'm gonna call the *po-po*."

Popcorn didn't want to talk though, he was all about action. He kicked Stunna all up in the ass, knocking him down to the pavement. That's when he got wild, using Stunna's face as a surface to practice tap-dancing on. All you saw was his head bouncing up and down off the ground as Popcorn imitated Sammy Davis, Jr. Stunna's blood was beginning to stain his ACG-boots.

Finally, the foreigner got on the phone and called *9-1-1*. However, that didn't stop Popcorn from playing soccer with Stunna's cranium. The two lil' basketball dribblers stood front row, watching a blood sport. It took for an old man coming in to play the lottery to pull Popcorn up off the boy.

Popcorn broke loose from the man and growled at him, showing his teeth like how a wolf does when it's about to attack. It was clear that the old man didn't want any smoke, he hurried up and threw his hands in the air as if he was being robbed or something. Popcorn loved putting people under submission, especially without having to get physical with them. To him, those were the sweetest victories of them all.

Popcorn turned back around and kicked Stunna dead in the ass as hard as he possibly could, just for good measures. Then he took off running out of the store, all the way back to the Fo'. Once he stepped foot on the block, the very thought had suddenly dawned on him, *Dammit, I didn't even get the fucking blunts!*

CHAPTER #8

IT CAME

Juice, an "Insane-Gangster," was currently serving out a natural life sentence for a heinous murder he had committed back in the 90's. The cold hearted killer had just came home from serving out a juvenile life sentence. Talk about catching bodies...this guy's count was about as long as his shoe size, and he had been stopped buying sneakers from Kids Foot Locker. In broad daylight one afternoon, right in front of Fenger High School, Juice ran up on another well-known gang member, with a sawed-off shotgun, and blew his face apart. The classic, high profiled murder was broadcasted all over the news. They called him the "shotgun-butcher."

Juice was Bible's day one homey, a brother from another mother. It was him who showed Bible the dark-side of the world. The type of terror Juice caused throughout the city was *Bin Laden-ish.* Pistol-playing was an obsession he would carry to the grave with him, some would say.

Juice and Bible grew up on the same block, both of their families were very close and looked out for one another on the norm. Before Juice caught his last homicide, he was very much on his way to becoming the leader of the Insane-Gangsters in the south region of the Chi. However, his aim was a whole lot farther than that; he had dreams and admirations of becoming the next **"Larry Hoover."**

Bible kept in touch with him throughout his bid sending him bread, books, and answering all of his collect-calls. Loyalty was a top priority for Bible, he placed it above everything, including money. Juice was back in the courts on a post-conviction relief. It seemed that the Judge had ruled in error, according to the Supreme Court Rule. This was a great discovery, being that *the natural-ball* the judge had given him was overturned; the judge had to re-sentence him to a lesser sentence. Currently, he had 15 years in…a resentencing hearing could possibly push him right out the door. He was in a very good position.

A lot of *guys* had counted Juice out, leaving him to hang dry like wet clothes pinned up on a line. From the very moment when the judge said, "Guilty on all accounts," nobody ever expected to see him hit the streets again. However, the tables have turned; and his moment was "up and coming." Murder was still on his mind, but this time the plot was against who he'd once killed for.

The slim shaped, mid height gangster slid across the dayroom with his head held high, giving cold stares and mean mugs to fuck niggas along the way. He went to the phone and punched in a series of numbers calling **"Big-Swole."** This was someone whom he would have died for at one point; however, now he couldn't wait to smoke his top.

"Thank you for using Securus, you may now start your conversation,"

"What up, big hoe, I mean…Big Swole. Long time, no money order or shit." Juice said, aggressively.

"What up, G-ball. Fool 'nem was just talking about your wild ass the other day."

"Aw yeah…I hope the discussion pertained to having them finances in order…all of them. I'm up now, I need those. I ain't gon' wanna talk at all. I'm coming to collect every penny that's rightfully owed to me, with interest." Juice warned. Big-Swole just giggled thinking the shit was a joke, but Juice didn't have the slightest smile on his face.

"I'm not bullshitting at all," It got a bit quiet on the phone till Juice began speaking again, "You muthafuckas been eating real good out there in 'nem streets and haven't sent me shit, not a fucking crumb! Ol' hoe ass niggas, if it wasn't for me folks 'nem would have been robbed and killed you bitches! Out there doing the sneaky talk with my name…let that bread don't be together when I touch."

"Man—" before Big-Swole could even start talking, Juice cut him off.

"—Man, my ass, just have my paper in order, *hoe-mie!* The shit ain't gonna be nice any other way."

"Damn, lil' bro…that's how you feel? How long you been holding that shit in?" Big-Swole said, sounding startled.

"You know what it is, partner. I'm the same muthafucka who took hot copper in the stomach for your fat ass and this is the thanks I get?" Juice argued. Big-Swole tried to weigh in on the conversation, only to get cut off again. "—Your days are numbered, bitch…that's on Rose." Rose was Juice's uncle who got killed in a stand-off with the police.

"*Click!*" Juice slammed the phone on the hook. He couldn't help but think to himself as he slid off from the phone booth, *I got something real bloody in store for that fuck ass nigga…these peoples bet not let me come home!*

A-1 waited patiently for the moment to come. He sat by the chuckhole and watched the correctional officers as they changed shifts. He examined every officer coming and going; however, he had his eyes set out on only seeing one guard in particular—C/O Adams.

"Where the fuck this nigga's at? Blood always be playing in his ass." A-1 complained.

"He's probably downstairs at holding trying to mack down Ms. Jones big-booty ass," C-Lord, A-1's cellie, replied.

Not a second later after C-Lord finished his remarks, C/O Adams came walking into the interlock with a McDonald's bag in his hand.

"Bingo!" A-1 said, looking over at C-Lord.

"That's him?" C-Lord asked, frantically. A-1 smiled and nodded his head.

Once C/O Adams got himself situated in the bubble, he came on the deck to do his count. When he made it to A-1's cell, he looked in and gave a good confirmation, "I got you already in the bubble, broski. Once I get done counting, I'm gonna let you out to clean up in the interlock for me...the move will be in the garbage."

"Alright, smooth then," A-1 responded, feeling good. C/O Adams continued counting and came back to let A-1 out of his cell. A-1 played it smooth, not fronting his move at all. He swept the deck up and made his way to the interlock. He grabbed a clean garbage bag and emptied the trash that was inside. *Umm*...he was loving it.

A-1 brought the trash bag back to the deck to the bathroom area where there were no cameras to watch him recover the McDonald's bag. He grabbed it and put it down his pants leg, then he came out of the bathroom and sat the trash bag back in the garbage can at the front of the wing. Swiftly, he slid back into his cell and put C-Lord on *"S"* (security) while he bust the McDonald's bag down—eagerly.

"Blam!" he said, as he pulled out the merch. It was 8oz. of some good smoke, a whole bunch of loose tobacco, and several Bic lighters.

"Yes sir, *charlie-wallie!*" C-Lord replied as he reached over and shook up with A-1.

True enough, the items weren't much to someone on the outside, but where they were, Cook County Jail max-division, it was surely a mil-ticket. The contraband was easily worth twenty-bucks or better. All they had to hit C/O Adams with was a band, tops. Kick-Dough financed the whole play.

"This is where doing time becomes fun, my nigga." A-1 advised C-Lord as he passed him an oz. to examine.

C-Lord was a 5-star universal, Conservative Vice Lord, "CVL," from out west. A-1 bumped into him when he first came into the county. Ever since then, the two been rocking hard with each other, no homo. C-Lord was official, he knew all the heavy-hitters throughout the city. Currently, he was locked up with a no-bond fighting a double murder. Him and A-1 had the same attorney, Chuck.

"We gotta move this shit around first before throwing any parties. We gotta be really low-key about this...by no means can we front our move. We might not ever get it as sweet as this again." C-Lord advised A-1 while smelling the bud. "This some good ol' green too."

"Yeah, I should've gotten some kush though," A-1 suggested.

"Nah, you did just good with the Reggie Bush. That kush shit is entirely too loud...we would've had a great task on our hands just off trying to contain the smell."

"True that-true that," A-1 replied. "Okay then, we gonna bag up four zones, all in 50's and 100's, and pass out G-bundles throughout the compound. Have lord 'nem stand on them funds, world to world Western Unions only. That way, we can run up a check right quick. You know, the right way!"

"Hell yeah! That's smart too. If twelve get a whiff of what's going on, it'll be hard to pinpoint where the juggs coming from with it being parties everywhere." C-Lord added.

"Right, then we take another zip or two and bust it down the same way to jugg and finesse ourselves. Before it's all said and done, we should see at least a salt-buck apiece. And that's after all the pass outs and partying." A-1 preached.

"I hear you church, it's gonna be so many muthafuckas on our dick...we're gonna have to purchase another one, apiece...no homo."

A-1 busted out laughing at C-Lord's slick remark. This was the type of shit he lived for, ever since he was a kid-a lot of attention. "No doubt Lord, we might as well make the best of this jail shit while we're here."

"The right way!" C-Lord hastened to reply.

The two criminals began breaking down the bud eagered to smoke some them damn selves.

A Novel by Pucasso

CHAPTER #9
CAUGHT LACKIN'

The **B.R.O**'s, Blood Related Only, were a family-orientated affair, being that the majority of their squad consistent of relatives. These were A-1's kinfolks. The clique of money-getters pursued to carry on the traditions of their predecessors—MVP. Their starting lineup was **Mac, Tom-Tom, Marshall, Justo,** and **Face.**

Mac was the head of the family's body; he called the shots and laid down the laws. Tom-Tom was the arms of the body; he enforced all the laws set forth by the head of the body—Mac. Marshall and Justo were the youngest of them all, so they were the legs; they made the moves necessary in order to get whatever the body needed.

Last but not least was Face—the big homie. He was the family's backbone. They say, *"Without a head, the body shall fall."* Well, in this case it's Face that holds the body together...Mac is just a front. Face made sure that the family stayed up through adversities just as well as the good times. Potentially-wise, the BROs were calculated to be the next best group of individuals coming out of Washington Heights...a power to be reckoned with. What can you say, they were only groomed by one of the **Most Vicious People** that ever stepped on the scene—A-1.

Shoota really didn't fit in with the BROs much. They just weren't his kind of peoples. Let him tell it...he was gutter-gutter, and the BRO's were privileged. He could've been a bit jealous of the way they looked out for each other as a close family. Shoota had been deprived of that kind of luxury. Ever since his mother got smoked, he'd been on his own scrambling out there in them streets. Him and his two lil' sisters, Meesha and Tina, were separated and brought up in different foster homes. He had to go against the adversities of society all by himself.

The closeness that the BROs shared amongst themselves just made him sick to his stomach. He hardly knew his father…last time he heard, the fucker was doing a mandatory life sentence in Menard Max Prison for Capital Murder. Word on the street was that he had killed a muthafucka, wrapped the body up, and then set it on fire. This happened sometime right before his mother got gunned down. Just terrible, huh?

Shoota done been in and out of different group homes and juvenile institutions, having to fight hard for reputation and respect. He felt that the BROs, on the other hand, didn't earn their stripes themselves…and if it wasn't for A-1, they wouldn't even exist. Shoota played the shit cool, only for a moment though. However, all he needed was a reason to play crazy with one of them, and it was on. The clash between two of Washington Heights' youthful gangs was bound to happen.

"Shoota!" Mac shouted out down the block. Shoota kept strutting forward, unaware of his name being called. Mac shouted out at him again, this time even louder, "Ay, Shoota!"

Finally, Shoota turned around sending his dreads swinging all across his face. Focusing in on the person who was calling him, he threw his hands up in the air and shouted back, "What up?"

"Check it out, bro'ski…" Mac yelled as he waved his hand, directing Shoota to come his way.

Mac was a sneaky muthafucka…he always having a hidden agenda or ulterior motive going on about himself. You never really could tell when dealing with him, you just had to be ready for whatever, something Shoota's been doing since his mother got changed. He kept a pole or two on him at all times. The two *drillers* met up in the middle of the block and exchanged palms, doing an infamous gang handshake. They both were originated from the Fo', which was the fourth block going into the Washington Heights Community—headquarters of "MVP."

"What up, bro?" Shoota said, moving his dreads out of the way of his face. Shorty looked identical to the actor Larenz Tate, *a.k.a* "**O-Dog**," off the movie *Menace to Society.*

"You seen a grey Charger sliding through the land?" Mac asked while zooming in on what appeared to have been the very car he was just describing. It was creeping up from behind Shoota.

"Hell nah, why—who was in it?" Shoota replied as he turned around to see what caught Mac's attention all of a sudden.

Mac reached under his shirt and pulled out a black and grey Glock .40. Instantaneously, Shoota drew his stick, ready to pop shots. "That ain't it, scud. That's a Magnum." Mac said, right before Shoota got a chance to clutch the trigger.

Mac withdrew his weapon, putting it back on his hip. However, Shoota kept his drawn, holding onto it with both of his hands and aiming it directly at the driver of the car as they rolled by. This shit was his livelihood.

"Them pussy ass niggas off the Tre just pulled up on me talking 'bout what all they gon' do once they catch you." Mac claimed.

"Straight up, who—Rio?" Shoota responded. He still had his 30-popper out, lowered down by his side.

"Hell yeah, him with Taz bitch ass riding shotgun. I couldn't see who was in the back with them." Mac answered.

Rio and **Taz** were a couple of young, dread-headed ass wannabe rappers, affiliated with an independent rap label called "Street-Fame Entertainment." They were from the Tre, which was the third block going outside of Washington Heights. It's been animosity against the two blocks since Genesis.

When A-1 started seeing some real bucks, he went ahead and squashed the beef with the Tre, making it safe for both sides to go to each other's turf. Being that Muscles was currently doing time behind some testimonies that came from the Tre, he didn't feel the move; but over some time, he bought into the play and understood how significant the peace treaty was to the land. See, A-1 was trying to expand MVP all across the city. Now that he was locked up, all negotiations were over.

"Man, them fuck niggas don't wanna see me...I ain't hard to find," Shoota said aggressively while lifting his pistol upwards and kissing it. "A-1 ain't here to save they bitch ass anymore!"

Mac gave Shoota a cold stare before smiling. "Hell yeah, on Scoobie's grave, we should go through that bitch and pop some shit up...show muthafuckas that shit ain't sweet." Mac suggested while lighting up a *loosey* (a cigarette).

This kind of jibber-jabber was right up Shoota's alley. He's been itching to wage an all out war against the Tre again. Quiet as kept, he already had been doing some drills of his own on them niggas. He didn't trust Mac like that but thought teaming up with him to *drill-drill* wouldn't be such a bad idea. Right now, the Tre was an imminent threat that needed to be taken care of.

"Shit...where you on yo' way off to?" Mac asked.

"I was heading to the park, but fuck that now...I'm ready to go op-shopping." Shoota replied, tucking his stick away up under his shirt.

"What, you talking about sliding through that bitch right now?"

"And you know it," Shoota replied, quoting a line from *O-Dog*.

"Shit, it's whatever—I never cared!" Mac said as he reached out and shook up with Shoota. Afterwards, they dropped three fingers-disrespecting the Tre.

"On Scoobie, I'm about to pluck a cluck or two." Shoota merched it, kissing four of his fingers and holding them up to the sky. Mac did the same.

The two gun-holders pimped off, up the block and through an alleyway, going towards the Tre.

Shoota hopped the fence swiftly and then came along Mac, following up behind the young savage. They both stayed low to the ground and inched their way on deadly grounds. This was a sneak attack, so they made sure not to front their move. Both were directly on cue with one another; they watched each other's backs as they did their own.

Shoota lived for this kind of action, especially when it was an actual reality. Playing the video game *Call of Duty* was quite entertaining and all, but he was more fascinated with being involved in hands-on combat out there in 'nem streets. The way he signaled Mac when making certain moves, you would've thought the boy was some type of military warlord or something.

Shoota and Mac crawled through the grass like some alligators coming up towards the back of a residential home. When they made it to the back door, they stood up and crept alongside of the house. They kept their backs to the wall with their guns out, ready to be fired…the right way!

Once they got closer, near the front of the building, the sound of two people's voices echoed through the air. It was dark outside, and the block had become deserted. Shoota glanced back at Mac, putting a finger up to his lips, signaling him to be quiet. He pointed the same finger towards out front, letting him know also that somebody was out there.

The two hunters crept up closer to try to make out who the individuals were. They got to the front of the house and then ducked down low behind some bushes, looking closely at the potential targets. Mac saw that it wasn't Rio or Taz and so did Shoota. However, it really didn't matter much to Shoota who the fuck it was out there lacking, he'd already put in his mind that he was gonna turn someone over to God tonight—if not two.

Zooming in closely, Mac paused in his tracks. "Wait, I know them. They ain't on shit, they're not even from around here. They go to Simeon High School." he whispered, grabbing Shoota's arm, stopping him from standing up all the way. He was already easing up from the bushes, on the verge of giving someone a standing ovation with his Glock .17. There were two basketball playing looking muthafuckas chilling in the front by a green 2000 Buick Park Avenue.

"What?" Shoota whispered back as he turned and looked at Mac like he was crazy.

"Them some nobodies, bro. We came over here for specific targets— Rio and Taz."

"So, what you want to do…lamp in these damn bushes till they show their faces, that could be all night," Shoota whispered, keeping a close eye on his prey. Mac just looked at Shoota with a blank expression. "Man, don't tell me we done came all the way over here for nothing. What…you're scared or something?"

Mac wasn't scared of a lil' one-eighty-seven, he just honored certain rules to the game. He let the innocent be, even if they were on deadly grounds. "Shorty, don't even try to run that *'you're scared'* bullshit on me. I'm no rookie to this *drill-drill* shit. I does it for real, nigga. I'm just not about to start shooting at innocent people—period!"

Mac tucked away his weapon and eased from the bushes, making his way back to the gangway. Shoota was in flames, he hated when muthafuckas went against his lead. That type of shit made him feel insecure about himself, which only made matters worse. He raised his gun and pointed it at the back of Mac's top, considering smoking it; but instead, he swung it around and stormed from the bushes in a hissy-fit. Mac didn't even bother to look back, he just took off running all the way back to the Fo'.

Ain't no such thing as being innocent, Shoota thought as he clutched the trigger. "*GLAH-GLAH-GLAH-GLAH!*" gunshots echoed the block, loudly.

When the slugs tore through the guy's chest plate, he went plummeting to the pavement. By that time, the other mark had a few seconds head start. Shoota swiftly turned his gun, slightly easing off the trigger, and took aim at the getaway runner. "*GLAH-GLAH!*"

Shoota ran up on the vic that was squirming on the ground, still firing shots at the other nigga who was running for his dear life. "*GLAH-GLAH-GLAH-GLAH!*" You could clearly see flames jumping out the muzzle of his gun.

Although the heavy-sprinter took shots to the shoulder, arm, and thigh, he maintained on his feet and he was destined to get away. However, his buddy didn't have the same fate. He was immobile, and crawling in the middle of the street. His number had come up for souls, and the Reaper was on deck waiting to send him in.

When Shoota made it to him, he stood over his body and pointed the stick down at his forehead. "*Always look a man in the eye before you kill him,*" the words of **Master-P** played back in his mind as he did just as the colonel said.

The vic was terrified; however, he managed to look up at Shoota seeing only a bunch of dreads draping down his face. He was the young, black **Michael Myers...** but with a gun. The boy flicked his eyelids shut and began reciting a brief prayer, "Our father—" was as far as he got before Shoota let the trigger fly. "—*GLAH-GLAH-GLAH!.*"

"JRW, muthafucka!" Shoota yelled joyfully as he took off running in the same direction as the other mark, holding his gun upward at the sky. Thick clouds of smoke steamed from out the muzzle and the handle was hot; however, he held onto it tightly.

Making his way towards the fucker, which had made it a few houses down the street and collapsed on someone's front porch, some bright lights suddenly beamed up the block. Several porch lights flicked on, and a series of house doors began opening simultaneously. Prayer works...that is, if you're able to get a fair chance to do so.

"Thank you, God!" the survivor cried out as an elder man opened the door where he was slumped at.

Shoota swiftly twisted his whole body around and tore ass all the way back to the land, in the same direction he had come from.

A fatal shooting on the southside of Chicago, one dead and another in critical condition, read the headlines on the Channel-9 News. Although the police didn't have anyone in custody or any relevant leads, they suspected the shooter to be Shoota. Skull-Cap and Ninja, two rookie detectives, came through the area in search of answers.

Shoota was in the park shooting hoops when twelve hit the curb and rolled through on the basketball court. He didn't even bother trying to run; he was clean, one of his shorties had his pistol and was blended in the crowd somewhere. Shoota knew the cops were gonna come looking for him, to interrogate him about the deadly shooting. He was eager to get the shit out the way.

"What's up, Charles Jones, or should I call you...Lil' Charles, the Shoota?" Ninja said, from out the passenger window. The squad car was parked in the middle of the court, blocking people from playing basketball.

Shoota kept shooting jump shots though, unaffected by the sudden defense.

"So, I see you like shooting around on and off the court." Ninja said, being sarcastic. The shit probably would've gotten under the average person's skin but not Shoota. He just kept shooting the ball, throwing up brick after brick.

"Looks like it to me, you got a way better shot off the court."

Ninja bailed out the car and then came his partner, Skull-Cap. When Shoota took the next shot, the ball bounced off the rim and came to Skull-Cap. He caught it and in one swift motion, bounced it once then shot it straight through the net.

"Swish, all pussy! Shooting basketballs is no different than shooting guns. Come on, you're supposed to know that, Shoota." Skull-Cap advised him while still holding both of his hands up in the air, following through on his shot.

Skull-Cap was a tall, white cop...a look-a-like of Dirk from the **"Dallas Mavericks."**

"Man, why y'all fucking with me? Y'all can't have shit else better to do!"

Ninja looked around and then down at his watch before speaking, "Nah, it seems that we don't, but solving a couple homicides might very well be something considered small to you."

Skull-Cap walked up on Shoota and made him assume the position. He patted him down thoroughly, even pulling down his trousers and looking in his ass. Just a standard procedure when dealing with some pigs. They found nothing but still slapped the cuffs on his wrists.

"What you locking me up for? I ain't even do shit,"

"We have an investigative alert out on you. We have to take you down to the station for interrogation." Skull-Cap claimed, shoving Shoota in the back seat of the squad car.

Ninja wandered off with his nose buried in the dirt, searching the promises like a K-9. Everybody on the playground began walking up on the cop, talking with aggression. "Let him go…he ain't do shit…black lives matter, you know…y'all just love bothering muthafuckas for no reason."

"Yeah-yeah-yeah, I know…tell it to the judge," Ninja replied. One juvie got kind of close to Ninja, and instantly, he upped his weapon aiming it. "Stand back or I'll shoot."

The whole crowd of people got out of the rogue cop's way. Skull-Cap signaled for Ninja. "Ay, partner…let's get out of here."

The two pigs bailed back in the car and peeled off in a hurry. With only half of a witness and no murder weapon linking Shoota to the crime, all he would have to do is keep his mouth shut, and he'd be free from any charges pending against him.

CHAPTER #10

GREEN LIGHT

Kick-Dough was chilling up north at his side bitch condo when his phone rang. Immediately, he answered the phone seeing that it was a collect call from someone in the county jail. *"Thank you for using Securus, you may now start your conversation,"*

"What up, king?" A-1 said.

"Shit, what's up with you, king?" Kick-Dough responded.

King was the new title the two titans started calling each other after Pops stepped down and gave 'em the throne.

"Nothing much, you got the better hand, my nigga."

"Nah...*we* got the better hand. I'm your right hand, and you're my left. Don't ever get the shit twisted...we're one, my nigga. It's just our left hand's temporarily injured and healing for the moment." Kick-Dough philosophied, feeling real smart from the good head Jessica was currently giving him.

"Slow down, Pops. I hear you, my nigga. You got the old man down packed already," A-1 giggled. Kick-Dough joined in on the laughter.

"Speaking of the old man, I haven't seen or heard anything from him in a while now. What about you?"

"Nah, he was supposed to come visit me before going on that little retirement trip he had talked about," A-1 replied. "Ever since then, he's been M.I.A. He was acting real weird when I saw him too. I think something's wrong with his health."

"Yeah, that's not like him to just up and disappear without giving us notice. I've been trying to get in touch with him for weeks now. I got some bread for him and everything." Kick-Dough informed.

"Damn, I hope ain't shit wrong with him...I'll go crazy in this bitch, for real."

"I'm already knowing, my nigga," Kick-Dough replied, trying to stop Jessica from completing the sloppy-top she was giving him. She was persistent though, and any other time, Kick-Dough wouldn't get in between her and her mistress duties. However, the thought of something bad happening to Pops had turned him off. Jessica sensed that Kick-Dough wasn't in the mood anymore by the serious look he gave her. She wiped her mouth off with her bare hand and got up to go to the kitchen to get them something to drink.

"What do Olivia have to say about Pops' disappearance?" A-1 asked.

"To tell you the truth, I haven't spoken with her in a couple of weeks. The last time we rotated, she hadn't seen or heard anything from him either," Kick-Dough recalled as he fastened up his Gucci jeans and belt buckle. "You know what, I'm up north right now...I'm gonna make it my business to slide on her and find out what's really good."

"If she don't know anything, something's definitely wrong." A-1 suspected.

"Hell yeah, I'm about to get dead on top of that right now," Kick-dough said. "What's up with you though, how you holding up in there?"

Jessica came back into the room holding two cups of Patron. She stopped dead in her tracks and gave Kick-Dough a cold stare, seeing him all dressed up getting ready to leave.

"I'm living the best way a king could possibly live while being locked up." A-1 said.

"I heard that, I'm bout ready to get up with Chuck to turn myself in. I just need to take care of a few more things. I say a lil' bit after my birthday, I'm gonna go ahead and do it. Chuck guaranteed he'll be able to get us both a bond real soon."

Kick-dough peeped the nasty look Jessica had on her face but played the shit smooth.

"Shit...even if them people do set bail for us, it's gonna be something outrageous," A-1 assumed, sounding fucked up about it. "Probably a half-a-mil apiece."

Kick-Dough paused in thought for a hot second, "That's something real slight to some muthafucking kings!"

"You ready to square off that kind of tab, my nigga?" A-1 asked.

"Man look...if that's the case then I could turn myself in today. I don't give a fuck what the tab is. I'm gonna make sure it gets taken care of...you can't put a price on a Hood Hero's freedom."

Kick-Dough walked up to Jessica and gave her a kiss on the lips then whispered in her ear, "I got to make an important run. Once I'm done, I'll be back to spend the rest of the day with you, baby...okay?"

Jessica didn't budge, she kept a mug on her face as if she was gonna go to the grave with it. Today was her birthday, and Kick-Dough had promised to spend some quality time with her. Oh well! She would just have to get over it...that or either get gone.

Kick-dough grabbed the cup of Patron out of her hand and slammed it in one swift motion. "*Gulp!* Aw..." he sighed as the alcohol slid down his throat. He put the cup right back into Jessica's hand and hit the door. No sooner than the door slammed shut, the empty glass came smashing up against it—shattering everywhere.

Jessica was in deep rage, but Kick-Dough paid the girl's mood swing no mind. He just kept it moving like a roach that's been partially stepped on. He had more important shit to be worried about than a funky ass attitude by a side-chick. Let him tell it *A bitch will run you crazy, only if you let them!*

A-1 was still on the phone chilling. The county jail sucked, but Kick-Dough made sure, every chance he got, that his partner-in-crime lived a lil' bit. For A-1, it was such an amazing feeling just to know that it didn't matter whatever the amount of his bond was, *as long as he got one,* someone would be coming to get him-real soon. It's muthafuckas who done got locked up and was given a measly thousand-dollar bond but had to sit still because no one would come get them…real talk.

Not A-1 though, he was just out on two bonds, one on top of the other, totaling out to about 40-bucks. He paid the tab straight out of his Rockstar jeans and then went to bond out a couple team members during the same period. Straight Boss Shit!

"Well, it's good to know that somebody cares about me out there." A-1 responded, speaking straight from the heart.

"Would you knock it the fuck off with all the theatrics? You're a king, my nigga…I'll die before I sit around and let you get treated otherwise." Kick-Dough said as he took a glance at the screen of his phone seeing back to back text messages coming from Jessica.

She was being very ominous…talking about how she was gonna confront Stacey and tell her about Kick-Dough's disloyalty…also saying that she was gonna kill Stacey, Baby-Aaron, and then herself as well. She claimed she was so serious this time; however, Kick-Dough done heard it all once before-*blah-blah-blah-blah!* He went ahead and discarded the bogus text and blocked her completely.

It got a bit quiet on the phone till A-1 broke the silence. "Hello,"

"Oh my fault, bro. I'm still here, I was just skimming through all these psychotic ass texts from Jessica. That girl is poison. Now, I see what **"BBD"** meant when they said, *"Never trust a big butt and a smile."*

"Missed her, kissed her, loved her," A-1 responded, feeding into the joke—giggling afterwards. A-1 and Kick-Dough both were some silly muthafuckas.

"Yo' ass still got them bitches, I see." Kick-Dough said, complementing A-1 on his ability to make a muthafucka laugh.

"Hell yeah, Why not? I ain't lost shit but a lil' time. My ability to make people laugh hasn't went anywhere," A-1 agreed about his undying humor. "But on the real, you need to leave that psychotic bitch alone before she snaps."

"I know, I just had to block her ass. She's talking about shooting Stacey in the face, stabbing Baby-Aaron up, and then hanging herself on the tree in front of our house."

"Damn, that's beyond psychotic, my nigga…that sound like some '*The Devil's Rejects*' type of shit. That hoe got **Rob Zombie** all in her blood." A-1 said.

Immediately, Kick-Dough busted out laughing. "You're shooting them bitches today, ain't you, man?" he replied. The dynamic duo continued laughing together.

"On some for real shit, I'm tired of these random ass bitches. I'm thinking about going ahead and popping the question to Stacey. She's the only girl who understands me just how I need to be understood."

Kick-Dough was back in his Porsche Panamera driving through the northside of the city. **Meek Mill** was playing low on the radio, "*Some of us go to college…some of us go to jail, some of us go to heaven…some of us go to hell.*"

"Stacey's my soulmate,"

"Word, that's what's up then. What the fuck you waiting for? Go right for it, my nigga—jump!" A-1 replied, happy for his rappy. "My bitch Sheila bum ass ain't good for shit. I'm about to hand that hoe her walking papers any day now, and I can damn near merch it."

"Come on now, my nigga. I done been to Kendall County, Livingston County, Cook County, and even DuPage County, but I ain't never...you hear me? I said, never been to Will County," Kick-Dough proclaimed, confusing A-1 a bit.

"Will County...what you mean, broski?" he asked.

"*Will* you knock it the fuck off!" Kick-Dough responded, suggesting that A-1 beat it with the jokes...talking like he was gonna really dump Sheila, his high school sweetheart. Everybody in the hood knew how much he loved that damn girl.

Once A-1 caught on to the joke, he couldn't help but crack the hell up. Kick-Dough was just as comical as he was, if not even funnier. He definitely had them bitches.

"Okay, I see you're returning fire. I set myself up for that one, but I'm serious, nigga. That bitch is cramping my style...trying to still live off me, and I'm the one who needs support. That's crazy, ain't it, man?"

"Hell yeah! But that's your fault, king. You spoil muthafuckas too much. Giving from the heart is obsolete now of days. One thing I've learned since you been gone was to stop enabling muthafuckas out here in these streets. I mean, I still give out blessings, that'll never change as long as I'm in the Lime-Lite, but a lot of that free hand out shit we used to do went straight down the drain with me. Once I realized that people's expectations of what they should be given had superseded their actual worth, I began making myself less available for muthafuckas." Kick-Dough preached.

"That's how I'm starting to feel too, bro. My lil' cousins out there *in the fucking way!*" I done showed them duck ass niggas so much jugg and finesse that they could of ran for the mayor slot in Atlanta and possibly got elected. Ain't no way in the world these niggas should be broke. I called Mac the other day about a quick jugg I was trying to bust, and he acted like he didn't have a dime in his pocket." A-1 complained.

"They all waiting on me to come through, but it's been too hot around there... you and I know that I don't need to get caught up in a jam right now. I been fake-fucking around with some cats from over by my momma's crib, just to keep the Lime-Lite glowing."

"Why is it so damn hot on the block, suddenly?"

"A lot of unnecessary drilling going on, somebody got painted on the Tre. Ever since then, it's been Battlestar Galactica. You 'bout could just guess who's the cause of it all, huh?" Kick-Dough implied, without mentioning any names.

"Yeah, I definitely got a good idea," A-1 replied, starting to catch a slight headache. Shoota had become an unmanageable problem to the livelihood of the Washington Heights Community. "I've been hearing a bunch of foul shit going on with the lil' fella...what's to him?"

"I don't know, he just came out the woolworks with this *drill-drill, gang-gang* shit. Shorty got a problem with listening. I used to slide on him and curve him well until he started letting big goofy get in his ear, feeding his mind with a whole bunch of bullshit."

Big goofy was a lil' nickname that the block had given Shoota's cousin Dino. It was a known fact that he had been corrupting the minds of the juvies, encouraging them to become more rebellious than they already were.

"I don't even bother reaching out to the lil' bastard any more, him or anybody in his lil' clique. They're all screwed up in the head. None of them got a jugg or finesse going for themselves but got the audacity to swag around the hood like they're bosses or some shit. All they're good for is drilling and jumping gates." Kick-dough informed.

A-1 already had a crucial drawing put together for the occasion. "Well, fuck it then…since muthafuckas getting a bit hungry and want to eat out of turn, I suggest you might as well go to KFC and order up a big ol' bucket of chicken." he said, talking in street codes.

Kick-Dough understood the drawing very well. He was given the green light to have Shoota smoked, him and whoever else that wasn't with the program. Both of the MVP representatives were thinking on the same accord. "The original recipe, huh!" he replied, letting A-1 know that the matter was understood.

"It's up to you to keep this "MVP" movement as relevant as possible. It's a tough job to do, especially without having no help, but you're the only one capable of doing so right now. The future of Washington Heights depends on the very moves you make out there, my nigga." A-1 lectured.

"So, you're telling me that if something happens to me then it's over with for the hood, broski?"

"It's sad to say, but yep…at least till me or Muscles touchdown." A-1 answered.

"Oh yeah, I just seen Bible the other day, and he was telling me that something new was about to go into effect, which could possibly kick Muscles out the pen soon." Kick-Dough informed his mans, with happiness all in his voice. "Bro been wilding out like Nick Cannon in that bitch though, getting wild with whoever—inmates and staff. Bible said that he lost a bunch of time."

"He'll get it all back, trust me. God loves us *Hood Heroes.* It's bro time to step into the Lime-Lite." A-1 suggested. "I tell you one thing though, it's gonna be a lot of muthafuckas sick behind him coming home. Bro was putting fire up under niggas, nobody expected him to hit the streets again. I just pray he be carcful and do the right things."

"And what's '*the right things*'?" Kick-Dough asked.

"Taking care of himself and the business…staying out of the cops' way…and far away from fuck niggas."

"The right way." Kick-Dough agreed.

"God forbids, but worst comes to worst, that's who we're gonna have to work the golden book. Bro's *gang*, I trust him with my life. He rep "MVP" to the depths."

"I already know. I used to always see him in the hood, fly as fuck, whipping up in something real slick. You and him started that taking off on the police shit. You, him, and Tino were all reckless as fuck."

"Hell yeah, what's good with T? I done reached out to him several times and still haven't gotten a response back." A-1 asked, assuming that T was out there in 'nem streets—*in the fucking way.*

"Fool be out here in the field doing his own thang, homework and all. He got his own lil' team and everything."

"He don't be trying to get up with you?"

"Hell nah…I guess he's still in his feelings." Kick-Dough figured.

"Oh yeah! Well, fuck him then. Ol' petty ass nigga think a muthafucka owe him something. That's the main reason why he's fucked up now." A-1 argued.

"That's crazy,"

"Yes, it is…but check it, I'm not even gon' clog your eardrums any longer, my dude. I done worked up a lil' sweat on this damn phone. Besides, you got a couple of things on your plate that need to be taken care of, immediately." A-1 said, trying to end the call. The shit about T had him heated.

"Oh yeah, one thing before you go. One of Stacey's friends had seen some of your old flicks and is really digging your swag. Her name is Meko, a bad ass chick too. She wanna come visit you. I told her that it was all good, but she insists that I ask you first." Kick-Dough delivered the good news to his homie at a most needed time. Talk about the art of timing!

"Hell yeah, I need a new friend right about now. Sheila's ass is out...I'm terminating her contract right as we speak, my nigga."

"Yeah right, merch it then," Kick-Dough said.

"On Scoobie's grave!"

"Alright then, dawg. I'm gonna let you know right now, you got a real brick-house on your hands—thanks to Stacey. She's always talking about you and shit. She misses you probably just as much as I do."

"Tell lil' sis that I love her and really appreciate the hook-up. You better hurry up and marry that girl."

"No doubt, keep your head up, nigga. Call me back later on, I should have been found out something about Pops by then. I'm almost at Olivia's crib now." Kick-Dough said.

"Okay, tell 'O' I said what up and that I'm gonna call her later also. Love, nigga!"

Both MVPians hung the phone up simultaneously. Not much longer after that, Kick-Dough pulled up in front of Olivia's crib. He dialed her number but got the voicemail. He sent her a quick text, *"Dis K-D, come o-s,"* and then honked the horn.

Helen, Olivia's foster mother, came out to the porch to let Kick-Dough know that Olivia wasn't there. He asked her if she seen or heard anything from Pops, and she informed him that she didn't. She claimed that she'd been trying to catch up with the old man for a couple of weeks now and haven't come close to tracking him down yet. Hell, she was hoping Kick-Dough knew something.

Kick-Dough apologized for any inconvenience he may have caused by honking the horn, interrupting her from whatever she was doing. Kick-Dough always been a gentleman. He told her to let Olivia know he came by and to call him asap. After that, he skated off, skipping going back to Jessica's crib...he had a bigger fish that needed to be fried.

Shoota kept his mouth shut in the interrogation room, he didn't even bother asking for an attorney. The cops had no other choice but to let him go. They had no physical evidence linking him to the murder, and the one witness that had survived the deadly shooting chose not to cooperate with the law. All of a sudden, he had vanished without the slightest trace.

The Tre was fucked up behind the murder. Instantly, they began seeking revenge against Shoota and his squad at the earliest convenience. **Butta**, one of the Tre's top shooters, had just come home from St. Charles Juvenile Prison and was eager to get it busting with whoever. The occasion was perfect for him, now he didn't have to waste precious time going *op-shooting*...specific targets were already determined.

Butta was to the Tre what Shoota was to the Fo', possibly even worse! He was a couple of years older than Shoota and had a menacing reputation in and out of the Dept. of Corrections. Taz and Rio played with pistols but not nearly as much as Butta did. While they were in the studio recording rap lyrics, he was somewhere in the bushes with two guns, lamping on the *opz*.

Now, what was really crazy behind the whole mess, Shoota and Butta were blood-brothers. Although both of 'em were well-aware of their kinship, they went at each other's necks persistently. Neither one of them really knew their father, so to them, they didn't share the same blood.

It was obvious though, the hatred that Shoota and Butta both possessed for their father gradually turned into animosity against one another. The two wolves went back and forth popping caps at each other's crew just like cowboys and Indians. The shit grew way out of hand.

Shoota was up north, going to visit his lil' sisters, when he bumped into this beautiful lil' redbone in Subway. He sized her up discreetly, from where he was standing at in line. The "PYT" definitely had the body of a goddess. Her breasts were well-developed...her waistline was amazingly fit...and her backside was just incredible. This young lady had the kind of sex appeal going on for herself that could of drove even a grown man crazy.

Although Shoota wasn't dressed up to part, he still felt the need to spark up a conversation with the "beauty queen." He caught her standing by the beverage fountain getting something to drink and made his move.

"Hey there, pretty...do you got a minute?"

The girl turned around seeing a dingy, dread-headed savage. "No, I don't!" she claimed, rolling her eyes at him.

"Well, there's no need to get bent out of shape about it...I just so happened to have a couple of them myself, let me give you one." Shoota struck a pose with his first impression; he had charm and charisma entwined with finesse.

He politely grabbed her cup and began filling it up with some pop. "Here, try this combination," he said, mixing Country Time Lemonade with Strawberry Crush pop. This was his favorite blend...also hers.

"I'm already up on that lick, playboy…that's that thang there!" she said, grabbing the cup back from him and taking a sip.

At first, the girl planned to act stuck up and give Shoota a hard time, but his approach was unlike the type of boys she was used to being around. He conducted himself like a "boss." That alone, gave him a whole bunch of cool points. She was flattered to say the least, she looked at him and cracked a sexy smile. This was all he needed, now it was time to turn his swag up on extraordinary.

"Oh my, look at that smile. Have you ever thought about modeling for Colgate?"

The question kind of caught her off-guard. "Nah, why you ask?" she responded, looking at him a bit confused.

"Because, you have an amazing set of teeth." Shoota replied.

Her smile got even wider, this time stretching out from ear to ear. "Why, thank you. I don't think anyone's ever told me that before. Who might you be, Prince Charming?" she asked, looking all cheesy at the face.

"Oh, I'm sorry, my name is Lil' Charles, but by you being so gorgeous and all, you can just call me your boyfriend." The young lady laughed at Shoota's slick remark, cool points were steady adding up in his favor.

"What's your name?" he asked while opening up the door and following her outside the restaurant.

"My name is Olivia, but my friends call me Livy."

"That's a wonderful name, but tell me…what do your boyfriend call you?"

"Why?" Livy hastened to reply.

"Because, that's what I'm gonna call you from now on."

Shoota got close to her and wrapped his arm around her neck. She couldn't resist his charm, he was laying it on real thick.

"Queen...wifey...bae...love—you know, things of that nature."

"Oh, so you have a boyfriend?" Shoota asked, quickly.

"Hell, the way you got your arm wrapped around me, I was beginning to think I did."

Shoota couldn't help but crack a crooked smiled. Livy definitely had a remarkable personality. "You have a beautiful smile yourself, where you from?" she asked.

"I'm from out south in the *hun-nits* (hundreds),"

"Double-O's and bullet holes, huh!" she responded.

Shoota let out a monstrous laugh before saying, "What does a pretty girl such as yourself know about bullet holes?"

Suddenly, Livy's gullible look had turned into a more sophisticated one. "Trust me, baby boy...I know." she responded.

Shoota's phone vibrated in his worn-out True Religion jeans, so he reached for it, taking his arm away from around Livy's neck. Already, she was beginning to miss his warm embrace. "Excuse me," he said as he looked down into his phone.

It was a text message from Ray-Ray that read, *"Baby, why you not answering your phone. I've been calling you for the past fifteen minutes, back to back. I got some horrible news, Popcorn just got shot in the park he's dead! Call me—asap!"*

Shoota's heart dropped down to his stomach, and he began feeling sick. It wasn't from the footlong Philly Cheese-Steak he ate either. *Not Popcorn,* he thought.

Livy sensed something awful had happened just by judging the look on Shoota's face. "Is everything alright?" she asked, concerned about Shoota's current mental state.

"I'm sorry, I gotta go. It's been a pleasure meeting you, Livy."

Shoota jogged across the street, beating on-coming traffic, and made his way to the bus stop.

"Lil' Charles," Livy yelled out. She couldn't help but try to extend a helping hand. "You need me to come with you?"

Shoota respected the kind gesture; however, his feelings were just too down to accept the offer. He didn't want her to see him the way he was. It was quite apparent that he was really hurt.

"Nah, thank you for asking though. It's very thoughtful of you. I'll catch back up with you some other time, hopefully on a better day than this." he said as he dropped his head down to the ground. The harsh reality of losing a real friend was beginning to take its toll, already. All he could think about was smoking a top or two—non-menthol.

Livy felt the boy's pain and understood that he needed to be alone. "Well, I work at that Wal-greens in the same parking lot as Subway. If you ever need me, that's where you can find me."

"That's what's up, I'll holla at you then." Shoota said as he hopped on the CTA-bus that pulled up beside him. He didn't even get a chance to see his sisters.

CHAPTER #11

TURN UP

Just moments before Shoota got the horrible text…

Rio and Taz slid through the outskirts of the Washington Heights Community, easing their way towards the Fo'. They were in a white Montana Van, Rio driving and Taz riding shotgun. Taz had a chrome Desert Eagle sitting dead in his lap with one cocked in the chamber. Their target was Shoota, but anybody from the Fo' would make do. They had grown tired of Shoota and his crew constantly coming through their hood popping shit up. Murder had become a top priority on their "to-do list." The Fo' was up on the score, and Rio and Taz sought to put the margin in their favor.

"Man, fam…as soon as I spot an op, I'm dropping 'em—man down! I don't wanna talk." Taz said, examining the D-E up close.

"On fo'nem grave, make sure you do them duck ass niggas real dirty." Rio suggested while sitting up, driving with both hands on the steering wheel. His antennas were turned up high, on heavy surveillance, in search of anybody who looked like they wanted some smoke.

Chief Keef was playing in the background, *"Riding with my chopper, aye…I'm gon' beat him like his father, aye…now it's blood on my Giuseppe's…I don't like no fucking Prada!"*

The two wannabe rap stars swung their dreads around relentlessly while rapping along to the song. They turned block after block—op hunting. Popcorn was leaving the park, making his way back to the Fo' when he spotted the white Montana van coming up the street. He didn't think much of it though, oblivious to the drill that awaited him.

"Ain't that that bitch ass nigga who stomped Stunna out?" Rio asked, looking closely at Popcorn from a distance.

Taz zoomed in on the suspect and replied, "Hell muthafucking yeah! That's Popcorn bitch ass...pull up on him real slow, fam. I'm about to blow this nigga's head off."

Taz let his window down and pointed the Dessy out of it, taking aim. Popcorn's face was buried in his phone, he didn't even notice when the van pulled up on him. Straight lacking, when it's cracking!

When Popcorn finally looked up, all he could see was-straight down the shaft of Taz's pistol...and he was the mission. Taz lined his ass up precisely, like a certified barber with a sharp-edge razor. Popcorn's knees buckled beneath his upper body, and his heart followed suit. He was stuck in position with nowhere to run for cover.

"Bitch ass nigga, what's up now!" Taz shouted as he leaned out the window and let the Dessy blow. *"DOOM-DOOM-DOOM-DOOM!"*

Popcorn caught two to the forehead. His lifeless body collapsed across the street curb as Rio punched the gas, sliding off in a dash.

The death of Cornelius Williams, *a.k.a.* "Popcorn," was broadcasted all over Chicago's news. The headline read, *"Another senseless killing due to Chicago's gun violence."* The homicide detectives didn't have any leads on who the shooter was. They flooded the Tre looking for answers. All they had to go off of was a partial description of a van. Good luck with that—the city was overpopulated with them shits.

Popcorn's mother was forced to make funeral arrangements to bury her only child on what was supposed to be her birthday weekend. The ceremony was jam-packed, everybody from across the neighborhood came to pay their final respects to the boy…everybody except for the BROs. However, they sent their deepest condolences to Popcorn's family along with a few dollars to help cover some of the funeral expenses.

Mac and his crew chose to keep their distance away from Shoota and the rest of the juvies. They blamed them for Popcorn's death, saying that it was only gonna get worse. Once the news got back to Shoota, any respect he may of had for the BROs was dead. It was at that very moment when he began plotting against them.

The majority of people at the funeral had on "R.I.P Popcorn" shirts, customized to each person's liking. Shoota's shirt out did them all. He had Popcorn spray-painted on the front, smoking a blunt with one hand and throwing up four fingers with the other. On the back he had two doves holding up a banner that said, "Pop goes a Legend…Gone but never forgotten." And he had a Glock .40 with popcorn popping up out of the barrel, at the bottom of the shirt.

Popcorn was Shoota's main man—right next to Do-Dirty. His death affected them both, deeply. They merched it that they wouldn't rest till they got pay back on Rio and Taz. Shoota was continuously on their asses', lurking for an opportunity to go back up on the score. The war was just getting started.

War between Fo' block and the Tre began heating up more each day. Shoota and his crew went on drills blowing down anybody caught standing on forbidden territories. It didn't matter if they were with the shits or not…somebody had to pay for what happened to Popcorn.

As soon as the Juvies finished a drill, Rio and Taz struck back. The Tre had gained a lil' aid and assistance from their homies on the **"Low-End."**

Instantly, the Tre fire power turned gigantic causing Shoota to call for reinforcements.

Bible pulled up in a Lexus LS460, a full-size luxurious sedan, and backed up into Shoota's grandma's driveway. He hopped out the foreign whip, all buffed up, looking like the rapper **50-Cent** in his hay-days. This nigga was a real live "work-out-aholic."

"What's up, big homie...what it do?" Shoota greeted, extending an open palm.

"Wud up, wud up," Bible responded, with a raspy tone. He took ahold of Shoota's hand and shook up gang signs with him and then he did the same with his lil' cousin Do-Dirty.

Bible had on Gucci from head to toe—including his underwear. He walked around to the back of his car and popped open the trunk. Shoota couldn't wait to see what type of gun Bible had for him. Bible reached in and brought out a *Drako*, a baby AK-47 assault rifle. Shoota's eyes got big as hell as Bible handed him the exclusive piece of machinery.

Shoota thoroughly examined the chopper from front, back, and side to side. "Hell yeah, buddy! I don't wanna talk...it's bussing!" he said while handing the *mop stick* over to Do-Dirty.

"Oh yeah, we're definitely gonna be on one with this here." Do-Dirty replied, taking aim with the chopper. He took the drum out and looked at how big the shells were.

"You hit a nigga with just one of them bitches and I bet a limb or two gonna fall off, *immediately*! Them shits like lasers." Bible advised Do-Dirty.

Shoota took back ahold of the gigantic power tool and flexed with it. "What you say you wanted for this bitch?" he asked Bible, knowing damn well that the big fella didn't sell guns...he buys them only.

"You stay fronting your shit, I see." Bible said while checking the time out on his iced-out Gucci watch. Shoota couldn't help but laugh at Bible's slick remark.

Twelve rolled by slow, not noticing them on the side of the trap with the foreign weapon. "Here..." Bible said, handing Do-Dirty a box of chopper shells from out of his trunk along with a couple of handguns. "Go tuck these away someplace safe along with the mop. Make good use of them...you got less than a week to handle your business."

Bible made his way to the front of his car, getting ready to bail back in and slide. One of the Juvies went to check which way the cops went. "They kept straight, going towards Morgan." he shouted out.

"I'm outta here...bout to go to Puerto Rico for my B-Day. Holla at you niggas when I get back." Bible said.

Everybody that was around wished him a Happy Birthday as he pulled off smoothly. Shoota and his team all ran inside the house to secure the armory. "Wait till the Tre get a load of me!" Shoota said to himself while walking right by his granny with the chopper out.

Butta ended up getting a kite from his father out of the blue. The letter read, *"First of all, let me start by praying by the time this scribe touches base with you that you're in the best health, mentally and physically.*

"I've been hearing a whole bunch of mess going on in the hood, and word is that you and your brother are at bats with each other. How is that so, son? Y'all got the same blood pumping through you all's veins. If anything, y'all should be trying to fend for one another in this crazy, mixed up world.

"I luv y'all both deeply and apologize for the absence I had on y'all lives. I was too busy caught up in my own lil' world. These people done

got my ass really good this time. A life sentence got a brother on ice forever. I dread seeing either one of you with the same fate as mine or possibly even worse.

"I know that I don't own the right to tell you what to do, but I'm inclined to give you some good advice. You and your brother need to come together and try to love one another. You're only here on this earth for a brief moment. Make the very best of it as much as you can.

"Lil' Charles is your blood brother; and from the way I hear it, y'all would make a good team. I'm not trying to tell you how to live your life or anything of that matter. I'm just asking you to put away your feelings and squash that beef.

"Just think about what all I said, son; try to take my words to the heart. You'll never know, your brother could be the very person that saves your life...or vise-versa. Take care and be careful out there in them streets. Luv, your father still—Buff!"

Instantly, as soon as Butta got done reading the scribe, he balled it up and shot hoops with it. "Fuck I look like!" he said to himself. Just receiving the letter pissed him the fuck off. He was tempted to grab the mop stick from out of the closet and then go hunt Shoota down...cut the damn sprinklers on the moment he spots him...be done with the shit, once and for all.

Butta had grown tired of his family talking that... *"he's your brother"* bullshit. Where he come from, your brother doesn't supposed to try to smoke you. It was Shoota who initiated first blood in the first place...all because Butta grew up on the other side and kicked it with his opz.

Sometime back, Shoota caught Butta and a couple other niggas he didn't like coming out of the corner store on the Tre. Without the slightest hesitation, Shoota opened fire at the group. He didn't intentionally set out to hit his brother, but hey...shit happens. Butta ended up getting struck in the leg. Ever since then, he's been on Shoota's ass trying to get his lick back and then some. He had blew at Shoota's granny house and Dino's pad on different occasions just as well as blowing at them both, in the same setting.

The only thing that saved Shoota from being gunned down by his brother was the run-ins Butta endured with twelve. He couldn't seem to stay out of jail. As soon as he was getting released from a cell, there was another bed being made up—specifically for his return. He's been home from St. Charles for several months now, which has been the longest freedom he had experienced thus far.

Butta went to his closest and grabbed his Teflon vest, putting it on under his Ralph Lauren Polo hoodie. Then he grabbed his 9-ruger and shoved a stick in it. He photographed his whole wardrobe and posted on Instagram, hash-tagged "Goon Wear."

Shoota, being one of Butta's loyal followers on and off the Gram, liked the post and commented on the subject posting a picture of his own. "That's a bit fresh, but check me out. I got on the same shit I had on yesterday, and I must say…I'm way more fresher." He posted a photo of him in army fatigue clothing, holding the Drako. Something was soon to happen between the two brothers, and the shit wasn't gonna be nice.

A Novel by Pucasso

CHAPTER #12

DREAMS AND NIGHTMARES

Kick-Dough and Stacey were living the American Dream. They had a luxurious estate settled on the outskirt of the Chi…all sorts of fancy automobiles covered their driveway…plenty money was tucked away and secured just in case of a severe thunderstorm, and more of it continuously came piling in, making it hard to find storage space.

Stacey was expecting a new bundle of joy, adding more life to their family. She had started a Nonprofit Organization called "G.I.R.L.S"-Get It Right Little Sistas. She sought to help teenage girls who were less fortunate, and lacked support mentally, physically, and financially. She also was gradually gaining in on becoming a doctor.

I guess you could say that life was marvelous for Kick-Dough, and I'd agree if he wasn't still wanted for a "Felony-Murder." A-1, his partner in crime, was locked up without a bond…conflict between the Fo' and the Tre began to put a cramp in his operations…his hands were so tied up that he had no time to try to patch the beef up between the two rival blocks. The more money you come across, the more problems you see— B.I.G. said it best.

Now, Kick-Dough got word that niggas were plotting on jumping his gate. Supposedly, they were gonna kidnap Stacey and Baby Aaron and demand an outrageous ransom in order for him to get them back.

For the past few days now, Kick-Dough's been really trying to find out Pops' whereabouts. He needed the old man now more than ever. However, Pops was in the Witness Protection Program waiting to go to trial and testify against a notorious drug lord—El Huncho. Pops wasn't in the position to be giving any advice...well, at least not to a street nigga who yells, *"fuck the police!"*

Shoota had Washington Heights on fire. Every other day, detectives were looking for him in questioning of another shooting. Every path he crossed, he turned into a battlefield. Not only was he wanted dead by them niggas on the other side, but also, by a few niggas on his own block.

Twelve began snooping around the hood too much, so all the Lime-Lites and drug juggs had to be put on hold, at least until Kick-Dough did something about Shoota. The troublesome boy was constantly bringing undue heat to headquarters, making Kick-Dough's name become more infamous than it already was. Shoota was like a malignant evil that spreaded destructively, a cancer that needed to be surgically removed from the body—one way or another.

"Ring-ring," Mac's phone went off again. He ignored it though, assuming it was just his son's mother, Shae. He had hung up on her extra ass just seconds ago. She had been calling his phone nagging about some money he didn't have at the time. She claimed that he was a poor excuse for a father and that he should just sign his legal guardianship over to someone else who knows how to take care of the boy...her new nigga, perhaps.

Jo-Jo, Mac's mini me, was about to graduate from kindergarten and needed an outfit to wear, picture money, and so on. With Shae, the list never ends. Now, the expense for the kindergarten graduation was petty money, true enough; however, gambling...getting wasted...and going ham in the strip club had caught up with the rockstar all at once. He didn't have a dime in his pocket, and this was a thirty-forty-thousand-dollar type of nigga we're talking about. He was…rich by day and broke by night.

Mac needed a reload on money, and he needed it the same way he spent it…quick, fast, and in a hurry. He loved his son dearly, spoiling him every chance he got. His B-M was just a drama queen who sought to kick him every time he fell down to the ground.

"Ring-ring!" Mac's phone continued to go off. The shit was aggravating as fuck.

"Man, why in the fuck this bitch keep calling my damn phone?" he argued to himself as he took a disgusting look at the screen of his phone. He came to notice that it wasn't Shae, instead it was Kick-Dough.

"Yooo," he answered swiftly, damn near breaking his neck.

"What up, lil bro…where you at?" Kick-Dough asked.

"In the crib, broke as hell. Why, what's up?"

Mac tried sounding pathetic as he could, hoping to come up on a Lime-Lite or two or at least some drugs to sell. Shit's been real rough ever since the war popped off with the Tre. So much shooting had been going on that the hood was a ghost town. The only gang that remained rolling around noticeably was "CPD."

"I fuck around and happen to have something slick for you. You gotta come and check it out for yourself though…you're mobile?" Kick-Dough asked.

"Somewhat," Mac replied, thinking about taking his mother's brand-new Chevy Impala SS for a quick spin, without her even knowing. She was asleep, resting before her work shift came.

"Meet me at the McDonald's on 127th, right off the e-way. Try to bring a nice set of legs with you too. Hurry up, with your…*'I'm broke as hell ass.'*" Kick-Dough said, giggling to himself.

"Fuck you, I'll be there in 5-minutes,"

"Alright...play in your ass if you want to, I'll have no problems with busting this move my damn self." Kick-Dough informed him, sounding really suggestive.

"I'm already in motion, and watch how you handle me too, nigga...MVP!" Mac responded, ending the call afterwards. Immediately, he ran up the stairs to go get Justo.

A-1 was up and ready to do all what he had been dreaming about doing to a beautiful lady sergeant named "Ms. Lathan." Ever since back when he first laid eyes on her, he'd been lusting over her amazingly figure, not to mention...her extraordinary swag. A-1 never really had a specific type of woman he liked, just as long as they were bad.

Ms. Lathan definitely exceeded the measures of being a bad bitch. Everybody who claimed to have some game about themselves stayed hawking her down whenever they saw her in traffic. Muthafuckas would do whatever they had to do just to get her attention...fake hanging themselves...upping their dicks on her...the whole nine.

Not A-1 though, he remained a boss. He hardly ever fronted his shit. He figured to just wait on a decent opportunity to finesse his charm on her and everything else would fall into play.

A-1 was laying down on his bunk when Ms. Lathan came strutting her stuff up the catwalk like she was a professional model from off **"Rip the Runway."** He sniffed out the fabulous perfume she had on from a distance. Instantly, his joint rocked up and stood at full attention, prepared to salute the fine correctional sergeant.

A-1's cellie was gone to Cermak, so he had the cell all to himself to get wild. He got asshole butt-naked and waited on his moment to strike a nasty pose...no homo! *Clapping* wasn't quite his thing, but being locked up suffering from lack of pussy made him become more horny for a bitch than he'd ever been. Whenever a bad female C/O came around, A-1 would often find him a nice spot where they could clearly watch him whip his dick out and go to work with that muthafucka...straight fuck their asses up! He never tried clapping Ms. Lathan, but that would change today.

Ms. Lathan was only a cell away, her sophisticated fragrance gave A-1 the heads up. The entire gallery was amped up whistling all sorts of shit. Walking down the catwalk was like going to a dick party to her. She got joints upped on her from every direction...the right way! Everybody banged on the bars looking like starving animals craving for a bite to eat.

A-1 heard Ms. Lathan making her way up to his cell and got hypnotized by the sound of her shoes stepping against the pavement. This was the very moment he had been waiting for all along. She came up to his cell wearing a very tight correctional uniform—from head to toe. This was a dream come true for him.

In the midst of just getting warmed up, A-1 had lost himself completely. She looked at him with satisfaction as he finished killing himself off. She smiled and bit down on her bottom lip afterwards. A-1 went *ham*, striking the greatest pose ever. Ms. Lathan quickly bent over and put her face up against the bars, catching the nut as A-1 bust. *"Skeet-Skeet!"*

A-1 wiggled his dick around until it wasn't a drop of cum left in it. Ms. Lathan didn't even bother trying to wipe her face off, she just licked as much of it as she could away from her mouth with her tongue. She turned around and pressed her big ass up against the bars, bending over touching her toes while shaking it. You could clearly see that fat monkey bulging out from in between her thick ass thighs. The sight of it was just bananas!

A-1 got in position while Ms. Lathan pulled her pants down letting them drop to the floor. She had no panties on, but that was a given...her camel toe was over puffy to begin with. He took ahold of his dick and shoved it in her pussy hole as far down as he could, being behind bars. He plunged into it repeatedly, back and forth like the classic **Aaliyah** song. All you could hear was the continuous pounding sound of his pelvis bone smacking up against her ass and the steel bars that was structurally planted in between them.

Ms. Lathan moaned out loudly, causing the whole gallery to get aroused. This was the baddest chick in Cook County Jail. Suddenly, A-1 opened his eyelids noticing that he was humping on his own pillow.

"On that compliance check!" an inmate shouted down the gallery.

A-1 paused for a moment, bent out of shape from being rudely awaken from a wet dream in the making. "Fuck...I hate this pussy ass shit." he said, loudly.

A-1's cellie was up already, getting the cell together. A-1 hopped up and grabbed his shank from underneath his mattress, tucking it away in the jock pouch of his thermal bottoms.

"Ay, lord...once I smoked this body and finally go home, I'm gonna have so much pussy lined up that I'm gon' have to get me a surrogate on the dick side just to help me fuck them all." A-1 claimed as he began making up his bed.

"Tell me about it, shorty. I'm so thirsty...I'd fuck a horse right about now." Lord replied.

A-1 gave him a weird look thinking to himself, *I ain't fucking any animals player, you're on your own with that shit.*

"I'm gonna come up on a shot of pussy in this bitch, solid. I just gotta run across the right type of bitch...someone who's just as thirsty as me.

Hell, I'll even give the *eater* a few bands to go with the dick." A-1 explained.

A-1 never had a problem with paying for pussy, he'd been doing the shit ever since he was a kid...before he even knew how to read and write well. It was no discrepancies about it at all, everybody who was quite familiar with A-1 knew that he was a "trick-off artist."

Mac and Justo pulled up into McDonald's parking lot flexing hard in Mac's mother's brand-new SS-Chevy Impala. **Lil' Durk** was playing low in the background, *"L's up for my hitters."* Thirsty muthafuckas...they already had the license plates off the car and in the back windshield.

Kick-Dough was parked in his bitch Stacey's whip, an all-white Audi Q7 SUV. "Where you at, boy?" he said to Mac, after answering his call.

"I'm pulling in right now," Mac replied, looking around the parking lot. "I'm in a black SS-Impala...that new thang."

"Okay, I see you...pull over and park somewhere. I'm about to come your way." Kick-dough pulled up on the side of the Impala and then got out, bailing inside with Mac 'nem.

"I see you want some money today, nigga...you got your ass up here quick," Kick-Dough said, taking a glance inside the new ride slightly amazed. "Who whip this is, lil' bro?"

"This my O-G shit, she just copped it last week."

"And she let yo' reckless driving ass get behind the wheel already...she must be sleep somewhere."

"Hell yeah!" Justo blurted out, giggling along with Kick-Dough.

Mac joined in on the laughter. "Fuck the jokes, what's the business. A nigga ain't even got enough money in his pockets to buy a Big Mack if I wanted one. I'm overly hungry." he announced.

"You see that Shell's gas station over there across the street," Kick-Dough asked. Mac just nodded his head while flaming up a square. "At about eleven o'clock or so, a regular person like me or you is gonna pull up to refill the ATM that's inside there. Them machines hold at least 15-bucks or better. Not the biggest Lime-Lite, but it'll definitely hold you down until all the heat passes over."

"Shit...right about now, I can use anything." Mac responded, while rubbing his palms together.

"I got a few more of these moves on hand—ready to be taken down. They're all yours if everything pans out alright with this one." Kick-Dough explained. "I'm not looking for anything back off these Lime-Lites either, just consider it a gift from your big cuz, A-1."

Kick-Dough couldn't help but see dollar signs bulging out of Mac's eyeballs. Mac didn't say anything, he just sat back and listened to Kick-Dough as he finished speaking, "It's something that needs to be handled in the hood though...something very urgent and important. A-1 feels the same way about this matter I'm bringing to you."

"What is it, big bro? Anything for you and A-1." Mac replied.

"I need you to go ahead and check Shoota's ass up out this shit."

"Damn...you want the lil' homie smoked?"

"Hell yeah, once and for all."

Mac had to flame up another square to fully understand what Kick-Dough was actually saying. Although Mac and Shoota didn't always see eye to eye, Mac still had love for the lil' nigga. Murdering Shoota wasn't a simple job, not to Mac.

"I mean, I know shorty's a hard-head and all, but damn, bro...that's a deep decision." Mac voiced his opinion.

Shoota's mother Missy used to watch over Mac when he was little, buying him ice cream off the Tasty-truck and taking him to the park.

Everybody in Washington Heights Community was real close with Missy; and twice a year, parties got thrown in memory of her. So, for Kick-Dough to request the execution of her son Shoota, it had to be for a good reason. Mac needed more encouragement.

"You know just as well as I do, shorty's gonna be the death of this MVP/BRO shit." Kick-Dough explained. "He don't give a fuck about nobody...not even his damn self."

Mac didn't bother going back and forth with Kick-Dough, he just continued listening looking for a more solid reason to jump on his bandwagon.

"Shoota don't listens to nobody...not me, A-1, or even his own family. He's constantly bringing undue heat to the hood," Kick-Dough continued to break the shit down to Mac. "I know you heard about him shooting up Jamaica's crib this morning."

"Nah, I didn't..." Mac responded while looking over at Justo. Justo just shrugged his shoulders. "What he do that for, Jamaica don't bother anybody?"

"That's what I'm trying to explain to you right now. Shorty's a rebel without cause. He's gradually putting a stop to our whole operation. We can't have that shit, now can we?" Kick-Dough asked.

Mac didn't hesitate to answer, "Hell nah!"

"Shoota's a cancer that needs to be permanently removed from the body in order for Washington Heights to live on. Our legacies deserve to be held up high until the end of time, not brought down to the ground and kicked on like shorty's doing." Kick-Dough began making sense to Mac and Justo. They couldn't help but agree with the murderous plot that was transpiring against Shoota. Hell, neither one of them could afford to risk letting shorty take them out of **"The Lime-Lite."**

"Fuck it then, if it's gotta be—it's gotta be!" Mac replied as he dapped up with Kick-Dough. "I'll get right on top of the shit asap."

"Trust me, Mac…it's the best solution to the problem. Me and A-1 went back and forth on the matter, and there wasn't any other way around it." Kick-Dough said, staring him dead in the face. "Can you handle this problem of ours? I know how touchy this is for you, I could very well find somebody else to take care of the hit."

"Nah, big bro, I got this. I'm gonna get right to it, we can't let the whole family go down all because of one rotten apple." Mac clarified.

"Smooth then," Kick-Dough said as he flicked his wrist to check the time on his icy Yacht-Master. "It's 10:50 right now, the Lime-Lite should be pulling up any minute. Let me get outta here so y'all can get ready to rock and roll. Hit my line later, Mac…alright Justo."

"MVP, nigga!" Justo shouted out the window, right before Kick-Dough bailed back in the Q7.

"Fo' life!" Kick-Dough responded, throwing up 4-fingers and getting back in traffic.

Mac pulled across the street into the Shell's gas station parking lot; and within the next minutes, a Volvo station-wagon came pulling up right in front of the entrance. An older man hopped out the car and walked inside the store holding a green-leather pouch full of money. Justo bailed out and ran up to the Volvo, spotting a duffel bag inside sitting on the passenger seat.

"Sweet one," Justo said to himself as he quickly busted the window and snatched the bag up out of the car. Instantly, he took off back to the Impala, swiftly hopping in, and Mac peeled off out of the lot. He jumped dead on the E-way, going back towards the land. The bag ended up having close to $40,000 inside it all twenties.

CHAPTER #13

ѕℵᴀᴋᴇ ᴇʏᴇѕ

Finally, Dino was up in the game for a change. He had a couple of cars...a decent amount of coke to jugg...and $10,000 put up in the ceiling. The war between his cousin Shoota and the BROs had opened up the block for him to start checking some serious bread. It didn't matter if the block had become a battlefield, cluck-buddies were still on the prowl searching for a bag of crack to smoke.

Dino stayed on point, consistently keeping some work on deck. It wasn't the best product a junky could find, but it definitely did the trick. Dino's spot was knocking a recognizable number, and he was loving every bit of it. He stopped Shoota and the Juvies from hanging out in front of his spot, making it hot.

Shoota began to grow a strong dislike for the big goofy, Dino. He felt like he was switching up on him now that his count was up. Dino had bumped a lil bitch named **"Lady-J"** and kept her around him day and night. He treated the infamous *dick-eater* as if she was some kind of queen when all the time, she was nothing more than a bum looking for a warm spot to rest her head. It just so happened...Dino ol' tender dick ass had room and boarding.

Dino clothed and fed Lady-J just as much as he did for himself, probably even more, in exchange for some washed up *top and bottom*. He kept her high out of her mind, hoping that she wouldn't ever leave his presence. However though, occasionally, she would wander off through the land doing multiple dicks along the way. A hoe's gonna be a hoe…ain't no way around it. **Future** said it best. However, Dino loved Lady-J and was willing to go to the depths over her.

Shoota hopped the fence and made his way to the back door of Dino's crib. Twelve was scorching, and he needed a place to lay low till they calmed down. Detectives were looking for him for a shooting that occurred just earlier in the day. They raided his granny's crib and assigned Skull-Cap and Ninja to stake the place out until his face popped up.

Shoota was running out of places to lay his head. Traveling back and forth from out south to up north, visiting his sisters and Olivia, was beginning to be a real hassle for the youngster. He needed some wheels— asap. Until then, Dino's spot was about the safest place for him to hide-out at.

"KNOCK-KNOCK-KNOCK!" Shoota tapped on the door and waited for it to be opened. However, nobody answered it. He knew Dino was there; both of his cars were in the driveway, and the lights were on inside the house.

"BOOM-BOOM-BOOM-BOOM!" he kicked the door as hard as he could, knowing somebody heard the shit. He was beginning to get infuriated.

Within the next split-second, Dino cracked open the door. "What's up?" he said, standing in the doorway with a lit blunt in his hand.

"Fuck you mean…'*What's up*'? What took you so long to answer the muthafucking door? A nigga could've gunned me down by now while you're in there playing in yo' ass!" Shoota argued, making an attempt to walk pass Dino to enter the house.

Dino stopped him in his tracks, blocking off the pathway-entirely. "I'm on something right now, cuz…you gotta find someplace else to chill." he said, looking down at Shoota. Dino was a tall-lanky muthafucka.

"What...man, cut it the fuck out," Shoota replied as he snatched the blunt out of Dino's fingers and continued trying to enter the doorway. "I ain't got nowhere else to go, plus twelve on my ass hard. Move your bitch ass out the way, goofy."

Dino was real adamant about the matter. He done had all he could take with suffering from Shoota's buck wild behavior...his spot had been shot up and raided, all compliments to the boy. Finally, the jolly-green giant was putting a foot down.

"Nah, cuz... I'm serious. I'm sick and tired of you fronting my crib off. I gotta live here—not you! You're into it with some of everybody, I don't need that kind of smoke around me."

Shoota was blew out of his mind. "You acting like a real bitch right now. Ever since you've been getting your lil count up, you been on some duck ass shit." Shoota responded, aggressively. All you could see were his dreads swinging from side to side and his pearly whites gritting.

"Man, fuck you! You don't give a damn about me...if you did, you wouldn't be bringing all this heat to my place. I'm not about go to jail, let alone die for yo' ass." Dino argued back.

Shoota just stood there, mean mugging Dino. The only thing that saved Dino from getting a hole blown through his forehead was the fact that him and Shoota shared the same blood. And only because of that, Shoota would spare his life...but not his pockets. Them shits would have to pay like they weighed.

"That's crazy, but it's cool, cousin." Shoota said as he threw his hoodie back on his head and turned around, pimping off like **Tupac Shakur** in the classic movie "**Juice.**"

Dino felt bad, but it was a decision he was willing to live with in order to get to the next level of the dope game. He just watched as Shoota slid off into darkness. Lady-J came up from behind him holding a fifth of Hennessy in her hand, drinking straight out the bottle.

"Why you just standing here with the door open, letting all the heat out?" she complained as if she ever paid a utility bill in her life. "Come back inside, baby."

Dino closed the door, locked it, and then went back to doing what he was doing right before he was rudely interrupted...sucking Lady-J's funky ass pussy. Talk about a real sucker for love!

Carla, Dino's oldest sister, was having a "40th-Birthday Bash" when Shoota decided to jump a gate...Dino's. Shoota had known about the party for a while now and figured it would be the perfect opportunity to hit the big goofy where it really hurts. It would be the easiest burglary he had ever committed; nobody would be present at the spot, which meant that all of Dino's pride possessions would be up for the taking.

Dino had fucked up by denying Shoota shelter in a great time of need. Twelve was on his ass and niggas wanted the lil' fella dead. Shoota was definitely living life on the edge; but to keep shit 100, he loved the feeling. This was just the kind of notoriety he had set out for in his treacherous endeavor of becoming the most feared person that ever walked the Washington Heights Community. He was an unpredictable individual who didn't care about shit.

Okay, here's where the finesse kicks in at. Shoota played along to Lady-J's fantasy of doing dicks and getting high off the shit. One day prior to the current moment, he had caught her off the block and layed the manipulation game down on her, real thick. He encouraged her into helping him rob Dino, promising her a chop off the move and some dick as well. Little did she know...she would never see neither of them shits.

Lady-J told Shoota exactly where Dino kept everything and agreed to keep him informed of their whereabouts while he robbed the joint. The shit couldn't get any sweeter than that. She would be Shoota's eyes and ears during the caper, but she had life fucked up thinking that she would get anything back in return for her involvement. Shoota wouldn't even give the bitch the slightest pat on the back...she fuck around and get two to the forehead. Shoota was just that treacherous.

He lamped in an abandoned garage, a couple houses down from Dino's spot, waiting for Lady-J to text him and let him know when the coast was clear. He was all alone on this mission, no worries about having to curve anybody other than himself.

A text message came through his phone, and he read it eagerly. *"You all good to go, there's nobody else at the house...it's empty."* Lady-J typed.

Shoota put his phone back inside his pants pocket and got right to it. Once he made it to his destination, he climbed through the side window that Lady-J had left open for him. Immediately, when he entered the place, he tossed it up like the Tupac song. He did the best job he could trying to make the burglary look random.

His phone vibrated in his pocket, so he pulled it out and began reading another text message from Lady-J. *"Oh yeah, it's two guns in the ceiling as well. Get them, I want one."*

"Dumb bitch!" Shoota said to himself as he kicked the door in and slid into Dino's bedroom. Instantly, he went straight for the gusto.

"BLOOM!" he said as he pulled a shoe box full of money from out of the ceiling. He grabbed an old duffel bag from under the couch and threw the rubber-banded racks in it, along with Dino's brand-new PlayStation 4 and Xbox One. Then Shoota hopped back on the couch and looked in the ceiling again, searching for firearms. He was eager to retrieve them guns.

After a few minutes of scrambling through a whole bunch of miscellaneous shit, Shoota had come up empty-handed.

"Fuck...where the butter and blickers at?" he mumbled as he grabbed his phone again and sent Lady-J a quick text. *"I don't see the drugs or them poles you were talking about."*

Shoota put his phone away and continued the search, ripping through the cushions of the couch and flipping over the bed mattress. Right when he was beginning to cut the search short, he got a text back from Lady-J. *"If it ain't in the ceiling, then go check in the wall by the washer and dryer. If it ain't there, then I don't know what else to tell you. Don't text me anymore, Dino's been trying to snatch my phone from me claiming that I'm cheating on him and shit."*

Shoota grabbed the duffel bag and went to the back door where the laundry area was. He pulled the dryer out a bit and went behind a loose piece of drywall, recovering a chrome 9-ruger and an all-black .357 Magnum. He continued the search, looking up... down...and all around for the yayo, but it was no place to be found.

"Fuck it!" he said as he threw both of the pipes in the bag. He done came up with way more than he had to begin with. He took ahold of the duffel bag and hit the door, taking off running into the darkness.

When Dino finally made it back to his pad that night, he couldn't believe his eyes. He was broken by the mess he had discovered. Truth be told, he wanted to cry a river. *Who the fuck had the audacity to pull this off?* he thought to himself as he went through the mess seeing what all had been taken.

Lady-J played along as if she didn't have the slightest clue who had jumped Dino's gate. "Who could do such a thing? It had to be some petty ass muthafucka, I bet." she proclaimed.

Dino looked at her and thought to himself for a hot second, *She fuck around and had something to do with this shit,* but quickly brushed his intuition off. He couldn't help but to…he was a sucker for love…a special kind of fool one would say.

Dino went over and hugged Lady-J with the warmest regards. "Don't worry, baby…we gonna get back from this minor setback." he promised her. His super duck ass was left with only a couple of ounces to try to bounce back with. It would be a long journey that Lady-J wanted no parts in.

MIDTRO:

RECESS

Tino sat on the living room couch of his granny's house playing the game. Times were tough, and being without money was causing him to slip into a deep state of depression. He never was quite the stick-up type; however, the pressure placed upon him was forcing him to consider the measure.

Something had to shake; he owed out too much money, and bills were steady piling up to the ceiling. He was deep in debt and needed a way out. He ended up losing the lil' dope line he had built. He couldn't come up with the re-up money, and nobody trusted him with any more fronts.

Tino was all out of helping hands. People would often ask him why he just won't ask Kick-Dough to put him in the Lime-Lite, but he would just ignore the question. His pride was too far in the way to go to kissing ass, especially to someone who he'd grown to despise so much.

The beef Tino had with Kick-Dough was kind of indirect, arising after Tino and A-1's bond broke. Tino and A-1 were the best of friends ever since kindergarten. If you saw one of them, then you seen the other one. Kee-Kee joined the crew shortly after, proving himself to be just as vicious as them—possibly even worse.

The three savages turned out to be a wicked trio, laying licks down wherever they went. Each of them played their part, all becoming bosses of the same gang—MVP. And when I tell you that MVP ran the streets, I mean that with an iron fist.

A couple of other cliques from around the way, "LOC," Lunatics, Outlaws, and Cutthroats, and the Tre-Block, envied the way MVP made moves. Together, these combative gangs confronted them with animosity; but after the smoke cleared, MVP stood to be the coldest group of individuals from the area.

In the beginning, Tino was the most deadliest person in the crew. His cockiness, arrogance, and "fuck the world" mentality made it very clear that MVP wasn't the clique to be fucked with. He stayed in the field trying to blow down an op or two. If I had to compare the old him to someone...it would be Shoota. The only thing that's different about the two is...Shoota never had shit to lose.

Tino and A-1 remained best friends for a long time doing everything together, even when it came to fucking on the hoes. They had the kind of attachment that most people called inseparable; however, the power of money and pussy couldn't have been a considered variable in the equation.

A-1 had always been the type of guy who did his best to make sure everybody on the team shine bright like a diamond. If anyone in his circle were ever short on bread, he curved them well...straight out of his pocket. From the jump, he kept a big ol' duffel bag on deck and giving out blessings was a part of his nature. Let him tell it...that's the reason why GOD had given him gifted hands.

Kee-Kee picked up the kindly gesture also, just as well as everybody else a part of MVP. Yep...everybody except for Tino. For some reason, he was quite stiff with his bankroll. It wasn't as obvious at first; but once people began taking some losses, including A-1, Tino's pettiness started showing.

It was a time when A-1 and the rest of the team was fucked up for real, and Tino had come across a nice piece of change from a settlement of a lawsuit…over 60-something thousand dollars. At this point, none of the MVPs had ever possessed this much money…not all at once. This was some time after Kee-Kee had went away to prison to do a stretch.

Tino definitely fronted his move, exposing his hand and not giving a nigga too much of anything out of it. A-1 had to wrestle around with him just to get him to come off the money he had loaned him until the lawsuit money had come through. The shit had A-1 bent all out of shape, causing him to look at Tino differently. A-1 didn't front his move though, he just continued chasing paper letting the cards play out.

Tino was riding high, copping whips and putting plenty cock in chicks. His claim to fame didn't last long though, a sudden change of wind came and knocked him clean off of his high horse. He ended up taking a fall down back to the very turf he had come from.

Simultaneously, just as Tino was falling off, Pops had introduced A-1 to the Lime-Lite. Instead of putting his alleged "right-hand man" up on the game of snatching bank envelopes, he turned the lick on to Kick-Dough. Ever since then, A-1 and Kick-Dough been jammed tight. They ended up becoming a dynamic duo, tearing off Lime-Lites with ease.

Tino was left out of the equation, completely. Don't get me wrong, he got curved off every move that A-1 'nem had busted. He just wasn't putting him in any Lime-Lites. At first, he was cool with the blessings A-1 and Kick-Dough was giving him; however, once the money began rolling in excessively…Tino started feeling some type of way. Let him tell it, the lil' handouts he'd been getting was insulting.

Tino expected a bigger chop, possibly even some Lime-Lites of his own. A-1 was in charge of the whole operation, and this was supposed to be his best friend. Some distance got in between the two running buddies, and the detachment grew wider each day.

Tino kept his cool and ended up learning the game on his own. He began going on moves himself...him and whoever he could get to tag along. None of his moves were like the ones A-1 and Kick-Dough was constantly taking down...$40,000 one week...$50,000 the following week...and $60,000 within the next week or so. The shit just kept getting better with time.

A-1 and Kick-Dough's relationship was solid, more than the one A-1 had once shared with Tino. Low key, A-1 was hurt behind the whole mess. He just didn't wear his emotions on his shirt. Besides, he felt like it was Tino's own fault for the way things had turned out between them. Hadn't he been so selfish and helped people out when he was in the position to, their bond would've remained unbroken.

A-1 was Washington Heights Superman, and "petty-ass niggas" were his Kryptonite. He kept them as far away from him as he possibly could, by all means necessary. Kick-Dough was Superboy, A-1's protege. He gave him the game just how it was given to him. That's where the beef came into play between Tino and Kick-Dough.

Tino felt like it was supposed to be him on the side of A-1, reaping all the benefits. Tino ended up coming across an allegedly "big-time move" to score on. Surprisingly, he pulled A-1's coat tail on it, attempting to break bread and mend a broken relationship with him. A-1 was cool with it, and Kick-Dough was offered to tag along as well.

The crew of bag snatchers went ahead and took down the lick, coming to find out that what was made out to be a hundred thousand-dollar finesse wasn't even a fourth of the number. They chopped the money up three ways, and it was suggested by A-1 that they all should curve Pops with a couple thousand a piece. This was said to be..."a blessing in good faith that Pops would keep them lined up with **Lime-Lites.**"

Once again, Tino couldn't hold back from being petty. The shit was embedded in his heart. He felt like Pops wasn't supposed to get a cut in on his move. It was Tino's lick, and he did all the homework. Giving a muthafucka a portion of his proceeds wasn't in the plan. Keep in mind now, it was Pops who had given them the game in the first place. Hadn't he put A-1 in the Lime-Lite, none of them would be eating on the level they were. Tino was narrow minded though, he only seen shit how he wanted to.

This situation was the last straw with A-1. He was done trying to reconcile the relationship between him and Tino. For all he cared, Tino could be broke, starving, and gangbanging and he wouldn't be affected by the shit...not even one bit. He had washed his hands with him.

Tino recalled the whole situation while sitting on the couch playing Call of Duty. His thoughts were vivid, more clear than spring water. However, sitting around remembering the past wasn't helping his current situation at all. He was broke, starving, and back gangbanging.

Tino tossed the game controller on the floor in the middle of going to war against a special opz team. The reality of not knowing where his next meal was gonna come from was eating him alive. His phone danced around on the kitchen table, and he broke his back to get it hoping it was some *good news* of any kind. At least, he would know that *it* still existed.

He made it to his phone and looked at the screen. "Bible," he said to himself, disappointedly. Immediately, he put his phone on silent and let the shit ring out. It didn't matter to him if anybody else would be trying to get ahold of him because the underlined fact was...he was too broke to even be bothered.

CHAPTER #14

THICKER THAN WATER

Dino could never quite bounce back from the loss he had sustained when his spot got burglarized by his cousin—Shoota. He had gotten robbed for every dollar he own,..close to 9-thousand. The next day after the robbery, Shoota went to the car lot and copped an '09 Chevy Impala-SS, out doing the basic one Dino had. Oh yeah...the lil gate-jumper wasted no time to "flex."

The night of the robbery, Dino had talked with Shoota asking him to keep an eye out in search of anyone who's suspect of robbing him. Shoota played the shit smooth, acting as if he hadn't the slightest clue who did the shit. He merched it on Missy's grave that once he found out who the thief was, he was gonna put a bullet in their head his damn self.

Dino asked to hold down one of Shooter's blickers, letting the obvious be known—that the burglar had gotten away with his pipes also. Shoota really didn't want to give him his gun, but he went ahead and did so. He did so out of finesse, avoiding from looking suspicious for the time being. The caper seemed to be going undetermined...that is until Shoota fronted his shit.

When Shoota came through the Fo', burning rubber in that SS, everybody from around the way knew the real deal...even Dino's dumbass. The rumor was out there..."*Shoota done jumped his own cousin's gate.*" The lil' nigga didn't even bother trying to deny the shit. To keep it 100, he never cared. Ever since his mother got smoked, he'd been all for himself.

Dino began making accusations, accusing Shoota of breaking into his crib and robbing him. *Duh!* As soon as word got back to Shoota, he went ahead and waged war against Dino's ass, shooting up his spot on a daily basis. That broke down gun Shoota had given to him was no match to his fire power. Dino couldn't help but fall back and just accept the fact that he had gotten *juked*…him and his tired ass looking bitch, Lady-J.

Shoota pulled up on his mans 'nem in his SS-Chevy Impala, all compliments to his cousin, Dino. Olivia was riding shotgun bumping **Fetty Wap,** *"Baby, won't you come my way."* This was one of her favorite songs, along with *"Trap Queen."*

Do-Dirty was out in **Harvey-World** chilling over one of his cousin's house. Shoota parked, and immediately, a bunch of niggas surrounded his car. He bailed out rocking a True-Religion jogging outfit with a pair of all white Air Force-1's on his feet. Instantly, he began congregating amongst the crowd of young savages.

"What's up, bitch?" Shoota greeted **Savage,** one of Do-Dirty's younger cousins. And oh yeah, the young nigga was living up to the name every bit.

Savage was tatted up with more street scriptures on him than an O-G who had done a stretch behind the wall. He even began getting work done on his face. The boy was an aspiring card-cracker known all across the city for finessing. The tall, athletic built teenager had dreads long like **Bob Marley's.** He swung them right in front of Shoota, showing off how much longer they were compared to his.

"What up, bitch ass nigga," Savage responded, shaking up with Shoota. "I see you went and copped you a lil whip…'bout time. Riding in steamers ain't quite cutting it anymore."

Savage was topless, so it was quite natural that he flexed around in front of Shoota's girlfriend. He was definitely a stunter, putting on a show was all a part of his finesse. Instantly, he took a picture of the SS and then uploaded it to Facebook saying, **"I just copped this lil bucket just to go do a couple drills in."**

"Aww, this ain't shit, bitch...wait until I jump this one gate...I'm really gonna be busting dicks then." Shoota claimed.

Do-Dirty came out of the trap with half of his hair braided, looking like **R-Kelly** in his *"I wish"* music video. "Okay...I see you scud...the right way." he applauded his homie while eating a pork chop sandwich.

Do-Dirty was impressed with Shoota's first whip. "This muthafucka is decent, bro. Leather seats and a moonroof...how much you fucked off on it?" he asked while checking it out entirely.

"A lil' bit of nothing, thanks to Dino's duck ass." Shoota replied. Laughter arose among the crew of troublemakers. Savage pimped around to the passenger side of the car to get a good look at who Shoota had riding shotgun. Olivia was leaned back in the seat listening to Fetty Wap while playing candy crush on her phone.

"And who might this amazing looking lady be?" Savage asked, politely greeting himself to her. "Hey there, princess. I'm Savage and you are..."

"Olivia...nice to meet you, Savage."

Do-Dirty looked in the car at Olivia and was even more impressed with Shoota. "Damn, she's bad as hell." he said, loudly.

"No doubt, and Shoota bitch ass just got her waiting for him in the car...all alone. The nerve of these niggas, right." Savage said, flirting with Olivia. "Man, why you got this beautiful girl cooped up in this hot ass car?"

Shoota just smiled mischievously as he sang along to Fetty Wap that was still playing on the radio, "All headshots if you think you can take my bitch." He formed both of his hands into imaginary guns and fired them off at Savage.

Savage and Do-Dirty both busted out laughing at Shoota's aggressive hand gesture. Not only because the shit was funny, but also, they knew the young muthafucka meant very well what he was rapping about. Shoota couldn't help but join in on the laughter, hoping to God that he didn't front his move.

The group of drillers walked to the porch and discussed hood politics. Shoota continued to brag about how he jumped his bitch ass cousin's gate. He put emphasis on taking down another sweet lick as soon as one became available. Between buying the car and fuckin' bread off on Olivia, he was about broke again. It was straight back to the drawing board.

Savage ran into the house and came back out with a couple of sticks, handing one over to Shoota. "Let's take a few flicks, scud." he said, whipping out his iPhone and started snapping shots.

Instantly, he jumped on Facebook-Live and waved the 30-popper around. A lot of words were currently being exchanged on social media between the Fo' Block and the Tre, and Savage felt the need to set the record straight.

"Y'all hoe ass niggas want to play rough...okay then, I'll show you rough." Savage said, mugged up at the phone looking like Tony Montana off the classic movie **"Scarface."** He recorded himself, Do-Dirty, and Shoota all at the same damn time.

"Say hello to my lil' friend." Do-Dirty said as Shoota upped the stick and aimed it right over his shoulders.

"*Bang-Bang*, you're dead!" Shoota shouted, coldheartedly.

You would have thought them boys was from O-block how they was swagged around in front of the camera. Savage positioned the camera directly on himself and talked his shit, "So, there you have it people, we're three young muthafuckas who don't give a damn about shit. Fuck your chief, king, or whatever you wanna call him. Tell him, we're coming to spill blood. You see, we got sticks in our hands and all blue faces in our pants."

Savage waved the 30 in the cam and then tossed it and his phone over to Do-Dirty to record what he was about to do next. He reached in the pockets of his Balmain jeans and whipped out a dookie-roll, all crispy bills properly organized. He unracked it and then flashed it outwardly as if it was a deck of cards, and he was performing some kind of magical trick.

"You see it, broke ass niggas! Please, don't ever get the shit confused...we got them bands!" Savage continued flexing, while opening and closing his bankroll—repeatedly.

Do-Dirty recorded himself as well, "It's JRW or death...free the guys-Muscles, Shawty-Rough, and Stix." and then put the camera on Shoota.

"R.I.P. Popcorn, you're gone but never forgotten. See you at the crossroads, my nigga. And to the son of a bitch who done the shit—" Shoota said, right before being interrupted by Do-Dirty.

"—*Bang-Bang!*"

"You're a dead man walking." Shoota finished his statement. Instantly, the live recording went viral.

Although the sun was out, shining bright like a diamond, it was a very dark and gloomy day for the people over on the Tre. Today was Henry Allen's, *a.k.a.* **"Grasshopper,"** birthday. He was the high school basketball player who got gunned down by Washington Heights very own—Shoota. Timothy Grant, *a.k.a.* **"Tim-Dawg,"** the other person who was with Grasshopper during the deadly shooting, was thankful to be alive.

Ever since Grasshopper's death, Tim-Dawg hadn't returned back to the Tre. The nightmare haunted his dreams each and every night afterwards. Tim-Dawg was Taz's first cousin and also, a varsity basketball player at Simeon Academy High School...him and Grasshopper. Neither one of them were involved in any street gangs, they were just at the wrong place at the wrong time.

Grasshopper's basketball jersey was hung up high in his high school's gym to honor his memory. He was a very admired person, nobody ever expected him to die at such a young age. His future was so promising, he had the great ability to jump out the gym. That's how he got the nickname, Grasshopper. All kinds of college scouts came to Simeon just to watch him play, it was a pleasant sight.

Rio, Taz, and Butta stood on May Ave, headquarters for the Tre, popping bottles and blowing gas. People who knew Grasshopper came through to show love and condolences for his glow day. It's been about 7-months now, since his death, but to Tim-Dawg...the shit felt like just yesterday. He had went against his better judgement of never stepping foot back on the block again. He just couldn't resist sliding through to celebrate his deceased homie's birthday.

Everybody lounged around the block in their exclusive R.I.P. "Grasshopper" t-shirts, conversating among each other. Shoota was out and about, watching the whole celebration transpiring on Facebook and Instagram. No doubt, the acclaimed moment had Shoota sick to the stomach. He was tempted to slide through and crash the party.

However, twelve was rolling thick in every direction. Going through the Tre and blamming a nigga, thinking he'd get away with it, was foolish. Shoota definitely played crazy, but he wasn't stupid. He had a trick up his sleeve though, a risky one, but hell...he was known for doing some daredevil shit.

Leaving his blicker behind, something he hardly ever does, he took a stroll down "memory lane." Instantly, he jumped on Facebook-Live to do some recording of his own. "Fuck Henry Allen and any other muthafucka that ever cared for the dead fucker," he said, with aggression.

"Matter of fact...I'm on my way to the party. Taz, get my cup ready. I'm cool on the gas, I'm already smoking on that Grasshopper!" Shoota continued talking real crazy.

Shoota dropped his phone in his lap and took ahold of the steering wheel with both hands, swerving recklessly while swinging his dreads. **Chief Keef** was playing loudly through his Bose-speakers, *"I been ballin' so damn hard sometimes I think that I'm Kobe..."* He sang along while whipping the SS, looking like he was performing a live-music video.

Immediately, Taz was alerted about Shoota's disrespectful behavior. He hurried up and got in mode, racing down the block trying to catch him sliding through. He had the .40 out, holding it down by his side. "I'm about to smoke this nigga's top!" he said to himself.

Tim-Dawg peeped the move and dipped off into his aunt's house. "I knew I shouldn't have went against my first mind. These people just don't know how to act around here." he contemplated, aloud. He knew better than to just be standing there waiting for bullets to start flying.

Shoota didn't attempt to ride down May Ave, he just flew up and down the side blocks that surrounded the area. He knew he was playing it real close, showing his face on the Tre at a time like this...and without a blammer. "Popcorn world, fuck Grasshopper and all the rest of y'all dead homies. Pretty soon, all of y'all gon' end up with bullets planted in ya heads...on the guys." Shoota shouted out the window at a group of people. He merched it that it would be a whole bunch of blood to come.

People began to duck down taking cover behind parked cars and shit, assuming that shots were about to be fired. Lucky for them, the young terrorist was unarmed. All he could do was threaten 'em with hostile words. "All you bitches gonna die slowly...oh, I'm on that fo'real-fo'real!"

Eventually, Shoota just pulled off tickled by the horror he had caused the bystanders. Taz and Butta was on the move, running in the direction of where Shoota was just at. Once they got to the corner of the block, Taz spotted the SS busting a "*U-wee.*" Instantly, he ducked off behind some bushes. Butta just played it smooth, walking along the sidewalk acting like he was unaware of Shoota coming towards him.

Deep down inside, Butta didn't want to smoke his lil' brother, but he figured that it wasn't any other alternative for handling the young villain. Shoota was untamable like a full-blown wolf...it was no getting' through to him. Besides, in Chiraq...it's kill or be killed.

When Shoota saw Butta walking unacquainted, seeming to be vulnerable for an attack, he knew something wasn't right with the picture. He examined the scene thoroughly, and that's when he peeped the move. Taz was easing his way out from behind the bushes waving the .40.

"I knew it was a rat-play." Shoota said to himself as he swiftly busted a sharp left turn, not even paying attention to the direction he was heading in. He never did! He kept his eyeballs planted on the blicker Taz had in his hand, pointed at him.

"*BOCAH-BOCAH-BOCAH-BOCAH-BOCAH!*" The sound of bullets coming out of Taz's gun echoed the block. Slugs shattered through

Shoota's car window. By this time, he was ducked down taking cover underneath the steering wheel, still operating the automobile the best way he possibly could without being smacked upside the head by hot copper.

Butta just watched, beginning to feel some type of way about the matter. Shoota was handling the wheel pretty well from under the dashboard until another storm of gunfire came thundering from out of Taz's weapon. *"BOCAH-BOCAH-BOCAH-BOCAH-BOCAH!"* He wanted Shoota dead more than anything on earth.

Bullets smacked up against the dashboard causing Shoota to let go of the wheel. *"WHAM!"* The SS smacked head on into a parked Suburban truck. Immediately, Shoota hopped out the car and tried getting away from the drill on feet.

Finally, Butta snapped back into mode and began clutching his trigger. *"FAH-FAH-FAH-FAH-FAH!"* Each shot, he failed to pin the tail on the donkey. This was a marksman I'm talking about.

Taz took off chasing after Shoota, intending to hawk him down with the .40 cal, was burning in his hands. He only had a few shots left, so he preserved them—specifically for Shoota's face. Shoota was a fast runner, but Taz managed to keep up with him. Besides, Taz had the advantage... they were on his stomping grounds. He ran after Shoota calmly as if they were just playing a simple game of *it*.

However, this wasn't nearly a simple game...it was a bloody sport that inspired "teardrops and closed caskets." Butta followed behind Taz with his weapon out in front of him, ready to blow a hole through someone. He'd been faced the fact that he must be the one who takes Shoota up out of this shit.

Shoota dipped down a narrow gangway and ran into a backyard that was enclosed by a cast-iron fence. There was no "jumping this gate." "What the fuck!" he said to himself, wondering what the hell to do next.

He glanced around the yard diligently, in search of something to try to defend himself with. He came across a long pipe leaned up against the building and grabbed it, putting his back to the wall.

Shoota inched his way back towards the gangway and listened as Taz's footsteps got closer and closer. Shoota braced himself and got ready to face a life or death experience. However the shit turned out he planned on remaining a real nigga.

As soon as Taz set foot into the backyard, Shoota swung the pipe at him as hard as he could, knocking the gun out of his hand. Taz fell down to the ground as well. Shoota dived for the blicker, but Taz managed to catch his leg right before he could get to it. The two arch-enemies tussled around on the concrete, trying to recover the gun. Taz was a bit bigger and slightly stronger than Shoota, so he ended up taking advantage of the situation real quick.

Taz took hold of Shoota's arms and began overpowering him, punching him in the face—repeatedly. Shoota became dazed and that gave Taz a perfect opportunity to retrieve his weapon. Once he had the gun back in his hand, he aimed it at Shoota's face. Butta came running up with his weapon drawn.

"Wait a minute, gangsta...don't shoot!" Butta said.

"What the fuck you mean...'*wait a minute*'. This Christmas, and that lil grinch over there just got caught trying to steal it. I ain't waiting shit." Taz said as he walked up on Shoota taking a close aim.

"I'm sorry, G...I can't let you do that. Lower your weapon." Butta advised his long-term homie, pointing his gun at him.

Taz turned around looking shocked as can be. He had his blammer buried in Shoota's face still, the slightest tap of the trigger and it was off with his head. Shoota was on the ground taking cover with just his arms.

"What the fuck…you really fronting your shit now," Taz said. Butta didn't budge, he was adamant about the situation. "So, what…you gonna kill me to save this op ass nigga? That's gonna be a whole bunch of blood on your hands, partner."

"Please, don't tempt me, G…just back away from my brother, and we can all walk away from this backyard alive."

Taz wasn't the type of nigga to let up, even in the face of a semi-automatic weapon. Butta could only figure that much, he was the one who created the monster. Taz trigger finger began itching rashly, and Butta seen it.

"I'm warning you, Taz. I'll knock your shit all across the gate over there. Please, don't force my hands." Butta continued to advise him.

Shoota looked up at Taz, into his eyes, seeing the Grim-Reaper in the flesh. The sight kind of reminded him of himself. However, he wouldn't have ever taken this long before squeezing the trigger. Let Shoota tell it…Taz wasn't quite crazy after all.

"Well, you gonna have to do what you gotta do because I ain't going." Taz informed Butta, tapping on the trigger. *"BOCAH!"*

Simultaneously, Butta followed suit. *"FAH-FAH!"*

The impact of shells colliding into Taz's head made him do a full cartwheel towards the fence with the smoking gun—still in his hand. It was a done deal for the Tre-Block rider. His brains were splattered out everywhere.

Immediately, Butta looked down at his brother worried to death, praying to God that he didn't catch some hot lead himself. Shoota was balled up against the fence. Butta reached down for him. To his delightment, he seen his brother was still alive and unharmed.

"Thank you, God," Butta said while helping Shoota up off the ground. "You're alright?"

Shoota was speechless and fucked up in the head behind what all just went down. He would have never expected his brother to save his life...not in a million years. The two brothers just stared at each other, it was definitely an odd moment. Just yesterday they were trying to blow each other's heads off, and now all of a sudden, they were smiling at one another as if they were about to hug or something.

Butta looked over at Taz's twisted up body. "I never really liked that tough ass muthafucka—anyway." he confessed.

Police sirens began to ring through the air, coming from afar. "Go ahead... get the fuck outta here before the cops arrive." Butta instructed his lil' brother, still smiling at him.

"What about you, big bro," Shoota asked, worried about Butta all of a sudden. "You gon' be good?"

"Yeah, I'll be Gucci. I got this, now hurry up and get the hell outta here before I have another change of heart and smoke your top like I done buddies over there." Butta stated, pointing his gun at Taz's slumped body.

Shoota found his brother's slick remark very funny. He went over and gave Butta a brotherly hug. This is what he'd craved for all along, someone to fend for him in the midst of danger. Ever since his mother's been in the ground, he had been taking care of himself—all by himself. Shoota definitely felt the love, and the feeling was mutual.

"Go on, now." Butta said, trying hard to fight back the tears.

"Love, big bro." Shoota replied, taking off running from the scene.

Butta just stood there, pistol in hand, unbothered about what was gonna happen to him once twelve arrived. Prison was his second home, so getting' locked up didn't make him any difference. Besides, even though he might end up losing his freedom again for the *umpteenth* time...he had gained a brother, and that alone was more valuable than anything.

CHAPTER #15

ᏂᎾᏞᎠ ᎩᎾᏌ ᎠᎾᏔᏁ

Shoota and Olivia hit it off well real early in the flick, enjoying every bit of the time they spent together. Eventually, the two newly love birds became closer than most and broke their backs to insure seeing one another more and more each day.

Olivia had sent her mother Destiny a picture of her and Shoota hugged up; and immediately, her stomach balled up as she recalled the very boy who she failed killing after succeeding with his mother. It took no rocket scientist to figure the shit out, Shoota still had a baby face as before. The only thing that changed was now he had dreads, an aspiring body count, and her precious daughter in his arms.

Dez looked over the picture many times, hoping that Shoota's face would magically vanish somehow. This was the very face that had been haunting her dreams, Freddy Kruger style, for the past 8 years. *How could this be?* she thought to herself as she sat on her bunk, crying.

For some time now, Shoota's been trying hard to take the relationship he had with Olivia to the next level. However, Olivia had made her mother a promise that she would save her virginity till she was of age and possibly married. Dez dreaded her daughter turning out anything like she was at her age.

For as long as Olivia possibly could, she fought off the sexual advances Shoota made. However, he was very persistent. Eventually, the temptations became unbearable for her—she finally surrendered and gave her innocence away—wholeheartedly. Sometimes, destiny has a crazy way of unfolding.

For several years now, Olivia's period had came on the same time each month. However, the current month was a bit different. She was deep in it and was beginning to believe that her period had somehow disappeared. When she went to the clinic, she came to find out that she was several weeks pregnant.

Shoota was the only person Olivia had told about her pregnancy. Instantly, he began hoping for a junior, excited about the matter. Olivia didn't know how to bring this subject up to anybody else, let alone to her parents...neither one of them. Although she was just as excited as Shoota was, deep down inside she felt a bit ashamed of herself that she had broken the promise she made to her mother, Dez. The main thing Dez had been praying and hoping that wouldn't happen—happened. And it happened with someone that she had done a horrible thing to. The drama continues.

Olivia was lost in the sauce, she decided not to trouble her mother with the doleful news. She hadn't seen or heard anything from Pops in a while now. Her foster parents were hardly ever around to discuss anything with. The Harris' stayed busy working, ensuring that Olivia was well taken care of.

Kick-Dough was the only other person besides Shoota that she felt comfortable with talking to. He slid through to check up on her and find out if she heard anything about the old man, Pops. Olivia was sitting on the porch when he pulled up on her. She looked through the car window and saw him maneuvering the European automobile into an open parking spot.

"K-D!" Olivia shouted as she hopped off the porch and ran over to the car. Kick-Dough smiled as he bailed out, covered in ice like he done survived a blizzard. "What's up, my wonderful sister, how have you been?" he asked while giving her a great big ol' hug.

"Aww, I've been cooling, just going to school and working."

"Is that right...what them grades looking like then?" Kick-Dough said. He took a sip of water from a Fiji water bottle and then followed Olivia over to the porch to cop a squat. "Ain't no lacking on them shits...not ever."

"They're on point, you already know I don't play when it comes to getting that lesson," she replied, thinking of a way to reveal her pregnancy to Kick-Dough. "I got all A's and B's with one C."

Kick-Dough was very proud of Olivia's grades; however, he still felt the need to encourage her that she should do better. "That's what's up! I'm definitely rocking with that, but you know they give out C's to the average person. That ain't you, is it?" he said, looking her in the face through his exclusive Versace lenses.

"I'm working on it, brother," she responded, deciding to break the news to him now. "It's something I wanna talk to you about but don't know exactly how to say it."

Kick-Dough turned aside towards Olivia, putting his hand on her shoulder, and spoke to her from his heart, "What is it, lil' sis? You can tell me anything and trust that it'll stay between just me and you...we're family!"

Olivia looked Kick-Dough in the eye, clearly seeing that he was sincere, and came out with it, "I'm pregnant."

Kick-Dough damn near choked on the water he was drinking. "You're what?" he asked, not quite believing his ears.

"I said I'm pregnant...about 5 weeks along now."

"Wait a minute...when did you even start having sex?" Kick-Dough asked, nearly choking again when he said "*sex.*" He grabbed the bottom of the Balmain V-neck he had on, and wiped his mouth off with it. He was totally caught off guard with the latest news.

"About 5 weeks ago," Olivia answered while holding her head down. She was beginning to regret even telling Kick-Dough about the shit.

"How did this happen? You done went from telling me you was on the honor roll to...'*I'm pregnant*'." Kick-Dough asked, looking confused.

After noticing that Olivia had dropped her head down, sobbing in tears, Kick-Dough put his anger to a cease. He reached over towards her, grabbing her chin gently and lifting her head back up. The sight of tears falling from her face melted his heart.

"Sis, don't cry," Kick-Dough said as he took his shirt off to use for drying her eyes. "Everything's gonna be alright...it's not the end of the world."

Kick-Dough continued comforting Olivia, holding her in his arms as if she was his daughter. "I'm sorry for coming off on you the way I did, but I just want the very best for you, sis." he said.

"I know...I feel terrible," she responded, beginning to feel a lil' better. "Not because I'm pregnant but because of all the people I've seem to let down."

Kick-Dough caught every tear that formed in her eyes, not letting one fall from her face. "Don't feel terrible...mistakes do happen, you know. Keep your head to the sky, it's up to you now to turn a negative into a positive." he replied while looking her dead in the eyes.

Olivia just listened attentively, taking an account on every word that came out of Kick-Dough's mouth. To her, it felt like she was having a one-on-one with her godfather, Pops. She was happy that she told Kick-Dough about her pregnancy.

"I'm gonna always be here to support you in whatever you do, just as long as it's righteous," Kick-Dough advised. "Who else have you told about this?"

"Just the father." she replied, ashamedly.

"What do you mean...*'just the father'*?" he responded, damn near about to blow up on her again. "You mean to tell me that you haven't even told your mother about this yet?"

"I don't know how to break the news to her without hurting her. She really stressed *'not getting pregnant'* to me." Olivia explained.

"You know you're gonna have to tell her sooner or later, it might as well be sooner," Kick-Dough said. "You don't want her to find out about it on her own terms."

"I know, I'm gonna tell her the next time we speak."

"Well, I'm glad you filled me in. It would've been bad for you if I had to find out about it through someone else. By the way, who's the father?"

"A boy I met several months ago named Charles." Olivia said.

Shoota? Kick-Dough thought to himself. He just knew she couldn't have been talking about the same fucker who he had just put out a hit on. Nah...not him.

"Do you have a picture of this Charles guy...big bro wanna size the fella up right quick?" Kick-Dough asked.

"Sure, I do," Olivia replied, grabbing her phone and scrolling through it. "Here...that's him, right there."

Kick-Dough took ahold of her phone and examined the photo. Instantly, he got an upset stomach and a bad pain in his neck. This was bad...very bad! *How the fuck did some shit like this happen?* he thought to himself.

What Kick-Dough didn't know was that Olivia's mother Destiny was Shoota's mother's murderer. No one had that much figured out yet...no one but Destiny, and she wasn't too eager to publicize that kind of information—especially not to her daughter.

Kick-Dough saved face, playing the whole situation cool as if it wasn't a problem he couldn't fix. He didn't feel the need to let Olivia know that he knew exactly who Shoota was, not just yet. He had to figure some more shit out first.

"How did y'all meet?" he asked as he reached over and handed her back her phone. Then he dug into his pocket, pulling out a dookie-roll and thumbing through it swiftly.

"We met in a Subway, right where I work. He was real polite to me, and we just start kicking it." Olivia answered.

Being pregnant with Shoota's baby made her love for him grow even more. It was nothing bad anyone could say about the boy, not to her face. Kick-Dough had that much figured out just off the fact that he was the first person she had told about the pregnancy. Olivia and Shoota definitely had a real tight bond.

Kick-Dough peeled off a few racks and passed it over to her. "Well, I'm not gonna kill your joy...bringing a new life into this world is such an amazing occasion. For the most part, it's a blessing from God. I'm happy for you...congratulations!" he said, faking a smile.

Olivia grabbed the money, smiling big like the Kool-Aid pitcher. "Thank you, brother," she replied as she wrapped her arms around his neck, giving him a kiss on the side of his face.

"Never hesitate to come to me when you seem to have come across a problem, not even for the slightest second." Kick-Dough said, looking at Olivia as she took a count of the wad of money he had just given her. "Are you listening to me?"

"Yeah, I got you, brother." she said, looking up at him—smiling.

"I mean it, and you need to hurry up and tell your mother, foster parents, and A-1 about the good news. Please, don't keep them in the dark any longer...they deserve better from you than that."

Olivia nodded her head in agreement with what Kick-Dough was preaching to her. "I'm gonna get right on top of that—asap."

"You still haven't heard anything from Pops?" he asked.

"Nope, I was just about to ask you that same question. It doesn't make any sense for him to just up and leave like that. Nobody knows anything about his whereabouts."

"I hope nothing is wrong with him wherever he's at." Kick-Dough said.

"What's up with A-1?" Olivia asked. "I wrote him a letter and sent him a couple cards."

"Oh yeah, he got them. He told me to tell you that he loves you and to be expecting a call from him soon."

"How's he holding up in there?"

"You know A-1, he's *Good* like Megan. The penal system can't break a real nigga." Kick-Dough said while scrolling through his phone.

Kick-dough's schedule was busy, so he began narrowing the conversation down. "I gotta get out of here...do your boyfriend know anything about me?" he asked.

"No, I haven't told him about you. I know how you are," Olivia responded, looking a bit confused. "Why you asked that though?"

"No particular reason, just asking," he replied as he stood up from the porch, shirtless. "Do me a favor though...keep it that way. At least till I run a thorough background check on him first."

"O.M.G. I got you brother...you just gotta stay bossed up, huh!" Olivia said as she hugged up with Kick-Dough and walked with him to his Porsche Panamera that was bolted up on Forgiatos.

Kick-Dough bailed in the car and fired up the Twin-Turbo engine. *"VROOM!"* Music came blasting out of the speakers. **Big Sean** was playing, *"I'm way up, I feel blessed!"* He turned the volume down a bit as Olivia leaned up against the passenger side window.

"When are you gonna let me push the foreign, brother?" she asked, infatuated with the fancy whip.

"As soon as you get them L's, I'm gonna take you to the lot and cop you yo' own."

"Merch it,"

"On Scoobie's grave! I can't allow my sister to be out here pushing somebody else's whip, not even if it's mine." Kick-Dough said.

Olivia knew the shit was official how Kick-Dough smacked four of his fingers on his forearm where Scoobie's face was tattooed at. He never lied on any of his dead homies. Good thing for her, she was already in Driver's Ed about to get her permit.

"Look, I'm really running behind. I'll be back in a couple of days to curve you a lil' bit better than I've done today. That was all I had on me to spare right now. I love you."

"I love you too, brother... take care."

Olivia backed away from the car as Kick-Dough pumped up the volume. *"I'm only here for a short time, not a long while. You know I...I haven't had a good time in a long while. You know I'm...I'm way up, I feel blessed...straight up-straight up. I'm way up, I feel blessed."* Kick-Dough sang along to the song as he chopped up the deuces to Olivia and wiggled his way out of the parking spot, getting right back in traffic.

After chopping it up with Olivia, Kick-Dough hopped dead on the phone and called Mac. "What's the business?" Mac answered.

"Check it out right quick, you know that one thing we was discussing at Mickey D's the other day?" Kick-Dough asked.

Mac dug deep into his thoughts trying to recall what he was referring to. "Nah, bro, try to refresh my memory."

"You know, about the cancer that had to be removed."

"Oh yeah, that's about to be in motion." Mac stated.

"Hold fast on that for a moment. Something just came up that I got to check into. Once I figure the shit out, I'll let you know if it's still a green light or not...okay?" Kick-Dough said, calling off the hit he had previously sanctioned against Shoota.

"You're sure, big bro? That order's set to go through." Mac confirmed.

"I'm positive, my nigga... put that on the back burner for right now. I'll let you know what's what in one sec."

"Alright, if you say so." Mac said, following the instructions very well.

"10-4, MVP!" Kick-Dough said, ending the call.

When Dez got the horrible news from Olivia, about her being a couple months pregnant by the very boy whose mother she'd killed years ago, her heart fell to the bottom of her stomach. Her haunting nightmares were now an actual reality...a terrible situation she couldn't avoid anymore. She began to regret not telling her daughter about the matter when she had first gained knowledge of who her boyfriend actually was...about how she ran up on his mother with a revolver, smoking her top, and then trying to do the same to him.

Maybe if Dez would've just told Olivia from the get go about the shit, things wouldn't have even gotten this far. But really, who's to say the outcome. You know how these lil' girls are when falling deeply in love with boys, Olivia could've just as well sided with Shoota against her mother. Besides, Dez didn't know where to begin explaining herself.

The whole predicament was disturbing and problematic, and Dez didn't know how to fix it. She blamed God, claiming to be cursed with "hell on earth." It was bad enough already that she was serving out a 20-year bit as punishment for her deadly behavior, but also had to endure the heartache and pain of becoming a grandmother to a baby whose father was someone she attempted to kill.

During this troubling time, Fate, Dez's girlfriend, did her best to comfort and support her. Fate was closing in on her prison sentence, only having several months left to do. The constant completion of academic contracts was bringing her release date closer to a reality each day.

Dez was very happy for Fate; she trusted that once her girl got released from prison, she would be able to make a way for the both of them. Fate had just received her Cosmetology license and planned to work towards getting her own hair salon called "Fate's Full Beauty." She had the skills and the right people behind her to help her dream come true. All she would have to do was come up with the finances. At the current moment, she hadn't the slightest sponsorship.

"Honey, everything's gonna be alright. It may seem all fucked up at the moment, but I have faith that things will get better. It's all a part of God's plan…everything happens for a reason." Fate said while styling Dez's hair.

Fate and Dez were in the cell alone, away from the presence of the other inmates. Fate had on a loose tank top and some super tight sweatpants, showing off her amazing figure. She was definitely one of the baddest bitches in the joint. Dez knew it and felt lucky for having her as an inmate partner. The couple had matching tats of each other's name on their necks.

Dez was sitting down on the stool half naked, only wearing panties and a bra. Although she had picked up a few pounds over the years, her body was still banging. The infamous scar that wrapped down the side of her face ended up becoming a distinctive beauty mark for the girl.

"Girl, I don't even wanna hear about God's plan right now. I gotta serious bone to pick with him...how could he let something like this happen?" Dez replied.

Fate didn't bother to try to answer that question, she was just as much confused about the event as Dez was. However, she fixed her mouth and said what she felt was appropriate for the moment. "They say God works in mysterious ways."

"Mysterious my ass," Dez responded, turning around and looking Fate dead in the eye. "It's quite obvious that the man upstairs is trying to destroy what's left of me and my family."

Dez turned back around, allowing Fate to finish doing her hair. "The great '*I Am*' got some explaining to do." Dez said.

Fate couldn't help but burst out into laughter. "Girl, your ass is a hot mess...you got them bitches." she replied, speaking about Dez's hilarious personality, something she'd grown to value so much.

The two lesbians were super-jammed tight, everybody in the joint rooted in favor of their relationship and expected to see them get married one day. Dez was beginning to feel a bit better now after discussing the matter over with her bitch. The sound of Fate's voice was starting to make her pussy wet.

The hell with getting my hair done now, Dez contemplated as she began playing with herself. Her pearl tongue was just craving for some urgent attention.

At first it was just a casual thing, but gradually, her hands turned the occasion out of control. Immediately, Fate caught her cue and began sprinkling kisses all across Dez's neck. She then reached her face out from around the back of Dez and planted a passionate kiss on her lips.

After a few moments of exchanging saliva, Fate let go of the wet lips on Dez's face and took a dive at the ones between her legs. By this time, Dez had come from out of her panties and bra. A lil' one on one girl action was exactly what Dez needed to take her mind off all the bullshit going on in her life. She cocked one leg up on Fate's shoulder and slid closer towards her face, spreading her pretty little wings out wide.

Fate took a couple of moments to enjoy the sight of Dez's playground before feasting. Dez's pussy got even wetter just off from being looked at voraciously. She squirmed around on the stool, yearning for Fate to eat her pussy.

Finally, Fate went in for her meal, licking Dez's vagina real sloppily like how a thirsty mutt does to some clean water in a bowl. All that was heard was a variation of slurping noises as Fate's tongue flapped up against Dez's G-spot. She'd been sucking her pussy long enough to know exactly how to make that muthafucka *jump*.

Dez's body began pulsating like a busy phone that's turned up high—on extra vibrate. Fate was doing the *wattossie* on that cootie-cat, forcing Dez to cum uncontrollably. She held onto Fate's face while letting her pussy hang all the way out. Fate kept sucking and licking on that joint like it was a fruity lollipop or something.

Enough was enough, Dez couldn't take anymore. She eased her goods away from Fate's over-accomplished tongue, feeling very satisfied with the work she had put in. *She killed that shit,* she thought, taking a couple moments to gather herself.

"Damn, baby," Dez said as she held onto herself, trying to stop her body from shaking. "Your tongue game is monstrous—every time!"

Dez began to gain control of her breathing again. Her hairdo may have been half-done, but her vagina was altogether. "That was the best head I had, thus far." she managed to say.

Fate just looked at her ferociously, with pussy juice dripping from her lips onto the floor. She loved giving Dez head, even more than getting it. It was an intimate way of showing how much she adored her. Fate was all in with the relationship and was bound to do what's necessary to keep Dez happy, even if that meant killing someone.

Fate stood up from the squatting position she was in. Seeing all the pussy drool hanging from Fate's mouth, Dez pulled her up close to her naked body and wiped it away. Fate sat down on Dez's lap and held on to her with her arms wrapped around her neck. Dez was a bit older than her, but age was just a number. The two lovebirds shared a ultimate bond, and that's what mattered the most.

"Baby, don't worry yourself about this Charles boy. He fuck around and don't even be in the picture for long. I can see him not being a problem to us at all." Fate said, speaking from the bottom of her heart.

Dez didn't quite catch onto what Fate was actually saying. She appreciated the fact that she was just being comforting in a time of need, but something had to be done other than just sitting around saying that everything would be fine.

"And how could you be so sure about that, Fee-Fee," Dez asked, looking at her sideways. "How do you know the boy isn't gonna be a problem to us?"

Fate smiled and then gave Dez another passionate kiss, maneuvering her anaconda-shaped tongue all through her mouth. She eased up off of her lips and cleared her throat for what she had to say next. She looked Dez straight in the eyes and gave it to her in the raw, "Because...I'm gonna smoke the bastard!"

CHAPTER #16

BOMB FIRST

The BROs threw a party at their grandma's house on the Fo'. Damn near everybody from the neighborhood was present. It was an open invitation for anyone from Washington Heights to attend, even Shoota and his squad. The event was epic.

Shoota, Do-Dirty, and Shawty-Rough slid through just to show their faces and to check to see if there was any action to partake in. Shawty-Rough had just gotten out of juvenile detention for an aggravated battery with a firearm charge he caught sometime back, and already he was eager to get wild. This was the perfect occasion.

Once Kick-Dough had called off the hit against Shoota, Mac let his guards down on the boy and welcomed him into his house with open arms. "What's up, Shoota!" Mac greeted Shoota and his squad, with all kinds of handshakes. Crazy right…just a week ago, Mac was plotting murder against Shoota, and now he's drinking and smoking with him. Talk about some back-door shit, huh!

Shoota was fake cool with the shit; however, him and Do-Dirty were both poled up just waiting for some smoke. Tino and a couple of homies came through blowing some dope as usual. Bitches were everywhere…all over the place and inside out. Every table was packed with food, alcohol, and kush. D-J Boss Life was on deck, bumping all of the hood anthems you could think of. The block was so packed that late attenders had to park their cars around the corner somewhere.

Shoota and Do-Dirty played the background and just watched while Shawty-Rough danced around, clocking the hoes. Tom-Tom, one of Mac's main hitters also cousin, was in the Cook County Jail fighting a weapons charge. The judge had given him a no-bond because of a probation hold. It was safe to say that the boy was *stuck like chuck*.

Face was out of town, as usual, checking a bag. Marshall, *a.k.a.* "M," was on deck running around with Justo. Both of them were high off the shits. Everything seemed to be going well until an argument broke out between M and a group of bitches.

It turned out that M wasn't any good at holding his liquor. He punched one of the hoes dead in the face and choked up another one, all because they didn't want to dance with him. Some off-brand ass nigga tried to grab ahold of M, and M swung on him, not realizing who he actually was. It was one of his lil cousin's homeboy.

The nigga swung back, giving M a two-piece spicy...hold the coleslaw. *"PECK-PECK!"* The gruesome sound of the boy's knuckles colliding into M's face echoed throughout the house. Everybody was paying attention to the whole thing now.

Shawty-Rough was the closest person to M, he didn't hesitate to take clean off on buddy ass. *"MACK!"* Instantly, he slept him.

M, trying to gain some control of himself, reached out and grabbed onto Shawty-Rough's Moncler polo shirt ripping it in the process. Once M got a hold of Shawty-Rough, he gave him a muff to the face. "That's bro you just knocked out, idiot!" he said, taking sides with the same nigga that just pieced him up something real decent.

Shoota and Do-Dirty took position, drawing their weapons like cowboys. Mac had left to go to the liquor store to get more alcohol, and Justo was currently outside playing mack-daddy with the hoes. Shawty-

Rough counter punched M, giving him a couple of haymakers to the center of his face. *"MACK-MACK!"* Instantly, M's nose turned bloody.

Hearing all the commotion going on, Justo ran in the house followed by a group of people. He tried to diffuse the situation, but Do-Dirty and Shoota both got in his way pinning him up against the wall.

"Let 'em fight head up, we ain't gonna jump in." Shoota implied, aggressively.

"Yeah, M tweaking hard," Do-Dirty added, mugged up at Justo. "He muffed bro in the face when all he was trying to do was defend him."

Finally, Mac pulled up back from the liquor run he had taken. He had plenty more bottles for the party-holics to pop. However, looking at how crowds of bad bitches were in a rush to leave, he could just assume that the party was just about over. "What the fuck done happened now!" he mumbled as he made his way inside the house.

M and Shawty-Rough exchanged a number of blows until Shawty-Rough did a side-step and caught M in the jaw with a nasty right hook. *"CRACK!"* Immediately, M hit the floor like the B.E.T hit series. The off-brand ass nigga that had poked his nose in some shit that didn't pertain to him, attempted sliding off and vanishing in thin air. However, Do-Dirty came out of the wool-works smacking him upside the head with his blicker, *"WHAM!"*

"Bitch ass nigga, where you think you're going?" Do-Dirty said as Shoota joined in on the fun trying to stomp buddy's ears together.

As Mac entered the house, he couldn't believe his eyes. "What the fuck is going on up in here?" he shouted.

Shoota and Do-Dirty didn't bother answering the question, they just kept playing soccer with homeboy's head. It took Mac to go over and break the shit up for them to stop. They weren't happy at all with Mac's interruption…not one bit.

"Man, I leave for a hot moment and this is what I got to come back to!" Mac complained, looking directly at Shoota and his gang.

"That ain't on us," Shoota replied, taking notice of how Mac was staring at him. "Take it up with your drunk ass cousin, M...he's the one who seem to can't handle his liquor."

Mac just continued staring at Shoota. *I see now why bro 'nem wanted this nigga smoked.* he thought as Shoota stared back at him—without the slightest blink. He wasn't the least bit terrified.

"He better be lucky I don't have Dirty *face-time* his bitch ass!" Shoota stated as him and his wolves slid right past Mac, leaving the house. D-J Boss Life was still spinning cuts playing some **Gucci,** *"Trap house 3 got to K with me and 3-bad bitches that stay with me."*

Shawty-Rough was the last wolf to exit the house, picking up his drank and finishing it first. "That's number 30 there, Mac." he said, clarifying the number of people he had knocked out. That boy had iron fist. The only count Shoota and Do-Dirty was ever interested in had the word "body" written in front of it.

"So, y'all just gonna disrespect my grandma's house like that?" Mac said, following behind Shawty-Rough.

The party continued to jam outside. Justo stayed behind, inside the house helping M get himself together. "He snaked me, cuz." M claimed. Once Justo got him up off the floor, he stepped outside with Mac to get down to the bottom of the matter.

M went to grab the blicker he had stashed in the ceiling earlier and came out of the house waving it carelessly, as if he was bound to shoot anyone.

"Wow, cuz...what the hell are you doing?" Mac said, noticing the chrome object in M's hand. "Put that away before you accidentally shoot someone."

"Nah, fuck that. That bitch ass nigga snaked me, cuz. It ain't gonna be no accident when I kill him." M shouted as he stumbled down the stairs.

"Man, you're fronting your shit," Mac said as he approached M and disarmed him. "Give me this gun before you do something dumb!"

Justo came up from behind, trying to help calm M down. By this time, Shoota and Do-Dirty had their weapons drawn and was easing their way back towards the party with "increasing the murder-rate" on their minds. Shawty-Rough stayed back in the cuts, and watched the drill play out from afar.

"Fuck's your problem, cuz...you trying to kill us all out here," Mac asked, holding the gun down by his side. "Pointing that gun like a mad man?"

A nice multitude of partiers lingered around in front of the house, still bopping to the music. Shoota and Do-Dirty both slid out from in between two parked cars, about a couple of houses away from the action. Mac, Justo, and M all stood by the porch conversating.

"You drunk, cuz, you don't need to be operating a gun tonight." Justo said, giving M a caring hug. "Go chill out and fuck with some hoes."

M pimped off mumbling under his breath, "These niggas be saving them bitch ass muthafuckas. I wish Tom-Tom was here, we would've plucked them duck ass niggas!" Mac ran inside the crib to tuck away the blicker he'd recovered from M. Skull-Cap and Ninja had been riding hard all day, and he wasn't about to run the risk of getting bumped off with it like his cousin Tom-tom did. If Mac got caught with another firearm, he would easily be charged under the **"Armed Habitual Criminal Act."**

Justo slid to the back of the house to take a quick piss. Do-Dirty and Shoota inched their way towards where M was posted up at. A few dick eaters that M were surrounded by had peeped the move and eased their way out of the direction the two menaces were coming towards. Before

M could even figure out what was going on, a bunch of gunshots had licked off, *"CLAH-CLAH-CLAH-CLAH-CLAH-CLAH-CLAH!"*

Bitches were screaming loudly as they ran for cover. Instantly, Mac rerouted his tracks and came out the house letting his gun talk, *"DARH-DARH-DARH-DARH-DARH!"*

Shoota and Do-Dirty both put Mac's front porch on rapid-fire, *""CLAH-CLAH-CLAH-CLAH!"* causing him to have to dive back inside the door. Instantaneously, Mac arose from the floor and began firing his weapon at them from out a side window, *"DARH-DARH-DARH-DARH-DARH!"*

Although Mac's shots were ineffective, he managed to get Shoota and Do-Dirty up off of his cousin, M. After emptying their clips at Mac's crib, Shoota and Do-Dirty fled the scene with Shawty-Rough tagging along right behind them. All three of them were laughing like the devil.

Obviously, the D-J wasn't spinning anymore records...the party was over! Everybody was hopping in their vehicles and getting out of there in a flash. By the time Mac came out of the house, the Juvies had vanished into thin air. A crowd of people circled around a body that laid slumped in the middle of the streets.

Noticing that the shirt the victim had on was once his, Mac's heart took a dive for the pavement. "Damn, lil cuz!" he said, moving in closer to the scene with his blammer still pointed outwards.

"Somebody call an ambulance!" one girl screamed out, loudly.

Mac dropped to his knees and prayed to God with the blicker in between his palms-still smoking. "Please, God... don't take my lil cuz from me. If someone must turn their soul over today, let it be me."

Finally, M crawled out from underneath a car, untouched. When he saw Justo's body twisted up on the pavement, he cried out like Ricky's baby did after seeing Dough-Boy and Trae carry his father's dead body through the front door in the classic movie, **"Boyz N the Hood."**

Justo lost a whole lot of blood from the gunshot wounds he had sustained in the shooting. He had taken bullets in the arms, ass, and leg as well. Also, the young fella had gotten skinned in the head by some hot lead.

The BROs were enraged—especially M, being that he was the cause of the whole mess. Nobody blamed him though well, at least not any of the BROs. The same night of the bloody shooting, Shoota went to Facebook with the shit sending subliminal messages saying, "Justo's blood is all on M's hands!"

It turns out that when Justo got done pissing in the back of the house, he returned back to the party outside only to walk across a line of fire that was intended for M. Again, another sad case of being at the wrong place at the wrong time. The results of it all left Justo having to walk impaired for the rest of his life. He was no longer the BROs best pair of legs.

Face was highly bent out of shape about the shit. For years now, he's been trying to get his cousins to relocate out of town with him, especially after A-1 had gotten locked up. Let him tell it...the Chi' was burnt up and the Fo' Block had taken its turn for the worst. Money was beginning to get dried up because of Shoota's theatrics, bringing unnecessary heat to the block. Face practically begged for his cousins to put Washington Heights behind them.

It's crazy how out of all the BROs who were offered a first-class ticket out of hell, M was the only one that accepted Face's kindly gesture. Even Justo turned the shit down, vowing to get his revenge back on JRW. Immediately, Mac and his lil' shooter squad went to war with the Juvies.

Keep in mind, these two street gangs shared the same home turf—Fo' block. These niggas was blamming at each other, back and forth, from directly out of the windows of their grandma's cribs...I'm talking about some across the street warfare type of shit.

The entire neighborhood done turned into a danger zone, it wasn't safe for anyone to be straggling through without protection...not even the elders. Both grandmas, Mac's and Shoota's, kept pocket-rockets on 'em whenever being chauffeured around the town. Hell, it was only a matter of time before someone played dirty.

The war went back and forth, Mac's crew shooting up some Juvies and Shoota's wolves returning the favor. Shoota began recruiting all the lil' shorties in the hood to be in his gang. It didn't matter how old they were, just as long as they knew how to shoot a basketball, he was blessing them in and putting guns in their hands. He sanctioned drills for them to complete daily.

The Juvies didn't let the beef they had against the Tre die down one bit. They came off one drill going straight to the next one, making it very hard for their opz to sit still. Shawty-Rough ended up catching a homi' on some fan of the Tre...shot a nigga dead in the face while riding the CTA bus, right after school. The shit was all over the news.

It turned out that the person Shawty-Rough had smoked was the son of a police captain. Law enforcements of all sorts swarmed Washington Heights like bumblebees, arresting Shawty-Rough in no time. He got charged with umpteen counts of first-degree murder and was looking at 100-plus years if found guilty.

The gun violence between the Juvies and the BROs died down, but not with the Juvies and the Tre. Them shits stayed lit like dragon's breath. In the midst of Mac going to war with Shoota, he went on to squash the beef he had with the Tre, being that they both had a mutual op they wanted dead. They didn't join forces or anything of that matter, they just lost interest in killing each other. Hell...everybody from around the way target was Shoota, he had become Public Enemy number one.

A Novel by Pucasso

CHAPTER #17

LOVE AND HATE

Stacey had never been the insecure type of woman. You know, the one who spends most of her precious day trying to figure out if her man is cheating on her or not. Nah…that wasn't Stacey's style at all. Not saying that she hardly ever was bothered about Kick-Dough's infidelities, it was just that she knew what she was getting herself into from the get-go.

Kick-Dough was a top-flight type of nigga, attracting a great multitude of people to him, and most of 'em were bad bitches. Stacey chose not to stress herself over the mediocre shit. She loved him and had faith that he loved her just as much. She had slightly bought into the notion…"all niggas are dogs" and…"nothing can change them, not even a cat woman."

Long story short, as long as Kick-Dough's affairs didn't hinder their happy home, Stacey didn't even bother tripping. And likewise, Kick-Dough did whatever was necessary to keep a smile on Stacey's face. He kept all of his side bitches in check like a notorious pimp. Yeah, he had his hoes in order…all of 'em except Jessica's crazy ass.

Time after time, he done let Jessica get away with shit that if it was one of his other hoes, he would of gave 'em their walking papers. To keep his shit 100, bro was beginning to catch feelings for her…deeply in love with the sloppy way she often topped him off. It was by far the best he ever had, and he wouldn't give it up to save his own life.

At some point though, Jessica must have forgotten her role and began *doing the most*. All that fake ass pillow talking Kick-Dough had been dishing out to her was now coming back to haunt him. She definitely was feeling like she was in a race for the number one slot, assuming that one day, Kick-Dough would leave his fiance and kid just to be with her...*A side chick's dream!* However, she would never see it. The more Kick-Dough tried confirming that to her, the more delusional she became.

She went as far as faking a pregnancy one time and threatening to tell Stacey about her and Kick-Dough's love child that was supposedly on the way. Each time, it was some new drama with her. It got to the point where Kick-Dough had to cut off all ties with the psychotic bitch before she wind up ruining his happy home. You seen the movie **"Fatal Attraction,"** this **Glenn Close** acting ass heifer was constantly cramping Kick-Dough's style, and even her monstrous head game couldn't keep him around any longer. He was done!

After noticing the disappearing act that Kick-Dough had pulled, Jessica began calling Stacey making ideal threats. She claimed that she was gonna come to kill her, her babies, Kick-Dough, and then herself as well. Stacey got straight on that with the hoe.

"Look, dumb bitch, if you keep calling my phone threatening me and my family, I'm gonna go and hunt yo' ass down with a machete and slaughter you like some cattle. I'm not fucking playing either." she yelled, through the phone.

Stacey paced back and forth through the front room, steady peeking out the blinds. She wasn't from the streets, but that wouldn't stop her from stomping a mud hole in Jessica's ass if she came her way.

"Bitch, you ain't gon' do shit but continue playing the perfect baby mama while I fuck yo' baby daddy the way he dreams of when he be up in yo' dried out shit. I'm the reason why you chose to take a few fellatio classes, remember? By the way, I heard you got a lil' better...you still ain't fucking with me, but I commend you on the effort though." Jessica replied, laughing sarcastically.

Kick-Dough always described Stacey as being green, mainly because she wasn't ghetto, but right now she was red—literally.

"Why are you calling bothering me all of a sudden?" Stacey asked, peeping out the blinds again seeing Kick-Dough pull up. "Aww, I know why…Kick-Dough must have finally given you your walking papers."

Kick-Dough slid through the front door singing **D-J Khalid's** hit song, "*I'm gon' hold you down,*" not knowing that Stacey was bout to explode.

"It was definitely sooner than I pressured him to," Stacey continued to verbally get under Jessica's skin. "In fact, I just so happen to know nothing about you until the current moment we're in, which brings to mind you must not have been on a crumb."

Kick-Dough came into the living room where Stacey was boiling hot at. From the cold stare she had given him, he could only assume bullshit was in the air. He walked over towards her and tried to place his lips on hers. Instantly, she turned her head aside and walked away hastily.

"I don't know why you side bitches just don't stick to the script," Stacey kept talking her shit to Jessica. "Y'all only good for sucking some dick and…hell, that's it!"

Kick-Dough knew a big argument between him and Stacey was up next to bat. He made his way upstairs to get prepared for it. Although the streets lights were on, and a full moon cover the sky, the night was still young…that is in Kick-Dough's eyes.

"If y'all just play the very short part given to you, everything would be cool, but nah…" Stacey argued, through the phone. "…y'all gets beside yo'selves and start acting like the shit's more than what it really is, and that's when the strings get cut—puppet!"

"Bitch, you talking real slick behind that phone," Jessica said, finally responding to Stacey's claims. "I know where you live, how 'bout I pull up on you and see if yo' lame ass can back up all that crazy you're playing."

Stacey didn't respond, she was too busy caught up in her thoughts. *I know this nigga didn't fuck her in my—*

"—What's wrong, you ain't got shit else to say?" Jessica blurted, interrupting Stacey's scandalous theory. "I'm gonna beat that baby out yo' stomach when I catch you, bitch!"

Jessica's buttons were pushed, she couldn't take talking to Stacey for another second. She ended the call without delay. She normally wasn't the type of woman who let other chicks live "rent-free" in her head, but it was clear that Stacey had managed doing so.

Stacey couldn't help but laugh, knowing that she had gotten to the girl. However, deep in her heart, Stacey didn't feel the least bit victorious. She walked to the kitchen and fixed herself a drink, a double shot of tequila-straight. After power slamming the shit down her throat, she played bartender again.

"Kick-Dough!" Stacey mumbled to herself, enraged. She reached in the silverware drawer and grabbed the first utensil she saw, a steak knife. Immediately, she fled towards the staircase with murder on her mind.

By the time Stacey finished climbing the flight of stairs, the alcohol began settling well into her system. Her emotions were all over the place...the product of an angry, black, pregnant woman. "Enough is enough!" she said, heading towards the bedroom.

Kick-Dough had just came out of the shower, he had a Burberry bath towel wrapped around his lower body. He flopped down on the bed and closed his eyes, not even bothering to put any clothes on. He just stretched out across the bed and listened to **Miguel** playing on the stereo, *"How many drinks would it take you to get with me."*

Stacey entered the room holding the steak knife tightly behind her back. **"This nigga wanna come in and go to sleep, huh!"** she sighed as she walked into the closet and swapped out the steak knife for a glock .17. She tiptoed around, making sure she didn't front the move. She eased up on Kick-Dough and cocked one into the chamber.

Stacey aimed the blicker at Kick-Dough's manhood and shouted, "Wake up, you dirty-dick muthafucka!"

When Kick-Dough opened his eyes, the sight was shocking. "What's going on baby...why you got that gun pointed at my dick?" he asked, while simultaneously thinking, *This bitch done lost her damn mind.*

"I just talked to yo' lil' girlfriend, and she claims that you be thinking about her when we're having sex..." Stacey relayed the message. "...Tell me, is that true?"

Hearing Stacey slur at her words let Kick-Dough know that she had been drinking, something she rarely does while being pregnant.

"What the fuck you're talking about," Kick-Dough replied, saying the first thing that came to his mind. "That shit sounds stupid, you must be drunk."

"Don't play on my fucking intelligence, Anthony!" she replied, waving the Glizzie at him carelessly. "What...my pussy ain't good enough for you?"

"Stacey, stop pointing that damn gun at me before you accidently fire it." he warned her.

"I'm sick and tired of being made a fool of," she cried out, still aiming the pole at Kick-Dough's joint. "I give you my heart, and instead of comforting it, all you do is wipe yo' feet off with it."

"Baby, you tweaking," he said, easing up in the bed cautiously. "Put that gun down, and let's talk about it."

"Just how much of yo' cheating do you think I can take, Anthony?" Stacey responded, raising the pistol up at Kick-Dough's face.

"Baby, I don't want any other woman but you, and you know that." he said. "What's up with all the theatrics?"

"When the hell are you gonna grow up and finally see that I am all the woman you need." she replied, pouring out tears.

"Baby, I know that already, you're my queen…" he stated. "…I couldn't even imagine living life without you by my side."

Kick-Dough always knew exactly what to say to get on Stacey's good side whenever she got to tripping about his infidelities. He was a smooth criminal with a lot of finesse. However, this matter was very different from the rest…Stacey had beared arms against him.

"Baby, you're the only woman for me. You're more than enough woman for me, and I promise I'll do whatever it takes to make you totally appreciate me. Just please, put the gun down before you slip up and do something that you'll regret for the rest of yo' life."

Stacey began coming back to her sense, calming down from the sudden rage she was just in. Never in a million years would she have sought to cause harm to Kick-Dough. She loved him deeply and was just hurt behind having to share him with another woman, even if it was only for a night.

Finally, Stacey lowered the Glizzle to her side, letting it fall to the floor. Kick-Dough sat up and grabbed her by the hand, kissing it softly. "I'm not gonna ever let another woman come in between us again…I promise." he said.

Stacey rubbed him across the face, giving him a big ol' juicy kiss. "You just don't know how much I love you, Anthony. The feeling is so crazy." she responded, still sobbing in tears.

Kick-Dough put his head up against her stomach, showering it with small kisses. At this point, he was sitting on the edge of the bed. Instantly, Stacey's pussy got wet. She had on a silk nightgown with no bra or panties on underneath. Kick-Dough swooped her off her feet, dunked her sexy ass on the king-sized mattress, and buried his face in between her thick thighs.

Stacey was very high maintenance, she kept her pussy shaved and cleansed. Kick-Dough made his way towards her goodies, pulling her pussy lips back with his fingers while sucking on the pearl tongue gently. As he sucked, he also licked his tongue around her clit in a circular motion getting all between her pussy's lips.

Stacey grabbed his head and let out a soft moan, "Aww, baby...that feels incredible."

Kick-Dough went to work like a dehydrated lion coming across a fresh drink of water. He stuck his tongue in and out, front and back, and side to side of Stacey's voluptuous "V." No spot in the perimeter of her vagina was off limits to him, not even her anus.

"Aww, baby...you gon' make me cum with all that nastiness." she murmured as she grabbed ahold of his head, pushing him deeper into her stuff.

Kick-Dough done went from sucking the pearl tongue to flicking his tongue back and forth on it while fingering her ass hole, all being done simultaneously.

"Ohh, baby, I'm about to cum...surf's up!" she said, sounding like she was finna cry. Her body began shaking, compulsively.

Kick-Dough sped up the pace, finishing what he started. He could just feel the weight of secretion hanging off Stacey's pearl tongue. She began to back up from him as if she had enough, but he followed, sucking on that coochie—voraciously.

"Baby, that's enough," she said as she climaxed. "I need you inside of me now."

Kick-Dough crawled up on top of her, throwing both her legs on his shoulders and positioned his cock right in between her wetness. He looked down at her, getting a mean fuck face, and said, "So, you're ready to ride this wave?"

Stacey held onto him and nodded her head. "Have me anyway you would like, just don't ever break my heart." she replied.

Kick-Dough placed a wet kiss on her lips and looked into her eyes. "I assure you, yo' heart is in good hands." he said, easing himself all the way inside of her.

Stacey's eyeballs widened as he repeated the process, maneuvering his dick back and forth in her—rhythmically. "Ooh, baby...I can feel it in my stomach." she claimed.

I hope she ain't talking about the baby. Kick-Dough thought as he sped up the pace. "I love this muthafucka pussy, girl...it's the best I've ever had by far. Don't ever forget that!" he said, talking to her while working the middle.

He reached up under her and grabbed onto her ass, pulling it towards him as he stabbed her goodies perpetually. All she could do was hum and try to brace herself as the wave got "tidal" along the way.

"Ooh, ba-by, I can feel it in my stomach touching my liv-er." she said.

Kick-Dough was all the way in it—literally. He began sucking on Stacey's toes, which was cocked up on his shoulders. Not once did he miss a beat on pounding her pussy. She came multiple times before he flipped her on her hands and knees. Doggy style was his favorite position. He pushed her back in and pulled her ass out, then squatted up into the pussy.

At first, he went slow...that was until he caught a decent rhythm. It wasn't long before he was riding the horse like a cowboy. He reached up with one hand and grabbed onto the canopyrail that was structured at the top of their four-post bed, hanging onto it like a gorilla as he went bananas in Stacey's forest. Before you knew it, he was hanging on with both hands, still beating up them booty-cheeks.

Stacey was loving the shit, she threw her ass in a circle while moaning, "Aww, daddy long stroke...work that shit. This is all yo' pussy, know that!"

Kick-Dough let go of the canopy rail and fell onto Stacey, pushing her down on her stomach and fucked her alligator style. Each time he stroked his stuff, he pushed as far down her tunnel as it went. Her face smacked up against the headboard like a tsunami crashing the shore. The bed rocked like a boat going through **"The Perfect Storm."** Stacey began to cry, only this time it was tears from ecstasy.

Kick-Dough softly nibbled on her back, neck, and ears while swimming like Mike Phelps in her octopus. She felt him grow large like a whale in her and knew exactly what time it was. The finale has finally arrived.

"Cum in yo' pussy, baby," she encouraged him. "It's all yours."

Kick-Dough did as much holding off as he possibly could. He was all sweaty and partially out of breath. The little energy he had left was just about to get exhausted until the strength of semen overpowered his testicles. Sperm rocketed up out of his dick into Stacey's universe, uncontrollably. Talk about astroNUT-status...Kick-Dough couldn't help but feel asteroids flowing through him while seeing astro's all across the room.

"Yes, bitch—yes!" he said, singing along to the song that was currently playing on the stereo.

The pussy was so good that he drooled at the mouth like a lil' baby. He let out a monstrous laugh as he wiggled all of the cum out of his dick, collapsing on top of Stacey afterwards. She had been tapped out several moments ago.

As Kick-Dough began to come back from his "outer body" experience, Jessica's face started fading away to the back of his mind. It was a fact that he just couldn't seem to get the psychopathic bitch up out of his system. She was a seductive lil' heifer. Only if Stacey was a mind-reader, Kick-Dough would have been pushing up daisies somewhere.

He looked over at Stacey and saw that she was asleep, snoring with her face planted in some drool of her own. He just smiled and gave her a soft kiss on her jaw. Through it all, he deeply loved her and would do whatever he had to do to keep her happy.

He reached over and smacked her on the ass, ready for another one. "Wake up, baby…it's time for round two."

Juice exited the front door of Statesville Maximum Prison as a free man. It'd been over a decade since the last time he seen the streets. It definitely was a beautiful sight to see, especially by it being the summertime. He looked up to the skies above and lifted his hands, giving praise to the Lord Almighty. He stooped down on his knees and kissed the ground. It wasn't everyday that a convicted murderer had gotten released from prison, ducking a life sentence.

Bible and his squad were there in the parking lot, getting the party started real early. Bible paid for a party bus and had arranged for specific strippers to perform on it. The ride back to the city would be a blast and possibly—the best time of Juice's life.

Bible walked up on Juice recording him on his phone cam. "Aww shit, J-Hoover's home…it's about to be a problem. What's good, fooly, welcome back!" he said, reaching out to give Juice a hug.

Tango and Boo-Bop, two young gangsters originating from Juice's set, both were on deck showing some love for their new chief. The tag-team drillers also had beef with Big Swole, both claiming that he was only out for himself and hardly ever did shit for the *guys*. They were glad that Juice was finally home and let it be known that they were at his every command.

Immediately, Juice took a liking to them, giving 'em a high slot in his new found organization **"F.O.E"**—Family Over Everything or rather…**"Fuckin' Over Everybody!"** Juice put Tango at region and made Boo-Bop the coordinator. Their territory was located just 10-blocks east of the Washington Heights community. Juice did most of his recruitments way before he was awarded an immediate release from jail. FOE was said to be…"the next best gang smoking in the city."

"What's up, chief? Welcome home!" Tango said as he handed Juice a Gucci bag with all Gucci attire in it.

Juice just smiled, feeling all the love that was given to him. "Welcome back, killa…it's yo' time now." Boo-Bop said, handing Juice an additional bag with all sorts of designer brands inside, from Ferragamo to Yves Saint Laurent.

"Aww, I guess I am loved out here," Juice said, joking around for the moment. "All these years, I was thinking something different."

Juice hugged up with his first two lieutenants, and they all got on the party bus. "Go ahead and change yo' clothes right quick, so we can get this party on the road, the right way!" Bible said.

Yo Gotti was bumping loudly through the speakers, *"You disqualified, bitch—you disqualified!"* Strippers were running around the bus ass hole naked, dancing and swinging across the miniature poles that were stationed in the back of the bus. A couple of niggas from Bible's crew were already turnt up, throwing money at the dancers. Drinks were unlimited and food was wherever they decided to stop and eat at.

Tango and Boo-Bop fell in line with the rest of the team, tip drilling the dancers. Juice was awestruck, just yesterday he was locked in a tiny cage eating Jack-Mack staring at the walls of silence, and now he was in the midst of **"ass and titties."** This was definitely a game-changer for someone who a judge had sentenced to **"no return."**

"It's a bathroom in the back," Bible said, handing Juice a brown paper bag full of money. "Hurry up and jump fresh so we can get this shit busting!"

Immediately, Juice looked in the sandwich bag seeing all sorts of dead presidents. Although he was off to a great start, real early in the flick, the premiere gang chief wasn't quite a **Duffel Bag Boy** yet...very vicious though.

"That's for you to get started with," Bible said while catching Juice looking confused. He signaled for one of the strippers to come over to him. "Aye, Rose-Gold...check it out right quick."

Bible saw that Juice wasn't ever gonna change his clothes, so he decided to go ahead and introduce him to some action. Rose-Gold's tall, big booty, redbone ass came clapping her heels their way. She was topless, showing off her double D's very well. Her hair was wrapped up in a bun with a rose-gold rod going through it, holding it up.

"What's up, Bible?" she said, smiling gorgeously.

"This big bro I was telling you about," he said, pointing at Juice. "Treat him like a king."

Bible gave Juice some dap and then slid off. Rose-Gold squatted down in front of Juice and bit down on his manhood through his fresh state jogging pants. It was a 45-minute ride home, and Juice would make the most of it. His thirsty ass never got around to swapping out the gear he had on with his new shit.

CHAPTER #18

EXTREME MEASURES

Bible was in the kitchen whipping up a 9-piece chicken dinner when his phone began ringing. He reached over to the counter and grabbed it, answering the call without delay.

"You have a collect call from Keyon Smith," the automated recording said. Immediately, Bible accepted charges. *"Thank you for using Securus, you may start your conversation now."*

"What's, up cuz," Muscles said, happy to finally have caught Bible.

"Wud up—wud up," he replied with a grim tone. He propped his cell phone in between his shoulder and ear, and then grabbed the Pyrex from off the stove. Methodically, he began stirring the gooey substance evenly altogether...like it was pancake mix. However, it wasn't flapjacks he was making...he was cooking coke.

Bible danced around the kitchen whipping the ingredient like a mad scientist. **Jeezy** was playing through the speakers of his stereo system, *"Got the Chevy sitting on 24's, you dig...lean with it, rock With it—Nah, I ain't dancing, I'm just whipping them grams up."* He diddy-bopped around, maneuvering his muscular physique to the beat while mixing the cake with perfection.

"How it's looking for you up in there," Bible asked, watching the coke closely as he whipped it hard. "I haven't heard shit from yo' ass in a minute."

"I'm gucci," Muscles responded. "Just trying to sucker duck for the most part."

"Tell me about it,"

"Yeah, the joint's done turned into a lollipop shop," Muscles claimed. "What's good with you though?"

"Shit, you already know...getting to this money...all day every day." Bible replied while making his way back to the counter where he had a bowl of ice water sitting at.

"Yeah, I see you've been busy," Muscles said. "A nigga can hardly ever catch you."

Deep down inside, Muscles wasn't trying to hear Bible's... *"I be getting to this money, all day everyday,"* bullshit. Bible knew it as well as he did, a person makes time for who or what he loves.

"Man, fooly...it seems like every time you call, I be just missing the shit," Bible claimed. "Why you don't be calling right back?"

Fuck I look like chasing. you down. Muscles thought to himself.

The coke inside the Pyrex began to lock up, so Bible sped the process of whipping the Arm & Hammer baking soda around in it making sure it blended in thoroughly. Every now and then, he scraped the scrapes from off the side of the Pyrex to ensure that everything came back right. Bible was a master at bringing back extras.

"Yeah, I figured that much," Muscles replied, downplaying the matter. "I don't be calling right back because I only have a short period of time to use the phone."

Bible was one of the few people who's been there for Muscles whenever he needed him. However, all of a sudden, Muscles was beginning to feel a little neglected. He assumed that the disregard he was experiencing from his cousin had everything to do with Juice being home.

Muscles didn't give a single fuck about Juice. When he was young, Juice used to always try to bully him. One time, he picked Muscles up in the air and dropped him down on the concrete. Bible did nothing about it.

It took for **Blue-Dough**, Bible's oldest brother, to come to Muscles defense. Blue-Dough cracked Juice upside the head with a miniature Louisville Slugger baseball bat, splitting his shit to the white meat. Blue-Dough ended up having to go to a juvenile detention center behind the incident.

Shortly after being batted on like a softball, Juice began turning up his savage coming to experience the juvenile detention system himself. Only thing different, his charges were a whole lot worse, "First-Degree Murder." Muscles ended up bumping heads with Juice again while doing time on his current bid. Juice was back in on his second body, the first one he was given a smack on the wrist because of his age.

This time the judicial system wasn't so lenient with Juice, they sentenced him to a natural-ball...that's life without the possibility of parole. The beef between Muscles and Juice got swept under the rug only because the relationship Juice had formed with Bible. Besides, the confrontation Muscles and Juice had was medieval, a thing of the past—supposedly.

However, tension arises again between the two arch-enemies, sparking up from a bogus violation Juice tried to sanction on Muscles. Allegedly, Juice sent four gang members to Muscles' *a.k.a.* "Kee-Kee," cell to handle the business. Kee-Kee wasn't having that shit though, the MVP representative sent all four of the foot soldiers running up out of his cell back to Juice with pumpkin heads themselves.

Juice would later go on to deny any claims of him having parts in what had happen, but Kee-Kee knew better. Kee-Kee didn't front his shit though...not even the slightest bit. Because the fact was very clear in his head, he didn't want Juice punched on—he wanted him dead. And when the time came for him to execute on the matter, it would be nothing Bible or anybody else could do to prevent Juice's grave from being dug.

Bible was a bit quiet on the phone with Muscles, he had his full attention planted on the coke watching it gradually lock up as he continued whipping the shit. The outcome of how good the coke turns out depended solely on this very moment. Once it was time for him to straight drop the the work, he grabbed the bowl of ice water and poured it into the Pyrex.

Instantly, the coke locked up all the way forming into nuggets of crack cocaine. Bible fished them out of the Pyrex and placed some paper towels down, letting the product air-dry on them. Any water left in them would be great for helping the shit to weigh out right.

"You know Juice's home," Bible said, finally speaking.

"Aww yeah," Muscles responded, sounding less enthusiastic.

"Yeah, folks been home for a few months now. I was just with him earlier." Bible stated. "Muthafuckas hate that folks back down...already he's getting to the money."

All the Juice talk was beginning to make Muscles sick to his stomach. He had to hurry up and change the topic or be subjected to vomiting—right there in the institutional phone booth. Bible didn't even have the slightest clue that his main man Juice was soon-to-be a pressed on picture on the front of a t-shirt, with the words "R.I.P." written right above it. Muscles planned to make sure of that.

"What's the latest news on the block," Muscles asked, switching the subject. "I hear a lotta crazy has been going on out there?"

"Nothing really, niggas out here playing in their ass." Bible replied while examining the crack he had drying out on the paper towel. "I slide through here and there, but it ain't too much over there for me."

This shit's glass! Bible thought to himself, referring to the cocaine he was cooking up. Let him tell it...he had the shit mapped out to a science.

"They're playing in their ass, huh," Muscles reiterated Bible's statement, waiting for him to tell him some more.

"Shit...if you ask me," Bible said. "Muthafuckas running around wild and lawless."

"Yeah,"

"Hell yeah! Since A-1 got locked up, the only muthafucka I fuck with around there for real is Kick-Dough. He don't even be messing around over there anymore. The Fo' ain't what it used to be." Bible explained.

Muscles wasn't hearing that...*"The Fo" ain't what it used to be,"* bullshit Bible was preaching. Let Muscles tell it...the Fo' would always be exactly what it is—"Glorious!" For the most part, Muscles knew that his cousin didn't favor the block too much, never had and probably never will. It didn't matter much to Muscles though, he repped MVP to the depth, and that was just that.

"Somebody was just asking about you the other day...damn, who the fuck that was," Bible said, trying to recall the person. "Aww yeah, A-1. That's who it was."

"Aww yeah, what's up with bro?" Muscles replied. "How is his case looking?"

"He's good. He told me to tell you that he love you and to keep your head to the sky." Bible said, still watching the coke as it dried out.

"The right way...my fucking dawg," Muscles responded, glad to hear something from his day-one nigga. "What the fuck Chuck's talking about?"

"Man, cuzo...I don't think they have been hitting his hand."

"Nah, you can't give it to me like that," Muscles said, finding the latest news hard to believe. "I know Face would never let something like that happen."

Truth be told, Chuck had been paid off in full after the first Lime-Lite Kick-Dough took down. Hell...he even gave Chuck extra-pay as a bonus to get them up out of that jam. Whoever Bible was getting his info from, they couldn't have known what the fuck they were talking about.

"Believe what you want," Bible said, boldly. "Either way don't matter to me."

Bible was slightly blue, and Muscles sensed it—immediately. Bible hated being contested, even if it was just not believing his words. However, Muscles was subjective to hear-say.

"Chuck said that their case looked good though," Bible said, giving some better news to Muscles. "And that it was just a waiting game now."

"That's good shit! Hopefully, A-1 will be touching down before me." Muscles said. "What's up with yo' case, fooly...them niggas still coming to court?"

"It don't even matter whether they do or don't," Bible replied, sounding a bit sad. "It's all in God's hands now, and I'm trusting that the Lord will take care of the problem."

"He will too, but I ain't gotta tell you that...all the blessings he's been laying down upon you."

"Yeah," Bible responded, dreary.

"Man, cuz, it seems like the shorter I get to coming home, the more aggravating niggas are to me. Every time I turn around, I find myself having to sleep a nigga or two."

"You'll be alright, stop trying to prove yo'self to them niggas up in there. It's already written in the books...you're official! Just fall back, read a book or something." Bible said, getting straight to the point. That's just what type of person he was—straight forward. You wasn't gonna get too much communion with him, he was incapable of sympathizing with people.

"Well, nigga send me something to read," Muscles said. "Some urban novels and magazines."

"I got you, cuz. I was just online checking out some books from this new author, **Pucasso**. He got this one book called **I am...M.O.B.—My Own Boss**, I know you'll find it interesting...I did. I'm gonna make it my business to send you some flicks too, I be forgetting. Don't blame my heart, it's the lack of time I have to execute everything I need to in a day." Bible proclaimed.

Sensing that the coke was done drying, Bible grabbed a digital ruler from the cabinet along with some sandwich bags. He began weighing up all the crack, totaling it out to 260-grams. *Perfect!* he thought to himself.

"I might have to go in on yo' boy Tino." Bible advised Muscles as he began bagging up the quarter-bird, all in ounces.

The Young Jeezy song that was currently playing had mixed over into another one of his greatest hits, *"I'm here now...y'all old news. Gotta couple Porsche trucks, couple old schools. I'll line yo' ass up, push yo' tape backwards. Cause I'm real nigga, and I don't like rappers."* Bible continued dancing around the kitchen, cleaning up the lil' mess he had made.

"Why, what happened?" Muscles asked, figuring already that it had something to do with some money.

"Shit really...nothing that I can't handle. The muthafucka owe me a few dollars and been ducking and dodging me. I ended up running into him at the liquor store with Mac 'nem...that's when he gave me some sorry ass story about how he was down on luck and shit. But the nigga was out popping bottles with my money. I don't know why niggas wanna play with me...he's lucky I didn't sleep his ass, right there!"

Muscles remained quiet on the matter, he knew that it wasn't shit he could say to make Bible think different. "He better hurry up and get me out the way." Bible added as he killed the lights in the kitchen and pimped off to the front room where he had company.

A couple of half-naked dick eaters lounged around on the plushed sectional couch. Bible was shirtless himself, showing off his tattooed body. If you thought Muscles was big then you haven't seen shit. Bible had the form of a "'Marvel Comic" super-hero.

"You gon' be good when you come home, cuz," Bible informed Muscles. "Yo' bit is almost over, everybody's waiting for you to get out."

"I'm already knowing, I can't wait my damn self."

"Yeah...well, stop fucking up the church's money," Bible replied. "Sit yo' ass down somewhere and wait for them people to call yo' name to go home."

Muscles really wasn't trying to hear that soft ass shit. He had become so accustomed to "getting wild" that he hardly knew anything else. Yard line was getting ready to be called, so Muscles went ahead and cut the conversation short. "They're about to run yard, cuzo. I'm gonna reach back out to you in a couple of days."

"You get that bread I wired you, right?" Bible asked, before having to hang up.

"Hell yeah, it almost slipped my mind," Muscles replied. "My fault, love, nigga!"

In all actuality, Muscles loved Bible greatly—even willing to shed blood for him, at the drop of a dime. He was just growing sick and tired of Bible always putting outside muthafuckas before him.

"I'm gonna put something else together for you in a couple weeks," Bible said, while checking out his two guests, all hugged up kissing each other. "Be strong, my nigga...only the strong survives."

"I already know, cuz," Muscles replied. "Be careful and tell the family I said love."

"Alright, bet."

Bible ended the call and tossed his phone right on the floor next to a fully-loaded glock .17 and several stacks of hundred dollar bills wrapped up in rubber bands. He pushed the pause button on the stereo remote, grabbed onto his manhood, and spoke, "I hope you lil' slut bitches ready to do this dick...it damn sure ain't gonna do its self!

Tino was beyond desperate and thirsty, he was into it with money and drastically losing the battle. It was like nothing he did worked. All the plots and schemes he had mapped out was to no avail, janky shit just kept happening.

It was time for Tino to get from behind the steering wheel coaching the play and hop in the passenger seat to finalize the **Lime-Lite** him damn self. Securing a victory was a must—his life depended on it. Shit done got real serious now, Bible was steady on his ass about an unpaid tab and not even Muscles could save Tino from a pair of ten and a half Wheat Timbs being kicked in his face...Bible's.

Bible knew how close Tino and his cousin were and sort of respected it, but that shit only went so far. Bible wanted his bread, and he was gonna come get it—even if that meant taking it in blood. Bible was a man of many principles, one of 'em being... "Let one muthafucka slide and everybody will think they can go ice skating."

Tino haven't had a good night's rest in a long while. Each day, he gets up early to start his bag-chasing journey off. Today was no different. He went on the low-end to snatch his boy, **Ziggy**, up to operate the wheel. Ziggy had wheel and was heavily with the shits.

At this point, Tino was just freelancing trying to come up on a quick lick. I guess his luck had finally took a turn for the better, he ended up coming back across an old lick he had missed out on some time back. It was an ATM money carrier who refilled the machines at all the Marathon gas stations in the south suburbs.

Tino instructed Ziggy to put a discreet tail on the car They followed the man for about 10 or 15-minutes before he pulled up at a Marathon gas station, right off the E-way. The money carrier parked right in front of the gas station's main entrance. Tino had the radio turned off and hadn't even thought about blowing any dope. He was over-focused.

"Alright, bro...pull in on the other side and flip around." Tino said, reaching in the back and grabbing the license plate from out of the rear window.

Tino came back to the front seat and got in position as Ziggy pulled around the gas pumps. Tino saw the man getting ready to hop out. He tapped Ziggy on the arm and layed down the lick, "Let me out right here. Drive real slow so by the time you come back around the car, I'd be done hitting the move. Once I get it, I'm gon' head straight towards the side street over there. That's where you're gonna come and scoop me up at."

The ATM man got out of the car, closing the door and walking into the gas station. Instantly, Tino took flight like a 747 airplane. When he made it to the car, he looked in and seen a duffel bag sitting on the back floor. He busted the window with his bare fist, reached in, and grabbed the bag. Before he took off running, he glanced inside the bag seeing that it was the real deal. *Bingo!* he thought to himself.

Tino's adrenaline was all the way turnt up. Ziggy was making his way around the last pump, coming back towards him. Tino signaled him with his index finger, telling him to slow down for a hot second. He wasn't done turning up yet.

Tino looked in the gas station diligently, seeing nobody coming his way, and then reached through the busted window opening the front passenger door and popping the trunk from the glove box. He went in the trunk and rambled through all sorts of miscellaneous shit until he found another duffel bag filled with money. "Jackpot!" he said to himself.

A man came out of the gas station shouting, "Hey, what are you doing in my car?" He whipped out his phone and began calling the cops.

Tino took off running towards the side street with both duffel bags in his hands, secured tightly. Ziggy followed, slowly pulling out of the gas station parking lot like an innocent customer. When Tino seen the car, he ran up and hopped in it, then Ziggy skirted off—right back onto the E-way. *Easy!*

"Somebody following us?" Tino asked, noticing Ziggy staring through the rearview.

"Nah, we're good!" he answered.

"Did anybody see us hop on the E-way?"

"We're good, bro, "Ziggy replied, while watching Tino pull wads of money from out one of the duffel bags. "It wasn't anybody else at the gas station...we're Gucci!"

Tino reached behind him and put the license plate back in the rear window. "Find a low-key Hotel so we can count up all of this *gwop!*" Tino said proudly, laughing to himself.

Ziggy shared the same vibe as Tino, happy that a lick had finally come through. "How much you think we hit for?" he asked.

Tino did a double take through the bags, trying to eyeball the amount. "We fuck around and got 40-bucks in each bag. I told you that we were gonna get some money today, didn't I, nigga?" he said, cutting the radio on and playing one of his favorite anthems. **"Duffel Bag Boy" by Playa Circle featuring Lil' Wayne,** *"If I don't do nothing, I'ma ball. I'm counting all day like the clock on the wall. Now, go and get yo' money lil' duffel bag boy...Get money!"*

Tino and Ziggy was on "ten" in the car, singing along as they glided up the highway.

When Tino and Ziggy got done counting up all the money from the lick they had tore off, the amount was damn near what Tino had speculated..."Seventy-eight thousand." While Ziggy wasn't paying any attention, Tino had cuffed 15-thousand of it bringing the grand total down to $63,000 for them to chop up amongst themselves.

Tino ended up paying off all of his debts, starting with Bible first. He even threw the big fella a few extra dollars just for the wait. However, Bible wasn't the least bit flattered and still wanted to go in on Tino after he didn't even have the decency to shop with him. Luckily for Tino, Bible left the shit alone and vowed not to ever front him any work again. It didn't matter much to Tino, he planned on taking off from this point on. He copped a half of brick of raw cocaine from A-l's big cousin, Face. He also copped 9-ounces of *dog-food* from one of his cousin's homies.

Tino went on a decent lil' shopping spree, copping all sorts of designers—Gucci, Louie, Ferragamo...you name it. He sent Muscles and A-l some bread too, not much but just enough to make commissary several times. It was more than A-l expected.

Tino pumped his drugs on the low-end, in the projects where Ziggy was from. The flip became so relevant that Tino went back to the store at least twice a week. Him and Ziggy ended up forming a very tight bond. They went up in strip clubs—The Factory, King of Diamonds, and Red-Diamond—showing their asses like famous celebrities do.

Tino may have only been playing with a cool huncho, but he sure in hell made the shit look like he was up a whole mil-ticket. Every bitch in the Wild-Hundreds were on his bumper trying to give him some pussy...even A-1's baby's mother, Sheila. She was one sack chasing ass bitch. I mean, it didn't bother her at all that Tino and A-1 were close friends. If Tino wanted some of that pussy then it was a deal in the makings.

Tino caught her up in Adrianna's one night...it was jumping hard too. **Yo-Gotti** and the **Migos** came through to perform. Tino had on all Burberry, even his underwear. Sheila was all on his dick from the moment they bumped into each other, all the way to the cheap Hotel room he ended up baking her ass in. He broke her off a hot *nick-nack* ($500) and promised her a spot on the winning team...of course, she accepted.

Although A-1 was Tino's main man, Tino didn't believe too much in all that

"L.O.E.," loyalty over everything, bullshit that A-1 was known to preach. Tino figured that if it was him on the other side, a muthafucka would definitely do him the same way—maybe even dirtier. Besides, whatever happened to the saying, *"Check the hoe, not the pimp."*

After a while, Tino went through a zone fucking everybody's girl who got caught out there flirting around with him. He didn't give a flying fuck who their niggas were, blood brothers and all. The game was cold and very unfair, but it was the business he was in.

Tino slid through the Fo' every once in a blue moon to fuck with Mac 'nem, but his days of repping that area was long over with. He had adopted a new land where he was willing to put it on for, the Low-End. He rolled through Washington Heights in a black and yellow, SS-Chevy Camaro on chrome Forgiatos bumpin **Young Thug**... **"Playin' with a check."**

Although Kick-Dough had way more money than Tino, Tino was enjoying himself way more. He had the luxury of not having to worry about the cops on his tail, looking for him for "murder." Tino flew right pass Shoota and his wolves slamming his sounds, not even bothering to honk his horn to acknowledge them.

"That was Tino's bitch ass," Shoota said while watching the Camaro go up the block. "Acting like he don't know a muthafucka."

Shoota was definitely feeling some type of way about the cold-shoulder Tino had just given him. Do-Dirty and one of Shoota's newest lieutenants, Sicko, were standing by with him. They were in search of a decent *gate to jump.*

"Man, fuck him then," Sicko blurted out. "He can get it too!"

"I'm gon' rob that bitch ass nigga," Shoota plotted, out loud. "I just haven't figured out how yet."

Shoota looked over at Do-Dirty who was currently giving him a suggestive look, flitting his eyes over at Sicko who wasn't paying attention to them scheming. *Aha!* A light bulb popped on in Shoota's head, leading him to catch on to what Do-Dirty was insinuating. *I can use Sicko as bait to jump Tino's gate.*

"Let's head back to the spot," Shoota suggested. "We got some preparing to do."

The group of Juvies slid off through a gangway of a residential home, *jumping gates* just to get to where they were going.

CHAPTER #19

SURVIVAL OF THE FITTEST

Stacey came through for A-1 putting him in the car with her best friend, Meko, at a time where it was most needed. Word got back to A-1 quick that Tino was baking his baby mama, Sheila. If A-1 wasn't already done with the lil' heifer, then he was now—altogether.

Meko was a dime-piece, beautiful like the morning sun. She was dark-skinned with long, wavy hair, not to mention also, she had an amazing body from top to bottom. Going to the gym to work out was one of her daily hobbies. The girl was also on top of her business, working hard to climb the ladder of success. She worked a good paying 9-5 job and helped co-run a nonprofit organization that her and Stacey had created, "G.I.R.L.S."

Meko had great ambitions to own her own company one day. She had a young daughter whose father was nothing more than a deadbeat dad. It didn't matter much to Meko other than the fact that she wanted her daughter, Sadie, to have a relationship with her father. Besides that, she couldn't care less about the fucker. She held shit down without his help or the government's. Hassling a nigga about help was so beneath her, she had too much class for that.

Long story short, Meko was a real woman and was in search for a "Hood Hero" to take on the world with. She had communicated with A-1 several times over the phone, before actually considering coming to see him. A-1 was delighted to swap out a woman who meant him no good, with a gorgeous lady who had a pair of wings and a halo…a Superwoman, one would say.

A-1 was up early, doing a few hundred push-ups in the cell, when a C/O came by to advise him that he had a visit.

"Damn, shawty," C-Lord said, leaning over looking off the top bunk at A-1. "Who that is you're about to go up on the dance floor to see."

"My new bitch," A-1 replied as he gathered his shower shit. "It's time for me to perform."

"What happened to Sheila?"

"Out with the old and in with the new, my nigga."

"I hear you," C-Lord said as he went back to reading "**Big Bertha— The Head-Hunter,**" written by an incarcerated author named **Pucasso**. "Just make sure you put me in the car with one of her buddies, shawty."

"The right way,"

A-1 fell into the visiting room looking so fresh and so clean. Well, at least as much as he could being locked down in Cook County Jail. He had on some Gucci chucks with matching lenses, and his hair was cut and lined precisely. Although he was fighting a natural life sentence, he still had an amazing swag.

When Meko seen A-1 stepping through the door, immediately, her pussy got wet. She had on a multicolored, Vera Wang blouse with her back hanging out; some Balenciaga fitted jeans showing off her curvy figure; and a pair of Ferragamo sandals with her toenails painted the same color of her shirt. Her hair was flat ironed into an immaculate wrap that had a fabulous bounce to it. All eyes were on her as if she was Nicki Minaj or Cardi B. She carried a small Ferragamo handbag and had on the belt to match.

A-1 spotted the sophisticated looking woman and came to realize that she was actually there to see him. *Damn, she's bad!* he thought to himself as he walked up to the stall—thankful as can be.

"Hey there," Meko said, smiling.

A-1 just took moment to examine the supermodel. "I'm sorry...I got caught up in your beauty. Hey, how are you doing?" he said, finally snapping into mode.

"I'm good," Meko responded humbly. "How about yourself?"

"It couldn't be more better for me right now at this moment." A-1 said, bringing a lil' laughter to the occasion. "Kick-Dough told me you were fine, but clearly that's an understatement...you're magnificent!"

A-1's remark put a Kool-Aid smile on Meko's face. "Why thank you, handsome. It's safe to say that you're a hunk yo'self, all cut up and shit. I see you Vin Diesel." she said while staring at A-1 biceps. They were bulging up out of his D.O.C. shirt.

Noticing Meko's eyes were mesmerized by the circumference of his arms, A-1 flexed them around as he talked. "I'm fair for a square, but you on the other hand..."

A-1 took a slight pause to lick his lips, LL Cool-J style. He was elated by Meko's presence. "Do me a favor, would you?" he said.

"And what is that?"

"Could you please, stand up and display that wonderful body of yours again for me?" A-1 had a couple of homies in the visiting room and he wanted them to see the eye candy he was working with.

"Sure, boss," Meko replied as she got up and spun around in a circle.

The entire visiting room eyes were stuck on Meko's glorious sculpture.

"Damn!" they said, altogether. Most of the detainees were there with their girlfriends, but that didn't stop them from "sightseeing." If A-1 wasn't the man already, this surely clarified it completely.

Meko gave a short bow to the convicts that applaud her presence and then sat back down. "If I do that again, it better be a whole bunch of money being thrown at me afterwards." she joked.

A-1 stared at Meko, biting down on his bottom lip as if he was thinking about clapping her. "I have to ask...why you ain't gotta man?" he asked, assuming there had to be a catch.

"Most men can't handle a woman like me," she explained. "Or should I say...know how to treat me the way I deserve to be treated."

"You make the shit sound hard or something," A-1 responded.

"Well, if you call pampering me all day with pure love and affection and fucking me good at night hard, then I don't know what to tell you."

"Who, me...you don't have to tell me *nathan* about how to please a woman, I do the damn thang." A-1 said, setting the record straight.

Meko couldn't help but smile, seductively. "Oh, is that right!" she replied.

"Mandatory!"

It was quite obvious that A-1 and Meko were feeling each other. A-1 liked Meko's open personality and enjoyed the way she expressed herself. He respected her ambitions in life and how hard she went for Sadie. He definitely needed her on his team as the head captain, running point.

Meko was feeling the vibe A-1 brought to the table as well. She honored how strong he was mentally, being in a life battling situation and still able to keep a smile on his face...not letting his current circumstances take control and get the best of him. She valued his company and cherished every word that came out of his mouth, he was very articulate.

A-1 was anything above petty, willing to give even if it meant him having to go without. Meko wanted him just as much as he needed her. It was just one thing she had to be clear about before going any further.

"Look, I'll never be number two," she began breaking the shit down to A-1. "And I'm a boss by myself so teaming up with you is more of an emotional need than physical."

A-1 just nodded his head, in full compliance with what she was saying. "I honor everything you've been saying 100%. Since I walked up in this visiting room, you had my undivided attention, and that's how we plan to keep it from here on out, right?" he stated, real silky.

"Mandatory!" she replied while rubbing her palms together, copying his infamous swag.

A-1 broke out in laughter, and Meko joined in sharing the moment with him. The two up-and-coming "lovebirds" went on to enjoy the rest of their visit, conversating about all sorts of shit. They were a match made in heaven.

Tom and Jerry were top-flight cops that got real involved in the streets. They were known for doing everything in their powers just to warrant an arrest. One time they crawled through Tino's house window while him and some more guys were parlaying, and raided the place without even having a search warrant. They confiscated several firearms and some drugs. Although the charges didn't stick, they were highly commended for getting some guns and drugs off the streets.

From day one, coming up out of the academy, Tom and Jerry had been making a name for themselves fighting hard against the war on crime in the city of Chicago. Their arrest list goes on and on, coming to collar some of the most notorious criminals in the Wild-Hundreds. These definitely weren't the kind of cops you wanted on your bumper.

Steve Murphy, *a.k.a.* "Tom," and Jimmy Miller, *a.k.a.* "Jerry," were best friends and damn good partners. Most of all, they were family looking out for each other—on and off the clock. Tom, a heavyset white *muthafucka*, operated the wheel while Jerry, a short-slimmed white *muthafucka*, rode shotgun ready to hop out and hawk a nigga down.

It was no getting away from this dynamic duo. Tom drove like a NASCAR race driver, and Jerry ran as fast as a cheetah. If these rogue cops were to ever get on your tail, your best bet would be to try to blow 'em down...real talk!

Now, every time Tom and Jerry flipped through the Fo', all the shooters went into hiding—even the ones on the basketball courts. They weren't fucking around one bit. They crept up through the alley and came out, whipping up right in front of Mac and his gang.

"Hey there, Mac Mann," Tom said, talking from out the window of his squad car. "I haven't seen you around here in a while, where the hell you been...on vocation or something?"

Tom had one hand on the steering wheel and the other one outside of the window, holding onto the roof of the car. This was his signature position while driving. Jerry didn't even bother to bail out, though he had his door slightly cracked. This was his signature move as well. Just in case he had to jump out and chase a nigga, he'll already be in motion. Nobody attempted to make a run for it though, they knew the drill.

"We ain't on shit, Tom," Mac pleaded his innocence, "Just out here enjoying the nice weather, see..."

Mac lifted his shirt up, showing Tom and Jerry that he didn't have any weapons on him. The rest of Mac's crew followed suit as well.

"Good-good," Tom replied. "I like to see a safe community, I must say."

Tom hardly bothered to look Mac directly in the face, he just let his eyes flit around the area carefully, examining like a watchdog.

"Who's the lil' fucker steady shooting shit up around here?" Tom asked.

"What's his name...Shoota, what's his problem?"

Mac just turned his head aside and played deaf. Although he had grown a strong dislike for the renegade, snitching on him never crossed his mind. It was a rhetorical question, Tom was just being funny as usual. He wasn't looking for any information, he actually came through to send a message.

"I hear Kee-Kee's about to get released from prison soon," Tom said, speaking about Muscles. "A lot of folks waiting to get revenge on that black fucker."

Mac and his squad just listen attentively as Tom spoke aggressively, "Look, you tell that son of a bitch that if he comes back to this neighborhood on the same nonsense he was on back in the days, I'm gon' personally put a slug in the back of his head my damn self."

Tom began waving his glock .17 around in the air carelessly while foaming at the mouth like a ferocious pitbull. "In case you lil' punks forgot, we're the biggest and most baddest gang in Chiraq...Blue Flames, muthafuckas—remember the name!"

Tom was out to send a warning to Muscles. He had caused the two seasoned cops and the rest of the department hell while he was coming up as a teenager. "Oh and yeah, tell K-D I said what's up...I'm trying to get put in the Lime-Lite. Take care, gentlemen." Tom said as he tilted his head and put his feet on the gas.

"They're gone!" Mac shouted out, towards the back of the house.

Seconds later, Sco came skipping from out the gangway with two blickers in his hands. He handed one over to Mac and tucked away the other.

"Man, Mac...if Jerry would've hopped out and came searching on the side of the house, I would of had to blow him down." Sco claimed.

Mac was beginning to feel like it just might be a good time to leave the hood—for good!

The Juvies didn't give a fuck about too much of shit, let alone some old-fashioned ass cops who were on a constant hunt to try to disarm them and have 'em thrown in the can. If the cops wanted them, they would have to just bring it on. Shoota had no problems with taking straight off on Jerry's old ass. Although Jerry had the legs of a greyhound, Shoota did also and he was more familiar with all of the cuts in the hood. The whole district would have to box him in to catch him...let him tell it.

Do-Dirty, Sicko, and Shoota were all chilling on Ray-Ray's porch when a maroon Ford Taurus flipped the block. The three Juvies were in the middle of scheming as the car got close up on them, becoming noticeable. Once the gang peeped the move, the vehicle and who were actually inside it, they knew it was a scrimmage.

Jerry bailed out the car before it even got a good chance to stop. All three of the Juvies hit the porch's banister simultaneously, falling on one another as the landed on the ground. Immediately, they took off running down the side of the house to the back where the alley was. Jerry hurried up and put some speed on his legs, gaining in close on their asses.

Shoota was ahead of the pack, sprinting like a gold medal Olympic runner. Do-Dirty was in the back trying to keep up with Sicko, who was in the middle enjoying the chase. All of 'em were strapped up like high-top Air Force Ones.

Tom didn't bother getting out of the car, he just punched it down the block trying' to cut them off in the alley. The hunt was on. "They kept straight through the backyard, going towards Green Street." Jerry chirped, through his Motorola. Tom skipped coming through the alley and headed straight for Green.

Shoota swung around the front of the house that he was running along side, doing a 180° turn from going east bound—back to west bound on the other side of the house. Sicko followed suit as well, but Do-Dirty's slow dragging ass chose to keep running straight, continuing going east bound. Jerry was gaining in good on him, chasing him right into the back seat of the police car Tom was whipping...at least that was the design play. Do-Dirty knew that much; however, he had gotten caught up in the moment of "getting little." He had a 40-cal on him, cocked with one in the chamber—ready to blow.

Seeing Tom speeding up the block coming in his direction, Do-Dirty decided to run northbound down Green to avoid getting trapped in between the cop on foot and his partner who was in the car—flying like a bat out of hell. Tom slammed on the brakes as Do-Dirty shot by him. He threw the car into reverse and then began chasing Do-Dirty while driving backwards.

Jerry was gaining in on Do-Dirty's tail. Do-Dirty seen shit was getting real so he sidestepped down the side of another residential home, trying to get some distance in between him and the cops so he could toss his weapon without either one of them seeing. He pulled it from off his hip and slung it like a Frisbee, on top of a roof before Jerry could turn the corner.

Do-Dirty kept it moving towards the alley and then ran down it, still heading north bound. "He's continuing moving north bound through the alley." Jerry chirped, once again.

Tom dropped the gear back into drive and punched it around the corner. He came up the alley moving like a rocket. Do-Dirty was all out of breath, he started to slow down figuring it was no need to keep running any more—he had gotten rid of the pistol.

Jerry moved in closer with his weapon drawn, pointed at the back of Do-Dirty's skull. "Freeze! Put your hands up high where I can see them and get down on the ground right.now!" he warned.

Do-Dirty stopped dead in his tracks seeing that Tom was right in front of him also, bailing out with his weapon in hand. "Get down on the ground, muthafucka, or it's barbeque for yo' ass!" Tom threatened the boy.

Do-Dirty eased his hands up and dropped down to his knees. Jerry came up from behind him, withdrawing his weapon, and slapped the cuffs on his wrists. Jerry searched him thoroughly while he was on the ground.

"What's your reason for running youngblood?" Jerry asked, as he pulled Do-Dirty from off the ground.

Tom walked up putting his gun away and flamed up a cigar. Do-Dirty was out of breath and could hardly say anything. "I think I gotta warrant." he replied, damn near about to cough up a lung.

"That's all them damn blunts you've been smoking," Tom said, blowing cigar smoke in Do-Dirty's face. "You know that shit can kill you, don't you?"

Do-Dirty was still wheezing a bit, trying to catch his breath. "You're not a very good runner. Now, your cousin Kee-Kee...that black muthafucka can sprint for miles. I miss hawking his ass down." Jerry said.

"Speaking of Kee-Kee, I hear he's about to get out soon." Tom intervened. He grabbed Do-Dirty by the arm and escorted him to the back seat of the squad car.

"I'm about to go back track his steps," Jerry informed Tom. "See what all I come up with."

Tom didn't pay his partner too much attention, he just waved his hand up in the air signaling him to go right ahead as he shoved Do-Dirty into the car. Do-Dirty began to sweat bullets, clearly fronting his shit, and Tom seen it. He punched Do-Dirty's government name into his computer's database and ran a quick check.

"David Donaldson, Jr...looks like you're not wanted for anything," Tom said, looking in the back seat at Do-Dirty. "Come on, tell me the real reason why you were running from us."

Do-Dirty just looked lost while Tom kept running off at the mouth, "I already know why Shoota was moving like a raging bull...it ain't a secret, that boy keep a gun on him like he does his dick. And that other nigga...what's his name?"

Do-Dirty remained quiet. "Whatever his name is, I hear he's moving up in rank these days, possibly taking over your slot soon." Tom said, trying to play mind games on Do-Dirty's brain. Do-Dirty knew better though, he refrained from feeding into the bullshit.

Tom just let the matter be, switching the subject a bit. "You had a gun on you, didn't you?" he asked. Do-Dirty was mute.

"If you tell me right now, I might can help you."

When Jerry came back from the search with the chromy object, Do-Dirty couldn't help but drop his head in his lap. *Fuck!* he thought to himself.

"I knew it was a gun." Tom said, giggling.

Jerry hopped in the car and Tom punched the gas again. Do-Dirty was on his way to another personal photo shoot.

Muscles wasn't out the hole for a month and already was on the verge of catching some good ol' wreck. Classifications ended up replacing his current celly, which was one of the guys, with a straight bug named **Cock-Strong.** Right off back, Muscles didn't like the nigga. Cock-Strong's vibe and movements were off beat. Immediately, Muscles put him on "no-talk" to try to avoid having to stomp a mud hole out of his ass.

Muscles was cuurently in the process of trying to restore the loss of good time he had jagged off earlier in his bid. He had caught multiple charges of assaults—on staff and inmates. A new law was about to go into effect, which could push him right out the door—immediately. The big fella wanted parts in that.

Washington Heights needed his presence, especially the Fo' Block. A lot of beef had been transpiring throughout the land among the shorties, and it was said that Muscles was the only one capable of settling the war. His new cellie was testing his patience though, and it was only so much he could take before going off again, catching more set-time.

Cock-Strong wasn't some lil' nigga he could just push around though. He was just as swole as Muscles was and bench pressed a similar amount, maybe even more. The rumor throughout the joint was that Cock-Strong had them hands. He was currently locked up for a beat down murder he had caught on an off-duty cop.

However, Muscles was the least bit flattered. All the rumors and gossip that went around...he never cared about. His buttons were being pushed, and for every action there's a reaction. Cock-Strong couldn't of known exactly what he was getting himself into...nitpicking with a straight savage.

Now, Muscles had given Cock-Strong fair warning about having respect for him while he rested his eyes. However, Cock-Strong continued to be inconsiderate about the matter, seeming to take Muscles for a joke. Muscles patience had ran to its limit, he had enough anger and rage in him to tear Cock-Strong's body apart. He hopped up off his bunk and threw on his state boots. It was "go-time." If Cock-Strong did have hands, the occasion was set for him to show and prove.

Cock-Strong slid back into the cell, talking loudly and leaving the door wide open. Muscles walked past him, going to the door and closing it.

"Ay, buddy," Muscles said, aggressively. "You must think I'ma bitch?" Muscles had his fist balled up tightly and was standing in combat formation. Cock-Strong was bent over digging in his property box, searching for something to eat. He stood up and turned around, seeing Muscles *suited* and *booted.*

"What you mean...'*I must think you a bitch*'?" Cock-Strong replied, while taking guard, "You must think I'ma bitch, approaching me sideways."

Cock-Strong tossed the few wet-packs he had grabbed out his box on his bunk, assuming some action was about to take place. "I done told you once already about breaking my sleep with all that running back and forth, in and out of the cell, hooting and hollering shit." Muscles said as he sized up Cock-Strong's jaw.

"Man, I'm not about to be tiptoeing around this bitch while you play sleep all fucking morning." Cock-Strong responded. "It's two muthafuckas living in this cell...you got me fucked up!"

"Nah, you got me fucked up if you think I'm gon' continue to go for this shit. I'ma slam yo' ass through the ceiling if you keep playing crazy in here, nigga!" Muscles warned.

Muscles really didn't want to talk, he was just getting in position to fully take off on Cock-Strong. He debated for a split second about what hand to strike with first, the left or right one. Both of them shits were lethal and considered "iron fist." Either one could easily put Cock-Strong down on his back pockets.

Cock-Strong must of thought he had one to go back and forth with, arguing and shit. Low-key, he tried using intimidation tactics on Muscles…flexing his muscles around while he talked. Little did he know, Muscles was above the bullshit and games.

"So, what you're saying then," Cock-Strong asked, assuming that Muscles would back down. "What you wanna do?"

"*PECK-PECK!*" Muscles took right off with a two-piece combo, cracking Cock-Strong dead in the mouth and nose. The impact sounded like a couple stacks of hardcover books had fallen off a shelf and smacked against a solid floor.

Cock-Strong was dazed a bit but hardly shaken up. He countered with a few punches of his own, striking Muscles on the side of his face. However, the shit felt like pillows to Muscles. He side stepped to the right and threw an ugly right upper-cut to Cock-Strong's chin. *"CRACK!"*

Cock-Strong felt his jawbone shift to the side. He stumbled forward almost falling until he caught ahold of Muscles shirt. Muscles punched him in the eye with the left—instantly, closing it.

Cock-Strong couldn't help but try to wrestle around with Muscles since he failed trying to stand up with him. He got low and tried snatching Muscles up off his feet, but Muscles got low right with him.

Although Muscles wasn't much a wrestler, he managed pulling off a few moves.

Cock-Strong ended up throwing Muscles in a bear hug position, squeezing him as tight as he possibly could. Muscles tried to power his way up out of it, but the hold was well-fastened...like a new born baby in their mother's arms. Muscles was impatient, tired of being enclosed by Cock-Strong. His adrenaline began rushing like the classic album by **Twista**. He needed to see some blood—ASAP.

Muscles glanced at Cock-Strong's face, lining it up for some kind of attack. He thought about head-butting him, busting the fuckers head wide open, but passed on the shit considering that he could fuck his head up just as well. He felt the urge to turn his savage up all the way—pitbull style.

Without any further delays, Muscles opened his mouth, showing off his sharp choppers, and sank them down onto Cock-Strong's nose. He pierced into his skin deeply, locking his jaw onto it as tight as the bear hug Cock-Strong had him in. Once he got one of Cock-Strong's nostrils secure in his mouth, he snatched back on it, ripping it straight off of Cock-Strong's face. "*Yum-Yum!*"

Immediately, Cock-Strong let go of Muscles and grabbed ahold of his face, screaming like a lil' bitch. "Oh, my God...you're a monster! You just ate my nose." he cried.

The sight of blood squirting out from Cock-Strong's snout was very satisfying to Muscles' eyes. However, his appetite wasn't quite fulfilled...not just yet. The ferocious fighter had a bite more on his plate.

"Bitch ass nigga," Muscles said, after spitting the chewed up nostril back at Cock-Strong smacking him dead in the forehead with it. "There you go."

Muscles began throwing a number of blows to Cock-Strong's face, knocking him down to the floor. People started to gather around the cell, peeping through the door at the fight. Blood was everywhere—on the floor, on Muscles, and of course, all over Cock-Strong.

Muscles dragged Cock-Strong's long body up out the cell and brought him to the dayroom. Bystanders made a hole as Muscle came through the hallway. Once he made it to the middle of the gallery, he flipped Cock-Strong on his stomach. Everybody stood around, watching diligently eager to see what Muscles was about to do next.

Muscles stared around at the crowd of individuals who were looking at him as if he was a gorilla at the zoo. Blood was on his mouth, hands, and boots. He reached over and snatched Cock-Strong's pants down to his ankles, spreaded his butt-cheeks, and spat in his ass. *Get that butt!*

Spitting in someone's ass was a symbolic message, showing total disrespect for the victim and labeling them as a great embarrassment to his organization as well as to himself. You had to be a "savage" to understand.

"Get down on the ground," officers shouted at Muscles, threatening to spray him with mace. "Get down, right now!"

Muscles just stood there in a zone, with Cock-Strong's bloody body slumped underneath his foot.

CHAPTER #20

LAY DOWN

Being that Do-Dirty had a background for getting caught up on multiple weapons charges, the judge set his bond at $100,000(d). That meant he had to come up with 10% of that to make bail. Without a doubt, he didn't have that kind of money and neither did anyone in his clique. His big cousin, Bible, was done bonding muthafuckas out of jail and not being reimbursed. He often told his lil' cousins to put money up for bond and attorney fees, but they would rather blow their dough on meaningless things.

The pressure fell all on Shoota to get his top lieutenant up out of jail. He had to come up with some kind of plan to make that happen. Trying to sell some coke was out of the question, Shoota wasn't a hustler of that kind. He didn't have the patience of waiting on hand-to-hand transactions, he would rather jump a gate for the cause.

Shoota already had his eyes set on a striking prospect—Tino. Now was the time for him to put the lick together and in motion. Money was real funny, something had to give...Do-Dirty's freedom depended on it.

Tino was just a sweet lick waiting to be taken down. Shoota and Sicko was in a Chevy Tahoe riding with a nigga called **"Bam."** Bam was a lame who just wanted to be down. Shoota and Sicko was just using him for a ride. They both were strapped up, and I'm not talking about seat belts.

Bam flipped through Washington Heights, from block to block, looking for a black and yellow SS-Chevy Camaro. "There he go, right there!" Shoota blurted out, pointing down Peoria Street.

A Novel by Pucasso

The trick was to have Bam slide up on Tino with Sicko riding shotgun, trying to cop a *Halsted* (63-grams of coke) from him. Being that Tino had an extensive background for gun charges, he refrained from keeping the blicker on him while just strolling the land. The threat of him trying to defend himself against the Juvies' ruthless attack was minimum…Shoota figured out that much.

They had to find a way to get close up on Tino without being looked at as a threat. Shoota planned to lay low in back of the truck. Just the sight of his face could very well raise Tino's suspicion level, which could blow the whole lick.

Tino was parallel-parked, rolling up some dope, when the Tahoe pulled up on him. Sicko had the window down trying to holler at him. "Ay, Tino," he said, signaling for Tino to roll down his window.

Tino didn't know too much about Sicko other than the fact that he was a JRW. It was a time when nobody wouldn't even dare try to rob Tino, he was Washington Heights' most feared shooter. After being shot multiple times, Tino began slowing his road. His reputation became less frightening, some would say. None of that really didn't matter much anyway. It was a new day of age, and these young muthafuckas was of a generation where there was no honor amongst killers. Muthafuckas were straight cutthroats.

Tino rolled his window down to see what the hell Sicko wanted. "What's up, shawty?" he said while finishing rolling up his blunt.

Really, Tino wasn't taking any sides in the beef going on between the BROs and JRWs. All he ever cared about was running up a check. And of course…fucking other niggas' bitches.

"You got some weight on the cola?" Sicko asked. "My cousin right here trying to cop a Halsted to go back out of town with."

Tino wasn't bought just yet, the shit seem a bit fishy to him. *Why they just didn't go to Bible?* he thought to himself.

"I don't wanna send him to Bible," Sicko explained. "You know he be taxing shit."

Tino antennas went down. If it was a hit, he figured he would've been dead by now. If they came to jump his gate, all they would get is a band or two—nothing worth losing his life over. He was safe as far as he seen it.

"Shit...I need 25-hundred for the shit I got," Tino advised Sicko. "It's some glass."

Tino bailed out the car, putting a spark to his blunt.

"That sounds cool," Sicko replied. "Hold up, let us pull over."

Sicko directed Bam to park the truck, he didn't want to run the risk of Tino walking up on the truck and spotting Shoota lurking with the stick in the back. Tino stood by his car while Bam parked the truck. Him and Sicko hopped out, leaving Shoota on "lurk mode."

"What they call you, homie?" Tino asked Bam as he shook up with him and passed him the blunt.

Sicko looked at Bam, letting him know through his facial expression to not give up his real name.

"B," Bam responded.

"B, huh," Tino reiterated. "Where you from, B?"

"Shit, I'm from the burbs, but I be all through the city, busting juggs." Bam said.

"What was the ticket on this bumble-bee?" Sicko asked, trying to switch subjects.

"When I first copped it, they wanted 35-bucks. I dropped a salt-buck and within a week, brought them another salt. Now, I only owe 15 on it."

Bam passed Sicko the blunt. He took it and slid towards the Camaro, examining it up close. "This bitch is wet as fuck. What made you get it in this color though?"

"Shit...everybody already had the black and red joint," Tino stated, looking over towards the Chevy Tahoe. "I just wanted to be different."

While examining the Tahoe, Tino noticed the back door opening up. Sicko peeped the move and drew his weapon to execute on the moment. When Tino turned back around to look at Sicko, all he could see was darkness—down the barrel of a P89.

"Get yo' muthafucking hands up high in the air," Sicko demanded. "Right where I can see them."

"What's going on, Sicko?" Tino asked while throwing his hands up, complying with Sicko's orders. "I don't want no smoke."

"Shut the fuck up and just do as I say," Sicko responded, ruthlessly. "Lay down on the fucking ground."

Finally, Shoota exited the truck and made his grand appearance on the scene. He had his dreads french-braided to the back, and walked like a coldblooded murderer—with the stick in his hand. "This ain't about you, T. This is just a simple jack-move. I'm in a tight position and need some finances, this is my only way out." he said, aiming the blicker at Tino's face.

Tino dropped to the ground praying to God not to get smoked over some petty cash. Shoota got right in mode, this was the very moment he had plotted for. He signaled for Bam to go and pat Tino down. Sicko just took guard with his pistol aimed directly at the back of Tino's skull. Bam grabbed a wad of money out of Tino's pockets, along with his car keys.

"Okay, y'all got what y'all wanted, now let me go." Tino plead. "I'm not even tripping over the shit...it is what it is."

"Shut the fuck up before I smoke yo' top just for the hell of it." Shoota warned Tino.

"Sicko, "Shoota called his lieutenant, giving him a command. "Get his keys and pop his trunk."

Bam tossed the keys to Sicko and waited patiently for any direct orders given out by Shoota.

"Give me yo' keys," Shoota commanded Bam, handing him his stick. "Here, guard him good. If the fucker make the slightest move, tap the trigger a few times."

Shoota walked up on Tino and snatched him up off the ground. "Get yo' bitch ass up...it's time to put this show on the road." he instructed Tino.

Tino stood up looking helpless. Shoota escorted him to the back of his Camaro where Sicko was guarding him also at gunpoint. The trunk was already opened up wide.

"What's going on," Tino asked, fearfully. "Where are you taking me?"

"Nah...the real question you should be asking is how much money we need to spare yo' life." Shoota said. "This shit is just business, not personal. Please, don't leave me to have to blow yo' fucking head off about this lil' money, T."

"I don't have any money, just some work," Tino tried explaining. "I'll give it to you, just please...let me go!"

"We'll see about that, T," Shoota said, heartlessly. "Now, get in the trunk, nigga!"

"I swear I'm telling the truth," Tino continued to plead his case. "Please, don't make me get in the trunk, I'm claustrophobic."

Sicko and Bam both broke out in laughter at Tino's alleged phobia. However, Shoota didn't find shit funny. He went and snatched his gun back from Bam. "Give me this shit, clown ass nigga." Shoota said as he pointed it down at Tino's dick.

"You think this shit's a fucking game," Shoota said, getting very hostile. "If you don't climb yo' ass in this trunk, I'm gon' blow yo' dick off right here and then shove you in it my damn self."

"Alright-alright, I'll get in," Tino agreed. "Just please, don't shoot,"

Tino went ahead and climb his ass into the trunk of his own car. Shoota closed it shut and made sure that it was locked. "Okay, now that the hard part is behind us, let us stand on the business at hand so we can get to the money." Shoota stated.

"Who's gonna come off the bread for him?" Bam asked.

"Ziggy!" Sicko answered, feeling good that the lick was coming together.

"My guess, Kick-Dough," Shoota assumed. "That's how we're gonna get the full amount."

"What's the ticket we're asking for?" Sicko asked.

"A cool huncho!" Shoota hastened to reply.

"You think they gonna come off that much money for him?" Bam asked.

Shoota looked over at Sicko, who was already counting unhatched eggs in his head, and then placed his eyes back on Bam. "Shit...they better, or they won't ever see him again—not alive!" Shoota said, tucking his blicker away and picking the blunt up off the ground that Sicko had dropped. It was still lit.

Shoota took a pull off the blunt and began giving out orders. "Sicko...get the Camaro and follow us. Come on Bam, let's get outta here."

The Juvies hopped into the vehicles and then took off. The Tahoe first, then the bumble-bee.

Shoota pulled the Tahoe up in an alley and parked it into an abandoned garage in a secluded area, over east. Sicko pulled the Camaro up right beside him. Shoota knew the area quite well, this was one of his aunt's stomping grounds. He bailed out the truck with the 30 out in his hand, then Bam and last, Sicko. They all crowded up around in back of the Camaro, getting back in character before popping the trunk.

Kidnapping someone for ransom money was a lot more complex than just jumping a gate. Really, this was a big boy's sport that Shoota and his squad had gotten involved in…Shoota had never taken part in this type of action before.

Sicko tossed the keys back to Bam, commanding him to pop the trunk. Shoota and Sicko had their weapons drawn, aimed directly at the trunk when Bam popped it open. Tino rose up from it looking terrified. The shit done went from looking like a potential drug sell to death—possibly.

"Please, don't kill me. I'll give you anything you want," Tino began begging for his life again. "Just please, spare my life afterwards."

Being stuck in the trunk for a short while got Tino straight in compliance to what was going on. He seen clearly that the shit was real. Hearing Tino comply was sweet music to Shoota's ears. He signaled for Bam to give him back his phone, which he had confiscated from him when he patted him down.

"Our so-called big homie is about to put us on, big time," Shoota said, giving Tino a grim stare. "Ain't that's right, T?"

Tino just bowed his head as Bam handed him the phone. *How did I let these lil muthafuckas catch me with my ass out and head in the ground?* he thought to himself.

"Listen up, my nigga," Shoota said while tapping Tino on the shoulder with his pistol. "I'm not about to be sitting here all night going back and forth with you about this and that. I need that duffel bag—boy...and I prefer to have it handed over to me in a timely fashion."

Shoota wasn't playing, Tino seen that clearly from the way he talked and how he looked. "It's only gon' be so long before I say the hell with the shit and just pull the trigger, leaving the top of yo' head all smokey like a chimney. You can try my patience if you want, but I warn you...them shit's short." Shoota advised Tino.

Shoota got real close up on Tino and demanded him to followed the instructions he was giving, "Now, get on the phone and call somebody who got a whole bunch of money and really loves you. I need a hundred-thou' for yo' life, my nigga!"

"A hundred-thou'," Tino replied, looking shocked. "I don't know anybody who'll come off that amount for me."

"Come on now, Kick-Dough walk around with that kind of cash in his pockets." Shoota said, waving his weapon carelessly at Tino as he spoke. "It'll be nothing for him to come get you."

Tino couldn't help but flinch at the sight of Shoota's stick as he continued waving it in his face. "I swear I'm not bullshitting you. Yeah, Kick-Dough's holding, but he don't fuck with me at all...Hell, I don't even have his number." he claimed.

"Well, who's gonna be the one to come to your rescue then because if I don't get the ransom soon, it's off with your head. You only got one chance to get it right." Shoota informed Tino.

"I can call Ziggy and get 10 or 15-bucks maybe, but a hundred thousand dollars is way out of my reach." Tino claimed.

Shoota looked over at Sicko frustratedly, in need of a lil' aid and assist. Sicko caught his cue and put it on thick for the cameras. "Man, fuck this shit...let's just smoke this nigga and go snatch up his homie, Ziggy. That's our mil-ticket there!"

What in the world have I gotten myself into? Bam thought to himself. It was quite apparent that Shoota and Sicko was prepared to kill in the event of getting what they wanted.

"Don't shoot until I give you the okay." Shoota commanded Sicko.

Sicko was squeezing the gun handle tightly, eager to fire off some shots. "No-no-no, please...don't do it, Sicko. I swear I'm telling the truth!" Tino cried out like a lil' bitch.

"Nigga, stop the crying and hop on the phone and call Ziggy—right now!" Shoota checked Tino. "Tell him if he don't come off 50 stacks within the next 30-minutes, the WGN News headlines are gonna read, *"Man Down, found dead—shot execution style twisted up in his own trunks."*

Tino wasted no time, hopping on the phone and calling Ziggy up. "What's up, T?" Ziggy answered.

"Ziggy, listen...I need you, bro," Tino said. "My life depends on how fast you move, I've been snatched up and being held for ransom."

"Get the fuck out of here," Ziggy replied. "Who's playing crazy like that?"

Tino looked up at Shoota and Sicko whom were both pointing their weapons directly at his face. "Man, bro...that's not important right now. They want 50-bands in exchange for me." Tino said.

"50-thousand," Ziggy blurted out, loudly. "Man, T...I don't even got half of that."

"You gotta make it happen somehow, or otherwise, I'm a dead man."

"I got about 18-bucks on hand and a gang of work." Ziggy responded.

Tino delivered the amount to Shoota, and that's when the young menace turnt up a notch—putting on a show just for good measures. Shoota took ahold of the butt of his gun and smacked Tino in the face with it. "*CRACK!*" The impact of the gun handle going upside Tino's face made a gruesome sound. Ziggy heard clearly what was going on through the phone.

"Aww—fuck...what was that for, man?" Tino cried out while holding onto his face with both of his hands. He had dropped his phone in the trunk.

Once he finally got himself back together, opening his eyes completely, Shoota had his gun pointed at the center of his forehead, ready to blow if necessary. "Shut the fuck up and pick the phone back up!" he demanded.

At this point, Tino was all shook up. Survival was the only thing that mattered to him.

"Tino, what happen," Ziggy asked, worried about his boy. "Are you still there?"

"Yeah, man...I'm still here," Tino answered, angrily. "But I don't know for how long if you don't come up with that tab."

"Okay, just tell me what to do when I get the money." Ziggy said.

Tino delivered the message to Shoota. Shoota got up close to Tino and borrowed his ear, telling him exactly what he needed him to tell Ziggy, "Tell him that he done wasted enough of our time already. The shit almost got you killed. Playtime is over...the next step I'm gonna take is gon' be fatal if he don't come up with the dough...Tell him he got 20-minutes to do just that. Bring the bread to the Shell's gas station on 79th and the Dan Ryan."

Tino informed Ziggy on what all he needed to do to get him back alive.

"Oh yeah, tell him to come alone," Shoota added. "And getting the cops involved would only make matters worse."

Shoota put his gun's muzzle up to Tino's forehead, pressing it against it, letting him know that he meant business. Tino got the message back to Ziggy and he got right on top of it, trying to save his homie from being *another one dead and gone.*

Ziggy came up as close to 50-thousand dollars as he possibly could, within a 20-minute time frame. He probably could of gathered up more cash if he had more time, he didn't want to risk his homey getting hurt or may be even killed over him taking his time to run the bread. He had 18-bucks that he put towards the ransom, Mac and his crew came off a salt buck, and Tino's baby mama, Tasha, dropped a knick-knack.

The grand total came out to 33-bands, plus Ziggy threw in 9-ounces with the cash just to insure his homey's survival. He really wanted his mans to come up out the jam alive and unharmed. He gave all he had not even worrying about if Tino had it to pay back.

Ziggy made it to the demanded location in a matter of a hour and called Tino's phone. "Yeah, you got it?" Tino answered, desperately. Shoota was there right in front of him along with Sicko, both of 'em still pointing their guns at Tino.

Bam was already making his way towards the Shell's gas station to pick up the ransom money.

"Yeah, I got it," Ziggy replied. "I'm up here at the gas station...where y'all at, bro?"

"He said he's up there with the cash." Tino informed Shoota.

"Tell him to just sit tight for a minute, somebody's on the way to get the money." Shoota responded. "And once he make it there, you will give him a call, and we'll go from there." Tino delivered the message and then ended the call.

"Seems like there's muthafuckas out there who do love you." Shoota said, standing tall with a smirk planted on his baby-face. He was just eagered to get his hands on the pot of gold.

Tino held his head down thinking about what he was gonna do to the lil' bastard if he somehow comes out of this situation alive. He contemplated taking it back to the days when everybody in the hood used to call him *"T-Murder."* He used to slay shit back then. If these lil' muthafuckas knew what was best for them, they'd kill him as soon as they get the money.

Bam pulled up in the gas station, parked, and dialed up Sicko. "What's up?" Sicko answered, immediately.

"I'm up here," Bam informed him. "I see a few cars parked, which one is it?" Sicko updated Shoota with the news.

"Tell him to sit tight and hold fast, right quick," Shoota commanded, looking over at Tino. "Call yo' homey!"

Tino got Ziggy on the line. "What's up, bro?" Ziggy answered while watching the scene from all angles—holding onto a semi-automatic handgun. Ziggy wasn't about to just go for the okey-doke; before he would let a muthafucka rob him blind, he planned to shoot it out first. Shoota coached Tino to say exactly what he needed him to say to Ziggy.

"How much money did you come up with?" Tino asked.

"I did my best to reach 50-thou," Ziggy replied. "I got 33-stacks and a 9-piece."

Shoota wasn't bent out of shape about the amount Ziggy came up with, it was more than enough for him. Besides, he didn't plan on chopping Sicko and Bam in on too much of anything, possibly nothing.

"Do you see the black Chevy Tahoe sitting in the parking lot?" Tino asked Ziggy, repeating Shoota's words.

"Yeah, I see it," Ziggy said. "It's a 2001, right?"

"Yep, that's it. It's gonna pull up on you," Tino said. "And when it does, you need to hop out and throw the money and drugs through the back window. You got it altogether in a duffel bag, right?"

"Yeah, but when are they gonna let you go...after this, right?"

"Once buddy get outta the vicinity of the gas station safe and sound, with the bread, that's when they're gonna let me go." Tino explained.

"Man, bro...how could you be so sure that they'll honor the deal?" Ziggy questioned. "I thought it was gon' be a fair exchange...this shit sounds suspect."

Shoota grew tired of Ziggy's stagulations and decided to give him the motivation needed to seal the deal. Without any further delays, Shoota smacked Tino across the face with the pole again, leaving a great big knot there. *"WHAM!"*

"Aww, fuck," Tino cried out, suddenly. "Please...stop hitting me, man. He got the money, damn!"

The impact of Shoota's gun colliding into Tino's face caused him to drop the phone again. This time, Shoota picked it back up and spoke into it, "Look, you're really testing my fucking patience. My nerves are shocked, I'm about to say the hell with this and just murk this piece of shit then come after yo' bitch ass!"

Ziggy remained quiet as Shoota continued his verbal rampage. "I fuck around and come out better holding yo' duck ass for ransom—anyway, especially once I start cutting yo' fingers off and sending 'em back home to yo' mother, you ol' hoe ass nigga!"

Shoota paused for a moment, taking a slight breather. Ziggy had worked his nerves up a bit. If it wasn't for his need for the money, he would've just blown a hole through Tino's cranium and be done with the shit. However, he was determined to get his right-hand man out of jail.

"Just do as the fuck you're told or go and get a head start run because trust me, I'm gonna come hunt you down. And when I catch you, I'm gon' put you on permanent bunk rest...you know what's good, nigga!" Shoota claimed.

Ziggy thought to himself, *That's Shoota!* Hearing the voice on the other end of the phone, he couldn't help but put a face to it. Shoota had a very distinctive sound when he spoke—raspy and grim. Ziggy knew the young fella's track record and figured that he was nothing to play with. Had he known that it was him pulling the strings to this caper, he would have been came up off the loot...probably even more.

"Alright, man—alright, you don't gotta hurt him anymore," Ziggy begged for his homey's life. "I'm in the blue Nissan Maxima sitting right across from the Tahoe. I got the bread, come get it. Just please, let T go afterwards."

"Cool then." Shoota replied.

Sicko got Bam on the horn. "Look, broski, it's a blue Maxima sitting straight across from you...you see it?" he asked.

"Yeah, I see it."

"Good, pull over there and let yo' back window down. He's gonna throw a duffel bag through it," Sicko explained. "Once he does, get outta there. Make sure that it's money and drugs inside the bag as you're doing so. It supposed to be 50-bands and a half of brick in the bag."

Sicko exaggerated the amount like Shoota told him to do, just to keep ol' Bam honest. "Where do y'all want me to start heading towards once I get it?" Bam asked.

"Go to yo' crib, but first make sure you ghost anybody who looks like they're on yo' trail, okay?" Sicko said.

"I got you."

Bam ended the call and pulled over to where the car was parked at, letting down his back window. Ziggy hopped out and threw the bag through it while holding on to his Glizzle tightly. Bam then pulled off, grabbing the bag from the back seat and going through it. All the cash was bundled up in rubber bands, looking like 30 or 40-something thousand to a good eye. He also seen the coke inside as well.

After checking the bag, seeing the money and drugs there, Bam took a look through the rearview mirror and seen nothing in sight...the coast was clear. He got back on the phone and gave Sicko an update. "I got it, and it looks all there...the money and cola."

Sicko looked at Shoota and smiled. "We're in the money, captain." he informed him.

Shoota felt great, like a king or something, but definitely didn't front his move. He kept his composure, staying in character through the whole flick. The heartless villain was built for these types of moments.

"Y'all have the money now...please, let me go." Tino pleaded for his life. "I can walk home from here, fuck that car!"

Tino knew this was a crucial moment for him, Shoota could easily go back on his word and just smoke him for the hell of it. To keep shit funky though, Shoota never sought out to kill him— especially not after being handed over the money he demanded. That's all he was after...not blood. Well, at least not this time. Tino was a first round draft pick in Shoota's means of bonding Do-Dirty out of jail.

Shoota ended up turning Tino loose, letting him live to see another day. He parked his car somewhere he could find it later on as directed. Tino shed tears of anger the whole time while walking towards the crib.

CHAPTER #21

TO BE AWARE IS TO BE ALIVE

Mac had been lamping in the bushes, trying to catch Shoota 'nem lacking for the pass week or so. He planned to smoke the young fella— once and for all. Shoota and his gang were constantly putting innocent people's lives at risk, more and more each day. Enough was enough, Mac sought to finalize the beef the best way he knew how.

Mac lurked in the cuts scoping the whole scene. Suddenly, he spotted someone coming from around the corner. It was in the *wee* hours of the night, so it was quite difficult trying to determine who the person actually was. He zoomed his eyes in and did his best identifying the moving object. It appeared to be Shoota.

Mac hit a switch on his weapon, cutting on the laser beam that was on it, and aimed it at the suspect. Shoota peeped the red light flashing across his body as he ran up the block. He stopped dead in his tracks and began searching in all directions, trying to see where the infra-red was coming from. Instantly, Shoota upped his stick and then ducked down low to the ground.

"Fuck!" Mac said to himself. He had forgot to take the safety off the gun before trying to fire it. The uncalculated mistake gave Shoota enough time to defend himself from the ambush he was supposed to be under. Mac had just missed his beat, the easiest opportunity to take Shoota up out this shit. Now, he had to come with it and shoot it out with his arch-enemy like an old western flick.

"Why don't yo' bitch ass come out from wherever you are so we can get to the bottom of this shit," Shoota suggested as he aimed his gun, professionally. "I know it ain't nobody but you—Mac."

Mac stepped out from the cuts pointing his blicker at Shoota. Although he had slipped up with operating his gun and missed his kill shot, he wasn't about to retreat just yet. He wanted Shoota dead, and now was still his moment.

"There he goes, y'all," Shoota said, talking as if there was an audience watching them. "All by himself for a change…BRO-*less*."

Without hesitation, Shoota swiftly aimed his gun at Mac and fired it. "*CLAH-CLAH-CLAH!*" Then he took cover behind a tree.

Mac ducked down behind a car as hot copper shot right pass him, missing his head by inches. He returned fire towards the tree Shoota was tucked off behind. "*DARH-DARH-DARH-DARH-DARH!*" You could see the slugs chipping away at the tree, knocking big chunks off it.

"Who's hiding like a lil' bitch, now?" Mac shouted out while moving in closer for the kill.

Shoota stood patiently, with his back pressed against the tree, waiting for an opportunity to lick shots again. Both of his hands were wrapped around his gun, which were pointed upwards towards the sky. He sensed Mac getting closer and dived out from behind the tree, doing a tuck-roll, then hopped back up on one knee.

Before Mac could even get an aim at Shoota, the young acrobat wrapped his finger around the trigger and curled it. "*CLAH-CLAH-CLAH-CLAH-CLAH-CLAH-CLAH-CLAH-CLAH!*"

Mac ended up catching multiple shots in his chest. Immediately, he plummeted to the pavement—backwards. Hollow-point tips left him laying slump in the middle of the street, looking like he was getting ready to take a quick nap or something. His weapon got knocked out his hands and was far out of his reach.

Shoota stood up and walked over towards Mac, aiming his stick directly at his face. Mac was helplessly trying to recover his gun, but Shoota kicked it all the way to the curb.

"You won't be needing that where you're about to go." Shoota said. He came back in front of Mac and looked him dead in the eye. Mac couldn't believe that his night had turned out like this. One simple slip up was about to cost him his dear life, a fatal price he had to pay for fronting his move.

Damn! Mac thought to himself. His whole life began flashing right before his very eyes as Shoota put the barrel up to his forehead.

"Tell God I said hi, my nigga!" Shoota said as he clutched the trigger. "*CLAH-CLAH!*"

Mac flinched and then his eyelids popped open wide as his body suddenly rose up from the bed. He was soaked up in cold sweat. It took him several minutes just to gather his breath.

"What's wrong, baby," Briana, Mac's girlfriend, asked. "You had another nightmare?"

Mac didn't say nothing.

"Talk to me, baby...it's alright now. It was just a bad dream." Briana said. "Come back to bed."

Briana wrapped her arm around Mac, trying to get him to lay back down. It took a nice while for him to fully snap back into reality...the shit seemed so real that he ended up pissing on himself. He got up and rushed to the bathroom, humiliated that he had wet the bed. Shoota's presence had him troubled—even in his dreams.

Once Mac made it to the bathroom, he stripped down from his pissy underwear and cut the shower on. He grabbed a towel and wiped his face off with it. While staring in the mirror, Briana came in and hugged him from behind. She kissed him on the neck and rested her head on his shoulder.

"Tell me about yo' dream, baby," she said. "I don't ever want this nightmare to come back and haunt you."

Looking at her through the mirror, as she showered his neck with kisses, Mac finally found the right words to say. "Go pack up our shit...we're getting the fuck out of here—tonight!"

For once in Shoota's life, he was looked at as a "big homey." He ended up bonding his top lieutenant out of jail and took him shopping, buying him all sorts of designers. He went ahead and broke Sicko and Bam off with a couple of racks apiece, something real slight for their partake in the robbery.

Shoota hit the car lot and copped a Lexus ES 330, with chrome wheels. He was smart enough to lay a decent amount of coke down in the neighborhood, giving all the youngster who was up under him a fair opportunity to come up. He bought more guns and issued them out to anybody that was down with JRW.

Eventually, he ran all the BROs from off the block and up out the neighborhood—for good. They couldn't come around without running the risk of being shot at. It was safe to say that Washington Heights was Shoota's domain and he would die before letting anyone take it from him.

Word got back that Tino wanted his run back for what Shoota and his crew had done, kidnapping and robbing him. Shoota was the least bit bothered about the shit though, he never cared! It was what it was—if Tino wanted revenge, then he would have to just get in line with the rest of the muthafuckas that JRW had fucked over.

For the most part, Shoota wasn't hard to find. He stayed posted up on the Fo' smoking some dope, surrounded by a bunch of shooters...*"Gang-Gang."* Youngeon 'nem loved the fuck out of him...he was like God to them niggas.

Butta, Shoota's brother, ended up being charged with second-degree murder for smoking Taz. He was facing something slight though, Shoota made sure he was taken care of during his short bit.

Rio remained on the hunt for Shoota's head, but the young gang leader had mastered the art of war. He kept the blicker on him like it was his I.D. He ran the hood with an iron fist, standing on top of the business—wholeheartedly. Although he didn't have a whole lot of money, he stayed bossed up everytime he stepped out the door.

It was the memorial day for a glorious Hood Hero—Marcus Reynolds, *a.k.a.* **"Scoobie."** This was Bible's beloved lil' brother. Just a couple of years ago, Scoobie had died in a horrible car crash, which happened on the Dan-Ryan Expressway. Scoobie died on the spot and Bible, who was also in the crash, was rushed to the hospital in critical condition. He suffered from broken bones all throughout his entire body.

Tino and Dino also was in the accident, sitting in the back seat of the Infiniti Scoobie and Bible had went through the front windshield of. Miraculously, they only sustained minor injuries. The shit was televised all over the news.

Nobody seemed to know what exactly caused the crash, but Dino had spread a rumor saying that A-1 had something to do with it. Bible ended up denying Dino's claims. Instead of showing support to Bible, in regards of him losing his lil' brother in the crash, Dino took him to court suing him. The things broke niggas do for money.

Every year since the fatal car crash, people would gather up from all across the city to pay homage to the late "Ghetto Star." A memorial picnic was thrown at the forest perserve in remembrance of Scoobie—all compliments of Bible. He covered all expenses, proudly.

At the picnic, everybody wore customized "R.I.P." Scoobie shirts and hats. Some even had pants and shoes to match. Scoobie was loved by a great multitude of people, it was such a tragedy that he had to die at a young age.

Scoobie left behind a beautiful lil' daughter, which Bible helped carry the burden of. He made sure his niece didn't want for shit other than her father being brought back to life. Unfortunately, Bible didn't have them type of powers.

DJ-BOSS Life was on deck once again, playing all the hood anthems. Bible barbecued some of everything you could imagine. It was a hurtful time for him, he loved his brother more than he did himself. He managed fighting off the majority of tears that tried watering his eyes; however, the few teardrops that he did shed...whoever around had to help him gather himself. His pain ran deeper than the ocean.

Above all, Scoobie's memorial was an epic event. Kick-Dough couldn't attend the picnic this year. Twelve was on his ass, and he knew that they would try to catch him lacking when it's cracking. Instead, he let Stacey roll solo, just her and Baby-Aaron, to the picnic. Later on that night, him and a couple of his team members linked up and fucked it off big-time at a high end club, downtown.

Bible showed up with a couple of his shooters to kick the affair off right. The door fee was $100 per person and another fee of $1,000...that's if you preferred a table. Each table came with a few bottles and V.I.P. access.

Kick-Dough and Bible bought four tables altogether. Kick-Dough had on an all-black Balmain leather jumpsuit with some exclusive Giuseppe's. His Balmain v-neck had Scoobie's face spray-painted on the front with all sorts of rubies on it. He topped it off with a pair of Cartier shades and matching wrist wear.

Bible never was the flashy type, but today was a special occasion. He took the term *"flexing"* to a whole 'nother level. He came to the club dressed up like he was attending the Grammys' Awards Show or something. He had on Versace all the way down to his shoes, which were some square-toed, crocodile Ferragamo's. V-V-S' were dancing all around in his right ear lobe and in the Presidential-Rolex that was wrapped around his wrist. All eyes were on him.

Bible have been getting money all his life, taking only a couple minor setbacks along the way—nothing major. Pitfalls wasn't deep at all to this giant, he was currently out on a $100,000 bond for a couple attempt murders he had pending on "the guys." All that buddy-buddy shit didn't mean a thing to Bible when it came down to him coming to collect an outstanding debt. He had given Chuck Simmons $50,000 right out of his pocket, just to make the problem go away.

Yeah, Bible seemed not to be worried about anything, even when the pitfalls began growing deep and deeper. Somebody kicked the door in at his baby mama crib, Latoria "La-La" Peatry, taking a brick and a half and $40,000 in cash. The same week, Dino broke ass ended up filing a lawsuit against Bible for the fatal car accident he was in. The courts found Bible liable, forcing him to have-to file bankruptcy to avoid losing everything he had hustled so hard for. It got to a point where he had fallen all the way down to his last few racks.

But like I said before, pitfalls were no biggie to a giant. Bible bounced back in no time. To the average eye, he never fell off to begin with.

"Man, I'll give anything to have lil' bro back here with me today. It's like nothing even matters to me any more without him being around. The money, clothes, hoes...none of that shit!" Bible said, drinking straight from a gold bottle—Ace of Spades.

The club was jam-packed and jumping through the roof. It was a surprise that Fire-Marshals didn't come and shut the place down. The rapper **Future's** aphrodisiac song, "*Codeine Crazy,*" was blasting loudly through the huge speakers along the wall.

"I miss bro a whole bunch too, my nigga," Kick-Dough responded. "I done learned so much game from him and fucked mad bitches just off mentioning his name...they sholl wasn't lying when they said *'the good die young'.*"

Kick-Dough sipped on his gold bottle and began vibing to the music. Everybody among the two squads had similar bottles to themselves. No cups were needed..."Boss-Life."

"What's up with A-l," Bible asked Kick-Dough. "He's good?"

"Most definitely, bro don't want for shit but a shot of pussy." Kick-Dough replied. "I told him to finesse one of them thirsty ass C/O bitches up in there, I give 'em whatever they want."

Bible couldn't help but laugh at Kick-Dough's statement, taking another swig off the bottle. "I tilt my hat to you niggas. Y'all got a tight circle...I like that." Bible said.

"That's MVP for you," Kick-Dough responded. "I was just talking to Chuck last week, and he said we were Gucci on the murder, and that the D.A. was trying to offer some time for the robbery."

Kick-Dough's phone began vibrating in his pants. He grabbed it and looked at the screen, seeing that it was his girl Stacey calling. "Give me a second, fool, I gotta answer this." he said to Bible.

"Go ahead, broski." Bible replied, waving his hand to let him know that it was all good.

"What's up, baby," Kick-Dough answered. "Is something wrong?"

"Hey, bae, nothing's wrong. I'm just calling to let you know that I'm gon' spend the night over my mom's house. My aunt and uncle is up here visiting from down south, and we are having a lil' sleep over. You don't mind, do you, bae?"

"Nah, I don't mind. Have fun, I might be coming home late anyway. Did you have a nice time at the picnic?" Kick-Dough asked while flirting with a sexy, chocolate, thick bitch who had just walked by.

"Hell yeah, Baby-Aaron enjoyed himself so much. He's asleep already." she replied.

"My main man is knocked out already?" Kick-Dough said. "Y'all must of had a ball then, he normally stays up until I get in."

Stacey began laughing, and Kick-Dough joined in on the moment. "I took a whole bunch of pictures too, just like you asked." Stacey advised him.

"Good, I gotta send A-1 some shit. I can just add the pictures with it. Give lil' fella a kiss for me, and I'm gonna take care of mommy as soon as I see you."

"I love you, bae," Stacey responded. "Be safe, daddy."

"I got you, baby...I love you too!"

Kick-Dough ended the call and got back to celebrating. He could feel the alcohol settling well into his system, which by the way was an incredible sensation. He looked over at Bible and then at the rest of the crew, seeing everybody was up mingling—drunk as fuck. "We're winning!" He said to himself.

The DJ mixed the song, and then Chief Keef came on, "*I ain't done turning up yet!*"

Kick-Dough looked around again, and the whole club was off their feet bopping to the music. He reached in his pocket and grab a wad of money, not paying any attention to the bills. He slung them all up in the air making it rain in the club. "I ain't done turning up yet!" he rapped along with Chief Sosa.

Without thinking twice, Bible followed suit slinging a even larger wad in the air. "I ain't gotta count it, I gotta money counter." he rapped his favorite part of the song. Normally, Bible don't handle money so carelessly, but he just couldn't pass on the opportunity...this was a moment of a lifetime. The feeling was electrifying.

Bible shook up with Kick-Dough and bopped along to the music. Before you knew it, the whole squad was throwing money in the air. The club was theirs for the moment, everybody around cheered them on— even the owners.

A few gate-jumpers played the background, studying the very movements of Kick-Dough and company.

"That's who got the bag, right there," one of 'em whispered, pointing directly at Kick-Dough. "I don't know about them other niggas, it's a slight chance that they fuck around and be flaging."

"I don't know now...big homie with the rolly on looks like he gotta hell of a check too!" another one implied. "I seen him pull up in a Lexus LS 460 on forgiatos."

"Well, he can be our next target," the ringleader said. "Right now, our focus is devoted totally on buddy with the Balmain jumpsuit on. I gotta real good feeling that he's our mil-ticket."

The **B.O.S.'**, "Big Ol' Sharks," were a treacherous pack of individuals who specialized in jumping the gates of high-profile, balling type of niggas. You know...them "Duffel Bag Boys." All throughout Chiraq, people were warned about the ferocious squad.

Rumor was, B.O.S. was responsible for a couple of pro-athletes from the city being kidnapped and robbed for a large ransom. Famous celebrities were their initial target, actually. These niggas weren't pussy-footing around the slightest bit.

Pulling kick doors, possibly having to blow a muthafucka's head off for the dough, was the exact business these guys were in. When the sharks hit, it was big and hard.

Duck, the ringleader of B.O.S., was the mastermind behind all the scandalous plots that the sharks carried out. Standing at 6'8, with the physique of a professional boxer, Duck wasn't just your average chip off the block. Nah, he was a calculated progressor destined to be the most vicious person alive.

Duck have been a menace to society since birth, and with his ruthless capacities, him and the sharks caused terror to sack-holders. His initial crew—**Skee, Tu-Tu, Rocko, Hungry,** and **Greedy**—were all groomed to be just as brutal as him, allegedly. He schooled them on a number of violent offenses, and by far, taking shit down was B.O.S. first nature.

Duck and his sharks have been scoping out Kick-Dough in the clubs fucking off a bag back when him and A-1 first got introduced to the Lime-Lite. However, at that time, they didn't quite qualify as being B.O.S.' top prospect. You see, when it comes to jumping gates, there's levels to the shit. Fortunately, A-1 and Kick-Dough didn't meet the price tag that Duck was aiming for...he was searching for a quarter-mil hop. At that time, neither one of 'em were even in the hundred-band club—not even if they were to put their bankrolls together.

Things done changed now, Kick-Dough had elevated his status to a higher plateau. With that being known, Duck and his sharks wanted in.

They began doing homework on Kick-Dough, mapping the felonious caper down to a science. They put tracking devices on his cars and studied his daily moves closely, learning all the boy's whereabouts. They knew where him and Stacey stayed and where Stacey's mother lived as well.

The Big Ol' Sharks were experts of all sorts and played a game way dirtier than your average jack-boys. They were down to do whatever to strike rich, even if that meant torturing and killing a whole bunch of innocent people. Duck and his "Great Whites" sat at the round table, discussing the money making mission.

"Time has come for us to cash out on this Kick-Dough muthafucka. I don't see any reason to stall on the subject any longer. All in favor show yo' teeth." Duck stated, letting his fangs stick out.

Within a matter of seconds everybody at the table began growling and foaming at the mouth like aggravated wolves. Clearly, they all were hungry, possibly even more than Duck was. Let the hunger games begin.

"Okay then, check out what the lick read," Duck said, showing his teeth even more. "I need each of you to be on yo' A-game at all times. Buddy moves like a savage of some sort...but what's a savage to some Big Ol' Sharks?"

"Nothing-nothing," Hungry responded, looking out of one eyeball only. He had gotten shot in the right eye a while back, during a hit he was involved in.

Skee was busy rolling up some dope for the squad to blow. Among the many skills he was equipped with, pearling blunts was listed at the top right next to taking a gun apart and putting it back together within a minute. "Let me get this straight...we're snatching up Kick-Dough and his bitch, right?" he asked, taking a small pause from twisting kush up in cigar wrappings.

"Nah, not the bitch," Duck answered. "She need to be free to go and get us what we want."

"True that," Skee agreed.

"We need to keep as many people out of the equation as possible," Duck advised his sharks. "We definitely don't need twelve poking their nose in the business."

"Hell, if we catch them both at the crib, we can tie 'em up and torture 'em until they come off of them dividends." Rocko added.

"What if the dough isn't in the crib?" Greedy asked.

"Oh, it's money there," Duck blurted. "Now, sitting here trying to determine exactly how much…that's another thang."

Skee flamed a blunt up and took a deep pull before speaking, "So we split up into two groups…one to guard Kick-Dough and the other to guard the bitch. That way we win either way."

Skee passed the blunt to Duck. Duck took ahold of the dope and let a cloud of smoke fill his lungs. He was impressed with Skee's idea. "I'm feeling that, great white." he said as he leaned back in his chair. Skee went back to pearling up some more dope.

Tu-Tu, a force to be reckoned with alone, was the last shark to impose his views on the matter. "So, we snatch both of 'em up simultaneously—one right after the other. We get the bitch first for leverage and then catch buddy before he make it out of the house to start his day. We already know that the bitch leaves the crib early to go and drop their kid off at her mother's crib. That's where we can snatch her up at. The bread's either gonna be at his crib or his bitch mother's house." Tu-Tu stacked his fist together two times, right over left. This was a signal letting it be known that word was bond.

Tu-Tu continued laying a crucial lick down, "Hold the bitch and whoever else's in the crib captive while we go in on the prime target. Make buddy comply with what's going down. Neither one of 'em would have to move once the shit hits the fan, the money's gonna be in one of the houses—possibly both."

"Double bub!" Duck responded, rubbing his palms together.

Tu-Tu was Duck's best shark. Oftenly, he plotted out schemes more calculated than Duck. The big fella stayed trying to get ahead. Duck respected Tu-Tu's gangsta and value the way that he made moves. However, for some unapparent reason, Duck had a funny feeling that Tu-Tu would try to *back door* him one day.

Everybody sitting at the table were in agreement with what Tu-Tu had suggested. All you heard were the constant sound of fists being stacked together and muthafuckas merching it, putting it on the B.O.S. That was just their way of confirming things, sealing the deal.

"Hell yeah, and if they don't wanna get down then we're gonna make 'em lay down," Rocko blurted. "Torture is my favorite!"

Rocko hit the dope and then passed it to Greedy. Duck looked around at his sharks in great admiration. It used to be a time when he had to come up with all the treacherous moves, now he had a squad of gangsters and thinkers working on the same accord as himself…Priceless!

Finally, Duck cracked opened one of the bottles of 1738 Remy Martin that was sitting on the table. By this time, Skee had multiple blunts up and running around the table—in full speed ahead. The entire room was covered in good smoke, setting the mood off just right. Duck and his sharks continued congregating among themselves about all the possibilities of the lick. This was their livelihood, and they weren't gonna let nothing or no one stop them from getting the "big feast."

CHAPTER #22

CATCHING A FISH

Stacey got up earlier than usual, being that today was the last day she had before Kick-Dough's birthday. She'd been planning him a surprise party for a couple of weeks now, and she wanted everything to go accordingly. Her mother had been constantly nagging at her about Kick-Dough's illegal affairs, warning her that if she didn't leave him alone she would end up dead or either in jail.

Whenever Ms. Jackie started talking nonsense like that, she was just getting ready to have her hand out for something—more than likely some money. Kick-Dough was getting sick and tired of Ms. Jackie's shit, and so was Stacey. The game she was running had gotten old.

Stacey decided not to even bother telling her mother about the surprise party, let alone inviting her to it. Stacey didn't invite her mother because she figured that all she would do is spoil the fun. Stacey rented out a hall room and sent out reserved invitations to only a selected few. She paid for the comedian **D'Ray** to perform a stand-up act and for **King Louie** and **Lil' Dirk** to take the stage—with some drill music.

Kick-Dough's surprise party would be an epic event, not only because of the celebrities that would be present there, but also, it was gone be the day Stacey asked Kick-Dough for his hand in marriage. He was taking too long to put a ring on her finger, so she decided to step up to the plate and take a swing at it.

Kick-Dough was still asleep like a lil' baby when Stacey left the house. First, she stopped by her mother's house to drop Baby-Aaron off for the day. Ms. Jackie was up cooking some southern-style breakfast for her and her drug addict daughter, **"Tee-Tee."** Stacey walked in and caught a good whiff of her mother's culinary art skills.

"Hey, momma," Stacey said as she set her purse down and then Baby-Aaron. "What's that you're hooking up...it smells great?"

"Aww, nothing much, baby," Ms. Jackie replied, receiving a kiss on the cheek from Stacey. "Some salmon croquette...white rice...and southern-style, homemade biscuits—you're hungry, baby?"

Ms. Jackie wiped her hands off so she could give her precious grandbaby some love and affection. "That's momma's baby there...yes shim is." she said as she made her way towards Baby Aaron, picking him up and showering his face with tender kisses.

"I gotta use the bathroom." Stacey said, racing towards the bathroom.

"Stacey, honey," Ms. Jackie said, happily. "Your sister's here."

Tee-Tee was Stacey's older sister who was strung out on heroine. She was known for committing a number of crimes just to support her habit—mostly, auctioning off her body for a high. Sometimes, she would be gone for days before Ms. Jackie could find out her whereabouts. Oftenly, Ms. Jackie would worry herself to death about Tee-Tee's well-being, praying to God that she didn't get killed out there in them streets.

Stacey didn't really fuck with Tee-Tee, the girl always was stealing miscellaneous shit from out of their mother's house—every chance she got. Stacey had grown sick and tired of her sister's mess; having to go out in them streets late at night, not knowing if she was dead or alive, was nerve wrecking. She hated how her sister had turned out.

It was once a time where Stacey wanted to be just like Tee-Tee, but that was before the monkey had gotten on her back. Now, Stacey didn't have too much of anything good to say to or about her sister. "She's still alive?" Stacey responded to her mother, from the bathroom.

Tee-Tee heard Stacey's ignorant outburst and decided to leave. She was currently upstairs looking for something valuable to take to the pawnshop and sell. However, Ms. Jackie had gotten smart, hipped to her daughter's gate jumping ways. She had taken everything that she could possibly think Tee-Tee might steal and hid it somewhere safe.

Ms. Jackie took Baby-Aaron by the waist and walked through the living-room, swinging him around in the air. Baby-Aaron just giggled himself to death, enjoying being treated like a miniature flight-jet. By the time she made it to the front room, she called out for Tee-Tee to come see her nephew.

Tee-Tee was the least bit interested though, she was too busy rambling through Stacey's Prada purse, which Stacey had left unattended on the kitchen table. It was a must that Tee-Tee got high, even if she had to steal from her own peoples. While going through the expensive purse, one of Kick-Dough's birthday party invitation flyers had dropped out on the floor without Tee-Tee's knowledge. She ended up coming out of the deal with some petty cash, just enough to curve her addiction for a short while.

Before Ms. Jackie made it back to the kitchen, Tee-Tee was in flight already—gone with the wind. "Tee-Tee?" she called out.

The sound of a toilet being flushed echoed the area as Stacey came out of the bathroom, fastening her Gucci belt buckle.

"You seen yo' sister?" Ms. Jackie asked, looking at Stacey as if she did something wrong.

"Nah, why," Stacey replied, walking over towards the stove to pick through her mother's delicious breakfast. "Where is the heifer?"

Ms. Jackie shoved Stacey away from the stove. "Don't pick over the food child, wash yo' hands and fix yo'self a plate!" she said.

"I'm in a rush, momma," Stacey responded while nibbling on a buttermilk biscuit. "I gotta whole bunch of business to take care of today, and I'm already running behind."

"Child, eating something ain't gonna take that much of yo' lil' precious time." Ms. Jackie said while rubbing on Stacey's belly. "Now, go ahead and put something on that big stomach of yours."

Although Stacey never told her mother about the coming of her second child, it was obvious to Ms. Jackie that her daughter was pregnant. "Eat something, girl, I made plenty!" Ms. Jackie said, walking away from Stacey.

"Not today, momma...I gotta go," Stacey advised as she walked over to Ms. Jackie, giving her and Baby-Aaron a kiss apiece. "But one of these days, I'm gonna come over and fix you up a delicious meal, I promise!"

Stacey grabbed her purse and made her way towards the door. Ms. Jackie just stared at her daughter, knowing very well what had her all tied up...*that damn Kick-Dough.* The door closed, and Stacey was off on her way.

"What am I gonna do with these girls, Baby-Aaron?" Ms. Jackie said. "Both of 'em strung out, one on dope and the other on dick—Oops...you didn't hear that, baby."

She sat Baby-Aaron down in his high-chair, noticing a lil' piece of paper lying underneath the table. She reached down and grab it, copping a quick squat afterwards. "Kick-Dough's Surprise Birthday Bash! I wasn't invited, huh!" she said, in a nasty tone.

Ms. Jackie was over-blue, rage began to build up inside of her instantly. "I said I was gon' fix his ass, it's time for me to start making good on the promise." she said to herself. Baby-Aaron mugged her as if he understood exactly what she was saying.

Ms. Jackie grabbed the house phone and dialed up an unforgettable number, 9-1-1. "Hello, you've reached the Chicago Police Department, how may I help you today?"

"I would like to report some valuable information about a wanted man...he goes by the name Anthony Moore."

Detective Hogan got an anonymous tip about a wanted man named Anthony Moore. The caller started to spill the beans until her daughter came barging in the house through the kitchen door. Ms. Jackie tried to play it off, holding the phone down in hopes that Tee-Tee would just go away this one time, but she didn't budge.

"Momma, I need 50-dollars," Tee-Tee said, begging as usual. "I just found a rehab that will accept me today. The admission fee is 75-dollars, Aunt Lori is gon' give me the other quarter."

Tee-Tee began scratching the side of her neck, down to the top part of her breast. It was quite obvious that she was fiending and trying to finesse for some *blow money'*.

"I don't have anymore cash," Ms. Jackie explained. "That 20-dollars I gave you earlier was the last piece of change I had on me...I told you that already."

Tee-Tee was persistent, forcing Ms. Jackie to have to hang up the phone right in Detective Hogan's face. He dialed up to the front desk clerk and had her put him back on the line with the anonymous caller who had information about Anthony Moore. The clerk dialed back the number and then merged it to line-2, Hogan's desk phone.

Detective Hogan pushed the blinking number on his phone's dial pad and waited as he listened to the ringing sound, hoping that the caller would answer. This was the one lead he'd been waiting on for so long now. He prayed the scarce opportunity wouldn't get away from him.

"Well, then can you go to the cash station and get it for me?" Tee-Tee begged, trying her best to look truthful as she possibly could.

Ms. Jackie wasn't buying what Tee-Tee was trying to sell. "I can't go anywhere right now, don't you see me watching over my precious grandbaby!" she said, reaching over and picking Baby-Aaron up giving him a great big ol' kiss. He could do nothing but giggle. It was a Kodak moment.

Not for Tee-Tee though, she was beginning to grow impatient. However, she managed to keep her composure. She definitely couldn't afford to front her move...not just yet. She was sick and needed a fix, Ms. Jackie was her quickest way to getting high.

Tee-Tee remained in perfect character, trying her hardest to get what she wanted...the art of finesse. However, if all fails, she wouldn't have a problem with going on to plan B, which was jumping a gate or two—starting with her mother first. Heroine is a powerful drug.

Tee-Tee went and sat down at the table where Ms. Jackie was sitting and pulled up her chair. "Momma, I really need to get my life together. This monkey that's on my back has taken its toll on my soul. I'm tired, momma...really tired!" she stated as she held her head down to the floor. The finesse was on.

Ms. Jackie didn't say anything, she just stared at her sick daughter suspiciously. *My poor baby, Lord, please help her!* she thought to herself.

Tee-Tee lifted her head, wiping away fake tears she had conjured up. Now...Ms. Jackie was beginning to buy into her bullshit. "This might be my only chance to get back right. Do you think I like giving my body away for drugs..." Tee-Tee said as she paused to look her mother dead in the eye. She seen that she had her right where she wanted her.

"Do you even know how many dicks I've sucked—"

"—Wait a minute, I don't need to be hearing about that mess up in here and neither does my grandbaby." Ms. Jackie complained, cutting Tee-Tee off from her explicit grammar.

"Oh, I'm sorry, momma," Tee-Tee replied, faking some more tears. "I'm just tired of this life I'm living, something has to change."

Tee-Tee put on an excellent performance, Ms. Jackie was sold. If Ms. Jackie did have some cash on her, she would of gave it all to her—no matter what the amount was. Ms. Jackie took a brief moment staring Tee-Tee up and down before speaking to her, "So, where's this rehab located?" Tee-Tee Oscar Award-winning performance has done it again.

Detective Hogan tried and tried to get back through to the anonymous tipper, but each time, he got no answer. He was able to trace the number though, it came back to one Jackolyn Henderson, Ms. Jackie, out of the Hyde Park community. He jotted the address down and grabbed his things, leaving the office in a flash.

This lead was all Detective Hogan had and he sought to execute thoroughly on it. As he passed the front desk, on his way going out of the department, the clerk called out his name, "Detective Hogan, your wife has been calling asking why you're not answering your phone."

"Just tell her I'm busy, and I'll call her later." Detective Hogan replied exiting the door. Nothing was more important to him at the current moment then arresting Anthony Moore and bringing him into the station.

The B.O.S. squad was up early on cue, splitting up into two groups just as they planned. Tu-Tu, Rocko, and Greedy covered Stacey while Duck, Hungry, and Skee lurked on their cash cow—Kick-Dough. Stacey left her man in the bed snoring, while she got out to handle some important business. Tomorrow was Kick Dough's birthday, and she needed to make sure everything was going accordingly as scheduled.

Stacey drove towards her mother's to drop Baby-Aaron off, to have more flexibility to do whatever else she needed to do. Tu-Tu and his team followed her discreetly, calculating the perfect time to snatch her up. They had planned to pull a simple kick door when Stacey first made it to her mother's crib, but right before they could take flight, Stacey's big sister came out the house throwing their scheme off a bit.

"I think I know that bitch from somewhere," Greedy claimed, pointing a finger at Tee-Tee trying to recall where he knew her from. *Tee-Tee.* he thought to himself.

The sharks were lamping in a Chrysler 300, tinted up, across the street from where Stacey's mother live. Greedy was behind the wheel, Tu-Tu was laid back in the passenger, and Rocko occupied the back seat. The mission was in progress.

"This lame ass nigga always knowing some damn body!" Tu-Tu said.

"Where you know her from, G?" Rocko asked Greedy, giving a grimey laugh afterwards.

"He probably done tricked off with her cluck-buddy looking ass." Tu-Tu said, assuming the obvious. All the sharks were aware of Greedy's fixation with fucking hypes.

Tu-Tu and Rocko both laughed in Greedy's face, not giving a single fuck about his feelings. That's what great whites do. They paused giggling for a hot second to see what kind of response he was gonna give them.

Tu-Tu hit the shit right on the head, Greedy had turned several dates with Tee-Tee. She prostituted on the strip where he was currently running a dope line called "Great White." Greedy wouldn't front his move to the guys though...not at the risk of continued being made a laughing stock out of. Tu-Tu and Rocko where the silliest muthafuckas in the squad; and whenever they joined forces, it was comic view on somebody's ass.

Tee-Tee looked at the 300, glancing up inside of it as she jogged pass. She caught the site of Greedy's face slightly, but not enough to pinpoint who he actually was. She kept it moving right along...curving her addiction was more important than trying to recall a face.

"Nah, I don't know her dope-fiend looking ass!" Greedy replied to Rocko's question, straight fronting his shit. A crucial lie like this could very much cost them their freedom, possibly even their lives.

"You sure you don't know her, G?" Rocko asked. "She sholl was poking her damn nose out a lil' bit too much."

Rocko gave Greedy a look that had "*you better not be lying*" written all across it.

"On the B.O.S., nigga!" Greedy said, stacking both of his fists together twice and then locking them. That was enough confirmation for the matter; stacking it on the B.O.S. was more honorable than putting your hand on the bible and then swearing to God...let the sharks tell it.

"Copy that," Tu-Tu said, flaming up a square. "Call Duck and give him an update."

Greedy followed instructions, getting Duck right on the line. "Yep," he answered calmly while laying low in the passenger seat of a Lincoln MKS. Skee was covering the steering wheel, and Hungry's Fetty-Wap looking ass lounged in the back seat. They had Kick-Dough's palace under heavy surveillance.

"His bitch is at her mom's crib. We were just about to go in on her ass until some random bitch came marching outta the house. She didn't peep the move though, my guess she was just a geeker." Greedy explained.

"Yeah, where's the bitch at now?" Duck asked, trying to figure some shit out.

"She's still in the house," Greedy answered.

Within the next second, Stacey came up out of the crib hopping into her Q7 Audi truck and pulling off.

"Matter of fact, the bitch just came out and left." Greedy informed Duck as he fired the car up and began following her again.

"Keep up, G," Tu-Tu instructed Greedy as he sat up in his seat.

"Don't let that bitch out of yo' sight."

Stacey had a real heavy foot, but Greedy managed keeping a discreet tail on her.

"Man. let me speak to Tu-Tu!" Duck said, seeming to get angry.

"What up, fooly?" Duck said, getting the phone from Greedy.

"What's the fucking hold up?" Duck argued. "Y'all supposed to be in the crib getting to the money by now, not playing cat and mouse!"

"I'm already knowing, chief," Tu-Tu replied. "We were about to get wild until a bitch came out the crib, throwing our timing off."

Tu-Tu continued on explaining his case, trying to make sense out of their procrastination. "Tell me what you want us to do at this point, we're following her right now." he asked.

It took no time for Duck to revise the scheme and put the mission back in motion. "Hunt the bitch down...First convenient stop she makes, snatch her ass up, but do it smoothly and keep the shit clean. Take her and her car back to the designated location and get wild!" Duck was an expert at calling last minute plays, a master at finesse.

"Case the crib good before y'all go in. Chances are, it may be other people there besides her mother and the baby. Once you get in safe and get everybody tied up, including the baby, hit my line, and then we'll go from there." Duck said, quarterbacking the play.

"Copy that." Tu-Tu responded, ending the call.

"Check it out...we bout to get busy," Tu-Tu explained to the sharks. "As soon as the right moment comes, we snatching lil' momma up out the truck and taking her back to her mom's spot."

Greedy and Rocko paid close attention to everything Tu-Tu said. "This shit ain't hard, it's just that simple! Rocko, you're gon' drive her truck while I hold her down in the back. Greedy, you stay put and just follow us."

Tu-Tu orchestrated moves like Tom Brady. "Y'all copy that?" he asked. Both of the sharks nodded their heads in complete agreement.

Stacey was a lil' distance away from her mom's house when her phone rang. Looking down at the face on the screen, she seen that it wasn't anybody but her nagging mother. "Yeah, momma," she answered, hopping that Ms. Jackie wasn't about to start bothering her. Ms. Jackie was known for asking Stacey to make frivolous errands whenever she dropped Baby-Aaron off at her house. Today was a very busy day for Stacey, and her time was limited. She had no room for doing any extra running around.

"I need a big favor, baby," Ms. Jackie said. "I don't have any loose money around the house to give your sister. She's trying to check into a rehab today, God bless her soul."

"Check into rehab, huh...I heard that one before," Stacey replied. "Tell her she gotta come up with a better one than that."

Stacey busted a sharp left, damn near missing her turn. Greedy had no choice but to keep straight. It was no biggie though, Tu-Tu was tracking her down with a navigational-tracking device he had planted underneath her car. Her current location was strategically being monitored—every stroll of the way.

"She's going northbound on Jeffery," Tu-Tu guided Greedy in the direction Stacey was heading towards. "Bust a quick left right here and another one at the end of the block to get back on Jeffery."

Greedy followed the directions accordingly. When they got back on route, Tu-Tu zoomed in on the tracking device pinpointing her exact location. "We're 'bout a quarter-mile away from her...speed up a notch." he advised Greedy as he sat upwards in the passenger. Rocko was tucked off in the back, enjoying the ride.

Stacey was still on the horn with her mother, conversating about Tee-Tee's dope fiend ass. "She's for real this time, I can see it all in the poor girl's face. She's serious about getting off that dope." Ms. Jackie said.

Stacey really wasn't trying to hear what her mother was kicking, her sister had fooled her too many times before already. Let Stacey tell it...this time was no different than the last. *She ain't gonna juke me again.* she thought to herself.

"She just need 50-dollars, Lori's gonna spot her the rest of the tab." Ms. Jackie said. "I hate to have to bother you from making your precious runs for King Kick-Dough, but your sister needs you right now."

Stacey took great notice of her mother sneak dissing and shit, trying to run the guilt trip down on her. However, it would take more to get her to bend. "Don't try to run that bullshit on me. The only thing that girl need is a real good ass kicking. And why the hell you got your nose poked up all in my business? I'm not the one on hands and feet, begging you for money. I mean, when is it ever gon' stop with that girl?" Stacey complained.

"Only the Lord knows how long, but I really trust that this is her calling to get her shit together and do something with her life. Don't you wanna see your sister succeed?" Ms. Jackie responded, defending her first-born.

Stacey thought the matter over in her mind for a quick moment. She knew her sister was full of it and would do anything in her power to get a blow. But on the other hand, Stacey often dream of the day that her sister would finally leave that dope alone. As much as she spoke bad about Tee-Tee, it was all out of emotions. Deep down inside, she hoped that her sister would get clean just as much as Ms. Jackie did. *What if this is her calling?* Stacey thought to herself.

"I don't know if I even brought any extra cash out with me." Stacey said as she dug through her purse looking for some money. *Damn, I know I had some dollars in here,* she thought to herself, searching in every corner but coming out empty handed.

"I thought I had some money on me, but I can't find it now." Stacey said to her mother, while pulling over into a Walgreens' parking lot. "It gotta be in here somewhere."

Ms. Jackie just remained silent on the phone. Stacey came to the terms that she had lost the money she had in her purse, she was quite sure she had left the crib with some cash. "Exactly how much does she need, momma? I'm 'bout to run up in Walgreens and make a withdrawal from the ATM." she said.

"Just 50 dollars," Ms. Jackie replied, happily. "God bless your soul, baby."

"Yeah-yeah-yeah, and if this girl's pulling another fast one, she's gonna need Jesus after I get done wealing on her ass." Stacey warned as she balled her fist up and slammed it down against the steering wheel.

"Oh, baby, don't think so negative…have a lil' faith."

"I mean it, momma," Stacey hastened to reply. "This is the last straw, I hope she's serious because I'm sure in hell is!"

Stacey ended the call, grabbing her purse and bailing out the SUV.

Greedy caught back up with the Audi truck while it was pulling into Walgreens. He pulled into the parking lot as well. Rocko watched the whole scene from the back seat.

"Check it out," Rocko said, tapping Tu-Tu on the shoulder. "There go twelve over there to the right, posted up."

Tu-Tu and Greedy took a glance at the undercovers parked right besides Walgreens.

"Fuck…what a coincidence," Tu-Tu shouted while snatching off the rolled up skully he had tilted on top of his head, slamming it down against the floor. "If this ain't some fluke shit, then I don't know what is."

"Just park somewhere low-key." Rocko directed Greedy.

CHAPTER #23
DEATH BEFORE DISHONOR

Big-Swole was clocking in more money than he could possibly count out himself. He kept a flock of birds flying in from across the country, which he sold for top dollar throughout the midwest. The drug operation that he conducted in Chicago brought him in a duffel bag of money— daily. His record label, "Street Fame Entertainment," was beginning to grow into a lucrative empire.

Yeah...Big-Swole was living "big and swole," he had plenty cash to throw around and look out for people. However, he chose to remain a petty ass muthafucka. He short-changed damn near everybody he came across or done business with. He couldn't help it, being ungenerous was all a part of his genetic make-up.

The only people he were ever fair with, as far as money goes, were his shooters. However, even they had grown to not like the overweight bastard. They wouldn't mind turning on him, all it would take is the right price to seal the deal. And like the old saying goes…"every dog has their day!"

You couldn't put a price on loyalty though; and when it came to it, Juice was about as loyal as they came. He operated strictly off all the laws and policies set forth by the honorable chairman—"Larry Hoover." Juice had only been out of jail for a couple of months now, and already, the streets were feeling his vibe. He rocked to a rhythm that the streets had been deprived of for so long, due to all the fuck boys with money flaunting around. Whenever he came around, them type of niggas crawled right back under the rock they came from.

Juice's team, F.O.E., grew notorious by the minute turning out to be one of the most deadliest mobs on the south side of Chicago. Their headquarters was located in the Roseland community, which was the most dangerous territory in the Wild-Wild-Hundreds. It stayed busting around them areas, non-stop.

Juice only recruited wolves into his gang, and he made sure that he fed them all accordingly. Whatever he had, they did also; and he made it his business that they understood the value of FOE, Family Over Everybody. Everybody had a design part to play, and they all needed to play it well. The organization got so much clout that muthafuckas were willing to kill their own parents—if it was necessary—just to be down with the squad.

Juice had the streets at his service—hands and feet. To him, forcing bitch-made niggas up out of the picture wasn't a bully move, it was just proper protocol. He was back from the dead, and it was only right that muthafuckas gave him all what he rightfully deserved...including interest.

First up was Big-Swole. Ever since Juice had been released from prison, Big-Swole been on Juice's bumper trying to make up for lost times. However, Juice wasn't interested in accepting any apologies, he just wanted his just due—Street Fame Entertainment. Big-Swole wouldn't have a choice but come up off the infamous label, either that or become a victim of a 100-round drum.

El-Huncho had sent for Popeye to meet with him at his luxurious estate out in Miami, Florida. It'd been a while since their last meeting. No one has yet to come through on the proposition El-Huncho had made, killing Sammie, *a.k.a.* "Pops," for the million-dollar reward he placed on his head.

El-Huncho was beginning to think that the job was too much for the people he had offered the contract to. Also, he had gotten word back from a crooked federal agent that there was possibly a mole placed somewhere in his cartel who had been feeding the FBI exclusive information about his ongoing criminal enterprise. The sinister crime-boss sought to get right down to the bottom of the shit.

El-Huncho was the "better safe than sorry" type of guy, he had begun killing off everyone who was present at the meeting he called discussing making "Sammie the Bull" disappear. First, he started with Mommi and Peebles, the two beautiful assault-rifle holders. If he had to murder a bunch of suspects just to guarantee getting rid of a rat then hey, so be it! Let El-Huncho tell it…the process is necessary.

Popeye was the last suspect on his list. He had been trying to get close to El-Huncho for some time now, making him suspicious of the actually reason why. Assumably, Popeye was either the federales or an aspiring drug-underboss coming to kill him for his position. Either way, El-Huncho wasn't having the shit. He'd been reigning king for over a decade now, and he didn't get this far from letting the law or ruthless thugs out think him.

It was time for El-Huncho to "clean house," kill off the old Cartel and create a new one. Popeye was oblivious to the matter at hand. In fact, he actually thought this meeting was a promotion for him to become El-Huncho's right hand man. He had been putting in extra work, overtime, trying to please the bossman in any way he possibly could. He did his best at trying to hunt Sammie down, he had a specific intent to chop his head off and bring it back to El-Huncho as a souvenir.

Popeye caught a flight to Miami and had a cab take him to the address that El-Huncho had given him. Once he made it to the palace, a couple of Spanish-man escorted him through the property. Popeye didn't think anything of it, not until he was led through the hallway...down some stairs...into a dungeon looking area. He didn't even get a chance to explore the glamorous parts of the castle, nothing more than a quick glance of the front corridors and alongside of the vestibule where the side stairs were. What Popeye had assumed to be a sightseeing adventure was now appearing to be a dark and gloomy narrow path.

Big-Swole pulled to his recording studio building, Street Fame Recordings, in a black and blue Ford Raptor pickup truck bumping **Rick Ross**, *"I think I'm Big-Meech...Larry Hoover. Whipping work...hallelujah. One nation...under God. Real niggas getting money from the fucking start!"* He bailed out rocking all Versace from head to toe, him and his number one shooter—**Psycho.**

Psycho had the 30 on him like Curry, and he was ready to blow it on first sight. Rumor on the streets was that once Juice caught up with Big-Swole, he was gon' pin the tail on the donkey. Although Big-Swole was a bit worried, he did his very best at downplaying the situation. He figured it was nothing that a bunch of money couldn't solve and if not, then Psycho would.

Big-Swole looked over at Psycho as they both headed towards the entrance of the building. "You can put that away now, shawty...we're safe up in here." He said, assuming everything was secure. They both entered the building, Big-Swole with a blunt in his hand and Psycho with the stick out, still visible.

Big-Swole just laughed to himself, feeling overprotected like back in the days when he had Juice on his side. Stepping into the lobby area, Big-Swole noticed that there wasn't anybody available at the front desk. The phone was ringing off the hook. "Muthafuckas always be complaining about their checks, wondering why they shit be coming up short...that's why!" he said while pointing at the phone, which was continuously ringing.

Psycho just stood on point as if he was waiting to be given an order to fulfill. He was on extra guard today for some reason. Big-Swole took it as he wanted an increase in pay and was working hard to prove that he deserved it. Fucking around with Big-Swole though...he'd never see it! He had put 20-bucks on Juice's head, and if the hired shooter got the job done, he would be handed over the prize, but nothing more.

Big-Swole was pissed off about the lack of work going on in his workplace. "What the fuck am I even hiring muthafuckas for...ain't shit getting done!" he complained while picking up the phone.

"Street Fame Recordings, hello, how can I help you?" Big-Swole answered. Whoever it was on the other end of the phone didn't reply, they just breathed lightly. "Hello-hello, is anyone there?"

The person on the phone remained silent causing Big-Swole to end the call.

"Nobody answered?" Psycho asked.

"Hell nah, I've been getting a bunch of empty calls lately," Big-Swole confessed while making all kinds of hand gestures. "I gotta good feeling that Juice and his gang is behind the shit...trying to scare a muthafucka, but my heart don't pump Kool-Aid. I fuck around and throw an extra *knick-knack* on his head, just off the strength."

On the outside, Psycho looked eagered, but truth be told, he wasn't flattered one bit. *Cheap ass muthafucka.* He thought to himself, giving Big-Swole a fake smile.

The lights were off throughout the building. However, from all the cars parked outside in the parking lot, you would've swore it was a party going on inside. "Where's everybody at?" Big-Swole asked.

"They're probably in the booth laying some tracks down." Psycho replied, getting the blunt from Big-Swole and hitting it.

"They better be," Big-Swole hastened to reply, as he slid down the hallway that leads to the recording area. "Even that dick sucking ass desk clerk, Jeanie!"

Psycho followed up behind Big-Swole, taking big pulls off the dope.

"Damn, yo' big lip ass must be trying to eat the blunt or something." Big-Swole said as Psycho passed him back the blunt.

Once Big-Swole made it to the recording room, he opened the door and stepped inside. The lights were cut off in the room as well. He walked over and flicked the switch. When the lights came on, an ugly plot unfolded right before Big-Swole's eyes.

"Big-Swole...just the person we've been waiting to see," Juice said, sitting down on a couch with an AR-15 in one of his arms and Jeanie in the other. "Come right in and have a seat, would you. I was just talking about you to the gang."

Jeanie sat in Juice's lap looking the least bit resistant while Tango and Bop stood on the side of the couch holding Glizzies—Tango on the left and Bop on the right. Both of 'em had infra-red beams dotted on Big-Swole's forehead. It wasn't anything the big fella could do but continue to hit the blunt.

Big-Swole took another puff off the blunt before dropping it on the floor and putting it out with his expensive alligator shoes. Afterwards, he slowly lifted his hands up in the air. "Juice man, what a pleasant surprise it is to see you. Tell me, what do I owe for this meeting?" he said, trying hard not to shit his pants.

Big-Swole couldn't help but look behind him, wondering what was taking Psycho so long to open fire. It didn't take long to figure out what was on Psycho's mind, his blicker was buried dead in Big-Swole's face. It was at that very moment where Big-Swole knew Juice meant business.

"Damn, Psycho," Big-Swole complained. "Where's the loyalty?"

Everybody in the room broke out in laughter at Big-Swole's contradictive remark—including Psycho. Here it is, a muthafucka who would betray his own mother is trying to preach about loyalty. He definitely was fronting his shit.

"How much you're getting for crossing me...at least tell me that much, Psycho?" Big-Swole asked his *ex*-shooter.

Psycho looked him right in the eye coldheartedly before answering the question, "This one's on the house, big fella!"

Big-Swole dropped his head, totally disappointed about the moment he was in. It wasn't too many times in his life where he had gotten out smarted. Juice had beaten him in playing his own game.

"So, there you have it, ladies and gentlemen," Juice intervened, clapping his hands and getting up from Jeanie's warm comfort. "Just another sad case of the good, the bad, and the pathetic...Being a fuckboy has deadly consequences."

As Juice walked up on Big-Swole, mopstick in aim, the big fella began to beg for his life. "Juice man...Let me explain...I'm sorry, killa, I never intended to leave you hanging. We built this company together, I just got caught up with trying to keep it running—all by myself."

By the time Juice was close up on Big-Swole, the nigga had fallen down to his knees crying like a lil' bitch. "Please, don't kill me for that,

Juice! Blame my situation, not my heart. Just please, don't kill me." He pled.

Big-Swole tried to kiss Juice's Giuseppe Zanotti sneakers, but the FOE chairman stepped his foot back to avoid letting it happen. Instead, Juice spat some phlegm down onto his face. Big-Swole didn't even bother to wipe it off.

"You're a great embarrassment to the mob as well as to yo'self." Juice said while he aimed the beam down on top of Big-Swole's head. "I take great pleasure in putting a couple of bullets in yo' skull myself."

"Oh no, please, don't do it!" Big-Swole begged, using his arms to cover up his head as if that was gon' block the slugs from penetrating his noggin—once Juice clutched the trigger. "Just tell me what you want, and I'll give it to you today...anything!"

"Anything?" Juice responded.

"Yes, anything. Just name it."

Juice didn't hesitate stating his demand, "I want this entire company signed over to me right now. Everything...from complete ownership and copyrights of all artists to the patents and trademarks of the brand Street Fame Entertainment as well as Street Fame Recordings."

"Damn, you want everything." Big-Swole blurted.

"The whole nine and a little bit more," Juice stated. "That's such a small price to pay in order for a bitch ass nigga like yo'self to stay alive."

"Alright...I agree!" Big-Swole, complied. "Just merch it on Rose that once I do this, you won't kill me still."

Although the red dot from the infra-red beam was planted in between Big-Swole's eyes, Juice's vision was still in the scope lining his adversary up. "On Rose grave, I'm not gon' kill you. Now, come over here and sign on all the dotted lines in this legal packet that Jeanie help put together for us." Juice advised.

Big-Swole got up and looked over at Jeanie, giving her a cold-stare. She gave him a hard stare back, happy to see him stuck in a position like this. He'd been short-changing her from the get-go. Making her give him sloppy-top had become a part of her daily job description, right along with whatever else he had lined up for her. Oftenly, he warned her about what would happen if she ever disobeyed him...fired and possibly even raped and killed.

Big-Swole went ahead and signed his John Hancock on each dotted line, page after page. Once Jeanie went through the forms, making sure he didn't miss a signature, she signed her name as a witness along with Tango, Boo-Bop, and Psycho. The shit was all set to be official, Juice would now be the new CEO of the record label, "Street Fame Entertainment."

It was only right that he made Jeanie the president of the label and put Psycho at head of his security. Tango and Boo-Bop mix-tapes were in the making, giving them a fair shot at climbing the ladder in Chiraq's rap-game. This was just the beginning of what Juice had in store.

Juice sat his assault rifle down and grabbed a bottle of Rose from off the table, letting it pop—"*POP!*" Champagne came bubbling from out the bottle onto the floor. Jeanie grabbed some glasses, and Juice began pouring everybody in the room a drinks—including Big-Swole. The whole team gathered up around where Big-Swole was at as Juice made a toast.

"Here's to success and capital gains in great abundance," Juice said as he pressed his glass up against theirs. "Street Fame Entertainment is schedule to take flight in five, four, three, two—one!"

When Juice got to one, he took his drank straight down the throat. It was a happy moment, everybody was cheering him along with only the exception of Big-Swole. The big fella was ready to go so he could plan his next move, retaliation against FOE. Let him tell it...the shit was far from over.

Big-Swole got up and tried to make his way towards the door...that is until Juice caught wind of the shit. "Where you think you're going, partner?" he asked while picking his chopper back up. Psycho went and guarded the door. Tango and Boo-Bop upped their weapons again. The whole scene kind of resembled how it looked when Big-Swole had first came into the room and cut the light on.

"Deja'vu, huh?" Juice said.

"You said if I turned over the record label, I could walk away alive." Big-Swole pled. "Come on now, Juice...you merched it!"

"I did say that, didn't I?" Juice began to lower his weapon. Clearly, he seen where Big-Swole had pissed on the floor at. It was all wet.

"Yeah!" Big-Swole replied.

"That's right, and a deal is a deal," Juice said, turning his weapon over to Jeanie. "I'm not gonna kill you, you big piece of shit."

Juice slid over to the table and poured him another shot of champagne, then he flopped down on the couch and took a sip. "Nah, I'm not gonna kill you, ol' pal...but I sure in hell ain't gon' try to stop Jeanie from getting her just-due. A deal is definitely a deal." he said while looking over at Jeanie. Juice had promised to let her be the one to put a bullet in Big-Swole's head.

Big-Swole could sense a red dot beaming in between his eyes. He shifted his focus over at Jeanie and noticed her standing with the AR-15 in her hand pointing it at him. He didn't even bother trying to beg for his life anymore, all the terrible shit he had done to her...it was no getting up out of this jam. The karma has finally caught up with him.

Big-Swole closed his eyes and began to pray, "Heavenly Father, forgive me for my sins—" was all he managed to say before Jeanie clutched the trigger. "*GLAH!*" His lifeless body melted towards the ground, landing face-first in a puddle of his own urine.

Juice and the rest of the gang huddled up around Big-Swole's slumped body and watched as blood gushed out the back of his head. Juice took his glass and held it high in the air, making a final declaration. "It's death before dishonor!"

Popeye was beginning to second guess the actual purpose of this trip; however, it was too late to try to turn back now. More than less, he held his composure and followed the lead of the Spanish man in front of him. The other ONE was in back of them, following as well.

They made it down the stairwell to a bank-vault looking door. The pisces in front spun the wheel on it around several times then pulled it open. The leading Spanish man let Popeye inside and the one in the back followed him in while his partner stayed behind guarding the outside of the door. It was no coming in or going out without their approval, which first came from the head nigga in charge—El-Huncho.

When Popeye walked inside the secluded room, he noticed a group of Surenos, armed with M16 assault rifles, standing around El-Huncho and what seemed to be a man in a guillotine. One of his hands were chopped off, laying on the pavement right in front of him. El-Huncho picked the poor guy's hand up and looked over at Popeye, waving at him with it.

"Popeye, come over here and join the fun." El-Huncho said mischievously as he wiped blood off the machete he'd just used to dismember dudes limb, onto the shirt of one of his soldiers that was standing nearby. The soldier didn't mind at all though…it was better that it was just his clothing being used like a dishrag and not his neck.

Popeye looked untouched…like seeing someone's hand butchered from their wrist was an everyday thang. As Popeye made it to the inner circle, he noticed that the man in the guillotine was Loso, *a.k.a.* "Carlos Santana." This was the federal agent who initially got El-Huncho all wild up, chopping muthafucka's body-parts off. How ironic that, at the current moment, El-Huncho didn't know he had just cut out the mole.

Popeye was lost in the sauce, he looked at Loso as he just trembled in extreme terror. The dismembered suspect done screamed and cried out so much that all he could do now was hum. *What the fuck did he do to deserve such torture?* Popeye thought to himself.

"Hey there, Popeye," El-Huncho said, waving Loso's chopped off paw around carelessly. "I was just telling brother Loso over here how much I despise a disloyal muthafucka…they just make my fucking skin crawl!"

El-Huncho had on a wife-beater with a vintage Gucci jumpsuit and the shoes to match. A pair of Gucci shades road the top of his forehead as he stood on the business with an iron fist. Just looking at him standing there talking with the machete in one hand—resting on top of his shoulder—and Loso's mitten in his other, reminded Popeye to never cross him.

Suddenly, one of El-Huncho's soldier's phone began ringing. "Hello, what the lick read?" he answered, listening closely to the information that was given to him.

"Aye, bro, tell boss that we just found out exactly who the rat is," the caller-said. "He goes by the name Carlos Santana, a short-husky, baldheaded muthafucka with a boat anchor tatted on his right hand."

"Uh-huh, is that right?" the soldier said, making his way over to El-Huncho to deliver the message.

Instantly, once El-Huncho learned the latest news, he looked down at the hand he was holding seeing that it was a left one. "Popeye, give me a hand, would you?" he asked for some support as if he didn't have enough helping hands already.

El-Huncho brought the machete down from off his shoulder. Popeye could only assume that it was time for him to make a "life or death" move...he dreaded ending up like Loso. El-Huncho's shooters would have to blow him down before he stand around and wait to be mutilated.

Right when Popeye had mustered up enough gut to take off, El-Huncho made himself more clear. "Here, hold this for me while I check something out right quick." El-Huncho handed Loso's severed palm over to him.

Immediately, Popeye felt a bit relieved knowing that his hands were still of some use to the bossman. "Sure, boss." he said gladly, grabbing onto Loso's severed limb.

El-Huncho went over to the guillotine, where Loso was locked in at, and swung away—like a mad lumberjack swiping an axe down on some wood. *CHOP-CHOP!*

Loso didn't even have a voice left to be heard, not even a hum anymore. He barely could shake. Blood gushed out of his amputated wrist from both parts, hand and arm.

El-Huncho looked back at Popeye, giving him a grim stare. "I could've been a surgical doctor of some kind...look how clean I make my cuts!" he said while pointing his bloody machete down at Loso's open palm that was twitching around on the marble floor.

"The first cut is the deepest." Popeye responded while looking down at it.

"You're damn right," El-Huncho agreed. "That's why I always measure once and cut however many times I have to whenever trouble comes."

El-Huncho reached down with the blade of his machete and fished the butchered limb in towards him, avoiding getting any blood on his Gucci-chucks. He grabbed the hand off the floor, clearly seeing that it was a perfect match. "Bingo!" he said, tossing it over to one of his soldiers, the one that delivered the message to him.

Popeye was a lucky man, if the call hadn't come when it did, he could have easily been sleeping with his fingers and the fishes. Seeing Popeye still standing appearing fearless in the face of death made El-Huncho think different of him. He was a fierce soldier, one whom he could very well use to help rule over the new Cartel.

El-Huncho walked back up on Popeye, wiping his bloody hands off on Popeye's silk Ferragamo shirt, and grabbed the back of his neck. He pulled his head close to him so he could clearly hear what he had to say. Popeye didn't resist, he knew better.

"I want Sam Walters dead and burned to the ground—prompto! If you can't kill him, I'll go kill him and then go kill you and yo' family!"

By no chance did Popeye take the threat lightly. Instead, he used it as motivation to hurry up and get the job done. El-Huncho handed him the deadly blade, taking away Loso's hand and finally shaking up with him. "Congratulations, my compadre...you just so happened to make the final cut. I'm making you my head lieutenant. But make no mistake about it, not even the slightest one...the consequence will be fatal." El-Huncho said, awarding Popeye supreme status.

"Now, do me a great favor and finish this bloody pig off for me," El-Huncho said, giving his right hand man his first command. "He's no longer a help to us or the FBI."

Without any delays, Popeye set his foot towards the guillotine, relentlessly swinging the machete like Jason. Seconds later, Loso's head came rolling up the marble floor like a bowling ball. El-Huncho was now beginning to trust Popeye.

CHAPTER #24

SHARKS ON DECK

When Stacey came up out of Walgreens, she was over agitated being that she had wasted unnecessary time, standing in the ATM line trying to withdraw some money for her drug addicted sister. This was the last day she had before Kick-Dough's surprise party, and she needed every minute of it devoted to getting the celebration together.

She hopped back in her truck and took off. Greedy got right back on her tail being as incognito as he possibly could, not letting her out of his sight. The sharks couldn't afford wasting any more time with snatching up the subject.

"This bitch is going in the same direction she just came from." Rocko said.

"You think the bitch made us?" Greedy asked.

"Not necessarily," Tu-Tu figured, scratching his Rick-Ross beard. "From the looks of it, she's heading back to her mother's house."

"Well, smooth then." Rocko said.

Tu-Tu grabbed his skully from off the floor and fixed it back on his baldhead, slightly tilting it to the right. Then he turned aside so that Greedy and Rocko could hear what he had to say. "Look, we're done pussy-footing around. It's go-time for real now! Rocko...you're ready?"

"Yep-yep," Rocko replied.

Immediately, Rocko began peeling out of his Moncler polo-shirt, slipping right into a red ComEd shirt with a matching cap. Then he grabbed the ComEd clipboard from off the seat. This was just a clever disguise, making it easy to jump a gate or two. He even had a fake I.D. clipped on to his shirt.

Stacey pulled back up at her mother's house, parking her car in the driveway by the side door. She hopped out and hurried inside. At this point, Stacey was racing against time.

"Pull down a couple houses," Tu-Tu instructed Greedy.

"Once you get inside and have everything under control, hit my line, nigga," Tu-Tu advised Rocko. "We're gonna be parked out back in the alley, waiting on yo' call."

"Copy that!" Rocko replied as he bailed out the car with the clipboard in his hand, looking very ComEd-*ish*.

Greedy pulled off slowly, and Rocko made his way towards the targeted house. Rocko took the pen out from the clipboard and began writing something down. He was now all the way in character. He went to the side door and pressed the doorbell, looking as professional as he could.

Ms. Jackie came to the door with Baby-Aaron in her arms. "Hello, how can I help you, handsome?" she said, trying to be sexy.

"Hey there, pretty lady. My name is Mark, and I'm a ComEd representative respectfully at your service today," Rocko stated properly. "We're inspecting the electricity flow coming from the circuit boards in the Hyde Park Community."

"Is that so?" Ms. Jackie responded, trying to show off her cleavage and in-shaped body. She had on a silk nightgown with a bathrobe slightly covering her up.

"Yes, ma'am, I just need to conduct a simple test on each fuse gauge," Rocko said, continuing to sound like he knew what he was talking about. "The whole process will take no more than 10 or 15-minutes."

A Novel by Pucasso

"Yeah, and how is this supposed to benefit me?" she asked, being flirtatious.

Rocko licked his lips and gave the woman a nice smile, showing off his wonderful white teeth. He knew he had her right where he wanted her. His next words would finalize the deal.

"Well, first of all, the test is guaranteed to lower your electricity bill by 25-percent." Rocko advised her, falsifying information.

That was enough music to Ms. Jackie's ears. Before Rocko could finish running down all the "fake" benefits to her, she opened the door wide. "Please, step right on in." she said, letting a coldblooded killer in her house.

Rocko entered the crib consensually, and the plot began thickening. Ms. Jackie shut the door and sat Baby-Aaron down, something she hardly ever does. Rocko flitted his eyes around the house observantly, casing the place like an inspector of some kind. He noticed Stacey and another girl, Tee-Tee, having a conversation in the dining room.

"Hey, young fella," Ms. Jackie called out, getting Rocko's attention. "Right this way."

She led him towards a door outside the kitchen by a short hallway. Stacey and Tee-Tee was sitting on a couch discussing something. Now was the perfect time for Rocko to make his move, he had all three of the girls gathered up—close by. It would be less chance for either one of 'em to escape. This shit was an art.

"Stacey, honey, come watch Baby-Aaron for a second while I take this fine young man downstairs to check the electricity." Ms. Jackie said, getting ready to open the basement door.

Stacey and Tee-Tee both got up and came towards where Ms. Jackie and Rocko was standing, only coming to stare down the barrel of an all

Thenon'

black FN-57. With great finesse, Rocko had upped his weapon on them while snatching up Baby-Aaron, simultaneously.

"Alright, everybody put yo' hands up and slowly get down on the floor," Rocko demanded, pressing the FN against Baby-Aaron's lil' chest. "I don't wanna have to blow the lil' one away."

Immediately, tears began falling from Stacey's face. "Please, don't hurt my baby!" she cried out, helplessly. Ms. Jackie and Tee-Tee just stood there looking stuck as if they smoked a bag of crack.

"I'm not gonna keep repeating myself, I asked kindly the first time," Rocko warned as he took the blicker off Baby-Aaron's chest and placed it upside his head. "The next step I'm gon' take won't be as nice."

"Alright-alright, please, don't kill my baby!" Stacey and her mother begged simultaneously while bending over and getting down on the floor—David Banner style. Tee-Tee followed suite as well; however, she was less emotional about it. She had been in this predicament many times before and knew exactly what it was about—*the money, baby!*

"Tell us what you want so we can give it to you and you can hurry up and leave." Ms. Jackie pled.

"Shut the fuck up, old lady…and keep yo' damn head down facing the floor," Rocko warned. "Please, don't force me to make good on my promise!"

Instantly, Ms. Jackie buried her head into the floor and so did both of her daughters. All of 'em were weeping like willows. Rocko went and placed Baby-Aaron in his high-chair by the kitchen table and then took a quick glance out the front blinds, making sure the scenery was safe and sound. After that, he hopped on the phone and called Tu-Tu.

"You got everything secure up in there, church?" Tu-Tu asked.

"Is pig's pussy pork!"

"Copy that," Tu-Tu said. "We're on our way through the backyard right now. Have the door open for us, okay!"

"10-4." Rocko responded, before ending the call. He grabbed a dish rag from out of the sink and then used it to open the door up, making sure he left no fingerprints behind anywhere. Baby-Aaron just watched cognitively as the shark slid back and forth through the kitchen. Within seconds, Greedy and the big fella Tu-Tu came strutting through the door, withdrawing their weapons.

Greedy had a small duffel bag with him. He reached in it and grabbed some masks and gloves, passing them around to the squad. The sharks danced around, putting the plot in its proper perspective.

Tu-Tu grabbed the duct tape and rope from the bag, throwing one to Rocko and the other to Greedy. "Get them all tied up, but first, pat 'em down and recover their phones. We don't need any surprises." he said while heading back to the window to peep the scene.

Rocko and Greedy got the girls together and wrapped up within a matter of seconds, sparing Baby-Aaron the "mummy" treatment. The boy wasn't capable of causing any harm to anybody—none whatsoever. Besides, they kind of like the lil' nigga. However, that alone wouldn't stop either one of 'em from smoking the kid if any games got played when it came time for Kick-Dough 'nem to run that bag.

Tu-Tu ordered for Rocko and Greedy to do a quick run through, making sure that no one else was there. Then, he hopped on the horn and called Duck.

"Demonstrate," he answered fearlessly.

"We're in shallow waters," Tu-Tu confirm his position. "Everybody's tied up like gym shoes."

"Okay then, how many heads you got up in there?"

"So far, three—not counting the kid," Tu-Tu replied. "I just sent the squad to do a thorough house check."

"Good-good...very good," Duck applaud him. "Shit done just got real, boys."

"About fucking time," Skee said, hearing the latest update. "I was just about to take a nap."

"Hell yeah!" Hungry added, giggling.

"Alright then, we bout to take flight and handle the business on our end. Just sit tight and let us do what we're great at. Once we're in the building, I'm gonna give you a call, and we'll just go from there, a'ight?" Duck instructed.

"Copy that, chief." Tu-Tu replied, examining the nickel-plated .45-llama he was holding.

"Well, BOS then." Duck said, ending the call.

Tu-Tu copped a squat and waited for Greedy and Rocko to make it back from the search. Once they got back confirming that the house was clear, Tu-Tu let them know what was up. "Bossman 'nem are moving in on buddy, right now. At this point, all we can do is just wait."

"Sound like pitch folks and hand grenades to me." Rocko said, stacking it on the BOS and throwing the rakes up with both hands, afterwards.

Hungry was an expert at breaking an entry, he had been pulling off burglaries since he was in the third grade. It wasn't a lock built that he couldn't pick; and when all seemed to fail, a good ol' flat-head screwdriver always did the trick. This shark had jumping a gate mapped out to a science.

Hungry made his way to the side of Kick-Dough's crib, carrying a duffel bag with a gun and some burglary tools inside. The plan was to enter through the side door while Skee, dressed up like a ComEd worker, distract Kick-Dough at the front door. The rest was said to be smooth sailing.

In the words of the top shark, Duck...*"The best robberies are those where a gun doesn't even have to get used. Once a gun gets fired, it alerts whoever's close by, letting them know that something bad is happening. The move is basically fronted then, one could only expect that the police had been notified and that they're on their way."*

This lick was precious to the sharks, not just an average gate being jumped. If handled accordingly, they could easily come out of the deal with a million dollars—that's 150-thousand apiece for them. This here was big fucking business!

Skee rang the doorbell, dressed identical to Rocko. Kick-Dough had been up for 30-minutes now and was in the kitchen, picking through the left over dinner that Stacey prepared for him. It was his favorite...steak and southern-style fried potatoes with some cheesy broccoli on the side. *UMMM!*

Although Kick-Dough had a decent appetite, he couldn't quite enjoy his meal. He had a lot on his mind, his main man A-1 was locked up with a no-bond; the police was looking for him for murder; Shoota was in the hood acting real crazy and had gotten his godsister pregnant; Pops was M.I.A. and nobody had the slightest clue where he could be; Ms. Jackie was steady sneak-dissing and hating on him every chance she got; Jessica was constantly threatening him and his family; muthafuckas was talking about robbing him when they see him; Stacey was currently pregnant with their second child, number three for him; and on top of all of this...his 25th birthday was less than a day away.

When Kick-Dough heard the doorbell ring, instantly, he thought about taking his chrome Desert-Eagle pistol with him to answer it. It was laying on the granite island, right where he was sitting trying to put something on his stomach. However, he went against his first mind and slid to the front door unarmed.

Duck was chilling in the cut, watching the scenery from all angles. He could see Skee and Hungry both at the same time. Kick-Dough made it to the door and took a peek out of it, seeing that it was just a ComEd worker, supposively. He was so oblivious to the treachery at hand.

"Who is it?" he asked while examining the person very well. Once he seen the I.D. clipped to the man's shirt labeled James, he waited for the correct answer.

"I'm James, a ComEd representative, and I'm here today inspecting circuit breakers." Skee responded, accordingly.

Kick-Dough lowered his antennas, everything seem to be safe so he went ahead and opened the door. Immediately, Duck got on the horn and gave Hungry the green light. Hungry went to work like **Cee-Lo Green**, prying the side door open in a flash as if he was a gorilla, and there was a bunch of bananas inside the house.

"What 's up, James?" Kick-Dough greeted the disguised gate jumper. "I'm K-D, how can I help you today."

"Hello, K-D, I'm here today running a service check on all the circuit breakers in this community. They had been considered faulty, and a recall had been put in on them." Skee exaggerated.

"Oh yeah," Kick-Dough responded, seeming to be interested in what he was talking about.

"Yeah, it's been several cases reported about circuit breakers catching on fire due to dangerous electric currents running, even when powered off. A simple test will take no more than 10-minutes to conduct, and with doing so, you automatically qualify for a 25-percent discount, which will be credited towards your next bill... are you interested?" Skee said, trying his best to drag the matter out to give Hungry enough time to invade the premises.

And Skee did good...by that time, Hungry was already creeping through the kitchen with his gun drawn.

"Why, sure I'm interested in anything that saves money coming from outta my pockets. Step right in, would you." Kick-Dough said, welcoming a stone-cold killer into his home.

Sweet-one! Skee thought to himself, entering the luxurious home.

"Right this way, homie." Kick-Dough said, directing Skee through the living room towards a side door that lead to the basement.

Duck, watching from afar, seen that both of his sharks were in the water so he went ahead and followed suit as well.

Remembering that he had left his blicker on the kitchen counter, Kick-Dough rerouted to get it. "Hold up a second." he said and then skipped in the direction of the kitchen. Before he could enter the extravagant scullery, Hungry, masked up with a Mac-90 in his hand, swung around the corner lining him up. The element of surprise had finally caught up with Kick-Dough.

"Put yo' muthafucking hands up," Hungry advised him, ruthlessly. "Now, nigga...don't make me bloody this place all the way up!"

At first sight, Kick-Dough thought that the gunman was a part of some kind of S.W.A.T. team sent to capture him; but once he heard the words come out of Hungry's mouth, he knew it was a hit. He turned around and tried to make a break for it, but Skee was right there on point with an HK 45—buried dead in his face.

Kick-Dough paused dead in his tracks and gently raised his hands up in the air, surrendering himself. Skee swiftly smacked him in the face with his H-K, "*CRACK!*" Instantly, Kick-Dough fell down to the ground and blacked out.

JUST MOMENTS LATER...

When Kick-Dough finally came to, back from the "Land of Nod," he was sitting in a chair tied up with duct-tape wrapped around his mouth. Skee was in front dousing him with some bottled water. Once Skee noticed him opening his eyes, he snatched the duct-tape from off his lips—dam near ripping his mustache off right along with it.

"Wake up, princess," Skee taunted. "It's time to get this show on the roll."

Hungry was somewhere searching the rest of the house, making sure it was secure. In no time, he came back and posted up with his sharks. "The house is secure, I see a couple of spot where safes might be hidden at too." he informed them.

Duck came up out the kitchen with a plate in his hands, eating the very meal that Stacey had put aside for Kick-Dough. "Ummm...this shit is smacking," he said, masked up with gloves on like the other sharks. These guys had come well-prepared, Kick-Dough seen that much already.

"Who put this lick together, Stacey or Jessica?" Duck asked, being hilarious; however, Kick-Dough didn't find the shit funny.

"What the fuck y'all come for, my life or just a bite to eat?" Kick-Dough said, appearing fearless.

Duck wiped his mouth off with his shirt sleeve and sat the plate down on the table, pulling out a chrome .45-Desert Eagle. This was the very gun Kick-Dough had left on the kitchen counter, right besides the pre-cooked chow. Duck cocked one into the chamber and aimed the gun at Kick-Dough's face.

"You know...you supposed to already have this fancy piece of equipment ready to blow and on you at all times." Duck broke some common street laws down to Kick-Dough. He walked up on him and pressed the pole into his forehead. "I want more than just a bite to eat, shrimpy. Yo' life means shit to me...whether you live or die is totally up to the weight of yo' wallet. I'm on a money-making mission."

Kick-Dough took a moment before responding, he seen that Duck and his squad meant business and would go to the extremes to get whatever they wanted, possibly. Let him tell it...he was a dead man either way, whether he complied or not. "I ain't giving up shit, you gotta take it in blood, nigga!" he said, coming to terms with the possibility of not seeing his 25th-birthday.

Duck giggled heartlessly, and the other sharks joined in on the laughter. "This nigga's a real live hard-ball...I like that." he stated, withdrawing the Desert Eagle from out of Kick-Dough's face and putting it into the small of his back. Skee and Hungry kept their blickers aimed at Kick-Dough with precision.

"You know...I really don't like guns," Duck confessed while walking around in back of Kick-Dough, whipping out a big Rambo-looking knife.

"For one, they're too damn loud...the sound hurts my fucking ears."

Duck put the knife up to Kick-Dough's neck, closely. The blade was so sharp that it sliced into his flesh with just the slightest touch. "Now, knives on the other hand...these are my buddies." Duck said, easing the blade up off of his neck a bit.

Kick-Dough wasn't shook still, even after seeing a lil' of his blood spilled. He kept the poker-face through it all as if he had been in worser situations. "Did you come to spill my blood or just to hold a conversation. Seems like it to me, you just wanna kick it. However, I don't have any legs right now, so let's get on with this shit. I got thangs to do, even in the afterlife." he said, profoundly.

Duck was flattered, he appreciated Kick-Dough's shark-life qualities. Had things been a little bit different, Duck would've just thrown the boy on his squad somehow. Duck favored real niggas; however, it was a bigger mission at hand and executing it meant big-bucks. Besides, the only thing on a shark's mind is *eat*.

"Well, since you don't wanna talk freely... let me give you a lil' motivation." Duck stated, jumping on the horn and Facetiming Tu-Tu.

"What's up, Jaws!" he answered, referring Duck to the most deadliest shark in T.V.'s history.

"Do me a quick favor, give me something small to show our golden boy here exactly how we're coming. I tried warning him already, but he's a stubborn muthafucka." Duck said.

Tu-Tu followed orders like the true disciple he was. He sat all of ladies upward on the floor and had Greedy stand on one side of them and Rocko on the other...both of 'em masked up with guns in their hands, pointed down at the victims. The clip looked something like a terrorists' hostage recording. Once Duck showed Kick-Dough the horrifying footage, the thrill was on.

"Oh...I didn't even know this nigga had tears." Hungry said, noticing Kick-Dough all water-eyed.

Duck continued to play puppet master. "Better yet, great white...show yo' fins, let this disobedient swimmer know he's in deep waters." he commanded Tu-Tu.

Tu-Tu went and grabbed Baby-Aaron from out of his high-chair then Face-Timed a selfie of him and the boy while holding his Llama upside his head. Duck showed Kick-Dough the footage again, and all that tough boy shit went out the window.

"Okay, please, stop this," Kick-Dough begged, breaking down crying. "I'll give you whatever you want, just please...let my family go first."

"See, that's where you got life fucked up, playboy!" Duck argued. "You ain't running shit right now, I do!"

Duck hopped on the horn and instructed Stacey to be kicked in the stomach. Tu-Tu delegated the chore to Rocko. Kick-Dough was forced to watch as Rocko stomped his 10 and a half, Air Max-95's down against her belly with force.

"Stop it, please! You made your point, just tell me what you want me to do, and I'll do it." Kick-Dough cried out, helplessly.

Duck walked back up on Kick-Dough and gave him several pats on the back. "Good-good, now we're talking. I knew you'd see shit my way." he said, putting away his blade.

"There's no price limited to be exchanged for a love one's life. All I'm asking is a quarter-mil apiece for yours. That's a million dollars, not counting you and yo' unborn child considering that it's still alive. And for the record, I came for a mil-ticket, not to spill blood. However, we can have it both ways if that's what you prefer." Duck stated, smoothly.

"All I got is 'bout a quarter-mil on hand," Kick-Dough advised him. "The rest of my money's being invested in different ventures."

Duck looked down at Kick-Dough sideways. "I don't believe you one bit. We've been scoping you out for quite some time now, and you've gotten fat. I bet you gotta cool million just laying around in here somewhere." he said, figuring Kick-Dough was holding back. He signaled for Hungry to do what he does best—-find the money.

"So, where would this quarter-horse be?" Duck asked as he picked the plate back up off the table and began eating from it again. Skee just sat still on the couch with his gun aimed at Kick-Dough's head.

Kick-Dough took a moment to think the situation out clearly. If he lead them to his stash in the house, the gate-jumpers would come up on more than just a fourth of a ticket. However, if they snooped around too much at Stacey's mother's house, they're likely to find the golden book. Them shits held over a hundred pages of Lime-Lites, totaling out to more than 50-million dollars. He couldn't allow that to happen, not at any expense.

"It's upstairs in the master-bedroom, underneath the floor of the right hand bed dresser." Kick-Dough answered without any further delay. "Just move it out the way and pull the carpet up...you'll see the safe there, buried in the floor."

Duck signaled Skee to go and check it out. "You bet not be shitting me. If so, the next time I jump on the phone—somebody's gonna die." Duck warned.

Within the next few minutes, Skee came back with a big smile on his face. "It's there boss, just like he said." he confirmed.

"Good, now all we need is the combination numbers so we can see what's all in there." Duck said.

Kick-Dough had no problems with coming off the code. Instantly, Skee was back on his merry way with a duffel bag in his hand. Finally, Hungry made his way back to the scene looking proud.

"I see two safes, one in the bathroom upstairs and another one in the baby's bedroom closet." Hungry said. "Some real good ones, if I must say so myself."

"Well-well, looks like our golden boy here is holding out on us," Duck said, looking at Kick-Dough disappointedly. "Now, what do you have to say about this?"

Before Kick-Dough could even try to explain, Duck interrupted him. "You must think I'm some kind of bitch, huh?"

"Nah, man...I don't think anything like that," Kick-Dough pleaded. "That's way over a million dollars. Take it, it's all yours."

The whole while, Kick-Dough had been trying to free himself from the rope his hands and ankles were wrapped up with. It was a tight hold though, and it was only a matter of time before the robbery was over. He could only assume that the sharks were gonna smoke him after they had gotten all what they came for and didn't need him anymore.

Hungry found a couple of empty duffel bags in a closet and headed towards the safes. Everything was going as planned. To the average eye, it seemed like the sharks were definitely in the money.

CHAPTER #25

ᗞOWᑎ TO TᕼE ᗷOTTOᗰ OF IT

When Skee and Hungry got done bagging up all the money from out of each safe, the total estimation was thought out to be over a mil——just like Kick-Dough said. The shit had Duck stuck wondering, *What else could this nigga possibly be trying hide? Why would he come off a hefty life's savings so easily? He got to be protecting something else that's worth more in Value.*

Duck, a methodical genius, paced back and forth trying to put two and two together. Skee and Hungry had gone fishing for a final time. It was something the sharks were missing, and the Duckster planned to get down to the bottom of it. A light bulb popped on in Duck's head as he thought, *Drugs...Where's the fucking bricks?*

Duck had came to the rationalization that Kick-Dough had a boat load of birds hidden at Stacey's mother's crib. "That's it...Stacey's mother's place is the safe house!" he thought out loud.

By this time, Kick-Dough had finally untied himself and was carefully positioning himself to make an attack on Duck. The great white was so caught up in thought that he wasn't paying any attention. Kick-Dough was defenseless, but he didn't let that discourage him from pulling a "Bruce Willis."

Duck jumped on the phone and gave Tu-Tu an update of what all had happened. He gave him a count of the money they came up on and ordered him to toss up Stacey's mother's spot, claiming that there were an unlimited supply of drugs somewhere there. Tu-Tu got right to it, putting Greedy on watch while him and Rocko went fishing.

When Duck came up out of the kitchen, Kick-Dough made his move. As soon as Duck walked by him, he took off full-fledgedly as if he was bailing out a car, going to snatch up a money bag. Duck couldn't have seen it coming. In one swift motion, Kick-Dough grabbed the Dessy from out the small of Duck's back and pointed it there—holding him hostage.

"Now, you put your muthafucking hands up and don't try to be smart about it!" Kick-Dough demanded.

Duck was caught by surprise and had no other choice but to follow the orders that were given to him. Hungry and Skee came down the stairs, seeing the twisted plot at hand. Instantaneously, both of 'em drew their weapons.

"Let him go or I'ma make the call to have yo' girl raped and then beaten to death, right in front of yo' kid!" Hungry threatened, aiming the Mac-90 at Kick-Dough. He couldn't get a good focus on the target though, Duck's body was all in the way.

Skee didn't bother to say a word, he just waited on a clear shot to take at Kick-Dough's head. He too couldn't get a good aim to fire shots without running the risk of possibly striking Duck. It was a very dangerous matter, and it wouldn't be long before someone tried making a sudden move.

Detective Hogan, *a.k.a.* **"Cigarman,"** drove at a decent speed, trying to follow up on a lead he had gotten from an anonymous caller—Ms. Jackie. He had her current address punched in on his navigational system, leading him directly towards her house. He was eager and determined to arrest Anthony Moore, "Kick-Dough," and bring him in for the crime of

Felony-Murder. He'd been wanted for over a year now, and the tip Ms. Jackie had partially given up was the only lead Cigarman had to go off of.

Although the time and dedication Cigarman was putting towards the case was slowly ruining his marriage, he didn't really give a fuck. His law enforcement career depended on making this arrest, which he felt was well-worth the risk of losing his wife and kids. He was getting up there in age, and his superiors constantly pressured him about resorting to a desk duty or maybe retiring. Nobody in the department wanted him as a partner…he was a grumpy old man who claimed to know everything.

Ever since his partner John Wright, *a.k.a.* "Super Cop," had gotten gunned down in the line of duty over a decade ago, he'd been going down in the slumps. Drinking had become a method he often used to help cope with Super Cop's death. Since the very day Super Cop got blown down in that convenience store, he had been blaming himself.

Actually, it wasn't Cigarman's fault for his partner's death...Super Cop was just living up to his name. The two savvy detectives were closing in on an armed robbery suspect, trapped inside the store. Cigarman and Super Cop had split up, forcing the robbery suspect into a corner—supposively. However, the gate-jumper had somehow hidden in one of the food shelves. He twisted the hunt around and got in pursuit of Cigarman, who was creeping up the side of an aisle. Right when the robber had Cigarman lined up and was set to clutch the trigger,

Super Cop came to the rescue using his body as a shield. He managed to push Cigarman out of the line of fire, but at a deadly expense. Super Cop ended up catching multiple shots all across his body.

Instantly, Cigarman returned fire giving the assailant a couple of headshots—no photography. The criminal died right on the spot. Super Cop fought hard to stay alive, but the Reaper's powers are irreversible.

He ended up dying on the operating table. He was survived by a wife and two kids.

Everybody in the department were hurt by the tragic death of, John Wright, especially Detective Hogan. As time went on, he felt that it was supposed to be him who got smoked, not Super Cop. Guilt began eating him alive.

Now, here's where the plot gets thickened. The Caucasian veteran man who allegedly died from injuries sustained in the robbery A-1 and Kick-Dough was involved in was Super Cop's father. From the very day of Clifford's death, Detective Hogan's mind hadn't been anywhere else, other than making sure the killers get brought to justice. Hogan's wife was beginning to bug up on him about his drawn-out obsession, divorce was her final decision.

Detective Hogan looked down at his phone reading through the latest text-messages he'd just gotten from his wife. *"I'm taking the kids and going back to live with my mother. I don't wanna be with you any more. My life is so miserable, and it's all because of you. We don't even fuck anymore...I'm filing for divorce. Sorry, but I just can't do this any longer."*

The Dear-John didn't bother Detective Hogan one bit. He figured as long as he could still see his kids he'd be alright. "Fuck her...fuck everybody! Once I make this arrest, the whole world's gon' be back on my jock." he said to himself as he flamed up a cigar and applied pressure to the gas-pedal, making his way to Ms. Jackie's residence.

CHAPTER #26

ΤΗΕ GRAND FINALE

Greedy waited impatiently guarding over the hostages while Tu-Tu and Rocko tore the house up—looking for an abundance of drugs. Greedy watched at the clock on the wall as the long hand began making itself around in a circle. *What the fuck...these niggas' taking all day,* he thought to himself.

Greedy looked over at where Ms. Jackie and her two daughters were laying, noticing them whispering amongst themselves. "That's enough of all that gossiping over there...either shut the fuck up already, or it's gon' get real hot up in here!" he warned as he waved his blicker around.

Ms. Jackie 'nem were congregating about coming up with a way out of the terrible predicament they were currently in. Baby-Aaron was still sitting in his high-chair, supposedly. Greedy's voice was beginning to ring a bell in Tee-Tee's head. *I know that voice from somewhere.* she thought to herself.

Ms. Jackie had came up with a desperate plan in the attempt of trying to save her baby's lives. She understood that sacrifices must be made, and risking her life for her family's was a meaningful obligation. Somehow, with her hands tied up behind her back, she managed getting up from the floor.

Greedy peeped the unauthorized movement and bugged the fuck up. "Bitch, what the fuck you think you're doing?" he shouted while pointing his pistol at her.

"Please, let my babies go," Ms. Jackie begged. "Keep me for your hostage until you get whatever it is you're looking for."

"Oh, you must think this shit is a game." Greedy replied, cocking a bullet into the chamber of his gun.

Stacey and Tee-Tee stayed put on the floor, terrified of what Greedy was possibly getting ready to do. "Please, don't hurt her!" they cried out, simultaneously. By this time, he was on the way over to where Ms. Jackie was standing, toting the cannon and an ugly mug. Ms. Jackie just stood there—stuck in complete terror.

Finally, Tu-Tu came from out of the basement seeing the situation getting out of hand. "What the fuck's going on up in here, G?" he asked, waving his Llama at Ms. Jackie.

"Man, this old bitch think I'ma joke. Somehow, she got up and began begging me to let them go. I was just about to handle my function." Greedy replied.

A light bulb popped on in Tee-Tee's head. *Greedy!* Finally, she put two and two together, matching a face with the voice she'd been hearing all along. How could she've been so unaware of the very vocals that oftenly moaned in her ears, telling her how much she was loved. Tee-Tee done sucked and fucked Greedy on numerous occasions. Hell, let her tell it...he was her man.

"Greedy, is that you?" Tee-Tee asked, hoping now that the dark situation she and her family were in would lighten up a bit.

Greedy just stood there looking dumbfounded now that his move was completely fronted. Hearing all the commotion going on back and forward Rocko shot down the stairs to see what was up. He was holding a duffel bag full of money and a notebook in one hand and his weapon in the other. He sat the bag and notebook down on the table and went to help defuse the situation.

Tu-Tu looked over at Greedy, very disgusted. He had specifically asked him if he knew the bitch, and he looked him dead in the face and lied. Tu-Tu wasn't the one to be betrayed or even given false information to. He gave 100-percent of loyalty out to his sharks and expected nothing less back in return. *I should smoke this nigga's top right here where he stand!* Tu-Tu contemplated.

Greedy sensed the animosity, he couldn't help but see hate burning in Tu-Tu's eyes. Truth be told, Tu-Tu never really liked Greedy. He always had his doubts about him being cut out for a *shark-knot* lifestyle. However, he tolerated the boy being around due to one fact only—he was Duck's lil' cuz.

Tu-Tu didn't front the move, popping some holes through Greedy's head, just yet. Now wasn't the time, it was other impressive shit that needed to be handled first...like for one, getting the current moment under control. Shit was beginning to fall apart.

Tee-Tee was persistent about trying to come up out of the jam that her and family were in. "Greedy, baby, please...don't kill us! Y'all can have whatever it is y'all are searching for, just let us go. I promise we're not gonna get the cops involved. Come on now, you know me, Greedy." she pleaded.

Rocko was completely confused behind what was taking place. He glanced over at Greedy, looking screw-faced, and then at Tu-Tu. "What the fuck did I miss?" he asked.

Tu-Tu just stood there, hot under the collar, with his arms folded. He gave Rocko a look of repugnance, rolling his eyes off of him and placing them on Greedy. Rocko knew very well what he was thinking.

"Man, G, control yo' lil' cluck fuck-buddy before shit get real messy!" Tu-Tu warned Greedy.

A Novel by Pucasso

It was at this very moment that Greedy realized he had fucked up…big time. He knew already that Tu-Tu really didn't give a fuck about him and was just looking for the slightest reason to push his wig back—Lebron James style. He felt the need to prove himself all of a sudden.

"If I have to tell you to shut the fuck up again," Greedy stated as he tried stomping Tee-Tee's ears together. "It's gonna be after I put a bullet in the back of your head first, bitch!"

Stacey cried out helplessly, "Please, stop it…you're gonna kill her!" she shouted.

Tu-Tu signaled Rocko, "Man, go over there and get that clown, would you!" he said.

Greedy was caught up in the moment of tap-dancing on Tee-Tee's skull when Rocko approached him. "Alright, fam, that's enough…I think you made your point very well." he said, grabbing him by the shoulder.

Tu-Tu began to inch his way closer to the action. Suddenly, Ms. Jackie lashed out at Greedy, head first, trying to take a big bite at his face. "You muthafucking hoodlum, pick on somebody yo' own damn size!" she yelled out. Just before she got her teeth close by Greedy's nose, Tu-Tu caught her in the jaw with a crazy left hook. *"WHAM!"* Instantly, she plummeted to the floor.

The sound of glass shattering against the hardwood floor echoed from the kitchen. In a sudden state of panic, Greedy swung around with his weapon right along with him—firing it twice. *"FAH-FAH!"* The gun shots sounded off harshly, bringing everybody in the house at attention.

Greedy hardly ever fired a weapon; and once he had a visual on exactly what he just done, it was quite difficult for him to remain standing. One of the bullets that he mistakenly discharged had smacked Baby-Aaron upside the face knocking half of his head off. The impact of the poor kid getting hit sent his tiny body tumbling backwards, all the way up under the kitchen table.

"What the fuck is wrong with you, scud? You really done fronted your shit now. Look at the mess you just made, how in the fuck you suppose we clean this up?" Rocko argued.

Stacey's heart was poured out on the ground, running right along with her baby's brains, which was pure and innocent. Greedy began pacing back and forward, looking as pathetic as can be. Stacey's cries grew loud and louder until Tu-Tu decided to put her in check.

"Bitch, shut the fuck up before I do you the same way—on purpose! That lil' boy's death falls on y'all dumb ass. Any more foolish acts and I'ma go back to back giving each one of you head shots…I mean it!" Tu-Tu warned.

All of the ladies just laid face down on the floor, quietly weeping among themselves. Rocko went to the front window and scoped the scene, seeing if anything looked out of the norm. Everything appeared to be fine. However, trouble wasn't far away.

"We gotta get the hell outta here, right now," Rocko advised. "The cops will be coming any minute!"

"Copy that!" Tu-Tu agreed as he made his way over to Greedy.

Greedy had taken a slight squat down, crouched upwards with his back against the wall. He had lifted up his skee-mask, revealing his face as he dropped it in between his palms—along with the smoking gun. It wasn't a secret that this was his first body, and being that it was done on an innocent two-year old had him emotionally imbalanced.

"Fuck-fuck-fuck!" Greedy repeated to himself as he pounded the murder weapon against his skull.

Tu-Tu was the least bit sympathetic towards Greedy. "Man, get yo' punk ass up so we can get the fuck outta dodge. You can beat yo'self up about that shit later…right now, we gotta jet!" he shouted.

Greedy opened his bloodshot eyes and looked at Tu-Tu… and then at Rocko. "Y'all go on ahead without me, I don't deserve to live. Please, God, forgive me for my sins…" Greedy pleaded as he shoved the barrel of his gun up into his mouth.

"No—Greedy, don't!" Rocko yelled.

"*FAH!*"

SECONDS LATER…

Tu-Tu stood there, in front of Greedy's lifeless body, watching brain matter gush out the back of his head onto the wall. When the shot sounded off, Tu-Tu didn't even flinch. He just stared deeply into Greedy's eyes as they began to go dim. From the looks of the shit, you would've thought Tu-Tu smoked his ass.

"Bitch ass nigga beat me to the punch." Tu-Tu said.

Greedy's hands dropped, letting go of the smoking pistol onto the floor. His body slid down the wall and twisted forwards, landing on top of the gun. Blood was all on the floor and wall.

Tu-Tu looked over at Rocko who was standing emotionless with his weapon aimed down at the females, waiting to be given the green light to blow 'em down—execution-style. Tu-Tu dug in Greedy's pocket and grabbed his phone and the keys to the getaway car, tossing 'em both over to Rocko.

"Here…go and start the car. Take the bag of money with you," Tu-Tu instructed his shark. "I'll be right behind you once I finish these bitches off."

Rocko snatched the money bag up, forgetting to grab the notebook…what an unfortunate move!

"When you make it to the car, call Duck and give him an update of what all just went down," Tu-Tu said as he recovered Greedy's gun and got in position to kill the hostages. "Tell him that we're on our way to the hideout, okay!"

"Copy that." Rocko replied, tiptoeing towards the exit door in the kitchen, making sure he didn't get any of Baby-Aaron's brain fragments on the bottom of his classic shoes. "Hurry up too, nigga…ain't no telling who heard them shots."

"I'm already knowing," Tu-Tu responded, getting ready to make some kill shots. "I ain't gon' be long at all."

Tu-Tu pointed the blicker downwards, right above Stacey's head. She was crying and saying her prayers, silently. The Grim-Reaper was definitely in the building.

Detective Hogan hopped out the car and made his way towards the address he had punched in on his GPS-system. Out of nowhere, he heard the firing of a gun coming from the house he was approaching. Immediately, he drew his weapon and took cover on the side of the resident. "What the fuck have I gotten myself into this time?" he said to himself, reaching for his motorola to report shots fired and request for back-up.

Detective Hogan came to realize that he had left all of his patrol equipment back at the station, right along with his bulletproof vest. Hell, moving so fast, he even left his phone in the car. He was forced to go into this situation without any "A-A," all he had was a gun and a good aim.

When Rocko came up out of the house, Detective Hogan swiftly turned aside seeing a masked gunman carrying a large duffel bag. The determined detective aimed his weapon with both hands and positioned himself to fire shots at the unknown suspect. "Freeze...this is the police." he warned the crook.

Rocko, not shook the slightest bit, turned around in an attempt to lick shots at the old copper. However, Detective Hogan was already on point—prepared to blow at any sudden move. "*GLAH-GLAH-GLAH-GLAH!*" was the sound of the cop's gun as he clutched the trigger. He caught Rocko in the shoulder and arm, knocking him down to the pavement.

Rocko crawled in front of Stacey's SUV and took cover. Tu-Tu, just a milli-second away from spraying down Stacey 'nem, glanced out the window and seen an old white man with his pistol drawn moving in on Rocko. He was taking cover laying in front of the Q7 truck, just waiting to return fire. Detective Hogan slowly inched his way closer to him.

"Surrender yourself, toss your weapon and come from behind the car with your hands held high," Detective Hogan advised him. "I don't want to have to kill you."

Tu-Tu posted up by the door, waiting on his cue.

"I'm going to ask you one last time to toss over your weapon and surrender yourself!" Detective Hogan repeated himself.

"Nah, I ain't going at gunpoint," Rocko shouted as he stuck his gun out from around the truck, preparing to open fire. "You die muthafucka!"

"*CLINK-CLINK-CLINK!*" Rocko popped off. Instantly, Detective Hogan took cover behind the vehicle. Rocko conjured up enough energy to hop up and take off running. Like a pro, he still was holding onto that duffel bag—with his dear life. Blood was all over his body, everywhere.

As soon as Detective Hogan sensed Rocko was done licking shots, he hopped up and aimed his pistol at the back of Rocko's head. *I'm about two kill this son of a bitch.now!* he thought to himself, getting ready to pull the trigger. However, before he could do the damn thang, Tu-Tu came charging out the side door busting two-guns...his and Greedy's.

"*FAH-FAH...BOCAH-BOCAH...FAH-FAH...BOCAH-BOCAH!*"
Both guns went off simultaneously, as Tu-Tu waved his arms around in circles like he was turning a rope, playing double-dutch or something.

Detective Hogan never seen it coming, he caught it all in the chest. Slugs had him doing full flips like fixer-uppers. He tumbled to the ground and blood came spilling out of his mouth, as he tried holding on to his dear life. It was gradually slipping away from him.

Hearing the violent shots fired, Rocko went diving to ground assuming that it was the cop blowing at him again. After realizing that he didn't get hit up, he looked up and seen Tu-Tu walking over to the cop, who was slumped on the pavement, and pop a couple slugs right into his face. "*FAH-FAH!*" It was good-riddance for the "Cigarman." He was now making his way to be reunited with Super Cop.

All you could hear in the air were police sirens coming from a far. Tu-Tu ran over towards Rocko picking him up, and balancing him on his shoulder, helping him get back to the getaway car. Once they made it there, Tu-Tu sat Rocko in the backseat and did his best at stopping him from bleeding out to death. Once he got his homie stable, he got the car keys from him, fired up the engine, and smashed off.

"Hang in there, champ," Tu-Tu said, while whipping the car discreetly, getting as far away from the crime-scene as possible. "I'ma get you some help real quick."

A fleet of police squad cars came flying pass them going in the opposite direction. Tu-Tu looked over in the duffel bag and seen a whole bunch of currency—at the least a quarter-mil. This was just a mere portion of what Duck 'nem had already came up on.

"I searched everywhere in that fucking house," Rocko managed to say, feeling extreme pain in his body from the hot copper burning. "And I didn't find any drugs, not even a blunt."

The more Rocko tried talking, the more his gunshot wounds burned. "Aww fuck, this shit hurts like hell!" he said as he braced himself for the excruciating pain that was continuously throbbing through his body.

"Just relax, my nigga," Tu-Tu advised him as he hopped on the horn and called Duck. "We're almost in the money."

When Duck's phone rang in his pocket, it was a perfect distraction giving him a small window of opportunity. He swiveled himself around, out of what seemed to be a tight situation, and upped his Rambo-knife stabbing Kick-Dough in his ribs with it. The shit looked like a scene from off an old Steven Segal flick.

Once Duck busted the move, stabbing Kick-Dough in the ribs, he dived out and away from him knowing that a whole bunch of gunshots were about to follow. Regardless of the stab wound he just sustained, Kick-Dough remained strong like a fierce soldier on the frontline of a war. Immediately, he opened fire on Hungry, "*DOOM-DOOM-DOOM!*"

hitting him up in the arms and knocking the machine-gun out of his hands.

Instantly, Skee returned fire as he ran for cover, *"BOCAH-BOCAH-BOCAH- BOCAH-BOCAH-BOCAH!"* Shots went blazing right pass Kick-Dough's face…he could just feel the heat dripping from off the hot lead.

By this time, Duck had crawled himself into the kitchen and taken cover behind the granite island. Kick-Dough got low as well, taking cover behind the other side of the wall from where Skee was. "Drop the gun and come out with yo' hands up, and I promise I won't make your family suffer for your stupidity." Skee said, faking a compromise.

Finally, Hungry had taken back control of his weapon. He was bleeding out all where he stood. "I'm hit…that bitch ass nigga hit me. I'ma kill him dead!" he shouted out as he rushed towards the section of the house where Kick-Dough was lamping.

Hungry had the Mac-90 pointed in front of him, aiming it as best as his injured self possibly could. He shot right by Skee, not even noticing him also creeping up alongside of the wall where Kick-Dough was hiding behind. *What the fuck is this nigga trying to do—get himself killed?* Skee thought to himself. He was about to try to stop Hungry, but the look on his face clearly stated…"bloody murder." Duck was *"ducking that action,"* in the kitchen *"ducking down"* hoping all of his *"ducks were lined up."*

"I hope you ready, muthafucka," Hungry yelled out, swinging from around the wall. "Here comes the pain!"

Hungry gave his trigger finger a slight work out. *"RAT-TAT-TAT-TAT!"* The sound of his Mac sprayed rapidly as he waved it around carelessly. Bullets ripped through the luxurious furniture that Kick-Dough was taking cover behind, skinning him upside the head.

Kick-Dough hid behind the couch as much as he could, trying hard not to get struck by another stray bullet. He only had several shots left in his gun, so he planned to make every last one count. However, Hungry was on a rampage with letting his gun talk, "*RAT-TAT-TAT-TAT!*" Kick-Dough had to come up with something in a hurry.

Skee was in flight, making his way to the shootout to end the shit once and for all. As soon as Hungry let up off the trigger, Kick-Dough hopped up on cue. Skee was just setting foot in the room when he heard the infamous shots. "*DOOM-DOOM-DOOM-DOOM!*" the Dessy sounded off as Kick-Dough held it firmly with both hands, aiming with precision.

When Kick-Dough eased up off the trigger, Hungry's head resembled a bowling ball. His eyes rolled to the back of his head as he melted his way down to the ground. Immediately, the Grim-Reaper took over his soul.

Looking out the corner of his eye, Kick-Dough peeped another masked gunman entering the room, aiming a pistol. Swiftly, Kick-Dough swung his gun and clutched the trigger, hoping to beat the buzzer.

Duck did nothing but watch as the grand finale unfolded right before his very eyes. **To be continued...**

OUTRO:

PLAY TIME'S OVER

Muscles laid on his bunk in the hole, daydreaming about all of the shit he had been through in life. His prison term had become a long life's lesson that he was gradually learning. However, the nightmare was beginning to seem like it would never end. He was constantly losing good time, which keep pushing his out date further back.

The one thing that made him feel good about himself and encouraged him to keep his head to the sky through adversities was the fact that he kept it gangsta throughout the whole flick. No one could ever say he was a mark of any kind. He carried himself prestigiously, every step of the way. His street cred grew more notorious from the work he had put in on the inside.

Muscles was a bit uneasy today being that...it was the day he had been scheduled to see the PRB, Prison Review Board. They had the power to give him more set time to do or possibly—grant him an immediate release. A new law had just passed, shaving some years off of his sentence; however, all the set time he caught, had him undetermined about when he'll be coming home.

Muscles went deep into his thoughts, back when before he even caught the attempt-murder charges he was locked up for. He had just bonded out for 10-thousand dollars on a home invasion charge he caught O-T. This was at the point of his life where he just started seeing some real money. Well, at least more money than the people around him were seeing—all compliments of Bible.

A Novel by Pucasso

When Bible came home from doing time off an armed-robbery case, it didn't take long for him to run up a check. Going O-T was just the move he needed, putting him in a league of his own. It was only right that he put his cousin Muscles, "Kee-Kee," on.

Kee-Kee began making 4-thousand dollars off an ounce O-T...that's more than 5-times the amount he was paying for it. In the city, he was barely even doubling his money, off the onion. In just a days work O-T, Kee-Kee would often come back to the city with at least 2-racks or better. The only muthafucka on the Fo' that could compete with that was A-1, "Shawty Bankroll".

Kee-Kee kept whipping up on the block in something new, only coming to either crashing it on his own terms or while in a high speed chase with the police. Just because Kee-Kee was clocking major figures didn't stop him from being a "vicious" person. He keep the blicker on him daily as if it was a part of his gear.

Eventually, Kee-Kee began falling off due to all the craziness he was playing in the streets. Instead of him stacking his bread like Bible advised him to do, he fucked it off carelessly—on cars, drugs, designer clothes, jewelry, and of course...his glorious MVP-team. Bible didn't take to well to the shit and ending up falling back off on him.

Suddenly, Kee-Kee began catching a number of offenses, all leading up to the critical charge that took him down. On one beautiful spring day, Kee-Kee was out sliding through the land in a four-door Cutlass Supreme bumping **Triple-Six Mafia**, *"Who Run It!"* At this point, the loose cannon was in to it with every mob that surrounded the Washington Heights community. However, that still didn't stop him from going wherever the fuck he wanted to.

While riding down the *opz* block, Kee-Kee ended up getting a brick thrown through his window. Immediately, he pumped the brakes and hopped out licking shots at everybody that was around, even at an older woman who was doing a lil girl's hair on a nearby porch. After striking a few niggas, Kee-Kee bailed back in his car and got out of there.

Kee-Kee was on the run for a couple of months before the law finally caught up with him, taking him off the streets and bringing him before the courts. The judge tried making an example out of him as much as he possibly could. Ever since his arrest, he's been subjected to what most prison administrators call rehabilitation.

However, as Kee-Kee, "Muscles," looked at himself through the blurry mirror that was bolted up on the wall, right above the steel toilet of the seg cell he was locked in, he clearly seen that prison didn't change him...it just made him even worse.

"Keyon Smith," an officer called out through the cell-door. "Is Keyon Smith in here?"

"Yes, that's me," Muscles answered.

"State your full IDOC number for me, would you!"

"R03547."

"Get dressed, the Prison Review Board is here to see you."

A Novel by Pucasso

Coming Soon

CHAPTER #1

RIDIN' AROUND & GETTIN IT

As I pulled up on the desolated block I noticed a grey-Dodge Charger sitting all by it's self parked on the right side of the street.

"That's you in that SRT-8?" I asked K-C, talking to him on Face-Time through the latest iPhone out. I've been on board with the device ever since Apple first dropped a phone. A boss stay upgrading himself in any way that's possible.

Kenny "K-C" Calloway was a natural born hustler, one of my top earners at the time. He went so crazy, in and out of trap-houses, everybody in the hood start calling him my lil' protege. I didn't mind either; bro conducted himself like a boss. He was smart, energetic, and very persistent. I had shorty up under my wing giving him a working analysis on this "Boss-Life" shit.

"Yeah, that's me, big bro," he replied, looking back at me through his phone.

"Aiight..." I said, while checkin' out the scene. We were too out in the open. My first mind told me to change the location to a better one. "Follow me right quick."

I was taught a very young age to always be aware of my surroundings. Like the old saying goes...it's better safe than sorry.

Living the life of a boss, there's a whole lot of shit you must watch out for at all times—Thirsty ass cops, gate-jumpers, a lot of opz, etc. Most of the times, all of these sorts of dangers work together against you that's why stayin' on yo' P's and Q's is a major rule to the game...no exceptions.

Good thing I had one of my "bout-it-bout-it" bitches with me, rollin' shotgun, while I'm out here getting to it...money that is!

Meosha "Me-Me" McMillain was another individual who had in training at Boss-Life Academy. She earned scholarships not only from the excellent brain she conducts on me but also from the bossly way she carried herself.

While leaned back in the passenger, Me-Me carefully thumbed through a large sum of bills like a seasoned bank teller. I often let her slide with a nigga while out juggin' around in the streets. I was pushin' anything between an eight-fee—to the whole thang. Business was going just well; when it came to keepin' me with glass, Slim didn't miss a beat. I was easily knockin' off a bird a day, sometimes even two...depending on how I felt; I was in the position to make that call, not Slim or anyone else for the matter.

Truth be told, I would of been way further up the totem pole right now if it wasn't for Fa-None's "Mr. shoot first and ask ques¬tions never" ass. Bro ended up catchin1 some serious heat with twelve, and I damn.'.near went broke getting the nigga up out of that jam. It was nothing though; that's what a boss suppose to do for a loyal bro in need. I don't get a pat on the back for that. Besides, a nigga bounced back well, just like an official NBA basketball.

I remember when my father use to cook coke up in the kitchen; I often would sneak and watch him perform what he called a "magical trick". The way he brought them extras back without taking away from the potency of the cocaine was extraordinary. No wonder why his bank¬roll stayed fat like a whopper-burger from "Burger King"... he had a miracle whip. The whole process seemed easy to me as a kid, but I'd learned as I got older that trial comes with error. Surely, I done fucked up my fair share of grams before my whip game became proper. Now you can call me Colonel Sanders how I cook a chicken.

Although I was taught "never let a bitch know yo' business," I made a slight exception to the rule. As long as it's beneficial and not detrimental to yo' health, mentally or physically, then hey...no harm, no foul. However, I highly recommend for potential students that's waiting to enroll in Boss-Life Academy to stick to the script—never go against law.

Okay, getting back to business at hand...I pulled up at a nearby grocery store parking lot and parked in between two cars. The whole time while driving here, I kept my eyes buried in the rearview mirror, making sure I wasn't being followed by the dangers I've spoken about earlier. K-C followed suit, pullin' in right behind me and parking as well. He belled out his car and came skippin' over towards mine.

I was in something real low-key at the time—the new Acrua truck, fully loaded. This was actually a good friend of mine's car, "Carmen". She needed some minor work done to it, so I volunteered taking it to the dealership to get checked out and gave her my GLE 63 Benz to get back and forth in. Boss shit! No biggie though, Carmen didn't have a man; and I was like a big brother to her. Besides, switching up vehicles is just a clever disguise to keep.me running from the cops.

K-C belled in the back seat looking astound. "Damn, big bro...every time you pull up it's in something real slick. I need to come and cop a whip from off yo' lot." he said, jockin' my style.

"This some slight shit, lil' homie," I replied, while checkin' out the time on the iced-out Audemar that was dancin' on my wrist. I was getting it, and it wasn't a fuckin' secret.

"Hell yeah," he responded, while whippin' out a whopper-burger and handing it over to me. "That's forty-five hundred right there. Give me another week or so, and I'll be coming for that Quarter-bird you'd been prepping me up for."

K-C took a glance over at Me-Me fine ass, noticing how swift she was with her thumb—skimmin' through the count. "Damn, that bitch bad as fuck!" he thought to himself. **Wale,** featuring **Rick Ross** and **Meek Mils,** was playin' low in the background, *"My bitch bad looking like a bag money."*

"Aw yeah... you coming for that sexy bitch, Nina huh!" I said, as I tossed Me-Me another wad of money to count. Not even for a split second, did I lose focus of what was going on around me. That kind of comfortability could have you put in an early grave. "Check it out, look back there on the floor and grab that brown-paper bag."

I grabbed ahold of one of Me-Me's thick ass thighs. She had on some black and pink cross-trainer leggings, which made her figure appear way juicer than it actually was. Tell you about a high level of focus...she payed me no attention; she just continued counting up the gwop. My fuckin' girl!

"Ay, big bro... you know it's two babies in this bag?" K-C informed me.

"Of course I do, my nigga. I'm the one who put 'em there," I responded, getting ready to announce a major upgrade. "Fuck... "another Week or so", It's time for you to turn up right now. No more baby steps for you, from this point on it's nine or better."

Providing the means and encouragement, these are just two of the things you must produce when tryin' to create a prototype of yo' self.

Lil' bro was very happy and grateful of the blessing he had just received—out of the blue. These be the kind of boosts some mid-level hustlers need, in order to make it to the next altitude. Most niggas don't ever get this opportunity.

"Right on time, big bro! I'm definitely bout to run up a check… something real decent." K-C thanked me from the bottom of his heart; I could feel the gratitude. Instead of runnin' the threat game down on him, about what I'll do to him if he don't have my money, I continued to encourage my mans 'nem.'

"Don't trip, next time you come back to the store, I'm gonna take you to the kitchen and show you a couple of magical tricks. I'm gonna make sure you win out here in these streets, boy!"

Most of the times, when "so-called" bosses bird feed their workers, it's mainly out of fear that if they were to nourish 'em well…eventually, they'll become larger than them in the game. I don't think that way. I want K-C to be a high-roller, the biggest boss of 'em all. If it ever came to a point where I was incapable of covering his order, I wouldn't have the slightest problem with introducing him to my connect. It makes no sense of holding him back; the more larger he becomes, the more money I make. That's just how the cycle goes.

K-C gave me a heart felt pat on the shoulder. "Bet 'em up. I'll be right back at you." he said.

"Well, smooth then. Let me get the fuck out of these people's parking lot before someone mistake us for some drug dealers." I was eagered to take Me-Me's ass somewhere and lay the dick down on her.

"Aiight, I'll holla. Love again, big bro…bye-bye pretty lady." K-C said, right before bellin1 out the truck and skippin' back off to his car. It was no secret at all that I had a lot of love for bro.

"What's the count so far?" I asked Me-Me, while discreetly manuevering my way through traffic. Driving dirty and getting away with it is a common design I've become so accustomed to doing.

"Shit... with the gwop shorty just dropped off, it's a quarter even."

Me-Me relayed the total count back to me with no problem. She's a very dependable and loyal woman, that's why I go an extra mile breaking her off with whatever she desires. Most of the time, all she want is some hard dick and something a bit, softer to put her stomach. Keeping a girl full off dick goes a very long way.

"Man, my tummy is growling right now. I can sure use a bite to eat," Me-Me suggested.

"What do you have in mind?" I asked, feeling hella hungry myself.

Me-Me leaned over towards me and unbuckled my Versace belt. I guess she wasn't referring to food when she said..."a bite to eat." She whipped my dick out and began massaging it, bringing it to a full attention.

"I don't know...something real meaty." she suggested, right before taking a dive down at my dick—mouth first.

Instantly, all I could hear was a collaboration of all sorts of slurping noises. She got right to it, toppin' me off. A few minutes went by before she rosed up from my dick, making a loud smacking sound. "SMUAH!"

It was so much saliva hangin' from off her tongue, down to my joint, you would of thought she tried to digest it. She looked at me like she was debating about something in her mind. When she wiped her mouth off and nodded her head, I knew she had fig¬ured the shit out.

"Some FIVE-GUYS -perhaps." she added, requesting me to take her to her favorite restaurant.

I am…"M.O.B."
My Own Bo$$

Seconds later, Me-Me was right back at—giving my dick "CPR". It was such a blessing that FIVE-GUYS, the famous hamburger joint, was located all the way out in the suburbs. That's how long Me Me! was good for sucking this muthafucka, there and back. Boss-Life!

CHAPTER #2

STEADY MOBBIN' 20

Terell "T-Drum" Drumming was a different type of boss, one set apart of what I was groomed to be. He thrived off warfare, promoting chaos and violence every chance he got. His clique, "MOB", Murder Over Ball, is part of the reason why Chicago's death rate's steady on the uprise. The notorious crew is known for playin' real crazy in the streets. They feared no man, not even "Jesus Christ."

MOB had so many opz that they went around yellin', WT0(we the opz). They got down on anyone that gave 'em the slightest tough-guy look—nippin' the beef in the bud. They breathe in carbon-dioxide, so a lil' gun smoke was like a breath of fresh air to them. Most definitely, this group of guys were very volatile.

T-Drum, MOB's "drill-sergeant", didn't just get the street titles "Drum" by abbreviating his last name. Nah...he earned the tag from oftenly sprayin' assault weapons that holds a 100-round drum or better. He had a bad habit for that shit. On any given Sunday, you could catch this nigga at a gun store—shoppin' for something new that pop a whole of shot.

Him and his shooters based their worth in life upon how many opz they had. Let them tell it... if a gang-member didn't have foes, then they were just in the way. T-Drum trained his wolves ferociously, commanding them to go look for trouble. But just like the old saying goes... "trouble ain"t hard to find".

$$$$$$$$$$$$

I am…"M.O.B."
My Own Bo$$

Leon "Lee-Lee" Banks was T-Drum's prime hitta—with and without means of a firearm. The boy stayed outtin' up, whether it was from puttin' a hole in a nigga's head or just several knots on it. This wasn't yo' average Joe from off the block; muthafuckas loved him and had no problems with ridin to the depths for his cause, even if it involved going against their own parents.

Officially, Lee-Lee was a real live gang member; however, there was this one thing about him that made him look kind of bad...he was a tender-dick ass nigga. He had a bad habit tryin' to force a bitch to be faithful to him. All of the woman he'd been in a relationship with, labeled him as being a complete control freak. The nigga done had more domestic disputes than "Ike Turner".

For a short while now, he's been seeming to control his compulsive ways—keepin' his insecurities in check. The new relationship he's in been going well, all up until he caught his girlfriend up in a random lie. That's when all the bullshit started back. One simple lie had him going through phones; ease-droppin' on private conversations; secretly following muthafuckas, playin' spy-games; puttin' tracking devices on cars and shit; takin' DNA samples from panties...the whole nine!

Good pussy is a common trap that, if "used appropriately," could get someone smoked. I was taught to never be head over hills for a bitch and that's including yo' own mother. Lee-Lee duck-duck-goose ass must have forgotten the rules to this boss shit—it's very much something like pimpin'.

Long story short, Lee-Lee was back to his old tricks, twisted like Keith Sweat 'nem... all over a bitch. At this point, anything going on in the streets didn't matter much to him. His only focus was getting down to the bottom of the unfaithful suspicions he had of his girlfriend, "Cassandra".

$$$$$$$$$$$$$

"My President is black, and my lambo's blue," the words of CTE's very own **"Young Jeezy"** played on the radio while Fa-None whipped the steering wheel of a souped up 96-Chevy Impala. He was heavily in traffic, sliding back and forth, handling his early morning affairs. Being in charge of multiple dope-lines, all at once, is a nice piece of work. But not for Fa-None...he made the shit look like child's play. To him, pushin' dog-food was a easy street.

I wasn't too involved with selling heroine; coca leaves was my drug of choice—60 push that is. As a kid, I sat and watched my pops make a killing off cocaine...I'm talkin' bout some, real-live come up "overnight" type of shit. After my eyes were exposed to seeing that kind success, I couldn't dream of being anything other than a coke boy

However, being that Fa-None was my mans 'nem and mixin' up a bomb on the D-side was something he did quite naturally, I helped foot the bill of his operation. I didn't look for anything back in return other than what he already was giving me—his loyalty. Besides, keepin' him busy with something he like doing (T figured) was the best thing I could of done to keep him out of trouble. However though, trouble somehow seems to find it's way without having any sense of directions.

"Ay, Sonic...check it out right quick," Fa-None shouted out the window to a tall, one-eyed D'boy who was "huggin' the block". After giving a couple of fiends the fix they needed, Sonic made his way towards Fa-None's car.

"What up, boss man?" he saluted, as he belled in the Impala.

"Shit, tryin' to make a dollar out of fifteen-cent," Fa-None replied, while checkin' out a text message that just came through his phone.

It read, "Good mornin'." with a heart emoji next to it.

Unfamiliar with the number or rather—who in the fuck this was that texted him, he sent a quick text back. "?"

"How is everything coming along with last batch we just put out there, how did the fiends react to it?" Fa-None asked Sonic.

"The blow heads lovin' it,"

"What about the shooters?"

"Most of 'em lovin' it too, but one or two complained about it cloggin' their needles."

"That's what I been hearing too," Fa-None said, as he checked his in-coming text message again, thinking to himelf, "Cassandra... who the fuck—"

"Oh yeah, I forgot to lock you in. Good mornin' ma!" he texted back, leavin' out the heart emoji. Then he reached in his armrest and pulled out a brown paper-bag that had several G-bundles of dope in it.

"Here, put this out there. Do a small pass out and then take flight from there. I bet you they ain't gonna have shit bad to say about this batch—I put that on the guys." Fa-None merched it.

"Wanna see you," the in-coming text on Fa-None's phone read.

"I'm in traffic... pull up on me." he texted back.

"What you want me to do with the rest of the other bundle?" Sonic asked, as he dug into his pocket and handed Fa-None a couple bands.

Just get it ready for me, I' m gonna take it back to the table and use it as mix. I"ll come back and get it later. Let me get off yo' hands so you can get to it." Fa-None said, noticing a nice crowd of fiends gathering up around the block.

"Be careful, my nigga."

Sonic showed some loved and then belled back out of the car, getting straight to the paper. Fa-None checked his phone again, seeing that Cassandra had sent another message. "Where?"

"Damn, this bitch thirsty!" he thought to himself, as he began textin' in a location, "Citgo...123rd & Halsted. Give me 10-min."

Before he could even set his phone down and take back off into traffic, he got a reply. "Cool!"

"Man, I'm bout to dog-walk" this lil' piece of pussy!" he said to himself, as he slid off.

$$$$$$$$$$$$$

30-minutes later...

The classic sound of my iPhone rang, snappin' me from out of the foreign planet I was currently in. Seeing that it was my mans 'nem, I went ahead and received the call, "What up, my dude?"

"What up, nigga...where you at?" Fa-None asked, sounding pissed off. Instantly, I sensed something was wrong.

"I'm on the e-way, on my way back to the land right now. Why...what happened?!" I replied, cuttin1 straight to the chase.

"Pull up on me once you do. I'm on the block at the trap house."
"Bro, what's really good. Let me know something now." I said. I hated dwelling in suspense, even if it was only for the slightest second.

"Man, just hurry yo' ass up. We'll rotate once you get here." Fa-None replied, refraining from speaking about it over the phone. He must of sensed that I had someone else in the car with me and didn't want them to overhear whatever it was he had to tell me.

"Aiight, bet... I'm about 15-minutes away. Stay put 'til I get there!"

I ended the call not knowing what to think. The sense of urgency that Fa-None put me under had completely turned me off from the sloppy-toppy Me-Me was giving me. "Boss lady, we gonna have to finish this another time. Something urgent has come up." I tell her, while easing her head up from out of my lap.

"Aw, daddy… I was just beginning to enjoy my desert." she pouted

"Check it out though," I said, getting ready to lay the business at hand down on her. "You got yo' license on you, right?"

"Yeah, why?"

"I'm gonna drop myself off on the block and let you take off with the truck 'til I get done handling somethings," From the way I had her undivided attention, I knew she understood the instructions I was giving' her. "It's two babies left in the glove box. I need you to take 'em back to the spot."

The spot was a lil' apartment I had her to lease in her name, over east. This was one of the few spots where I often stash drugs, guns and money at. Nothing more than Me-Me was uncapable of handling.

"Put the coke and gwop up in the safe, and sit tight. Wait for me to give you the next word. When that time comes, I'm gonna need you to come back and scoop me up; but leave the truck behind and use yours."

Constantly belling in and' out of different cars is not only a smart method used to dodge certain dangers; but also, it magnifies your boss-like demeanor.

"You follow me well, boss lady?"

"Yeah, boss daddy—100! I hope you don't take all day. My pussy's soakin' wet right now… It needs to be taken care of."

"Don't worry, baby. It's gonna get taken care of real well, once I get done handling my business, okay?"

"You promise, boss daddy?" she asked, pouting her mouth out like a lil' kid. I love it when she does that.

"I promise, that's on the "BOSS"." I replied, while stackin' my right fist over the left—two times and then lockin' them together afterwards. Now that's a real live iron fist for yo' ass, right there!

The hand gesture was all the confirmation Me-Me needed, to know that I meant what I said. She kissed me on the neck as I put some pressure down on the gas petal, thinking to myself..."What the fuck had Fa-None done gotten himself into now?"

CHAPTER #3

INVESTIGATIVE ALERT 27

Danny "Dt.Danz" Cook was the head homicide detective present at the scene where a deadly shooting had taken place. He's been with the department, in the homicide division, handling 9-1's for quite some time now. Him and his partner Frank "Kukoaks" Castella was responsible for solving some of the most mysterious murder cases in the city of Chicago. When it came to retrieving physical evidence, these boys were like bloodhounds; they could smell the shit from a mile away.

"One shot to the chest and another one to the forehead…the shooter sure as hell knew what the fuck he was doing!" Dt.Danz said, while examining Lee-Lee's dead body. It was stretched out in a Citgo Gas Station parking lot.

"What do you suspect, more gang violence?" Kukoaks asked.

"I don't know. It's hard to tell, this early in the flick. I can assume, but I rather not; I don't wanna make an ass of myself.

"Oh, like how you did when you ruled that one murder a suicide when, in fact, it was a homicide…according to the autopsy report." Kukoaks replied, slightly insulting his elder partner.

"Need I be reminded of that again," Dt.Danz said, as he looked at Kukoaks bitterly. "Okay then… since we're playin1 the memory game, I got one for you."

Instantly, Kukoaks dropped his head, ashamed of what possibly his partner was about to recall. "Damn, I need to learn how to stop thinking out loud." he thought to himself.

"I remember a rookie homi' detective who witnessed a man layin' dead with his brains blown out—through the top of his skull," Dt.Danz recollected, while laughin' a bit. "Not only did the rookie barf all over his tailor-made suit, but also, he slipped on some brain matter and ended up fallin' across the murder victim...what a fuckin idiot!"

Dt. Danz wasn't the one to try to front on; he fought fire with gasoline. "Shall I continue?" he asked his partner, seeing if he wanted to keep playin' the memory game.

Kukoaks remained quiet. He knew better to not try to come back with a rebuttal; Dt. Danz had them shits 'til the doors rolled. (all day long)

"Yeah, I thought so you "officer Hoyk" looking muthafucka." Dt. Danz said, bringing a lil' humor to the stiff moment.

Kukoaks couldn't help but to laugh at the joke his partner's slick remark. Oftenly, Dt. Danz made fun of him, claiming that he looked similar to the actor Ethan Hawkins" off the hit movie "TRAINING DAY".

"Nah, for real though what do you suspect?" Dt.Danz asked.

I don't have the slightest clue; but whatever the cause might of been, it couldn't of been worth this guy's family having to arrange a close casket ceremony for him." Kukoaks responded, expressing his feelings for the matter.

Dt. Danz looked up at his partner, from where he was squatted down at—Viewing Lee-Lee's dead body, and set him straight once again. "I'm gonna tell you like I've told you several times before...don't take none of this shit personal. It's all business and just that. It's our civic duty, as Homicide Detectives, to solve murder cases—not to try to save the world. That's their fuckin' job!"

Dt.Danz pointed his finger at a crowd of police officers. "They're the super heroes, not us."

"Then—who are we, Mr. Lonzo?" Kukoaks asked, referring his partner to the character "Denzel Washington" played in TRAINING DAY.

Dt.Danz gave Kukoaks a malicious look, showing off his front row of teeth, just how a wolf does when it's getting ready to attack. He took a few seconds grinning before sayin, "We are...the unspoken words that needs to be heard. Don't ever forget that, partner."

Kukoaks wasn't buyin1 into all the..."civic duty"…"unspoken words" bullshit that his partner was tryin' to sell him. However, he kept his opinions to himself for right now. He just stood there with a disgusted look planted on his face.

"Look...if you really wanna know why this muthafucka in front of us got scheduled for a visit with the undertakers than I suggest you get up out of yo' feelings for this tatted face hoodlum. Hell, it'll be a greater service of you to just lay down and take the fucker' s place instead of cryin' about the shit—that or just change professions, maybe become a humanitarian or some shit of that nature. Either way means me no good. I'm tryin' to solve a murder case." Dt.Danz gave it to him in the raw. that's just the type of person he was—straight and forward.

Crime Scene Investigators laid down number plates by both of the empty shell casings that was found- on the scene and blocked it off with yellow and red tape.

"Dt.Cook," a very attractive lady officer called out, tryin' to get Danz attention. He was legally deaf in his right ear forcing her to have to raise her voice. "Dt.Cook!"

"Yeah, right here." he answered, waving his hand up in the air.

The lady walked over to him, escorting the gas station manager who was present at the time of the deadly shooting. "Good afternoon, sir. I'm officer Butler, and this is Raul Gomez, the store manager." she said flirtatiously. It was quite obvious that she was tryin' to climb the ladder of success and didn't mind being sexually exploited in doing so.

"I wouldn't mind bending her fine ass over and shoving my dick down her pussy hole." Dt.Danz thought to himself, as he shook her hand and then Raul's. "Good afternoon officer butler and Gomez. I'm Dt. Danny Cook; but please, just call me Danz. This is my partner, Dt.Castella."

"Hey there, please to meet you. Call me Kukoaks." he said, greeting the two individuals.

"Take us to the surveillance camera. I need to playback the footage, in and out of the store." Dt.Danz commanded, while sizing officer Butler up—discreetly. Although his reckless eyeballing was some-what "low-key", officer Butler managed to peep game. The chase was on.

"Sure," her and Raul said, at the same time.

Raul looked over at her, thinking to himself, "This bitch over thirsty. I guess investigating dead bodies is a complete turn on. I need to change professions."

"Oh, I'm sorry Mr.Gomez, go right ahead." officer Butler said, while excusing herself out of the way letting Raul take the lead.

"Thank you... right this way, detectives." he replied, leading them inside the gas station and behind the counter, into a small office room. Officer Butler tagged along as well—walkin' right behind Dt,Danz.

$$$$$$$$$$$$$

T-Drum was in the middle of checkin' out an "AR-15" at Buck's Gun shop, when he noticed "Just-Blow" tryin' to FaceTime him. Instantly, he answered the call, "Wud up," He spoke with a grimey delivery naturally and the more drugs he took, the more grimier his voice got.

Just-Blow was one of T-Drum's hitters and also, Lee-Lee's best friend. Bro had great potentials to becomea full-blown wolverine one day, especially being under the construction of T-Drum's commands. All he needed was to go through a few more drills.

"Man scud, have you heard anything from Lee-Lee?" he asked Drum, sounding a bit concerned.

"Nah, why?"

"He was suppose to slide on me earlier to check this one thing out, but he never showed up."

"What happened when you hit him on the horn?"

"His shit just kept ringin'... now it's going straight to the voicemail." Just-Blow informed him.

"Who all you tried callin', maybe he's laid up with a dick-eater somewhere." Drum suggested.

"I called Cassandra, but her shit's doing the same thing—going straight to the voicemail."

"Where... there you have it. Scud is spending some quality time with his bitch and don't wanna be disturb. Yo' nerd ass need to try to find some pussy to lay up in. Ain't nothing wrong with bustin' nuts too." T-Drum said, as he walked around the gun shop holdin' an AR-15.

"That's not like him though, he would of atleast texted me back and let me know something by now. Something must be wrong."

T-Drum brought his attention away from the topshelf, which was stocked with all sorts of luxurious weapons, and place it on Just-Blow—undividedly. He rubbed his beard methodically, while unraveling through the gloomy thoughts that was traveling inside his head. "Scud fuck around and probably got checked up out this shit..."

"What you thinking, scud?" Just-Blow asked, seeing "Godzilla" appearing in T-Drum's eyes.

"Fuck you mean... "what am I thinking"? I'm thinking yo' ass need to go and find out where the fuck Lee-Lee's at before yo' ass come up missin...forever!" T-Drum slurred through the phone right before ending the call.

The gun shop worker who was assisting T-Drum could only assume that the boy was a stone-cold "killer"... and boy was he so right.

"Would you like for me to show you more of our stock on assault rifles?" he asked nervously.

"Not today, I'm running short on time right now."

"Well, have you found anything you1Id be interested in purchasing today, sir?" the worker asked, constantly tryin' to force a sell upon T-Drum.

T-Drum looked at him aggravatedly, while setting the AR-15 down on the counter. Although the man meant no harm, the current conditions T-Drum was under allowed him to take the man's eagerness—quite offensive. "I should smack the shit out of this honky and shove the AR-15 up his ass!" he thought to himself, while giving the man a cold stare.

"I'm sorry, did I say something to offend you..." he asked. T-Drum didn't bother replying, he just kept giving the man a hard look. "Cause if so, then I truly apologize, sir." T-Drum could do nothing but turn his anger someplace else, understanding that the man wasn't the problem.

"It's cool, just give me a couple of them glock .40's over there and 100-round drums as well. A few boxes of shells apiece too." T-Drum said, as he upped a big bankroll.

The worker bagged up everything and then gave him his total. "Will that be all you need today, sir?" the worker continued practicing common courtesy for the customer, he definitely wasn't tryin' to piss the "Drumster" off again. The consequences could be fatal—possibly.

T-Drum just paused in thought for a moment, before answering the the worker. "Shit, fuck around and get real live, if something done happened to my mans' Miem...Maybe I do need to prepare myself for the worst."

"Better yet...add that whole top shelf over there to my cart as well. I may have to go "duck hunting" soon!"

A Novel by Pucasso

DUFFEL BAG BOYS

&

MOST VICIOUS PEOPLE:

BOOK #1

"THE LIME-LITE"

ACKNOWLEDGEMENTS

Thank you "Father God" for giving me purpose and allowing me to put my talents to work while being stuck in between a rock and a hard place.

To my belated mother "Karen Y. Adams"...thank you for loving and supporting me, even through all the foolishness I was involved in. I'll be forever indebted to your love...rest in heaven, momma.

To my belated grandmother Gertrude "Gerdy" Adams... thank you for giving me mental strength, instilling relevant principles in me and showing me how to work with what I got-even if it ain't much.

Thank you "Grandma Rose" for always being there for me, my mother, and my siblings. When times got hard, you went out of your way to make sure we were Gucci. One of these days I'ma return the same kind of favor. Big ups to John "Mr. John" Andrews for also being a supporter...thank you!

The reason why I'm going "HAM" with this writing shit is all from the inspiration my daughter gives me. Thank you, Clarissa Adams, *aka* "Bundlez," for coming into my life and blessing me with the greatest happiness a father could have. Daddy loves you, silly girl, don't let anybody try to tell you anything different. To my cool ass nephews—Ree, Ron, and lil' Gio"...turn up, my dudes.

Thank you, "Wanda Mae", for always keeping it real with yourself just as well as with others regardless of what the topic is. I love so much, I promise I'ma take good care of you when I get my check on the first of the month. Shout out to my uncle "The Moon Man," I want government money too. R.I.P. to my grandfather "James." I bet if he was still alive and I told him I"ve written a book, he would've said..."Well, whoop-de-muthafucking-do!"

Much love to all my family from around the globe...the Adams', Burch's, Harvey's, and Bonner's. There's far too many of y'all to sit here and call out names. If you think I don't fuck with you then I probably don't.

To my fucking dawg, the original "Duffel Bag Boy," Jerry "J-B" Brown... I salute you and can't wait for you and Stevie "Boi" Smith to touchdown, I already know y'all" gonna give the block CPR...Mount Vernon.Park please stand up! To my nigga, even if he don't get any bigger-Joshua "J-T" Townsend...no matter how many times you fall down, keep getting back up—like you've been doing. Failure is just a stepping stone leading to success. The sky is the limit! To my brother from another planet-James "Pooh" Johnson.... thanks for sparkling my brain with a little of that "Earth God" wisdom. I got you planted in my heart forever! Shout out to my boy, Big Sidney...remember when you used to send me them dope ass urban novels to read, who'd ever guess me to author one of my own. Nino Brown...get "Spike Lee" on the horn, tell him I gotta script for him. "ChiRap" coming soon!

How could I ever forget my lady Latasha "Passion" Kennedy... keep yo' head to the sky, girl. Remember that when the storm clears up, sunshine shall follow. We're Capricorns...fighters...soul survivors. We find opportunity within the midst of adversity. I love you, baby...the best is yet to come!

To my brothers who've made it outta prison and claimed freedom wholeheartedly—-"Cole Cutz, Ryan (Blood Ain't As Thick), and Rob...Get that money! I wish I' could've helped prove the recidivism rate wrong like y'all did. I tilted my hat to y'all and whoever else that done got out and put the penitentiary in their rearview...never looking back. To my homie-Rashun "Buff" Cole...nothing pay out more than hard work, keep on pushing, my nigga. Emmanuel "Manny" Dosunmu...man, don't let the finesse just go to waste. Let's run up a crazy check!

Eriends...how many of us have them 'em. I send a great big ol' shout out to a good friend in need—"Samm Ram"...couldn't have done it without you, partner. Now, let's take this shit to the next level. Imagine how it's gonna be next time around when we tear them streets up...fuck around and burn the city down. Stay focused, "Grade-A-Books" gon' be the dopest company on the market. To my graphic designer—"Tavis"... keep them icey ass book covers coming my way, love, my nigga! Thank you, "Sharon Holiday", for putting your editing touches on my manuscripts and sending me in the right direction for guidance. Thank you, Leah Ward-Lee, for taking the time out to read my synopsis and sending it to a great editor-D. Razor Babb. "DRB" ... thank you for helping me with my manuscripts. 1 definitely look forward to working with you in the future, if possible.

To a person who I'm highly aspired by—Katrina "Tree-Tree" Adams... thank you for believing in me when others didn't. Keep heading down the entrepreneurial path and all of your dreams' will come true. I'm here for you—always! I couldn't of picked a better person to go into business with, much love. To Daniel Pierson...thanks for helping bring my manuscripts to life, formatting and typesetting it. You came through right at the buzzer..."swish!" To a real live "MBK" representative—Young Maine...thank you for your support and for coming through with that dope ass author logo. Continue to stay on top of your game, and keep the legacy alive. Shout out to all my lil' cousins out there trying to make a dollar out of fifteen cents- "O-Dog On That," "Man-Man," "Pooh-Pooh" and "Tyree" just to name a few.

To my big homie, my dad-Clarence "Guitar Man" Adams... thank you for being understanding, patient, and loving. Continue to get up on your pivot foot, in the event of pursuing your dreams. I'ma proud supporter of your cause...let's get to it! Shout out to my brother "Gee-Gee" and my sister "Kee-Kee," **I love y'all** deeply.

I send much love to all of my loyal readers...Shaun Mack, Coon, Keystone, Dirty, Carey, Free, Trap, 5ive, Donnie, Bond, Pride, Corey, K-O, Ray-Ray, G-Ball, Head, Saint, Jerome "Jerhonimo" Lawrence, Smoove, T-Mac, China Man, Philco, Blue, Goon Town, Dave, Gapp, Tommie, Renegade, B<-Way, Chucky, Moo-Moo, Joe, Flaka, Paul "Pee" Woodard, Reginald "Reggie" Pritchett, Twin, Ba-Ba DRB, Sharon Holiday, Samm Ram, CB, J-T, Keanna "Kee-Kee" Adams, Nino, Cole Cutz, Dan Pierson, J-Reed, Bryant "Shaggy" Carter, Poppa Snake, Tavis, Katrina "Tree-Tree" Adams, LAFA, Vino, Greg. "G-Money" Amos, East Side, Shannon, and all my social media family and friends.

Free the good guys...G-Money(MVP), Ray, E-Dubb, Too-Too, Carey, Lesile "lil' Lez" Dyrant, Toby(Platinum Thug), G-Maine, G-Red, Donnie, Face, T-Mac, Tone, G-Ball, Vick, Twin, Ben-Ben, Rell-Rell(cuzo), Gee-Gee(brother), Shaun Mack, Poppa Snake, .Black, J-B (MVP), Boi (MVP), Grass(east STL), Beam(STL), Q(east STL), Lil^ Larry, Win-Ball, Willie-.D, Skee, Tay-Tay, Vino, Dale, .Willo, Herman(MVP), Day-Day(MVP), Rell, Mateen, Bull, Anthony "Wayne" Davis, Gangsta, Piazo, Co-Co, Mono, Rabbit, Demon, Dirty, Ben-dawg, J-Smoove(MVP), Hustle, 5ive, Smack, Head, Fuss, Kenny B, Mikey-

A Novel by Pucasso

WooWoo(MVP), Ba-Ba, Bird, Jigga, *Lil' Ed, U-G, Ray-Ray, Philly, Twin(Keith), A-R(MVP), Kydra(MVP),* Dough-Boy(BOCO), and of course...Me

To my cousin in the FEDs—"June-G"...Don't even stress over the minor setback, the comeback is gonna be major—I already know. I never stopped counting on you. I'm working hard to be accountable as well. Much love, big bro! Shout out to all my peeps in the FEDs..."Ant," I haven't forgotten about you...keep it real! Rose(BOCO)...told you I was gonna publish a book.

R.I.P. to 4-Block's dearly departed. . .Mrs. Lovett, Vannie, G-Bo, Mrs. Brown, Shirley, Tanya, James Strickland, Momma Claire, Mr. Fouch, Dennis, Cookie, Mrs. Snowball, Mr,,-and Mrs. Carter, Gannie, "The Twins," Red, Mr. Mail, Alex, Gertrude(my grandmother), James(my grandfather), Dominique "Nique" Bullitt(my cousin), Adonta(my cousin), A-Jax, Karen Y. Adams(my mother), Eggard "Snuggles" Wells, Lanett, Pee-Wee, Mr. Stokes, and anybody else that I might've left out. I miss you all. And last but not least, to all the people who went out of their way trying to make me feel like I'm worthless or that I'll never amount to shit...thanks for the motivation. "You can hate me now!"

DUFFEL BAG BOYS

&

MOST VICIOUS PEOPLE:

BOOK #1

THE LIME-LITE

ABOUT THE AUTHOR

Clarence "PUCASSO" Adams is an incarcerated black author who's pursuing his passion for writing-wholeheartedly. Born and raised in the "Wild Hundreds," on the southside of Chicago, IL., Pucasso had become exposed to the wickedness of the streetlife at an early age, which lead him down a narrow path.

By the age 18, Pucasso was sent to prison to do a lengthy sentence for a number of violent offenses. After kicking out a 12-year bit, Pucasso returned right back to the hood that had taken him under and proved the statistics of the recidivism rate to be accurate by getting locked right back up.

Although Pucasso's life seemed to have taken it's toll, it was in a jail cell on his second bit where he learned about his love for writing. Instead of letting his harsh circumstances get the best of him, he chose to work hard at his new found talent in the pursuit of becoming a famous author. Duffel Bag Boys & Most Vicious People: Book #1-"The Lime-Lite" is Pucasso's debut novel, coming from a multi-series. He's currently in the lab working on various projects.

If you would like to know more about the author, you can reach him at...pucassosway@gmail.com or write him directly—Clarence Adams I.D# R03547, Pinckneyville C. C, 5835 State Route 154, Pinckneyville, Illinois 62274

www.ingramcontent.com/pod-product-compliance
Lightning Source LLC
Chambersburg PA
CBHW030918260626
47169CB00002B/297